To those of you facing big or possibly terrifying choices. May you be guided by your heart in finding answers and fueled with the courage needed to claim your future.

TEMPTED &
TAKEN

RHENNA MORGAN

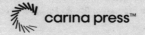

carina press™

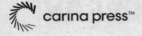

ISBN-13: 978-1-335-00618-9

Tempted & Taken

Copyright © 2017 by Rhenna Morgan

Recycling programs
for this product may
not exist in your area.

Printed in U.S.A.

TEMPTED & TAKEN

Chapter One

Classic Coach in black, or Michael Kors in plum? For secondhand store purchases, both bags were in exceptional shape and worked perfect with Darya's skinny jeans and fitted tan button-down.

She wiggled her toes inside her grape-colored Chuck Taylors, sorely missing the designer shoes her former boss and benefactor had kept her supplied with. On the meager income her skip tracing jobs provided, it was shoes, or bags, but not both and never ever new. In the end, she'd rationalized purses were quite literally easier to run with than heels, and God only knew when her past was going to rear its ugly head and fire the starting gun.

The Coach tote sat prim and proper on the edge of her bed. It would call less attention for sure, but the Michael Kors boho saddlebag with its tassels and gold grommets had a whole lot more sass and was an almost perfect match for her Chucks.

Life's about living. I'm counting on you to live enough for both of us.

JJ's words. She'd pounded the statement into Darya's head for months and made her vow she'd never forget them.

And living didn't mean blending in.

She snatched the saddlebag off the bed and started swapping out the contents from her well-worn Patricia Nash bucket bag with the long hippy fringe. JJ was right. Darya had made it nearly two and a half years since she'd fled her home in Russia without one single indication she was still on anyone's radar. Did she need to be cautious and keep her online presence limited? Absolutely. Just functioning day-to-day under JJ's identity was risky enough. Never mind doing something stupid enough to catch the attention of the killer she'd left behind. But that didn't mean she had to turn herself into a shadow dweller who only ventured from her box of an apartment at night. She could live. Could soak up every amazing moment of the heat-laden home she'd made for herself in Dallas, Texas, and make a fresh new life for herself.

With one last check of her appearance in the mirror, she hustled into the living room, humming the new Bruno Mars song she'd downloaded the night before. She paused beside her makeshift office in the tiny dining space beside her galley kitchen, shook the mouse to wake up her computer and typed in her password. The sync process for her mail application kicked in the second she opened it. Rather than sit and watch while her overnight spam filtered in, she sauntered into the kitchen for a fresh cup of coffee.

Maybe, just maybe, today would be the day she'd hear from Knox.

A whole week she'd waited. Seven anticipation-laden days filled with the compulsive need to check her messages on at least an hourly basis. She'd lost count of the number of times she'd reread his initial response to her first email, checking and rechecking to see if she'd mis-understood his meaning.

I'm always open to business ventures. My software company's got a new release coming out this weekend. Let me get that tucked away and I'll see if I can free up some time to meet.

Not a hard no, but not a yes either.

She slid the coffee carafe back onto the warmer, the nutty depth of the rich dark roast scent weaving an ele-ment of early-morning calm into her anxious thoughts. Sipping the bold brew, she leaned a hip against the coun-ter and savored the words on the white-washed sage plaque mounted on the wall. The white font was whim-sical, but the words never failed to pack a punch.

Dream as if you'll live forever. Live as if you'll die tomorrow.

That was her goal. The mission she'd accepted the day she'd claimed JJ's life as her own.

And Knox Torren was a pivotal part of her plans. The foundation for the future she wanted to build—or rebuild, as it were.

Three quick dings from her computer signaled the finalized download from her three accounts; one for business, one for JJ's personal correspondence and one for junk mail. She pulled out the simple ladder chair that matched her Shakespearean writing desk. When she'd left San Diego behind, she'd brought very few of JJ's possessions with her, but this was one of her favor-ites. Finished in rustic cherry distressed wood, it was a stronghold of old-world elegance in her otherwise fru-gal existence. Her new life had been born behind this desk, masterminded by the real JJ Simpson—her own guardian angel.

She forced herself to work through the spam folder first. Sales she tucked away for reference later. Outlandish claims for fly-by-night software and cheap clothing outlets she deleted with a weird amount of satisfaction. At first, she'd taken the time to unsubscribe from the bothersome promotions, but then she realized if she kept up the tidying task, she'd get almost no email at all. And wouldn't that be a depressing reality?

Finished with her spam, she clicked on her work. Two follow ups, three new jobs and an inquiry on pricing from a new company.

Well, at least that was promising. Since relocating to Dallas nearly nine months ago, she'd managed to pick up six new companies, all of them focused on collections or repossessions and offering steady income. She jotted out a quick response to the new vendor, attached her pricing sheet and scanned the rest of the emails. Nothing there that couldn't wait until tomorrow for her attention, which meant she could finally give in and get to what she hopped was the good stuff.

She clicked her personal account.

Too fast, her brain processed the senders. Her shoulders slumped and she slouched against the hard backrest. No Knox. Not even anything worth reading. She snagged her coffee and glared at the calendar displayed in the corner of her mail application. Whether she liked it or not, it might be time to face reality. Knox was a successful businessman with more than enough opportunities to keep him occupied. What were the odds he'd be interested in anything she had to offer? And the truth of the matter was, he wasn't the only person who could help her reach her goals. It was just he'd been introduced to her life in such a serendipitous way she couldn't help but think reaching out to him was the right move. Too many times she'd followed that same gut instinct only to have it save her life. She wasn't about to ignore those signals now.

Guiding her cursor to her work files, she opened the one labeled *Research* and double-clicked the file at the top.

The image she'd saved from an online Dallas news article a few months ago filled her screen. Seven men, all vastly different in appearance yet obviously comfortable in each other's presence, faced the camera with open smiles. Most were standing, some with a casual arm thrown around another and others lifting their drinks in salute, but two of the men leaned against gleaming motorcycles. One had dark hair down to his shoulders and a wicked gleam in his eyes. The other was Knox.

With his butt perched on the edge of his seat and his ankles crossed, he smirked at the camera as if he had a naughty secret he was just dying to tell. Where the rest of the men favored either extremely short hair or styles long enough to buck convention, Knox's was somewhere in the middle and cut in a way that made him look like he'd just surfaced from a good tussle in bed. His jeans were worn enough she'd bet they felt as soft as spun cotton, and his green T-shirt with faded white lettering molded his lean but sculpted torso. A tattoo peeked from the edge of one shirtsleeve and another marked his bared forearm. No matter how many times she'd tried to zoom in on the graphic, she'd yet to make out the details, but it definitely had a tribal flare. Edgy to match the thick leather cuffs and bracelets he wore on each wrist. According to Jason, he was the ultimate geek and hacker all rolled up into one, but on the outside he looked like a rock star.

She flipped to the next picture, one pilfered from a technical review article shortly after he'd released his successful Lystilizer app. It was less candid. More professional than the one with his friends and lacking his genuine smile, but accented his gray eyes.

The next picture was her favorite. Used for a story about his aiding the government after giving up his blackhat ways, they'd ironically used a mugshot taken when he was eighteen. Even then he'd been attractive, aiming his smug grin at the camera and demonstrating not the least bit of remorse for whatever he'd been caught doing. Honestly, she wouldn't have been surprised if he'd been flipping the bird at whoever took the picture.

Knox was smart. Brilliant. Even if Jason hadn't told her so over and over for the last many months, anyone would glean the same impression with one look at him. Challenge and charisma poured out of every image.

Sighing, she closed the pictures and all the background applications. Her infatuation was stupid. Of all the people for her to turn borderline stalker on, she had to pick a top-notch hacker. Not a great idea for an average girl. A horrid idea for a woman desperate to dodge any kind of unnecessary attention. But Knox was the best. A man who'd built an amazing life for himself from almost nothing and had a history for taking talented people under his wing.

Reality was reality, though. If he didn't respond in the next few days, he probably had no intention of doing so, and the last thing she'd do was beg. She might not have the natural ability he possessed, but what she lacked in innate skill, she more than made up for in tenacity. Otherwise, she'd still be in Russia and a kept toy for a tyrant.

She logged out of her computer, stowed her empty coffee mug in the dishwasher and tidied up her desk.

JJ's laughter-rich voice moved through her thoughts. *Relax, Darya. The world's not going to crash in on you if you don't keep things lined up just so.*

Hitching her purse on her shoulder, Darya paused beside her desk. Her coaster sat perfectly aligned with the top of her wireless keyboard, and her paper clip holder, stapler and Post-its were all neatly lined up beneath her monitor.

She pushed the Post-its out of their orderly formation, leaving the neon yellow stack cockeyed, and grinned. So what if Knox hadn't contacted her. Today wasn't about strategy or planning for worst-case scenarios. It was about living and giving. Enough for her *and* for JJ.

Chapter Two

Open air, speed and good music. Normally, Knox could count on the combination to unravel even the worst mood or problem, but today it wasn't working. The fact that he'd just racked up a solid ten hours' sleep after a two week stretch of cat naps at best should have had him at top speed. Instead, guilt squatted on his shoulders with all the pleasantry of the grim reaper. Hell, the dark and gloomy fucker might as well just put that scythe of his to work and gut him while he was at it. God knows, he'd just done the same thing to a sweet girl who'd done nothing but help him be a somewhat normally functioning human for the last six months.

He whipped his souped-up Audi Roadster off Highway 75 and onto the service road, the top down and the wind hitting him on all sides. Marcy Playground's "Sex and Candy" pulsed through the car's interior and drowned out the mid-morning Monday traffic. What he needed to do was pull his head out of his ass and do it pronto. The last thing he needed while sweeping a target's home was a muddled head and he needed intel on one JJ Simpson pronto.

A block away from JJ's apartment building, Beckett's nondescript white Chevy sedan sat curbside. All five cars they used for tailing people were the same, just in varied colors, though this one was in serious need of a wash. It also was a long damned way from Beck's preferred mode of transportation—a refurbished 1970 candy apple convertible Corvette.

Knox slid his electric blue ride in behind Beckett. Across the parking lot, JJ's apartment on the second floor was barely visible. The tan paint job did a decent job of covering up the apartment's age and the thick hedges lining the buildings gave the place a little color, but overall the look was mighty sterile.

The woman was an enigma. After helping his brother Trevor out a few months ago, he'd started digging around to find out more about the mystery skip tracer, only to find her online footprint had all but dried up over a year and a half ago. Worse, there were conflicting photos he'd traced to the same Jeannie "JJ" Simpson. Then she'd gone and amped his need for information up by reaching out for an alleged business opportunity. If she was really out to talk shop, he'd listen. But if her so called business deal so much as hinted at blackmail against the brotherhood, he wanted leverage to put her in her place. Plus, he was just plain curious. It was a helluva feat for someone to hide from him when he was in the mood to dig, and he'd dug plenty with her.

Eyes aimed on the landing outside JJ's door, Knox hustled to Beck's sedan. The power locks snapped two seconds before Knox's fingers slipped around the door handle, and a blast of cold air billowed out into the July morning the second he opened it. He slid into the passenger seat and shut the door. "You know these models have an automatic thermostat in 'em."

"Don't see me givin' you shit for sweating your balls

off in that four-wheeled crotch rocket you call a car, do you?"

Goddamn Beckett. All of his brothers gave him a hard time for his Audi, especially since all of them stuck to trucks, luxury sports cars or custom rides. He still wouldn't trade it. The color alone made him smile. A giant *fuck you* to conformity. Rather than fire back with a retort like he usually would, he chin-lifted toward JJ's apartment. "You seen her yet?"

"Nope." Beckett dialed down the radio so only the drone of the AC registered inside the car and gave him a solid once-over. "For a guy who just got more than eight hours' sleep for the first time in a while, you look pretty damned keyed up."

Playing it off was tempting. Damned tempting. But the fact that his jacked up sleep problem and all-around trust issues had hurt yet another decent woman was kicking his ass. If he could lay his shit out with anyone it was Beckett. "I cut things off with Tiffany."

Beckett kept his mouth shut.

Knox shifted against the tan leather seat. He hadn't expected an argument. God knew, Beck had given him enough stick over the years about the rigid rules Knox kept in place with the women he hooked up with. So much so he could say plenty without uttering a word.

"How'd she take it?" Beckett finally asked.

"Probably plotted at least twelve ways to cut my nuts off before I'd hit the parking lot, then talked herself out of doing anything by the time I hit the highway." He shrugged and focused on the quad of apartments closest to the property's edge. Over the last week, he'd done his share of time monitoring JJ's comings and goings, but he'd never been one to catch sight of her. "Tiffany'll rebound. My guess, she'll find what she's after faster without me jerking her around."

Beckett nodded, his gaze locked on the same target as Knox. "What about you?"

"What about me?"

He paused a beat. "You gonna rebound as good as Tiffany?"

So much for Beck keeping his mouth shut. "No need to rebound when you never fell."

"Wasn't talkin' about rebounding from her. Was talkin' about rebounding from the guilt."

Knox let out a heavy exhale, anchored his elbow on the window ledge, and raked his hand through his hair. "I don't like hurting them. I'm honest. I tell them over and over I can't do a relationship, but it always ends up like this."

"Then we find another way."

"What other way? Booze and pills put me too far out of it. That's an occupational hazard in our line of work. Exercise doesn't work. Work doesn't work. Sex *does*. And as much as it might make me a fucking pig, I like the sex. I like the women. I like the challenge. Fuck, it's the ultimate throw down to see how many times I can get them off."

"And therein lies the rub."

The unexpected comment snapped Knox's attention from JJ's front porch and straight to Beckett, who just shook his head like he was dealing with an idiot. "What's that supposed to mean?"

"Brother, you get them off. Repeatedly. Like it's your God-given mission to sex them into the stratosphere. Then, when you pry your brainy ass out of their bed, you dote on them like a proud big brother. No amount

of honesty or reiteration is going to keep them from
reaching for the brass ring."

Goddamn it. He forced his gaze back to their target's
apartment, frustration and self-condemnation burning
him from the inside out. "I'm fucked up."

Beckett chuckled at that. "No more than the rest of
us."

True. But at least it wasn't just him and Beckett anymore like it had been growing up. Now he had five more
brothers, each with their own cross to bear.

"We're in motion," Beckett said with a jerk of his
chin toward the apartments.

Sure enough, a statuesque blonde in tight jeans and
a simple tan top appeared on JJ's landing, stopped long
enough to throw her deadbolt into place, then practically bounced down the stairs to the parking lot. Actually, calling her blonde was an injustice. Unlike the
California gold many women strove for, JJ's ran closer
to white. Like she'd been birthed from some mystical
winter realm.

Unless it was fake like some of the women he knew.
Oddly, he hoped like hell it wasn't.

"Interesting car choice," Beckett said. "Danny would
say that's a notch in her favor."

Fire-engine red with black rally stripes, the Dodge
Challenger JJ folded herself into looked like something
one of his brothers would pick out. "Good taste in cars
doesn't mean trustworthy."

"Told you, you're bein' paranoid."

"Took me twenty-three years to get the family I
wanted. Not gonna let some unknown player rip it apart
if I can help it. If that makes me paranoid, so be it."
Knox shook his head. "Besides, something's nagging

me on this one. Can't put my finger on it." And until he was sure his family wasn't impacted by whatever it was, he wasn't letting up. No matter how much shit Beckett gave him.

The Challenger's roar rumbled all the way to where Beck and Knox waited.

"That's my cue." Knox popped the passenger door. "Give me a call when she gets wherever she's headed."

"Yep. You got your keys?"

Knox patted his front pocket where his bump keys were stowed. "Might not have been a Boy Scout, but never met a locked door unprepared."

Beckett grinned and waved him off. "I'll make it easy on you. It's a Schlage. My guess, a five pin."

Knox laughed and pried himself out of the front seat. "And there you go, stealing all my fun." With that, he slammed the door and jogged back to his car. He'd barely made it back in before JJ pulled the Challenger out of the far parking lot exit that emptied out toward the service road.

Beckett followed, but Knox held his spot. Too damned many times he'd rushed in for a job only to have their target circle back for some forgotten item. The last one he'd moved too fast on had forced Knox up-close-and-personal with a holly bush to keep from getting busted. That damned shrub had worked him over harder than the twins he'd dared to take on solo the night of Jace & Viv's wedding, but it'd also taught him the value of patience.

Ten minutes later, he powered up the top on his roadster and backed into an ideal parking spot with a straight shot for the main road. Another lesson he'd learned through the years—always plan for a fast getaway. He dug his trusty Texas ball cap out of the glove box, pulled it on and ambled toward JJ's place. With his backpack slung over his shoulder, the odds of anyone viewing him as anything more than a friend of JJ's were slim and none, but any job done in broad daylight was a risk.

The scariest part? He was totally jonesed on the rush. Not the B and E part, but the anticipation of what he'd find on the other side of her door. There was something there. A shotgun muzzle pressed between his shoulder blades couldn't have spurred him for answers any more effectively than the impulse buzzing beneath his skin.

At the top of the stairs, he tugged his bump keys out of his pocket and snagged his mini-hammer out of the backpack's side pocket. Angling his body to better hide his actions, he slid the key in.

Set. Smack. Pop.

The lock on the main doorknob twisted smooth as butter.

Shifting to the deadbolt, he repeated the process, this one taking three bumps and a little more finesse than the first.

Feminine voices sounded on the walkway below just as the deadbolt twisted.

Home free.

He pushed the door open, ducked inside and shut himself into the blissfully air-conditioned living room. Outside, the women he'd heard continued their chatter, the clarity of their words diminishing as they moved farther away.

Turning, he scanned the tiny apartment. Standard layout. Living room, galley kitchen and small dining area on one side, with a bedroom and adjacent bath on the other. The tan carpet was low-grade and the walls were the dreary grayish white loved by every landlord in the nation, but the vibe of everything else hinted at a demure, but playful personality. A couch covered in gunmetal fabric and dotted with Caribbean colored throw pillows lined one wall, and the coffee table was little more than a slab of glass and rose gold legs.

He paced the front room's perimeter. Where most people left anything from fliers and unpaid bills to chargers and knickknacks laying out in the open, JJ's place was immaculate. Not a single thing out of place. She had a thing for wolves, though. On the wall hung a wide painting of three of them, each in varying shades of gray and prowling through a winter storm. What few other decorations she had were a mix of carved or porcelain depictions of the animals in a variety of poses, but otherwise, nothing at all worth his deeper inspection.

The desk stationed where most people would put a small dinette? Now, *that* was worth some attention. Though, tempting as it was to dive into her electronics right away, he knew better. The second he got into the laptop perched on top of her desk, he'd be fighting a black hole time-wise. Better to case the rest of the place first and leave the big job for last.

The bathroom was just as tidy as the rest of the place. Mirror spotless. Everything in its right place. Neatly folded towels draped over the towel racks. He inched deeper into the cramped space, drawing in the room's unique scent. Kind of like the roses one of his foster moms had grown, but with a crisper edge. Brisk, like a morning after a hard freeze.

He shook off the odd observation, spun for the bedroom and got one hell of a shock. The walls were the same drab white as the rest of the place, but what they lacked in color, the bed more than made up for. Spread across the full-size mattress was a bloodred comforter that was worn but looked insidiously soft. The top had been pulled back the way you'd expect from turndown service at a high-end hotel exposing sheets barely a shade lighter. A wooden ring stained to match the rich espresso headboard hung from the ceiling with sheer scarlet panels flowing out toward either side of the bed, and pillows of every shape and size were artfully strewn in front of the headboard.

Yep, one look at that bed and every predisposed notion he'd had of his mystery skip tracer got turned on its head. No way did the woman who slept in that bed match either of the pictures he'd seen online. It was pure sex. A refuge you slipped into with a long list of decadent intent and didn't roll out of for hours later.

Fuck, who was this woman?

He made quick work of her dresser, carefully checking the contents of each drawer for any stashed information or clues he could leverage. Like everything else in her place, the clothes he found were good quality, but a little shabby. As if she'd bought well to start with and hung on to them a long time, or got them secondhand to start with. Except the bras, panties and silk nighties. Those were still in great shape and covered every sinful hue imaginable.

The closet was more of the same. Nothing stashed away in boxes but the shoes that belonged there. No pictures. No notes. No nothing. Hell, now that he thought about it, he hadn't seen one damned picture in the whole damned place. Chicks loved pictures. All JJ had were an abundance of wolves and an apparent appreciation for quality merchandise. So, where would a woman with an appreciation for tidiness keep her secrets?

Under the bed.

Grinning, he set his backpack full of tricks on the floor, kneeled beside the sex-o-topia she'd created and tugged up the dust ruffle.

Bingo.

He slid out the two-by-two black plastic tub, making note of exactly how she'd had it positioned as he did so, and popped open the lid.

His chuckle filled the room's silence, a mix of chagrin and pure delight moving through him. Not exactly the secret he'd been after, but one he couldn't help appreciating. Arranged on a black velvet cushion was a thick black dildo, a pink finger vibe and a slender violet butt plug.

Oh, yeah. The bed and sexy underwear weren't a mistake. Whoever JJ was, she had a naughty side. Curious, he plucked a thin box from one corner of the plastic tub and thumbed open the lid.

A simple chrome four-by-six frame sat perfectly nestled inside, the picture inside it drawing his focus to a laser point. Two women stood beside the Dodge Challenger JJ had driven off in this morning, their arms around each other and smiling huge for the camera. Whoever had taken the picture was far enough away to get the whole car in the shot, making details of the women too obscure, but there was no mistaking who they were. One was the woman he'd seen leave the apartment this morning—the same blonde currently reflected on passport and driver's license records for one Jeannie "JJ" Simpson. But the other was the early-thirtyish strawberry blonde he'd found on older online records buried in obscure but now dead social and professional sites.

A random mix up of identities online he could buy. In today's technologically centered world, it happened. But the same two women arm-in-arm claiming to be the same person? Hell, no. The whole thing reeked of identity theft, if not something worse.

He snapped a picture of the photo with his phone, tucked everything back up the way he'd found it and headed to the computer. That had to be where the real info was. Hoping for no password and an easy in, he powered up her PC.

No dice.

Powering it back down, he pulled out his laptop, disassembled her hard drive and connected it to his serial ATA. Five minutes later—*voilà*. No password required.

He scanned her hard drive first. No hidden partitions. No special settings in her BIOS. No locks to prevent or slow unauthorized access, so probably not doing any hacking on the side. He checked her router's default DNS servers and set them to those at his office so he could monitor future traffic.

Satisfied he had the basics in place, he turned his attention to her search history. Lots of shopping, no social media outside of Pinterest—which had no user picture associated—and some heavy traffic on search sites for skip tracing work. Otherwise, her online presence over the last thirty days was pretty dull.

He opened her file browser. Like her house, it was well organized and easy to follow. Finances were tucked away in one spot, her last few tax returns showing a healthy savings despite a somewhat meager income, which definitely pointed to those clothes and shoes being secondhand. In another folder were her subcategories for each of the companies she provided services for. In another were recipes, most of the selections having a Slavic tilt. At the very bottom was a folder labeled *Future*.

He clicked on it, expanding the folder and a short list of no more than ten saved articles off the web. His phone vibrated in his back pocket as he opened the first, and an ominous buzz shot across his shoulders. The article was from an entertainment feature Viv had scored from this year's fund-raiser for Catherine's Kids, a biker rally where motorcycle enthusiasts from Texas and surrounding states pulled together to finance summer art programs for disadvantaged and financially strapped kids. The picture at the top of the article featured him and the rest of his brothers in a semi-candid moment centered around his and Jace's bikes. The shot was great. He'd actually saved it himself when the story had been posted, but seeing it on JJ's computer slaughtered his hopes of JJ being on the up and up.

The vibration from his phone kicked in again.

Knox checked the caller ID, slid the answer button and tucked it between his ear and shoulder. "I take it JJ's Monday morning excursion is no longer a mystery?"

"Nope," Beckett said. "Not anymore."

Clicking on the next article, Knox asked, "Anything interesting?"

"Not unless you find volunteering at a retirement village the height of entertainment."

Knox frowned at the new page he'd opened, a technology feature he'd earned after helping the Feds nab a nasty blackhat in bed with a Columbian drug lord. He moved to the next file. "Say again?"

"I said she spent the morning doting on some old folks at a run-down retirement center. Now she's in a dojang about three miles from her apartment changing clothes for a taekwondo lesson."

The information was interesting, for sure, but nowhere near as eye-opening as the star in all the rest of the files stored on her computer. He slouched against the back of her desk chair. "Not exactly what I expected."

"Nothing about this chick is what we expected," Beckett said. "Have you looked at her?"

"Blonde. 5'6". Skinny. Blue eyes. Doesn't like makeup."

Beckett huffed out a chuckle. "That description might hit the salient points, but it doesn't do her justice. Whatever photos you've been looking at, they downplayed the reality big time."

Knox ran his finger along the almost perfectly arranged desk items beneath her external monitor. Two women who knew each other at one point in time, now sharing the same identity, one of which was AWOL. Official photos close enough in appearance to match real life but not exact.

He straightened the Post-it notes so they lined up with the paper clip holder and stapler. "I've got a hunch she's hiding. Probably using a stolen identity. If so, doctoring up her passport and driver's license photos would help throw off facial recognition. It would also explain her working at a nursing home. Plenty of opportunities there for an industrious person needing a fresh identity once someone kicks it."

"A problem for her, maybe, but not one that impacts us. Unless you found something else?"

Knox filtered through the contents of the file one last time, still floored at the number of stories and pictures amassed. "Oh, I found something else. Except it's not the brotherhood she's digging into. She's digging into me."

Chapter Three

"You want me to take Beck's order back and keep it warm until he shows up?" Knox's waitress asked. Like all the other girls who waited tables at Trident, she was dressed head to toe in black T-shirt and jeans, but her attitude fit the outfit. All emo and one hundred percent don't-give-a-fuck like everyone else in the place. Then again, when Jace had set out to launch his first club, that had been his attitude, too. God only knew how many years later, the vibe still stuck.

They also had the best damned bar food in Dallas. Knox motioned for her to go ahead with the delivery. "Nah, he's no more than a few minutes out. Once he bites into those wings he's not gonna care about temperature so much as you keepin' the beers coming."

She shrugged, slid the basket of nuclear goodness to the counter and took off.

Too starved to wait for his brother, Knox tugged his own order closer and dug in. He'd just polished off the first wing and was halfway through draining his draft for relief when Beckett rounded behind him and pulled out the stool on Knox's right. "You got the hot ones, right?"

Like he'd get anything else. The celebration party

welcoming him and Beckett to the brotherhood had taken place at this bar and, whether it'd been intended or not, the scalding wings had ended up both a rite of passage and tradition born all in one shot. He nodded and dug in for another round. "Just came out a few minutes ago. Jessie's working the grill, so you can bet your ass we're gonna pay for this later."

Beckett unrolled the napkin from around his silverware and shook it out like a man braced for combat. "Worth it."

"Yep."

Pausing only after he'd laid waste to this first wing, Beckett knocked back a giant slug of beer and asked, "So what's this shit about JJ digging into you?"

Knox shrugged. "Hell if I know. The articles weren't anything important. Just random commentary that covers everything that's common knowledge from the last eleven years."

Beckett hesitated. "Eleven years?"

Throat on fire and eyes watering enough to make him wonder why the hell he kept torturing his stomach the way he did, Knox nodded and wiped off his fingers. "All the way back. You remember that piece that came out after I helped the Feds?"

"The one with the mugshot from your first bust?"

"Yeah, that one. She had it. Not entirely sure, but it wouldn't surprise me if she had every story that's been published with my name on it."

"But not the rest of us."

Knox shook his head and went for another round. "Nope. Just one from last April's rally that had a picture of all of us in it."

"And you think she kept it because you're in it."

"Don't know what to think. On one hand, I wanna give her cred for bein' so thorough. On another, I want to unravel what's got her so focused so I can tie it off and redirect."

"Could just be she's got a crush."

"No way. She's never met me. Doesn't add up."

Beckett frowned and tossed the decimated remains of one wing to his basket. "Not like you live under a rock. You could've run into her anywhere. As much as you and some of your girls hit the bars, it's not a stretch she saw you, and you never saw her."

"They're not my girls."

Rolling his eyes, Beckett pushed his basket away and snagged his beer. "Hookups. Stable. Whatever. You fuck. A lot. The way she reached out to you on that job with Natalie's ex, it would explain a lot." He leaned both elbows on the bar and grinned. "Might be you've got your own stalker."

"JJ seem crazy to you?"

Levity disappearing in a heartbeat, Beckett aimed his gaze toward the bar, but it was distant. "Nope. Not even a little. Everyone I saw her with acted like she was a ray of sunshine. Real touchy feely, but not in a bad way. More caring than anything."

The waitress dropped off two fresh beers and spun away without pausing long enough to see if they needed anything else.

"By the way," Beckett said, "JJ's taekwondo's not bad for a beginner. Probably has another three to six months before she'd be solid enough to use the skills in a real-life situation, but she's got a natural ability for it."

"You watched her?"

"Fuck yeah, I watched her. So did every other being

on two legs with a dick and a pulse. And that includes the old farts at the nursing home."

The image he'd found of JJ in her apartment pinged in his head. It'd been taken at a distance, but even without the facial detail she'd seemed softer than in the state and federal pics. "I still think she's hiding under this JJ person's ID."

"Why?"

"Because I've got conflicting photos on the same social."

"So? That shit happens all the time these days. You know that."

"Between strangers, yeah. But I bet I could count on one hand the number of times it happens where the two people in question know each other."

Beckett set his beer back on the bar and gave Knox his undivided attention. "What's that supposed to mean?"

Snagging his phone out of his back pocket, Knox thumbed up the photos he'd saved from his online searches, starting with the older version. "This is the Jeannie Simpson—aka JJ—I found on an outdated trade site." He flipped to another picture. "This is the JJ Simpson on file with the state of Texas and the Feds."

"Like I said. Not an uncommon mix up."

Knox flipped to the picture he'd snapped this morning. "This is the photo I found in JJ's apartment. I already dug deep for death records that might explain the mix up and came up with nada."

"You think she killed the woman?"

"Maybe. Maybe not. Just think it's mighty damned fishy they knew each other and one of 'em isn't showing up anywhere these days."

For at least fifteen seconds, Beckett sat and turned

his beer in a circle. He shook his head. "She's not the type. Doesn't feel right."

"Might not feel right, but it looks pretty bad on the surface."

"I'm tellin' you, I didn't get that read off her. She's a volunteer at a fucking retirement home."

"I explained that. Best place in the world to canvas for a new social security number."

Beckett frowned. "You're wrong on this one. Can't give you any concrete evidence, but I'm willing to bet you're diggin' up the wrong tree."

"Gotta start digging somewhere. I got nothing but old data and dead ends online."

"Then take the meet she asked for."

Damn it, he hated not having the upper hand. "I don't like it. Maybe I need to take another pass and see what I can uncover on the older woman."

"Fuckin' A, brother." Beck hung his head as though digging deep for patience, then pinned Knox with a serious stare. "She can't weigh more than a buck twenty sopping wet and while she might outsmart one of us, not a chance in hell she can get past the collective brotherhood. You want a thread to follow? Then get up close and personal." He leaned in for emphasis. "Take. The. Meet."

More than anything, Knox wanted to fidget. To get up, pace the length of the bar and give his mind some unencumbered space to work. Better yet, he'd appreciate a high-octane LAN connection and a lot of uninterrupted time with his computer. Instead, he pulled up the picture he'd taken at JJ's apartment and gave it another once-over. "She's something to look at, huh?"

Beckett chuckled and fisted his pint. "Good enough

I'd be willin' to bet you're angling to have her fill up Tiffany's spot inside of one face-to-face."

"Yeah, that's not gonna happen." He pulled out his wallet for money to cover the tab, the need to get back online and see if he'd missed any loose ends making him as itchy as an addict with the promise of a new high on the horizon. "Looker or not, I'm not crossin' sex and work."

"One grand," Beckett said.

"One grand, what?" Why he even bothered acting dumb after all these years was beyond Knox. He knew exactly what Beck meant. After all, he'd been taking his brother's bets even when they were ten. Although, back then they'd wager with stolen booze or cigarettes instead of cold hard cash. Still, luring Beckett in was half the fun.

Beckett tossed a twenty on the bar and spun to face Knox. "One G says you cross the line with JJ and you do it inside of a month."

Oh, yeah. This one was gonna be a cakewalk. No way was he going to sleep with someone with secrets like JJ's. He grinned and held out his hand. "You're on."

Starved, sweaty, and still tingling from the afterburn of adrenaline, Darya trudged up the staircase to her apartment. She'd always thought the people who compared Texas summers to hell on Earth were being a little melodramatic, but after experiencing ninety-five degrees on horseback she was starting to think they were right. And here she'd thought after escaping her homeland there would never be such a thing as *too hot*.

She unlocked the deadbolt and put a hip to the door, practically stumbling into her air-conditioned apartment. First order of business—water. Lots of it. Right after that, she planned to stand in a lukewarm shower for at least thirty minutes. Though, if her butt got a say in the agenda, it would probably want another thirty minutes soaking in the tub. Nothing made a woman realize how certain muscles were used less than others like a two-hour trail ride.

She wouldn't trade the experience for anything, though. All her life she'd wondered what it would be like to ride such a beautiful creature, and now she knew. Not from books and not from movies, but in real life.

One more experience to add to her ever growing list of accomplishments.

An hour later, she padded from her bathroom in cotton pajama bottoms and ultra-soft T-shirt feeling mostly recuperated and noodling over what her next adventure might be. JJ had tried to get her to go skydiving once, but Darya had chickened out over the jump point. Maybe she was ready for something that daring now. Or bungee jumping. She'd heard the Texas State Fair was pretty impressive and had some miniature-sized bungee attractions. Maybe she could start there and see if she could actually follow through.

She pulled out her desk chair, powered on her laptop and settled in to see what not-so-extraordinary things had happened while she was out conquering the world. As always, a healthy string of spam filtered in. She paused on the latest sale notifications for J.Crew and Banana Republic, taking note of all the latest styles. Someday she'd be able to afford whatever clothes she wanted, and *she'd* be the one to buy them. Not a benefactor, no matter how kind or selfless. Definitely not some megalomaniac out to rule her life.

Distracted by her thoughts, she clicked on the next email.

No pretty pictures or bold graphics.

Just text.

Frowning, she scrolled back up only to have her breath hitch in her throat.

Knox Torren.

Finally!

She straightened in her chair, blew a shaky exhalation through her lips and started at the top.

JJ,
You still up for talking? My upgrade's done and have some time freed up early next week. I'll have Katy put you down for Monday the 18th at 2p.m. at Citadel Security. Let me know if that date doesn't work for you.

He accepted. Maybe he hadn't exactly waxed poetic with his response, but he'd given her a solid time to meet. So what if it didn't come with a bunch of extraneous words. If she could sell him on her idea, she'd be that much further along in making her future her own.

Okay, granted, she'd be sporting a future with someone else's name, but it would still be *hers*.

But more than that—she was actually going to get to meet Knox Torren.

She anchored her heels on the edge of her chair and wrapped her arms around her shins, a barely contained schoolgirl squeal pushing up the back of her throat. Not since she'd landed her personal assistant position with Yefim had she been this happy. This filled her with delight and certainty. It was like winning the lottery and landing a date with your high school crush all in one fell swoop!

Now for how to reply. He'd been brief, so he'd probably appreciate the same approach. Maybe a simple one-liner affirming that the time worked for her and she'd see him then. Or maybe even that would be too much.

She released the bear hug around her shins, reached for her mouse to click the reply button—and froze. Hand still hovering inches from the desktop, all she could process were the three items lined up perfectly beneath her external monitor. She'd moved the Post-its before she left. She was sure of it.

Her heart thrummed an angry, erratic rhythm, and a frantic buzz fired in her ears. One look at the front door confirmed the deadbolt was secure. The blinds were closed and no one was in her apartment, not unless they were hiding under the bed. Scrambling to her feet, she hurried to her bedroom.

You're being silly. The boogeyman doesn't exist. You're just imagining things.

But she'd moved them on purpose. That much she remembered clear as day.

Dropping to her knees, she yanked up the dust ruffle, peered beneath the bed and let out a shuddering breath. No one. Just the box where she kept her toys and the one reminder of JJ she'd dared to bring with her sitting exactly where she'd left it.

She stood and wiped her shaking, sweaty hands on her hips as she scanned the room. Everything else was perfectly tidy. Not a thing out of place. So why did she feel like a thousand eyes were on her?

Ruslan's face flashed with crystal clarity in her mind, the possessive leer he'd given her the last time she'd seen him roiling her stomach as it always did. It had been a warning and a promise. One she'd run from and never looked back.

Taking two steps to the closet, she fisted both sides of the doorjamb, her gaze locked on her suitcases lining the highest shelf. The safe move was to run. To make sure Ruslan never had a chance to make good on his promise. He wouldn't kill her. To do so would defeat his purpose, but she'd end up an empty shell all the same. She'd seen it too many times with men like him. Powerful men who used women as trophies at best and whores at worst.

She swallowed and took two more steps into the closet. Her pulse fluttered at her throat. A butterfly desperate to escape.

Live enough for both of us.

The last words JJ had spoken. Yefim hadn't extracted the same promise in words, but his eyes as he'd set her escape in motion had said the same.

And running wasn't living.

Squaring her shoulders and gritting her teeth, she stomped out of the closet and into the living room, checking every detail along the way. She settled at her desk chair and forced herself to take slow, deep breaths. There was always the possibility whoever straightened her things wasn't Ruslan. After all, if he'd tracked her down, he'd simply cart her away kicking and screaming no matter who heard. *Avtoritet*, what Americans would consider captains in the Russian *bratva*, answered only to their *pakhan*.

No, it was entirely possible someone else had moved her things. Maybe even someone as harmless as a maintenance man. Granted, them touching anything was grossly out of line, but the idea wasn't beyond reason.

Still, she'd be wise to stay on the alert. If Ruslan really was after her, she'd need to think smart. Pay attention to her surroundings, fortify her resources and build what allies she could. She zeroed in on the email she'd left pulled up, resolve thickening even as her fingers settled on the keyboard. Step one was solidifying her future.

Chapter Four

One week Darya had waited. Waited, watched her every step and worked herself ragged. Outside the rearranged Post-its on her desk, not once had she glimpsed any indication Ruslan or anyone else had found her. In fact, her life had settled into its usual routine so easily she'd wondered if maybe she hadn't imagined leaving things askew on her desk.

Regardless, the time to meet Knox was here and hopefully, the leg up she needed to go with the introduction. Parked in front of a single-story building with plain-Jane concrete walls, she stared up at the brushed chrome Citadel Security sign and rehashed the pitch she'd spoken aloud at least twenty times a day. Cool air pumped from the car's vents against her clammy skin, barely making a dent with all the adrenaline coursing through her veins.

The clock on the dash flicked from 1:54 p.m. to 1:55 p.m. Either she could sit here until straight up two o'clock and let her anxiety climb all the way up into the stratosphere, or she could pry herself out of her car and hope a slightly early arrival showed an extra level of professionalism.

She popped the handle and shoved the heavy door

open, swinging her resale Jimmy Choo–shod feet out onto the concrete parking lot. What the tan pumps lacked in pizzazz they more than made up for in accentuating her legs, especially paired with the matching pencil skirt that ended just above her knees and the delicate ivory camp shirt with its mandarin collar. Putting the outfit together had been both a joy and a welcome distraction, a brief trip back to a time when she'd been able to enjoy fine fashion instead of constantly trying to blend in.

Before her hand connected with one of the glass entry handles, the click of a lock being released sounded. She pulled the door open and a wave of chilled air to make her Challenger's AC seem weak blasted across her skin. Even with the ample light spilling through the double doors and windows on either side, it took her eyes a second to adjust from the bold midday sunshine.

A pretty blonde dressed in jeans and a T-shirt stood from behind a curved reception desk stained a soft ebony and accented in soft chrome. Her eyes were an enviable green and her hair styled in a tousled pixie cut. She reached across the tops of three monitors arranged in a perfect semicircle and offered her hand in greeting. "You must be Jeannie Simpson. I'm Katy, Knox and Beckett's assistant. Can I get you something to drink?"

Two or three shots of vodka would be nice. God knew she needed something to loosen up her tongue. While the outside of Knox's building had been nothing short of plain, the inside was jaw-dropping high-end contemporary. Like Katy's desk, the walls on either side of her were dark—not quite black, but charcoal gray, and fashioned from some kind of metal rather than paint. The wall behind Katy's desk, however, was a beautiful dove gray that added extra depth to the limited space. Classy yet edgy cylinder pendant lights with frosted white glass hung above either end of her desk, and two impenetrable steel doors flanked her on either side. "If it's not too much trouble, water would be nice."

"No trouble at all." Katy cocked her head, curiosity glimmering behind her assessing gaze. "Your accent is amazing. I'm guessing Russian?"

For a second, Darya's thoughts flatlined. With limited daily interactions beyond her normal routine, it was seldom she met new people. So much so she'd forgotten the need for explanation. "Yes," she said, realizing all too quickly Knox would expect the same. "Not too hard to understand, I hope."

"Not at all. It's actually beautiful." Katy punched a few buttons on her computer and waved Darya to the small seating area to one side of the front door. "Just give me a minute to grab your water and let Knox know you're here."

"Thank you."

"Don't mention it." She splayed her hand on a black screen beside one heavy door and a heavy clunk that sounded on par with a bank vault being released resonated through the room. Only then was Darya left alone in the intimidating environment.

Slowly, she paced toward the iron-colored leather couch and the oblong marble coffee table. Sitting was out of the question, not if she wanted to exude any kind of calm. She might be technically alone in the room, but the cameras anchored in every corner made it relatively certain there were eyes on her somewhere. She squeezed the handles on her briefcase a little tighter and pretended to study the landscape outside one picture window. What really held her attention was the glass itself, multiple layers thick and no doubt capable of stopping bullets. But then such measures made sense for a security company. As did the secured doors. At least she hoped that was the reason for such stringent measures. The last time she'd been in such a tightly controlled environment was the day she'd met Ruslan, and her world had gone from pampered to hell in all of five minutes.

The door *kachunked* behind her.

Darya turned, the pleasant smile she'd intended for Katy evaporating along with all the air in her chest. Instead of Katy strolling through the large door, Knox ambled her direction, a smile in place potent enough to disarm the most jaded woman and a bottle of water loosely gripped in one hand.

And he was gorgeous. So much more than what the pictures she'd scrounged up promised. More intensity. More charisma. More *everything*. Like in all the photos she'd seen, he wore faded Levi's and military-style black boots. His T-shirt was a deep gray that accentuated his lean, but muscled torso, and tattoos peeked out from each sleeve.

It wasn't until he moved within reaching distance and held out the water he'd brought her that the white graphic on the T-shirt registered—a classic Impala and the phrase, *Get in, loser. We're going hunting.*

"You like *Supernatural*?" she blurted.

His smile deepened and he wiggled the bottle still in his outstretched hand. "Not even officially introduced yet and you're already scoring points for good taste." A rugged leather watch with a thick camel-colored band covered his wrist, while a darker brown cuff and two smaller bracelets made of turquoise and red shells circled the other. Total rock star.

She took the water, wishing she could press the ice-cold plastic against her flaming cheeks, but juggled it with her briefcase instead and offered her hand for a formal introduction. "Sorry. I'm JJ."

His grip engulfed hers, the warmth of the contact and the way he leisurely perused her from head to toe scattering her barely resuscitated thoughts. "Not a thing to apologize for from where I'm standing." His gaze settled on hers, the impact of it stoking grossly inappropriate thoughts. Vivid, carnal and deliciously wicked thoughts. His voice lowered and rasped with pure sexual promise. "I'm Knox."

Oh, yes. Definitely dangerous territory. Absolutely the worst trespass her mind could make with plans to pitch her future so close. She forced herself to relinquish his hand. "I'm very pleased to meet you."

His beautiful gray eyes sparked with mischief and he grinned in a way that said he hadn't missed the huskiness in her response. He sidestepped and swept his hand toward the door, but rather than use the movement to add more distance, he splayed his hand at the small of her back. "How about we get out of the lobby and give you a chance to get your bearings before we talk shop?"

Walking was good. Distance would be even better. Although, for the first time since she'd started wearing heels, she wasn't sure if she could put one foot in front of the other without looking like a newborn deer.

Behind the industrial steel door, the air was even colder, the steady draft tunneling between the glass walls on either side of her gently lifting the hair off the back of her neck. "You must really hate July in Texas."

"My servers hate July in Texas. I learned to tolerate it like every other native before I left the cradle."

Behind the glass, server racks stretched tall and wide in precise rows. Her heels clicked against the industrial tile, mingling with the steady hum from the machines. "This is all for your security company?"

"Some of them. The rest support the traffic from my apps."

Well, that was silly of her. The very reason she was here and she'd not been smart enough to realize he'd need a sizable infrastructure to support the business he'd built. She slowed her steps, appreciating how the wires ran in neat rows up the back of each stack then disappeared into the iron racks above. Combined with the soft blue light emanating from the ceiling can lights she felt a bit like she'd entered a sci-fi flick. "It's quite overwhelming."

He chuckled and placed his hand on yet another bio scanner beside a black wood door. "Overwhelming is when a server goes down and pissed off customers start calling in." The lock released and he opened the door for her. "There've been a few drills I'd liken to an electronic version of a needle in a haystack, but hey. Nothin' like a challenge to keep a man sharp."

For some reason, the image of Knox knee-deep in a challenging situation sent a charge through her strong enough to power half the machines they'd left behind. True, he was handsome, but nothing captivated her more than a man's intelligence. Considering Knox had both in spades, it was a wonder she'd been able to string more than three words together, let alone remember her name.

She trailed behind him into his office. It had the same contemporary feel as the lobby, only less intimidating in its colors. A soft gray chenille sofa and two club chairs covered in a matching patterned fabric were arranged near a window on the far side of the room. In the center was what she assumed was Knox's desk, though it was far more unconventional than the standard arrangement. Where most people chose to arrange their furnishings with their back to the wall and a bird's-eye view on the entrance, Knox's wide steel desk faced an astounding number of monitors mounted on the far wall, each of them streaming what she assumed was live footage from a number of businesses. Even more impressive were the four oversize computer monitors arranged in a semi-circle in the center of his desk.

In the monitors hanging on the wall, people went about their daily activities, innocently working, drinking and eating without so much as a clue they were being watched.

The muted tap of fingers on keys sounded and the screens went dark.

"They're a distraction until you get used to them." Knox spun his sleek black office chair around, rolled it toward a smallish collaboration table on her right and motioned to the guest chair behind it. "Have a seat."

She did, unpacking her laptop from her briefcase as she did so and setting it on the tabletop.

Directly across from her, he leaned in, rested his forearms on the brushed chrome surface and cupped one fisted hand with the other. "So, you mentioned a business opportunity. What's on your mind?"

So much for easing into the topic. And had she really referred to it as a business opportunity? Now he'd think she'd pulled some kind of bait and switch to earn his attention. She cleared her throat and smoothed one hand across the top of her computer. "Business opportunity might not be the right way to describe it."

His expression blanked, the warmth and lighthearted mirth that had shone in his beautiful eyes chilling in an instant. As though she'd not only angered him, but disappointed him as well. Without the vibrancy in his gaze, his eyes looked tired. Pinched and weary around the edges as though he'd gone for far too long without rest.

She forged onward, drawing from the countless rehearsals she'd spoken out loud while pacing her apartment. "You remember when I first reached out to you—when I emailed you on my tracking services—I mentioned I'd learned your name from someone you'd mentored."

He nodded, though the movement seemed cautious. "Jason Reynolds."

"Yes." She fidgeted in her seat and curled her fingers around the farthest edge of her laptop. "Jason's told me many stories about you. About the men you call your brothers and how you've made a successful career for yourself. He holds you in very high regard."

"Not sure how that plays into a business opportunity."

This was it. In the grander scheme of things, it wasn't nearly as big a risk as taking on JJ's identity or fleeing Russia, but it could still catapult her future. She pulled in a slow breath and held his commanding stare. "It's important because I want you to mentor me."

His eyes widened, a little of the emotional barricade he'd put up easing as he spoke. "Jason's a coder."

"I know. He's the one who first gave me the idea."

"And you know him how?"

"He comes to visit his grandmother every Monday.

At a retirement home. His grandmother isn't very talk-ative, but he always comes and brings his computer. He told me you've been known to teach people with an in-terest and, if they do well, give them a leg up."

"I teach people with *talent*. No matter how much in-terest a person has doesn't mean they can be success-ful in the long run."

Emboldened, she sat a little taller and leaned in. "I can't tell you if I have talent, but I can promise you I'm tenacious. I've already completed two of the self-teaching courses you recommended to Jason and have started a third."

He reclined against his chair back, one arm still draped atop the table while the other rested casually at his hip. It was a relaxed pose, but the intensity that crackled around him said she'd be a fool to assume he wasn't assimilating each and every detail to the nth de-gree. "You're looking to expand on the skip tracing?"

Always stick to the truth, JJ had coached her. *Or as close to it as you can get.*

"I'd like to move away from that business," Darya answered, "to build a career that's less reliant on com-panies but is still transportable." Realizing the unin-tended kernel she'd left uncovered, she clarified, "So I can travel."

For several seconds, he merely studied her, the quiet amplifying until it droned as loud as the servers in the other room.

"The skip tracing is good," she said, needing to fill the silence. "With my contracts, I can keep a steady income, but I don't like the feel of it. I don't like find-ing people who don't want to be found. I don't want to worry that they'll learn who found their information and take their anger out on me."

Without moving so much as a muscle, his entire demeanor shifted. A shrewd observer one second and a lethal predator on alert the next. His voice was deceptively smooth. "Has that happened?"

Not exactly. Not to her anyway, but it *had* happened. "Once. A collection company wanted to locate a man past due on his car payments. He was living at his ex-wife's address in a town only thirty minutes away. The company secured the car, but the collector inadvertently mentioned who had located the debtor's new residence."

"And?"

She shrugged, recalling the none-too-pleasant altercation that had happened only a few months after she'd gone to work for JJ. "People who lose their possessions tend to be very angry. They also want someone to blame for their misfortune, and this man in particular wanted to voice his displeasure. In person." She paused for a minute, looking for the right words to help him understand without exposing too much of her own predicament. "I don't want to experience that again. I want to create something. To build a career where my success will be limited only by my abilities."

He pulled in a slow breath, sighed as though he questioned having scheduled the appointment and sat up in his chair. "You realize there's a lot more to this than syntax and technique, right? Even with persistence, you need damned good ideas and a hell of a lot of luck if you want to be more than just a hired coder."

"I will make my luck."

His eyebrows hopped high and his lips curled in a

sly grin. "You quoting me because you believe it, or to let me know you've done your homework?"

"Because I believe it. This isn't the first time I've taken risks, and I doubt it will be the last, but every person has to make their own way. If the path doesn't exist, it's up to every individual to make one. You took your love of music and movies and made a niche for yourself. I can do the same."

"You use my app?"

Her and everyone else eager to find new leads for their playlists or Netflix binges. Lystilizer had originally focused on music only, but had been expanded to include movies a little over a year ago. The algorithm behind it was amazing, evaluating each user's individual libraries and making spot-on recommendations for new purchases. "I use it all the time."

"Music or movies?"

"Both."

"Favorite band."

That drew her up short. "Can you actually narrow your favorites down to one?"

One corner of his mouth twitched. "Fair enough. How about your top favorites in the last six months?"

"Halsey, Eve to Adam and Chris Stapleton."

He cocked one eye and crossed his arms across his chest, but his grin was playful. Clearly, he not only loved music, but he was familiar with a broad spectrum of genres. "Alternative, rock and country. That's a heck of a spread. I'd have pegged you as a top forty girl."

She shrugged. "I like music that fits my mood. Why limit yourself to only one format when you can explore many?"

"True." He cocked his head. "So, what about movies?"

For a second, she ducked her head, then remembered who she was talking to and shook off her embarrassment. What difference did it make what he thought of her burning through pop culture lists off IMDb? "*The 40-Year-Old Virgin* and *The Princess Bride*."

His smile deepened. "'Wuv,'" he said, imitating the clergyman near the end of the movie. "'True wuv.'"

"'You killed my father!'" she fired back with her own impression of Inigo Montoya. "'Prepare to die!'"

He laughed loud enough to fill the room, the rich rumble of it soothing away the remnants of her fears. "A classic. I'll bet I could drop at least twenty-five quotes inside of five minutes. Maybe less."

"I'm watching *Airplane* next. Jason says it's insanely old, but has just as many quotes, if not more."

His laughter died off slowly, and while none of the suspicious tension she'd picked up on before returned, he studied her through slightly narrowed eyes. As if she were a puzzle he couldn't quite put together. "How long have you lived in the States?"

Every time someone asked that question all she wanted to do was bolt, but denying her heritage wasn't an option. She'd long ago accepted her accent was too prominent to eradicate without serious training, but that didn't mean she was comfortable opening doors that might lead to more questions.

The tattoo on his forearm drew her attention. Bold and drawn only in black ink, it resembled a tree but with a tribal style and surrounded a rugged H in the center. A mark with purpose, yet nowhere near as sinister as the tattoos she'd become all too familiar with in Russia. Was Knox dangerous? Absolutely. Her instincts with people were seldom wrong and for Knox they insisted he had an intellect not to be trifled with. She'd even uncovered rumors of him and the men he called brothers having ties to criminals. But sitting with him now—watching him and interacting with him—she sensed fairness. Honor and determination paired with an indomitable courage. If she expected him to take a chance on her, he at least deserved the same willingness in return, even if it gave him a lead toward discovering who she really was.

She took a deep breath, straightened her spine and fisted her hands in her lap. "I left Russia about two and a half years ago."

Chapter Five

Beckett was right. Jeannie Simpson, or whoever she really was, had to be one of the most beautiful women Knox had ever met. And not uptight and untouchably beautiful either. No, JJ's allure was an intoxicating mix of wide-eyed guilelessness and earthy sensuality. The girl next door and a seductive winter nymph all rolled up into one, complete with white-blonde hair, bright blue eyes and lips a pale watermelon pink. A woman who'd tempt a saint to throw his vows and caution to the wind with no more than a single look.

He was definitely no saint. Not with the string of urges that had queued up the second he'd watched her walk through the front door.

Another bigger observation—she was innocent.

Maybe not from the identity thing, but no way had she offed anyone to claim Jeannie Simpson's name. What was absolutely certain was she was hiding. She might not have come right out and added that she'd run from her home over two years ago, but the tone behind her confession said plenty. A plea and a request for privacy all at once. And damned if it didn't make him want to cart her off someplace safe and obliterate whoever forced her to run in the first place.

He motioned with his chin toward her laptop. "So, tell me what programming languages you've worked with."

She let out a relieved sigh and smiled, the sheer gratitude and vulnerability in her expression further cementing her innocence. Folding her hands on top of the table, she leaned in with the same prim and proper interview stance she'd used when she'd first sat down. "Jason said you encouraged him to learn native languages instead of cross-platform development tools, so I focused on Android and iOS separately."

Three times now she'd mentioned Jason and every one of them had stunned him a little more. Yeah, the kid had talent, but he also had the attention span of a gnat. The fact that he still remembered Knox's name, let alone anything from their mentoring, shocked the shit out of him. And what was a woman as gorgeous as JJ doing hanging around a rail thin geek whose idea of a hot date happened on online role playing games?

The first answer that came to him pissed him off on about twenty different levels and made him ask without thinking, "You and Jason are a thing?"

She blinked a few times, a nonplussed expression leaving her a little slack-jawed. "A thing?"

"You and Jason. Together. Are you dating?"

Her eyes widened and she flinched as though he'd literally shocked her. Just as fast, her cheeks turned a soft pink. She shook her head and ducked her chin. "No, I'm not seeing anyone."

Why the hell her answer calmed him as much as it did he couldn't say, but hearing those simple words unwound a good chunk of his tension. As for the blush, she might as well have dangled a red cape in front of a bull. One way or another, he was finding out what was behind it. "So, you want a mentor?"

She lifted her head, hope flashing brilliant behind her arctic blue eyes. "Yes. And maybe a chance to work for your company once I gain the sufficient skill."

He fought back a smirk and rubbed his palm across his mouth to cover any tells that slipped by. He'd give her kudos for gumption. Katy hadn't dared to utter the word *employee* until she'd lived and breathed all things programming for a year, and it'd still taken her another six months to make it on the payroll.

"I know it's a time investment on your part," JJ said. "So, I'm willing to trade my services in exchange. If you need anyone found, or need someone in your company to do entry level work, I can do that. I'm a fast learner. I'm not afraid of hard work."

Damn it. Nothing reeled him in more than willingness and a killer attitude. If she had talent to boot, he'd be stupid not to give her a shot. He leaned his elbows on the table and nodded at her computer. "You bring samples of your work?"

The smile she gave him was bright enough to give the mid-afternoon sun a run for its money. Eagerly, she opened it up, tapped out her password and guided her fingertip along the trackpad. "I don't have anything fancy. I've mostly taken simplistic existing applications and tried to replicate them on my own. I figured learning technique to start was more important than trying to create right away."

Funny, because that was the same approach he'd taken early on—although when he'd been doing it, he'd been scamming to make a quick buck or two instead of wholesome learning.

She double-clicked the trackpad and spun her computer around. "I've got four I've been working on. They're all in this folder."

"All right." He plucked her laptop off the table, wheeled in his chair to his desk and hooked the device up to his external monitors. "Pull your chair over here and let's see what you've got."

His focus was instant, the draw of the syntax in front of him lassoing his attention until the rest of the world fell away. Or at least it did until JJ slid her chair beside him and perched on the edge. No more than six inches away, her prim and proper skirt had ridden up to reveal a good span of creamy thigh. And her hair. Christ, it was long. Perfect for a man to wrap his hands around and pull her to him while he fucked her from behind.

Bad idea.

As in don't even think it, dumbass.

He shifted in his seat, willed his cock to calm the hell down and scrolled farther down in her code. The structure was good. Rudimentary still, but a solid beginning. She'd even found some creative ways to streamline her code in places other people would have been thrown off course. He closed out the first app and opened the next.

Her scent gently curled around him, the same winter rose he'd appreciated in her apartment only more potent when combined with her presence. Even without looking, he felt her gaze on him. Studying him. Probably with that same doe-eyed wonder she'd nailed him with when he'd found her cooling her heels in the lobby. And damned if he didn't want to turn his head, palm the back of her neck and give her something that would really rattle her world. He forced himself to focus and asked, "How long did this one take you?"

She kept staring. No answer.

"JJ?" He slanted a quick glance just to make sure she'd heard him.

Big mistake. That wasn't doe-eyed wonder on her face. That was infatuation wrapped up in an insane amount of lust. Her lips were free of lipstick, but the lower one was shiny as though he'd just missed her tongue wetting it. And they were parted. Ready and begging for attention.

"How long did this one take you?" he asked again, though the repeat was a whole lot more grated than the first.

Her gaze lowered to his mouth, pure craving written on her face. "A few days for each."

Fuck.

He wasn't sure what turned him on more—the fact that she'd worked through how to make the apps work in a short amount of time, or that she hadn't so much as flinched when he'd busted her openly eyeballing him. "Did you make any design changes, or copy the apps outright?"

She swallowed and some of her professional distance returned. As if she'd realized her dream was over and it was time to crawl out of bed. She faced toward the screen, evaluated what section of code he'd stopped on, then motioned for him to scroll down. "I took time to evaluate where the user interface could be stream-lined. Places where the user could do more with less steps. This one had too many subpages to navigate in the settings menu, so I streamlined them into more in-tuitive groupings."

A fantastic answer. Even some of the most gifted de-velopers he'd worked with in the last ten years failed to maximize user interfaces. Whether she'd figured that out on her own, or picked the best practice up from one of the self-teaching modules, it demonstrated a whole lot of promise. Or at least the ability to actually listen and learn.

So, it wasn't just willingness and a great attitude she brought to the table, but aptitude, too. The damned trifecta as far as he was concerned. And while his instincts had been way the hell off to start with, he was pretty sure he was spot-on in guessing she needed a leg up big time.

The downside? He'd catalogued at least ten different ways he'd like to screw her since the second he'd laid eyes on her. Even if she were some random woman he met socially, that kind of preoccupation reeked of complications, but mentoring her? That made her strictly off-limits. Besides, she wasn't the no-strings type. He'd bet his state-of-the-art server room on it.

No, JJ was the type of woman a man stayed with for the long haul. That he'd protect. Spoil and pleasure. Definitely *not* the type of woman Knox wanted or needed in his life.

He spun enough to face her, crossed his arms over his chest and pulled in a deep breath. "You understand I run a check on every person who works with me?"

So what if he'd already done it. That wasn't the purpose in the question. The response, however…that was the key.

Her gaze cut to the screen still displaying the code he'd scrolled through. For a minute, he thought she'd back down and tell him she'd go it alone. Instead, she nodded as though making some internal decision and lifted her chin a notch. She looked him straight in the eye. "I understand."

"Will that be a problem?"

She shook her head but it was tight.

"Will I find anything?" he asked.

"I hope not," she whispered.

And there it was. The truth without admitting a thing. But if they were going to work together, she needed to understand the level of scrutiny that came with the relationship. He held her jittery stare, leaned forward and rested his elbows on his knees. "JJ, what I'm asking is *am I going to find anything*?"

Comprehension registered on her face and her creamy skin blanched to a sickly white. She swallowed huge. "You've already looked."

He could lie. Hell, it might be the more compassionate approach. Then again, if she couldn't handle this, she wouldn't last a day with him in the office. "If Jason learned anything from me, it's that I'm thorough. Surely, you assumed I'd do my research before we talked."

"I knew it was a risk."

A risk. Not a certainty or a necessary evil, but a risk. As in willing to expose her secrets in exchange for grasping a new future. "Gonna ask you a question and I want the truth."

She nodded.

"I understand secrets," he said. "We've all got them. But I've got a career and a family to protect, and I have to gauge what kind of exposure your involvement with me and my company creates. More than that, I need to know if I can trust you with my records. So, I'll ask again. Are any pieces from your significantly lacking background gonna come back to bite me, or my family?"

She held his stare, so much emotion moving across her face he couldn't grasp it all. Fear for sure, but there was something beneath it. Resignation maybe. Plus a mother lode of hope. "If my past comes back, it will come for me. No one else. All I want is a simple life. To build a career that will support me and create things I'm proud of."

Oh, yeah. Definitely running. And as pretty as she was, odds were good the one chasing her had a dick and a nasty attitude to go with it. Whoever said asshole was, their chances of ever getting their hands on JJ dropped to nada the second she'd strolled into his office. No way in hell was he letting any man bully a woman.

"All right then," he said. "Let me talk with my brothers. If they're up for an addition to staff, I'll take you on and teach you." And if they said no, he'd find another way to help her stop running.

Chapter Six

Surrounded by his family, Knox kicked one boot-shod foot up on the ottoman and stretched out further on the entertainment room's butter-soft leather sectional. It'd been two hours since they'd all staggered away from the dining room, stuffed full of Trevor's steak-and-potato dinner selection, and Knox's stomach still felt like it was going to explode. Although, over-stuffed on KC Strips or not, he'd still kicked everyone's ass in some old-school *Mortal Kombat*.

Gabrielle, or Gabe as the crew referred to her, yawned and snuggled deeper inside the crook of Zeke's arm. "Who picks dinner next week?"

"Knox," Ninette said with a smirk.

Everyone groaned in a well-synchronized chorus and Knox grinned huge. In the last three years, he'd pushed their tradition of one person picking dinner for family night by picking every kiddie favorite he could come up with. He'd thought Jace was going to put a hit on him the week he'd picked fish sticks and cherry Jell-O. "What? Someone's gotta keep this group on their toes."

"You're not keepin' us on our toes, brother, you're keepin' us fat," Danny said.

Trevor's wife, Natalie, smiled and smoothed her

sleeping son's overlong blond hair away from his eyes. The poor kid had passed out with his head resting on Trevor's lap an hour ago and hadn't so much as budged. "You guys might not appreciate Knox's taste in food, but Levi's a huge fan."

"That's because they're both wee lads at heart." Sylvie stood and started gathering up empty dessert plates. Where Knox kept everyone guessing with food, Sylvie's personal mission was to find the perfect sweet to go with whatever meal was chosen. Tonight, it'd been a traditional cheesecake, made one hundred percent from scratch. Plates in one hand, she paused next to Knox, patted his cheek and winked. "Don't let 'em get ta ye, love. Whatever ye pick is fine with us."

Axel grumbled and thumbed through the screen's television guide. "Christ, Ma. Don't encourage him. We'll end up eating frozen Kid Cuisines again."

Vivienne snickered, stood and started helping Sylvie. "You guys are so dense. He only does it to get your goat. If you'd relax and go with the flow a bit, he'd find some other way to make you nuts."

Yep. Jace's woman was smart as hell. No wonder the Haven leader had given up his solitary ways to claim her.

As if spurred by some innate womanly cue, Ninette and Gabe joined in with cleanup detail, their quiet voices as they divvied up tasks and shared plans for the next day drifting through the room with a pleasant warmth.

Out of nowhere, the conversation he'd had with JJ popped in his head. He'd done that a lot the last few days, churning through the possible ways of how to bring her request up with his brothers along with his suspicions, but this time he couldn't help but wonder how she'd fit in with the rest of the women. If she'd be as comfortable as Viv, Gabe and Nat were with his brothers.

Knox shoved the thought aside, closed his eyes and focused on the moment. Family night never got old. The other guys grumbled every now and then when Sylvie and Ninette demanded their presence each Wednesday, but not him. He'd waited his whole damned life for this. Watched the other foster kids he hung with finding permanent homes while he bounced from place to place, hoping each new placement would be different. But it never was. At seventeen he'd given up and accepted Beck would be the closest to family he'd ever get.

And then he'd met Axel.

One private security gig, a whole lot of hacking questions and a full year later, Axel, Jace, Trevor and Zeke had welcome him and Beckett into the fold. Only twenty-three years to get the family he'd wanted, but man, the wait had been worth it. So yeah, Ninette and Sylvie might have to browbeat the rest of his brothers, but it'd take an act of God and a probable loss of limbs before he'd miss this weekly sabbatical from the world.

Still chattering amongst themselves, the women ambled out of the room and toward the kitchen downstairs.

Jace scanned each of his brothers. "Who's bunking down here for the night?"

That was the cool thing about Jace and Axel's ranch on the outskirts of Allen, Texas. Every brother had their own suite away from Dallas's chaos and no one but family was allowed. The massive estate was exactly what Jace had named it—Haven. A safe place where they could get away, say what they thought without censure and cover whatever business needed handling without fear of prying ears.

"I'm in," Knox said.

"Me, too."

"Yep," Beck and Danny said in tandem.

Trevor cupped his son's shoulder, the pride on his face as he did so rattling long dead hopes inside of Knox like a box of brittle bones. "Can't tonight. Levi's got a thing in town with his best friend in the morning."

Man, but Trevor was lucky. Levi might not be flesh and blood, but as of a few months ago, he was Trevor's boy as far as the courts were concerned. And he was a helluva kid. Rambunctious. Smart. Honest to a fault, too, which meant no one could never predict what jaw-dropping comment was gonna fly out of his mouth.

Zeke raked his fingers through this hair and yawned. "I've got a day shift tomorrow, so me and Gabe are gonna head home."

What a difference a woman made. A little over a year ago, Zeke had been as hard to unwind as Knox, yet here he was at barely ten o'clock, yawning and ready to head home with his old lady.

Out of nowhere, the memory of JJ and the way that she'd looked at him during that one, unguarded moment during their meeting hit him hard. He'd had women look at him with lust before, but she'd focused on his lips like she'd die if she didn't get a taste. He shook off the image and forced himself to focus. "Got something I need to run past you guys before anyone heads out."

Axel folded up the footrest on his black leather recliner, stood with his empty crystal tumbler and tossed the remote next to Jace on his way to the wet bar. "Brother, you ate two baked potatoes, all of one strip and half of Gabe's. Not sure you how can think after all that food."

"No shit," Danny said. "For a skinny guy, I don't know where you put it."

Jace chuckled and took up scanning through the television channels. "He works it off with the women in his little black book."

Beck gave Knox a look that said he was about a nanosecond away from spilling how long Knox had gone without sleep before he'd caved and hooked up with Tiffany.

Knowing that would get him a whole lot of attention and a lecture he didn't need from Zeke, he redirected the conversation before Beckett could speak. "You guys remember that skip tracer who helped us with Trevor's deal?"

Axel glanced back from the wet bar. "JJ, right?"

"Jeannie Simpson on paper," Knox said, "but me, Beck and Danny have been digging into her, and I've got a hunch that's a bogus identity."

Jace paused with his scotch halfway to his mouth and asked, "Just a privacy thing or something else?"

"My gut says something else."

Beckett crossed his arms as though he were settling in for a good debate. "For the record, his gut was paranoid a week ago. Then he met her and realized I was right."

"Right about what?" Zeke said.

Danny snickered, but otherwise kept his silence. He'd barely been a brother for a year, but he'd settled into his place among them like he'd been there his whole life.

Knox scowled at Beckett. "Give it a rest, already.

You gonna tell me you'd have thought any different if you'd found that picture?"

"Bloody hell." Axel turned from the bar, leaned against it and crossed his feet at his ankles. "You three wanna quit the Larry, Curly and Moe routine? Found what picture?"

From Beckett's place on the sectional, Axel was behind him, but Beck cranked his head Axel's direction the best he could. "Knox got an email from JJ saying she wanted to talk about a business opportunity. But, Knox being Knox, he assumed she was out to blackmail the lot of us after helping us out with Natalie's ex, so he dug deeper online for counter-dirt."

"And?" Jace said.

Knox focused on Jace. "The JJ Simpson we worked with is squeaky clean. Only, if you go back in time about three years, she looked a hell of a lot different than she does now and lived in San Diego."

Trevor frowned. "Not sure I follow."

The same buzz Knox got anytime a decent puzzle or problem presented itself fired beneath his skin, nudging him past his lingering food coma. He pushed up on the couch and planted his elbows on his knees. "The online pictures I found of JJ Simpson three years ago and further back show a woman in her early thirties. Curvy body, gold-red hair, green eyes and 5'6" according to legal records. Not a ton of online shots, but at least some candid ones on old social media accounts. Not exactly a country girl, but I'd bet she comes from a blue-collar background." He shifted his attention to Axel, pacing closer. "Today all I can find are state and federal headshots and the woman in them has platinum blonde hair and light blue eyes."

"So?" Zeke said. "Identities get mixed up all the time these days."

"Yeah, well, I wanted to know for sure, so we combed her place." Knox whipped out his phone, flipped to the image he'd snapped from the box under JJ's bed and passed it to Jace on his left. "I found this shot of both women."

Jace set the remote aside and zoomed in on the picture. "So, where's the redhead now?"

"No clue," Knox said, "but I can't find any recent pictures of her."

Axel rounded behind Jace on the sofa and studied the picture over his shoulder. "You're thinkin' foul play?"

"Thought," Knox clarified. "I set up a meeting two days ago to see what her business deal was, and Beckett's impression after tailing her was right. No way she's a killer. If she is, she's the best damned actress I've ever met. But she's definitely hiding. Or more accurately running. From who, I still don't know."

"What was the business deal?" Trevor asked.

Beckett aimed an *I told you so* look at him and Danny chuckled.

Knox rolled his eyes and blew them both off. "She found out I've got a history of mentoring coders and wanted to offer a trade—my coaching in exchange for her services. Traces or administrative work. Whatever I need."

Zeke leaned forward and plunked his empty Bohemia Weiss on the oversize wood tray situated in the center of the huge ottoman. "I thought she was a skip tracer."

"She is," Knox said, "but she wants more. Says she doesn't like finding people who don't want to be found."

Danny tipped the top of his beer toward Knox. "Which ties in with the whole assumed identity. If she didn't like the job, why start it in the first place?"

"Exactly," Knox said.

Jace tossed Knox's phone across the ottoman to Zeke and Trevor's side of the couch. "So, what happened to the first JJ?"

"She's MIA," Beckett said. "No death certificate. No new sightings. She's just gone."

"And you think blondie engineered all this?" Axel said to Knox.

"Not sure *engineered* is the right word. My guess, it's more a case of her taking advantage of an existing situation. I do know this. She wants the chance to work with me enough to risk a lot to make it happen."

"What makes you think that?" Trevor said.

"Because she's got a seriously thick Russian accent. Just showing up for the meet made it clear she wasn't born on US soil and the *real* JJ Simpson was born in San Diego thirty-two years ago."

Zeke cocked his head. "You call her on it?"

"Yep. Asked her point blank how long she'd been here. For a minute, I thought she'd scramble for some lame excuse, but she copped to moving here two and half years ago."

Danny muttered over the top of his beer, "Definitely a runner."

"But honest," Beckett added.

Axel lifted his tumbler in salute. "That counts in my book."

For a few seconds, silence filled the room, each man looking from one to the other. Per usual, it was Jace who spoke first. "So, what's your play? You gonna teach her?"

And there was the question. His instincts had already gone off half-cocked once and now he couldn't decide if he was solid enough to make the call. Especially considering how she'd scrambled his head through the last part of their meet.

Knox shrugged. "She's got attitude and aptitude. I needed a leg up once. Seems the right thing to do."

"But?" Trevor said.

"But without knowing who she's running from, there's no telling what kind of attention we'd attract. Plus, I'm going on pure gut. She could still be a hell of an actress. I don't like the idea of putting her in contact with any of our systems without several second opinions."

Beckett slouched deeper in the cushions. "Already gave you my spin. Give it a go."

Danny chuckled and shook his head. "You're just angling to win the bet."

Zeke perked up and swiveled his attention to Danny. "What bet?"

Grinning huge, Danny zeroed in on Trevor and Zeke. "She's hot. Like Christmas fairy hot. Beckett ponied up one large that says Knox'll add her to his black book inside of a month."

"Not gonna happen," Knox said. "If anyone knows what a bad idea it is to fuck someone you're teaching or working with, it's me."

In all of a second, Beckett went from laid-back to upright and pissed off. "Oh, give that shit a rest. You were barely eighteen. Not a man in this room that could think with anything other than their dick at that age. Especially with a thirty-year-old teacher built like a brick shit house out for attention. JJ's thirty-two. That's a whole different situation."

"No, her *records* say she's thirty-two," Knox argued back. "No way she's that old."

Beckett scoffed, stood and stomped to the mini fridge. "Whatever. She's way older than you were so cut yourself some fucking slack."

Not the least bit bothered by Beckett's outburst, Jace grinned and focused on Knox. "Gotta say, sometimes mixing work and pleasure works out for the best."

"I'll second that," Trevor said.

Of course, they would. Both of them had found their women through work. Sort of. Trevor had truly gone after Natalie while she was on payroll, but Jace had to bribe Vivienne into a job first and *then* lured her in.

"You guys are makin' too much out of this." Granted, he'd had a whole host of ideas slide through his head on things he'd like to do to JJ while she was sitting next to him, but who the hell could blame him? With those high as fuck heels she'd had on and her sinfully long legs, he'd have had to be a eunuch not to conjure up a ton of dirty thoughts. "The only reason I'm considering what she asked is because she seems to need the help. That's what we do, right? Just because she doesn't have a dick doesn't mean I should tell her no."

Beckett paced forward with his fresh beer, took a pull, then murmured, "Mmm hmmm."

Trevor grinned at Beck's subtle jab but gave his attention to Knox. "Ignore him. If you want more opinions, just set it up so we meet her."

Danny barked out a laugh. "Yeah, that's an incentive to keep a girl from running. Line her up in front of seven men with a ton of questions."

"Not like that," Jace volleyed back. Like they handled this kind of arrangement every day when in fact, they only met as a group for brothers. Or meeting a woman a brother wanted to claim. "We'll set up something casual. She doesn't have to know what's up. Just a chance for us to get a read on her."

"A family thing," Zeke added, though his gaze when it slid to Knox had a mischievous glimmer that made Knox want to stand up and pace. "Wouldn't be the first time we'd gotten together to meet a girl, would it?"

The fucker. That wasn't what this was and he damned well knew it. Still, if he protested, the rest of the guys would just jump on the bandwagon, so Knox ignored it.

Axel leaned his hip against the couch and rubbed his jawline, working his fingers through his thick beard. "We could meet her Saturday night. That's the next Bikers and Blues Rally."

As laid-back venues went, the summer-long gimmick Axel had set up to promote a new outdoor music venue in Dallas was perfect. The premise behind the bi-weekly gatherings was that if you could get people out on a regular basis in the hottest months of the year in Texas, you could damn well support a steady music venue year-round. So far, he'd been successful as hell, packing Klyde Warren Park to the gills with a slew of bikers and every other music lover in Dallas.

"That could work." Beckett shuttled his gaze from Jace, to Trevor and Zeke. "The girls will be there, right?"

"Yep," Zeke said. "Music. Food. Laid-back. Perfect for letting JJ's guard down."

Jace studied Knox, the uncanny shrewdness behind his eyes saying he was thinking the same thing Zeke was. "That gonna work for you?"

Well, they could eyeball and tease him about mixing work and pleasure all they wanted, but this was nothing more than a meet with a prospective employee. Not some fabricated excuse to get his family's blessing on a long-awaited girlfriend. Knox shrugged and reclined against the couch back. "Yep. Works for me just fine."

Chapter Seven

Three sharp raps sounded against Darya's front door, jerking her out of a dead sleep and upright in bed. Her heart kicked and sputtered while she blinked and brought her eyes into focus. Soft early-morning sunlight slipped past her bedroom blinds and blanketed her room in a muted glow. The dim drone of traffic from the highway sounded in the distance, but otherwise everything was quiet. Peaceful.

She shoved her hair out of her face. Maybe she'd dreamed the sound. It wouldn't be the first time she'd been jolted awake by a nightmare, but she'd hoped after a six-month stretch without one, they'd finally ceased.

She dropped to her back, rolled toward the nightstand and fumbled for her phone. Her favorite wolf graphic glowed on the lock screen, a bold 7:02 a.m. displayed across the black-haired predator as he howled up to a full moon.

It had to be a dream. Beyond the occasional maintenance man, she never had visitors, and they'd never knock on her door this early. She laid back down and curled on her side, tucking one hand under her pillow as her eyes slipped closed.

Knock. Knock. Knock.

Her eyes snapped open and she squeezed the phone still nestled in her palm so hard it groaned. No way that was her imagination. Pulse lurching to a jog, she swept her legs out from between the cool sheets and snagged her fluffy gray robe off the floor where it had fallen sometime in the night. She crept toward the living room, careful not to make a sound. It couldn't be Ruslan. Knocking was too foreign of a concept for a man like him.

Then again, it could be he'd merely caught a lead as to where she lived and was flushing her out. He might be arrogant, but he wasn't stupid enough to draw unnecessary attention. She belted her robe with a firm tug, gently pressed her palms against the door's cool surface and rolled up on her tiptoes for the peephole.

Sunlight shafted from the eastern horizon, casting whoever stood outside in a vibrant halo. They lifted their hand to knock again, blocking the sun's rays just enough to bring their face into focus.

Knox.

His knuckles connected with the thick wood and she jumped back, the lingering vibration zinging through her body as powerful as a live current.

"Just a minute." She winced at her obviously frazzled voice and combed her fingers through her hair. So much for making a solid follow-up impression. She might not wear heavy makeup most days, but she'd at least like to have a little on when face-to-face with a prospective boss. Even nearing her third year in America, she'd yet to shake the need impressed on most Russian women to primp and prepare before presenting herself in public.

On the bright side, her short robe was cute with silver worked into the gray chenille and did a decent job of hiding her stick figure. She flipped the deadbolt, braced long enough to suck in a steadying breath, then pasted on a bright smile as she opened the door. "Hello."

Knox turned, his hands planted on his hips and a scowl on his face that made her rethink having opened the door.

Until his expression shifted.

One measly second and the predator on her doorstep morphed from impatient bystander to focused hunter. Slow and steady, his gaze trailed the length of her, the heat in his gaze thicker than the hottest Texas afternoon. His attention snagged on the deep neckline of her robe and, for a second, she'd swear he'd clued in to her lack of clothing underneath.

Her breasts grew heavy and her nipples puckered against the soft fabric. She fisted the lapels above her heart to try and cover her body's all too willing reaction. "Is everything okay?"

Whether it was the huskiness in her voice or the question itself that broke his focus, she wasn't sure, but his gaze shot to hers and his voice came out deep and rumbling like it was hard to speak it all. "I woke you up."

"I worked late last night." Granted, the last hour before she'd nodded off had involved a few toys and a whole lot of sexual frustration, but he didn't need to know that. She stepped back enough to motion him through the doorway. "Do you want to come in? I can make some coffee."

He glanced at the parking lot, frowned as though questioning the wisdom of being there and raked his hand through his already mussed hair. Instead of turning her down like she expected, he stepped across the threshold. "Coffee's probably a good idea."

She shut the door behind him, pausing a moment to watch him unhindered while he openly perused her space. The barest hint of his subtle but sexy scent lingered in his wake, a rich black currant mingled with woodsmoke that made her think of cold winter nights spent tangled and sweaty in bed with a lover. His navy blue T-shirt was a little rumpled and had a caption styled like a neon beer sign that read, *Live Every Day Like It's Taco Tuesday*. On anyone else it would have looked cheesy, but on him it was cute.

And crazy sexy.

Forcing herself out of her visual indulgence, she hurried to the kitchen and set about prepping coffee.

"Sorry about waking you up," he said. "I don't sleep much. Sometimes I forget the rest of the world doesn't suffer that problem."

She stole a peek over one shoulder.

He stood with hands planted on each hip and stared up at the winter wolves painting JJ had given her for her first Christmas in America. Even without Knox's attention aimed her direction, energy fairly poured off him. So much so, she wasn't entirely sure plying him with more caffeine was a good idea. He already looked like he'd downed three pots of coffee and a few Red Bulls for good measure. "It's okay. My alarm would have gone off in another thirty minutes anyway."

As soon as she pushed the brew button, he faced her, which made her wonder if he hadn't been clued in to her every move the entire time. He prowled forward, eyes roving her apartment as though cataloguing every inch. Glancing back toward her bedroom, his gait

hitched the tiniest bit when his gaze landed on her di-
sheveled bed. He recovered fast, though, locking stares
with her and motioning toward her desk chair with a
jerk of his head. "Sit."

"It would be rude to sit while you stood." She motioned to the couch behind him. "We can sit there if
you like."

He grinned, leaned his shoulder against the wall that
separated her galley kitchen from the living room and
crossed his arms. "If you're gonna argue every time I
tell you to do something, me teaching you isn't gonna
last long."

"But—"

"I'm not the formal sit-on-the-sofa-and-chat type. I
sprawl. Usually with a computer or a game controller
in my hands. Considering I barely know you and my
laptop's out in the car, I'm not gonna kick my feet up
on your pristine cushions and make myself at home. At
least not yet. Now, sit."

She bit back pointing out that she wasn't a dog, but
just barely.

The full-on smile he shot her said she'd conveyed
the thought regardless. "You sure you want to work
with me?"

Lifting one brow, she practically stomped to her chair
and planted her butt in the seat but did it sideways so
she kept him in her direct line of sight.

His attention dropped to the hem of her robe where
it rested mid-thigh and his smile slipped.

For a second, she couldn't breathe. Could only focus
on the building pulse and ready slickness between her
legs. The way he looked at her, the intensity behind it,
she could almost imagine his touch, warm and confi-

dent as it slipped between her knees up the insides of her thighs until he cupped her sex.

He pushed off the wall and meandered to the kitchen counter, thankfully shattering the moment before she did something stupid like peel her robe back and take care of business herself.

"You might as well learn up front, I'm bossy as hell," he said. "I've got a certain way I do things. Nothing half-ass." He opened the cabinet right above her coffee maker and snagged a mug like he'd been there a thousand times before.

She snapped taller in her chair. "How'd you know where the cups were?"

"Why'd you put 'em right above the coffee maker?"

"Because that's where they're most convenient."

He glanced back at her, smirked and shut the cabinet door. "That's how I knew." He scanned her tidy countertop. "You do milk or sugar?"

"I can make my own."

"Didn't ask that. I asked if you take milk or sugar."

"No. I like it better black."

"That because you don't have a sweet tooth, or because you like to hurry up and get down to business?"

She swallowed, the tone in his voice making her question if they were talking about coffee preferences or something far more personal. "I like to get down to business."

He nodded, but his lips twitched as though fighting back another smile. Turning, he rested his hips against the countertop and curled his fingers around the edge. "Where were we?"

"You're bossy and nothing half-ass," she said before her brain could check the flippant retort.

This time he didn't even try to hide the grin. "When Jason was extolling my virtues, did he also happen to mention I'm arrogant, compulsively organized, controlling and nosey in a way you're sure to hate inside of one week?"

"I promise you, I've met men far more arrogant and controlling than you, and I'm certain I could top your organizational skills if given a chance. So, if you're trying to scare me off, it won't work. If you don't want to take a chance on me, then speak your mind and move on, but I'm not stopping until I'm successful. The only uncertainty is the path I take to get there."

She wasn't sure what response she'd expected her rant to generate. Surprise maybe. Irritation for sure. After all, he'd pushed her buttons this morning, so turnabout was fair play. But instead of either, he clipped a quick nod. "Good answer. God knows, you're gonna need that attitude to get you through the next few months."

Behind him, the coffee machine spewed and gurgled the last of its cycle.

Knox pushed off the counter, turned and pulled the carafe off the burner. "I doubt you've checked your email since I woke you up, but you'll find three links to different training programs I've set up for you."

"You did?" She spun to her computer and waggled her mouse to bring her screen to life. "There wasn't anything when I went to sleep last night."

"Like I said, I don't sleep much." The clunk and slide of the coffeepot moving across the warmer sounded behind her mixed with the hiss of a few coffee drops sizzling against the plate. "That's another thing you'll have to get used to. I do most of my code reviews overnight so expect to get hit first thing in the morning."

Zeroing in on his email the second it loaded in her inbox, she clicked on the first of the training links. A browser session opened listing at least fifteen modules with descriptions too dense with information to process with him watching over her shoulder.

Movement sounded and his voice drew closer. "You want to work with me, you've got two hurdles to clear. First, I want you to finish all the sessions on the first course I listed and get me the sample code you generate from it by 5:00 p.m. Friday. You make it to that point without jumping out the window or calling me to cry uncle, then I'll pick you up at eight on Saturday night for the second leg."

He plunked the coffee down on the desk right beside her hand, dug his wallet out of his back pocket and fished out a business card. He waggled it a few times then plunked it down next to the mug. "You want to wave the white flag, here's my number."

For the longest time her mind struggled to catch up, the sheer logistics of completing what he'd asked in two days' time scrambling her wits. The sessions she'd done before had taken her twice as long, and she'd bet a carte blanche Neiman Marcus shopping spree he knew it.

Knox stared down at her, that edgy charisma that clung to him sparking twice as hot and a blazing dare burning in his eyes. "You think you can do it?"

Maybe. She'd have to give up sleep and possibly meals to pull it off, but she wouldn't tell him that. "Absolutely."

"Good." He turned and ambled toward the door.

"You're leaving?"

"Yep," he said without looking back.

"But you didn't drink your coffee."

"The coffee's for you. Trust me. You're gonna need it."

He opened the door.

She glanced down at his card beside the coffee cup. What had he said about Saturday and a second task? She scrambled to her feet. "Wait."

He paused mid-closing the door behind him, one hand still wrapped around the knob as he looked back and raised both eyebrows.

"What's the second hurdle?"

One corner of his mouth crooked wickedly, all bad boy promise and devilish delight. "You meet my brothers."

Chapter Eight

Knox backed his Harley into an open parking spot outside JJ's apartment and killed the engine. At eight o'clock on a Saturday night, the world around him was anything but quiet, but it still seemed tame in the absence of his bike's throaty rumble. Smiling to himself, he jogged up the steps. Tonight would be interesting for sure. Not only had JJ delivered the code generated from the first lesson he'd assigned her, but it had hit his inbox two hours early.

Knox,
My code is attached. Hurdle one is complete. Assuming the quality meets or exceeds your exacting standards, I'll be ready to tackle task two at eight o'clock tomorrow.
Sincerely,
JJ

Oh, yeah. He'd definitely fired her up with his Thursday morning visit. Which sucked for him because the attitude was a total fucking turn-on. Especially paired with her crazy-quick wit and serious intelligence.

Still, there'd been a purpose behind him prodding

her temper, and it had worked just like he'd hoped. She had a long way to go before she had so much as a prayer of making a living writing apps, and the best way he sensed he'd help her was with some good old-fashioned challenge.

He rapped his knuckles against the old wood door and studied the highway in the distance. Much as he hated to admit it, his head had spent way too much time the last few days rehashing the last time he'd stood in this spot. Or, more to the point, the image of her in that short robe with her sinfully long legs on prime display. No way had she had anything on underneath it. He'd been suspicious when she'd gripped the lapels between her breasts and waved him in, but seeing how much of her thighs were exposed when she sat behind her desk cinched it. How he'd stopped from dropping to his knees, anchoring her thighs over his shoulders and tonguing her cunt until she screamed was a damned miracle.

The deadbolt disengaged and the door opened.

Damn.

Talk about a gorgeous woman. Why it hadn't occurred to him to spell out what she should wear he couldn't say, but seeing her in her sheer white top, tight black fuck-me skirt and matching heels was damn well worth the miscommunication.

He prowled forward not waiting for an invite, taking his sweet time as he did so and giving her a solid once-over. "You look great."

Interestingly enough, she waited until the last possible second to step aside and let him pass, and if he wasn't mistaken her lips pursed with a barely restrained smirk. "Thank you. Although, I hope you'll forgive me if I say the effort was for your brothers and not for you."

And there was the attitude again. It might have been veiled under a polite and formal response, but the bite was there none the less. Totally hot.

Her television remote sat on one end of the glass coffee table, perfectly perpendicular to the edge. As if her smarts, sass and sex appeal weren't already enough of a package, she had to go and give his compulsive drive for neatness a run for its money. Sighing, he rounded the table, snatched up the remote and made himself at home on her couch. "Sweetheart, if you didn't have them eating out of your hand with your accent, you'd definitely seal the deal with your legs. Only problem is, where we're going, you're going to need to dress a whole lot more casual."

She frowned, checked her appearance, then shot her gaze back to him. "But you said this was an interview."

"No, I said you were going to meet my brothers. Big difference. Between where we're going and the way we're getting there, I'm thinking you'd be smart to ditch the skirt and wiggle into some jeans. Boots, too, if you've got 'em."

"Boots?"

He punched the power button and fought the need to kick his feet up on the coffee table. Comfort was one thing, but mucking up the clean surface seemed a dick move even if he was out to build some professional distance with his demanding behavior. "Yep. Whatever kind you've got. Or close-toed shoes if you don't have those."

"Why?"

Thumbing through the guide, he scowled at the

screen. Basic cable only. He'd have to fix that. As-suming she got a thumbs-up from the guys and things moved forward. Then again, as busy as he planned to keep her, movie binges wouldn't be in her future for a while. He punched CNN and dialed back the volume. "Because while you'd look badass wearing those heels riding on the back of my bike, they wouldn't do much to keep your pretty toes protected."

"Your bike?" It was just two words, but with them a whole new demeanor swept over her, the sharp-edged battle-ready businesswoman replaced with a kid pre-Christmas morning. "You mean motorcycle, correct? Not bicycle."

For some stupid reason, his mind coughed up the lu-dicrous image of him peddling his old hand-me-down dirt bike with her perched in the center of the handle-bars. "That depends. Is your enthusiasm in favor of the motorized variety? Or do you have a thing for self-powered means of transportation?"

The smile she shot him was blinding. Pure, unadul-terated joy in the making. "I'm very much in favor of motorcycles."

Fuck.

Her accent was sexy enough when she was throw-ing him sass, but mixed with the husky rasp it was downright lethal. Thank God he was sitting down and stretched out to give his dick room to swell or he'd be damned uncomfortable. "Are you a fan because you've ridden before, or because you want to?"

"I've never been, but I've always wanted to."

Well, wasn't this a delightful revelation. He'd get to feel her body pressed against him and he'd give her a first. A win-win for everyone. He jerked his head to-

ward her bedroom and prayed she'd be too preoccupied
in her excitement to notice how much he was looking
forward to popping at least one kind of cherry. "Then
get a move on. We need to get you saddled up and
ready to ride."

Riding on the back of a Harley with Knox Torren had
to be on the top of Darya's best-ever experience list.
Everything seemed so much closer. So much more vibrant and tangible than it did from the safety of her
car. With her chest pressed against his back, her arms
banded around his solid abs and his rich masculine scent
mingling with the whipping wind it was pure heaven
on Earth. An extraordinary rush.

Knox leaned into a turn that took them through a
major intersection and steered them toward a park on
the opposite side of the highway bustling with at least
a thousand people. A well-manicured green stretched
the length of two city blocks, dotted on each side with
slender pin oaks and old-fashioned street lights. At the
farthest end, a huge stage had been set up, it's red, blue
and white lights pulsing in time with music that registered even above the motorcycle's roar.

She smiled and hugged her arms tighter around
Knox. JJ would have loved this. Every second of it.
Although, knowing JJ, she wouldn't have been content
as a mere passenger. No, ten minutes into the ride, she'd
have devised a plan to buy her own bike and would've
launched her first solo trip shortly after. Nothing had
ever held JJ back. Not her fears and certainly not her
past—which was the main reason she'd been so ada-
mant to help Darya right up until the day she'd died.

Too soon, Knox backed them into a line of other

motorcycles in a makeshift parking lot. All the others were similar in size to his, but none had the same edgy appearance. Where the others were all shiny chrome and flash, his was lean, mean and all business with ebony paint and matte black pipes. He killed the engine and the thrumming beat of a blues song surged in to fill the void.

So, this was what a live concert was like. Directly in front of the stage, the crowd was thick with people standing shoulder to shoulder, but farther back clusters of attendees had set up sport chairs or thrown down blankets to enjoy the show. Most fascinating of all were the variety of people. Young, old and everyone in between. Social status didn't seem to equate here. As if all the world's biases had clocked out for the night and simply opened its arms to everyone.

Knox craned his head just enough to grin back at her. "If you hop off, I'll get you in the thick of it instead of making you soak it up from the parking lot."

"Oh. Right. Sorry." She braced her hands on his shoulders, barely stifling the urge to savor the compacted muscles beneath her palms, and set about getting herself vertical. Thankfully, the dismount came off a lot less awkward than when she'd climbed on. Then again, after the exhilarating ride, she was so pumped up on adrenaline she probably could have levitated off the machine if she'd put her mind to it.

The second she cleared the seat, Knox popped the kickstand, put the bike to rest and swung his leg over the back like a modern-day cowboy.

Maybe it was the energy around her, or the genuine smile he gave her as he turned and stuffed his keys inside the pocket of his faded jeans. But in one overpowering moment, all the emotions she'd kept carefully contained since the day JJ died surged to the surface, knocking aside every scrap of common sense and decorum in favor of unadulterated gratitude.

She wasn't alone. For this moment in time, she had companionship, was very much alive, safe and living free with the promise of a new and exciting future. She jolted forward, wrapped Knox up in a huge hug and rasped, "Thank you."

His arms came around her, slow and gentle at first, then growing in strength. As though he'd intuited the storm roiling through her and sensed her need to be anchored. "Goes without saying, I like the way you show appreciation." He slid his hands along her spine, splaying one between her shoulder blades and the other low on her back. Not quite on her ass, but low enough to make her body come alive and crave an entirely different connection. When he spoke, his voice was low and grated. "Not thinkin' that's a good idea though if I'm gonna be your boss."

As fast as she'd lost control, reality snapped into place and she tried to pull away.

He held fast, forcing her hips more tightly against his.

He wanted her. If the heat behind his thundercloud-colored eyes didn't convey it clearly enough, the impressive erection pressed against her made the realization irrefutable. Her heart kicked hard enough to rival the steady beat from the bass drum, and while she tried to temper her voice with a casual lightness, it came out breathy and ragged. "I'm so sorry. I was just…well, happy."

"So am I now. Very much so." His gaze dipped to her lips and he inhaled slow and deep, but instead of taking the kiss she hoped for, he relaxed his grip and eased her away. "Just not willing to cross that line with someone who wants to be my employee."

"Of course." She nodded and put more distance between them, hating the uncomfortable situation she'd created with her actions. Logically, she saw the reason behind the boundary. He was a businessman. A highly creative, driven and successful one. Unfortunately, common sense didn't seem to be something her mind generated in high supply where Knox was concerned. "You should know, I didn't intend it inappropriately. My family was very open in their affection and I tend to be the same. Sometimes impulsively so. I didn't mean to make you uncomfortable."

He crowded closer, eradicating the buffer she'd created. "The last word I'd use to describe the feel of you next to me is *uncomfortable*. Stunned, maybe. Stoked and ready to go, absolutely. But even if I were willing to mix business and pleasure, I am not the kind of man you want to go there with. I may have only known you a handful of days, but I've seen and sensed enough to know you deserve a whole lot more than I'm willing to give any woman. Understand?"

Not really. Her instincts about people were seldom wrong, and everything they said about Knox was that he was not only trustworthy, but deeply loyal and caring. Then again, processing anything rational with him standing this close was impossible. She dipped her head in a crisp professional nod and forced herself to meet his stare. "Absolutely."

He hit her with his killer smile and motioned toward the crowd with a jerk of his head. "Good, then let's get you a tour and see if we can't track down my family."

The tour consisted of a leisurely stroll past five different barbecue vendors that left her mouth watering, an overflowing beer tent and three more booths specializing in wine, liquor and band merchandise. The closer they got to the stage, the stronger the music thrummed through her and the thicker the crowds grew, but throughout it, Knox kept his silence, guiding her this way and that and letting her soak up every detail.

Near the center of the venue sat a roped-off section full of round tables with a private bar stationed in the middle. Knox splayed his hand low on her back, pointed toward it and leaned in close. "We're headed there."

To her left, a burly man with shoulder-length salt-and-pepper hair barked out a laugh, spun from a large cluster of men dressed as rugged as he was and stepped directly in her path.

Before she could dodge out of the way, Knox shifted his hand from her back to her hip, swiftly pulled her out of the big man's trajectory and shielded her from any impact.

Burly man lifted both hands apologetically, scanned the two of them and beamed a full-toothed smile at Knox. "Hey, Knox, I wondered if I'd see you here." His gaze shifted back to Darya for another much slower perusal before he returned his attention to Knox. "You lookin' for your crew?"

Knox shook his head. "Nope. Clocked 'em in the VIP section already."

"The perks of Axel bein' the one who put this gig together I take it?"

"Something like that." Knox squeezed his hand still anchored on her hip. "JJ, meet Seth. Seth, this is my friend JJ Simpson."

Friend? That was an interesting choice for an introduction. Better than associate or colleague, maybe, but still not what she'd expected.

"Man, you've got a lot of *friends* and every one of them is hot." Seth held out his big hand, heavy calluses lining his palm and two chunky silver rings adorning his fingers. A tangle of tribal tattoos snaked up and down his forearm. "Nice to meet you."

His grip when she placed her hand in his was surprisingly gentle for such a big man. "Nice to meet you, too."

He kept his hold, letting the possessive clasp linger as he assessed Knox, then dropped his hand and edged back. "You two hanging around awhile?"

"At least until the band wraps up." Knox dipped his head in a way that indicated he was done with the conversation and nudged Darya toward the reserved section. "Let me get JJ situated and we'll catch up later."

"Oh, yeah we will. Count on it." With that, Seth winked at her and sauntered off to wherever he'd been headed before he'd kamikazied into her path.

"Seth is a friend of yours?" she asked as they wove through the people.

"More of an acquaintance. He works for a guy who's got business with my brother Jace."

Before she could ask what kind of work a tough-looking man like Seth specialized in, they reached the restricted entry to the private area. Two men guarded the gate, both in tight-fitting black T-shirts with *Security* emblazoned in big letters on the back. Rather than ask them for names or identification as she'd expected, the mocha-skinned man with dreadlocks down to his shoulder blades flashed Knox a familiar smile and lifted his hand for a high-five greeting. "Hey, man. Wondered when you were gonna show."

Knox greeted him in kind, an entirely different level of familiarity registering than what he'd shown Seth. "Hey, Ivan. Didn't expect to see you on shit detail tonight."

Ivan shrugged and rubbed the back of his hand against his chin. "You know how it goes. Axel needed help, so I ponied up."

A look passed between them, one she couldn't quite categorize, but seemed loaded with meaning.

"It all counts," Knox said. "Doin' time is worth it in the end."

"I get it." He jerked his head toward a table just beyond the private bar and food vendors set aside for VIPs. "Your crew's dead ahead. Have a good time."

Capturing her hand in his, Knox led the way, nodding and lifting his hand in greeting at different people along the way.

"You know a lot of people," she said from behind him.

He glanced back and grinned. "My brothers know a lot of people. If left to my own devices, I'd probably never get out from behind my computer."

Just as they approached the table Ivan had indicated, Knox released his hold. The band ended their song and announced they'd be back after a short break, and the crowd let loose with resounding applause.

A deep rumbling voice sounded from somewhere on the other side of Knox. "Thought we were gonna have to send Beckett out for search and rescue."

She inched forward to see who'd spoken just as Knox stepped back and brought the whole table into full view.

The impact was staggering. Even having shamelessly studied each of them in the picture she'd saved from the rally earlier in the year, the men Knox called brothers were twice as impressive in person. Next to three of them were equally beautiful women, each comfortably situated close to their men with happy, contented expressions.

Knox waved to the man and woman closest to him. "JJ, this is Jace and Vivienne. The two goobers next to him are Beckett and Danny. You'll get more than your fair share of dealing with them if you end up on payroll."

Darya nodded, all the nervousness she'd managed to ignore in the last hour surging back to the forefront along with a healthy fear she'd bungle this meeting altogether.

Not pausing to let anyone get a word in edgewise, Knox kept going. "The happy couples over there are Zeke and Gabe, and Trevor and Natalie. Both newlyweds and utterly disgusting to watch."

The dark-haired woman he'd introduced as Vivienne frowned up at Knox. "What are we? Chopped liver?"

"It's been a year and half," Knox grumbled back. "You're just a garden variety couple now. And I'm still convinced you two are piping suspicious shit into the water at Haven. All the lovey dovey's contagious."

The grate of metal on concrete sounded on her left, drawing her attention to the one brother she'd yet to meet. He was tall, at least six foot one, and would have been intimidating with his long russet hair and full beard if it weren't for his tailored slacks and fine button-down with rolled up shirtsleeves. Despite the heat, he looked utterly comfortable among the rest of the casual crowd and not the least bit wrinkled.

Not waiting for Knox's introduction, he stepped in close and offered his hand. "I'm Axel McKee."

Darya placed her hand in his, expecting a polite shake, only to have him lift it to his lips. "It's nice to meet you," she managed, the sheer devilment in his wicked gaze hitting her harder than the kicks she'd earned in her last sparring session.

Axel grinned, his smile and the soft tickle of his whiskers against her skin sending goose bumps up her arm. "Christ, that accent's gonna do me in." Straightening, he kept hold of her hand, tugged her closer to his side and pulled a chair from behind them next to his. "What's say you settle in next to me and ply me with it for a day or two?"

"Yeah, that's not gonna happen." Knox slid the chair away, scooted it into an open slot on the far side of Jace and steered her that direction. "A word to the wise. Axel thinks it's his God-given mission to seduce all the women in the tristate area. Sit next to Jace. He's too busy getting into Viv's panties to try and score yours."

"You wound me, brother." Axel settled into his chair, his eyes still on Darya as he raised his glass in salute. "And for the record, it'd be unsporting to limit myself to only our wee neck of the woods."

Knox shook his head and focused on Darya. "Gonna make a drink run. You want something?"

A wide variety of wine, mixed drinks and beer rounded the table. If it were an interview, any kind of drinking would have been a horrid idea, but Knox had gone out of his way to emphasize this was a casual meeting. Plus, a little something to steady her nerves wouldn't be unwelcome. "Vodka, please."

"And now I'm in love," Axel muttered as he leaned forward to catch her attention. "Ye sure ye don't want ta set w' me, lass? I'll match ma scotch with yer Russian brew and we'll break all kinds o' international barriers."

"Can it with the brogue, you dirty Scot," Knox said. He splayed a hand on Darya's shoulder, scanned the rest of his crew with a warning look and headed for the bar.

He'd barely made it three steps before Vivienne twisted in her seat. "So, you're from Russia, right? What part?"

And so it began. She'd thought long and hard since learning Knox wanted her to meet his brothers about how to handle her past, and the only thing that had felt right was to be as honest as possible without sharing much in the way of details. "Yekaterinburg, but I moved to St. Petersburg once I completed my schooling."

Dressed in simple navy blue tank top and cutoff jeans, the pretty honey-blonde woman Knox had introduced as Gabe piped up. "How long have you lived here?"

"Almost three years. Though most of it was spent in San Diego. I've only been in Texas for the last nine months."

Vivienne chuckled. "Your first Texas summer. How are you holding up?"

"It's different. Much warmer than Russia in summer, which is nice unless you're on a horse. I went on a trail ride a few weeks ago and realized maybe I should have waited until fall."

The blond brother with the ponytail perked up. Of all the men, he and Beckett had been the two she'd recognized on sight—Beckett because he'd been listed in some of the articles with Knox, and Trevor because he'd been the focus of a client request several months ago. That had been the job that had given her the courage and impetus to reach out to Knox to start with. "You like to ride?"

His wife, Natalie, snickered and rolled her eyes. "Oh, now she's done it."

For a second, she thought perhaps she'd stepped into a topic she shouldn't have. Then she remembered the ranch that had been included in the pre-packaged information she'd passed on to Natalie's ex-husband at Knox's request. "I'd never been before but always wanted to, so I treated myself."

Trevor cocked one eyebrow. "Yeah? What'd you think?"

"It was amazing. Though I would have liked it better with fewer people and a little less structure."

"Well, we can swing that." He hugged Natalie closer to him. "We've got horses out at our place and lots of room to roam."

Danny leaned forward and crossed both arms on the table. "Man, I'll take a Harley to a quarter horse any day."

"Yeah, you said pigs would fly before you did, too," Trevor said. "Now I can't get you out of my Cessna."

Shrugging, Danny lifted his beer for a drink, but smirked right before he tilted it. "That was before I knew how good planes were for impressing chicks."

Gabe twisted enough to aim a frown up at Zeke. "Are you telling me the whole flying-on-a-first-date thing is a ploy you all use?"

Unlike the rest of the men, Zeke had a certain *GQ*

appeal. Mostly short dark hair except a little longer and tousled on top with just enough scruff on his chin to give him a sexy edge. He smiled down at his woman, not the least bit ruffled by her sass. "You've got my rock on your finger, so I'm thinking it worked."

"Mmm." Natalie set her wineglass down on the table and cocked her head toward Gabe. "I'll give you the pilot thing being hot, but it was seeing Trevor on the back of a horse that did me in."

"See?" Trevor said to Danny. "Don't knock horses. Women love 'em."

"Screw that," Jace grumbled. "Take the direct approach and bribe 'em. It's faster and more effective."

Well, that was an interesting crumb of information and surprisingly in line with the approach many of the men she knew in Russia were prone to take. She was just about to open her mouth and ask if he had any Slavic ancestry when Knox ambled up behind her, leaned in and plunked a short tumbler of vodka directly in front of her. "What are you guys talking about?"

Vivienne smirked at Jace then craned her neck toward Knox. "Somehow we've gone from polite weather chitchat to how best to snag a woman. Not surprisingly, Beckett and Axel have stayed tight-lipped."

Knox moved in on Darya's right, glared at Beckett until he moved his chair over enough for Knox to sit between them, then plunked himself down. "So, basically you're rubbing your marital bliss in everyone's faces?"

"Something like that," Jace said. His gaze rested on Darya for all of a second before he refocused on Knox. "If you want, we can rewind and start over so you can pick up a few pointers."

Knox scowled back at him. "JJ's angling for a coder slot. Not a hookup or a husband."

Not a husband, no. But if Knox was the hookup in question, she'd absolutely sign up.

Jace winked at her like he'd overheard her thoughts then smiled at Knox. "Whatever you say, brother."

"Knox said your real name's Jeannie, right?" This from Gabe, who seemed either blissfully unaware of the good-natured razzing bouncing back and forth between Jace and Knox, or simply too accustomed to their banter to worry about it.

Darya sipped her vodka and nodded.

Gabe cocked her head. "So, what's the JJ stand for?"

As fast and easy as Darya had settled in with the group, an icy wave of discomfort settled over her. It wasn't the first time she'd been asked the question, and it certainly wouldn't be the last, but every time she had to answer it drove a jagged spike through her heart. Reminded her of the woman she'd left behind and the risk she navigated every day parading herself as someone else.

One by one, she met the gazes of those around her. Every one of them stared back at her. Patient. Invested. Kind, but watchful. For fifteen minutes, she'd happily sat at their table and sensed only goodness. An open love for one another, as well as honor and protectiveness. Aside from the time she'd spent with JJ, she'd only felt the same sense of belonging with Yefim. A man who'd taken her in, taught her how to navigate the real world and saved her at high risk to himself.

Twice before, she'd trusted her instincts, and now they said to leap once more. To believe and take a chance at building something good while she could. JJ

might not be beside her physically, but she could feel her
steady presence as sure as a comforting hand pressed
between her shoulder blades.

Live enough for both of us.

Yes, this was right. She felt it clear to her bones.
"The truth is, my name isn't JJ. Or Jeannie." She met
Knox's steady gaze and swallowed. "My real name is
Darya Volkova."

Chapter Nine

Darya Volkova. Knox must have silently rolled the name around in his head at least twenty times since she'd dropped the truth on him and his family an hour ago, and every time it fit a little better. Way better than JJ or Jeannie, neither of which had sat well with him. She'd been white as a sheet for the first thirty seconds after she'd shared. A reasonable response considering the tension that had whipped around the table and the seven laser-focused men staring her down.

"I haven't harmed anyone," she'd said and quickly looked to Knox for support. "My past is behind me, but I wanted you to know the truth. To give you some token that any chance you give me is valued."

Silence crackled and snapped, amplified by the white noise of reality around them, but eventually Jace had shifted his focus to Knox and lifted a questioning brow. A non-verbal *You got this?* that Knox had promptly answered with a nearly undetectable dip of his chin. No matter how much his family had taken it in stride and acted like it was NBFD, it *was* a big fucking deal. One he'd dig into as soon as he got reconnected to his sources. That was unless she opted to pony up the details when he took her home.

The lady working the vendor stand delivered two platefuls of barbecue ribs and pulled pork, dragging him back to the present. He slid a twenty across the counter. That was another thing he'd learned about the cute little skip tracer now known as Darya. Where some women picked at their food in an attempt to watch their weight or look delicate, Darya openly savored what she liked—and she liked barbecue and vodka. In abundance.

Turning from the counter, he stepped forward and nearly ran into Seth.

Rather than step aside, Seth glanced back at Knox's table then jerked his head in that direction. "You got a minute before you head back?"

He did, but he wished he didn't. The last few hours had been some of the most relaxed he'd been outside of Haven in months, so spending time juggling whatever had put a calculated look in Seth's eyes didn't give him a whole lot of warm and fuzzy. Still, Seth worked for Otter, and Otter was a key factor in keeping dangerous drugs out of Jace and Axel's clubs. *Key factor* meaning he got exclusivity in peddling all the weed he wanted at Crossroads, so long as he didn't get caught doing it and kept all the other heavy players out in the process.

Knox shrugged and motioned to a side table set up with napkins and condiments. "Sure. You talk. I'll load up."

He'd barely set his plates down before Seth kicked in. "Didn't realize you'd taken an old lady."

Pausing with his hand midway to the napkin dispenser, Knox frowned back at the guy. "Come again?"

"Your friend. JJ, right?"

Knox blinked. Then did it again. Frankly, he was surprised his body managed that much considering the pleasant surge vibrating through him at the thought of

Darya being his. Except she wasn't. His place was to teach her and look out for her. Nothing more and nothing less.

He shifted his attention to the napkins and shook his head. "Nah, she's a friend."

"No shit?" With eyebrows hiked high enough they gave his hairline a run for their money, Seth glanced at the brotherhood's table and locked his sights on Darya. "Man, you're out of your mind not grabbin' on to that."

A sentiment his thoughts had echoed at least fifty times since he'd woken her up a few days ago, but it didn't change reality. "She's long-term material. I'm more the multiple-choice type."

Seth grinned huge. "Still not up for an old lady, huh?"

"Nope. Not in the cards."

Seth nodded, shoved his hands in his jeans pockets and slid his attention back to Darya. "What about the rest of your crew? She tight with any of them?"

Oh, hell no. Knox straightened to full height and pushed his shoulders back, a whole lot of unexpected fury whipping a firestorm in his gut. He knew that hungry look. Had cast it on a slew of women himself. And while Darya might not be his, he'd be go-to-hell if a player like Seth got his hands on her. "JJ's a free agent, but if you're anglin' to get laid, pick someone else. She's better than that."

Completely undaunted, Seth chuckled. "Man, I got that with one look." He lifted his beer in salute and turned to leave. "You might have a problem with long-term, but I don't."

Knox stayed rooted in place, the plates all but forgotten as he tracked Seth's path back to the rear table Axel had set aside for Otter and his crew. Nursing his anger was stupid. Totally out of character. But in the space of two seconds, he'd gone from laid-back and happy to ready for murder, which was hands down *not* his thing. Fists and head-to-head was Beckett's gig. Knox was more the cut-your-nuts-off-on-the-sly-and-smile-while-doing-it type. So, why the fuck was he so uptight?

Convinced Seth was going to keep his ass at a distance, Knox headed back to his crew. If there'd been any lull in conversation while he was gone, it didn't show by the time he got back. If anything, Darya looked like she'd been friends with his brothers and their women for years instead of hours.

He settled into his chair and passed the plate he'd gotten for Darya two seats over. Somehow Beckett and Danny had lured her between them all of twenty minutes after her info bomb and hadn't stopped talking her ear off since. More than once he'd caught her giving one or the other a light touch. Her fingertips on Danny's shoulder, or leaning her head against Beckett's shoulder as he pulled her into a side hug. Funny how the simple affection looked right with his brothers, but he'd wanted to rip Seth's head off for just looking at her.

She lifted her gaze to his, smiled an unspoken thank you and picked up a rib.

He picked up his own rib and dove in.

"She's pretty," Viv muttered low beside him.

Pretty was an understatement. Her eyes alone were the kind of shit people wrote poems about, a mixture of ice and a clear spring day. Added to her winter-blonde hair, she was nothing short of otherworld regal. "She's smart. Driven."

"Mmm hmm," Viv said. "I'm sure it's the smart and driven part that's got you watching her like a hawk, too."

Fuck.

He tore his attention away from Darya and wiped his fingers. "Just trying to get a handle on how she ticks. I'll teach her better if I understand her."

Jace swiveled his head and cocked a shit-eating grin. He might not have actually joined in on the conversation, but his look said he'd heard every word and was crying bullshit foul right along with Vivienne.

Danny barked a resounding laugh and Darya stood, a tiny smile playing on her lips as she scanned everyone around the table. "I'm making a drink run. Anyone need a refill?"

"Me."

"Me, too."

"I could use another scotch."

This from Beckett, Danny and Axel as they stood and reached for their wallets like synchronized swimmers. In the space of ten seconds, all three had bills outstretched and wavering in the soft summer breeze.

Gaze moving from one hand to the next, Darya giggled. "I think I can cover the expense of four drinks."

Vivienne propped one elbow on the table and rested her chin on her palm. "You're sitting at a table overloaded with testosterone. If you don't let them pay, you'll wound their male egos."

"She's right," Nat said. "Take the money. You have no idea how bad these guys can pout."

Darya rolled her eyes, eyeballed Axel's, Beckett's and Danny's outstretched hands, then snagged Axel's hundred-dollar bill. With a playful mew aimed at Beckett and Danny she said, "You two can pick up the tab next time."

Axel snickered, reclined against his seat back and

crossed his arms like he'd just trounced his brothers in a world class debate. "The lass has taste."

"Hardly." Gabe curled her hand around Zeke's bicep and grinned. "More like she figured out you'd pout the longest."

With a quick woman-to-woman smile, Darya side-stepped between Beckett and the table and headed toward the bar. "Something like that."

Zeke waited only long enough for Darya to make it out of earshot before he shifted into serious mode. "Big play, her sharing her real name. If she's runnin' like you think she is, that's a huge vulnerability. Takes guts. I like her."

Trevor nodded. "Me, too."

Axel and Danny chimed right behind him.

"Yep."

"Agreed."

Beckett shrugged in a classic I-told-you-so move and pinned Knox with a superior look. "I never misread people. I told you she was good."

Jace shifted enough to give Knox his full attention. "You wanna take her on, you've got the all clear from us."

"And if that past of hers comes calling," Axel added, "you let us know that, too. She might not be one of us yet, but we're not lettin' her swing alone."

With his focus squarely centered on Darya's swaying ass as she made her way to the bar, Knox's brain lagged at least five seconds before Axel's quip registered. "What do you mean she's not one of us *yet*?"

Trevor grinned over the rim of his longneck. "He means the way you've been eye-fucking her all night, he thinks it's only a matter of time before you're callin' rally and throwin' down."

He opened his mouth to tell Trevor to stop with the bullshit then promptly lost his train of thought.

At the bar, Seth ambled up beside Darya and leaned his elbows atop the makeshift surface as if settling in for a long chat.

Cock-sucking no good son of a bitch. Which part of *she deserves better* did the asshole not get?

Darya ducked her head at something Seth said, laughed and tucked her beautiful blonde hair behind her ear to reveal a pretty blush. A blush another man had put there.

Beckett's sharp voice cut through his thoughts. "Knox?"

He whipped his head around to face his best friend. "What?"

Smirking, Beckett cocked his head. "Asked when you're gonna put her to work. We need to get her prints scanned in if she's spending time in the office."

Knox let his gaze slide back to Darya. She'd put some distance between her and Seth while she placed her order, but what little she'd created, Seth gobbled up with a sly advance.

Beckett chuckled. "I'm so winning this bet."

"Calm the fuck down. I'm lookin' out for her. Nothing else." Only taking his attention off Seth long enough to cast Beckett an annoyed scowl, Knox chin-lifted toward the play going down not thirty feet away. "She's not into him. You think I'm gonna leave her without an out if she needs one?"

Trevor swiveled in his seat to check things out for himself. Grinning, he spun back around, wrapped his woman up in the crook of his arm and zeroed in on Beck. "Any chance I can get in on this action?"

"Jesus." Knox snatched his beer off the tabletop and planted his foot on the rung of the empty chair next to him. "Stop thinkin' with your dicks and look at her. She's tried to head back this way twice and he's cut her off."

"I don't know." Vivienne pursed her mouth in a considering way, but it didn't do enough to hide the smile behind it. "She seems like a sharp girl to me. Pretty sure she can shut Seth down if she wants to."

Darya handed Axel's hundred dollar bill to the bartender, but Seth wrapped his big paw around her wrist, pulled it back and offered his own cash.

Motherfucker.

He stood, slammed back the rest of his beer and plunked the empty bottle on the tabletop. "She wants to go for it, that's fine, but if she wants an out, she's getting one."

"Oh, I'm thinking she's getting something," Zeke said as Knox walked away.

Not to be left out, Axel's and Jace's razzing comments trailed right behind it.

"Probably has a mind to show her his oversize hard drive."

"Go get her, tiger."

Knox flipped them all the bird without looking back and kept moving. He stepped in behind Darya and laid a possessive hand on her shoulder. This close, her scent hit him hard, barely there roses and crisp winter even while the summer heat pressed around them.

She shivered beneath his touch, her body going from relaxed to full scale alert in a second.

He squeezed in what he hoped she'd process as a comforting gesture. "Everything okay?"

Seth turned from the counter and tucked the change in his pocket, open annoyance written all over his face.

Darya twisted as much as she could with him crowding so close, her gaze resting briefly on his hand before she lifted it to his face. It was a look, nothing more, but he'd swear it sparked with an electric current. But was that for Seth, or for him? "I was just talking with your friend," she said to Knox before she faced forward again. "Seth, right?"

"Yes, ma'am." Seth's gaze dropped to Knox's hand then shot Knox a knowing smile. "There a problem?"

"Nope." At least not one he was willing to analyze. Not now, tomorrow or any day after that. "JJ just looked like she could use a hand with the drinks."

Fuck, he hated that name. Now that he knew the real one, it felt wrong on his tongue, but risking the bogus identity with anyone outside of family wasn't an option either.

"You didn't need to do that," Seth said. "I'll give her all the help she needs."

Yeah, Knox knew exactly what kind of help Seth had in mind. "No need." He forced himself to release his grip and handed two drinks off to Darya. "You grab these, and I'll follow you with the rest."

She hesitated only long enough to study his face, way too much scrutiny moving behind her stunning blue eyes before she turned back to Seth, all poised politeness. "Thank you for the drinks."

Seth moved in close, cupped the side of her face with a gentleness that shocked the shit out of Knox.

"Darlin', anything you want, I'm happy to give. You just say the word."

Not going to happen.

Knox cleared his throat.

Darya took a big step backward. "Right. Well, thank you." With one last piercing glance at Knox, she wove her way back to the table, Seth's stare rooted on her ass the whole way.

"How much are you out for the drinks?" Knox asked.

"My treat." Slow, like he didn't have a care in the world, Seth leaned one arm against the bar. "Any chance any of those are for you?"

Knox snatched the last two drinks off the bar. "Nope. You just shucked out a handful of cash for a no-go and drinks for Axel, Beckett and Danny."

"Too bad."

"I know. Sucks when you crash and burn."

"Not what I meant." Seth pushed upright, his holier-than-thou smirk firmly anchored in place. "Meant it was too bad one of the drinks wasn't for you. You're gonna need something strong when reality kicks in and you realize you're a goner." He jerked his chin up in a manly see-ya-around. "You got a good thing with that one, Torren. Try not to fuck it up."

Chapter Ten

Darya hurried up the steps to her apartment, Knox's heavier footsteps sounding on the concrete pads behind her with the same driving punch as her heart. God, what a night. Four glorious hours of comfortable interaction with wonderful people, fantastic music and enough delicious food to make her belly ache. Not since before she'd left Russia had she had so much fun. Simply let loose without fear of who might see her. But with Knox's family it was easy. As if within their presence, her past couldn't penetrate and sully the moment.

Pausing outside her door, she dug in her purse for her keys.

Knox slid up beside her, slipped them from between her fingers and wedged himself between her and the door. Unerringly, he flipped to the right key and slid it into the deadbolt. "You have plans for tomorrow?"

Her heart tripped at the question, the same staggering response as when he'd intervened between her and Seth and all but claimed her with a touch. For a man who verbally insisted anything sexual was off-limits, his actions from the moment she'd opened the door to him had conveyed an entirely different desire. "No."

He pushed the door wide, handed her back her keys

and stole inside ahead of her, sharply assessing her living room. "Good. I'm sending Danny over before noon to change out your deadbolts." He held up a hand for her to wait. "Stay here. Let me check the rest of the place."

"Why?"

He stopped long enough to frown back at her. "You might not have said it outright, but it's clear you're running from something or someone. I'm not bringing you home and leaving you here without making sure you're safe before I go."

Well, damn. She'd hoped him following her inside meant he'd decided to waive his no-sex-with-employees policy. And while she appreciated him looking out for her, she needed help taking the edge off the burn he'd created with his heated looks and casual touches way more than she needed a security team. "No, I meant the locks. They're perfectly fine. Why change them?"

He flipped on the light in her bathroom and strode inside. The swish of her metal shower curtain rings echoed out of the tiny space. "They're not fine. You need bumpless locks at least." He reappeared, flicked his attention to her briefly before moving to her bedroom door. "You could use a security system, too, but I'll have to sweet-talk your landlord before I can make that happen."

"Bumpless?"

He disappeared into her room without answering and a second later light from her bedside lamp spilled out of the opening.

Ignoring his command to stay put, she padded across her living room, too drawn by the promise of seeing him in her private space to do as she was told. She rounded the corner in time to find him on the far side of the room staring down at her bed, his mouth clenched in a firm line and his hand fisted at his side.

His gaze sliced to hers. "Thought I told you to wait."

She shrugged. "I was curious. Besides, this isn't the first time I've come home alone and it won't be the last. I can take care of myself."

He cocked his head and prowled a few steps toward her. "Curiosity can be a dangerous thing. Leads you into places and tempts you with things you shouldn't know."

"Like?"

"Like knowing what you keep under your bed and being all too capable of picturing you splayed on those sheets and using them to get off."

She gasped and took a jagged step back, one hand pressed against her chest to still the jackrabbit rhythm of her heart. No way had he had enough time to see what she kept stored in her box. To see it, yes. But to take inventory, no. "How did you—"

"Like I said. Bumpless locks. You need some. Bad."

The Post-its.

He'd been the one to move them. And if he'd been at her desk then that meant… "You broke into my place. Looked at everything."

His mouth curled in a wicked smile, not the least bit repentant. "No one gets close to my family without me knowing everything there is to know about them. You came clean with my brothers tonight, so I'm returning the favor now. And before you get too fired up about me invading your privacy, there's not one person on mine or the brotherhood's payroll with the potential of getting close to our records who doesn't get the same sweep. The only difference between you and them is you actually know it happened."

She swallowed, her mouth too dry to do the job properly. "Then why tell me?"

"Because you're vulnerable. How much so, I'm still waiting for you to share, but the best way I can help you is to lay it out so you'll be more inclined to let me help you fix it."

Her files. She had to have at least a dozen articles solely about him. "You knew I'd been researching you."

"I knew you had a lot of stories with me in them, yeah. Why you had them, I didn't have a clue."

"And JJ?"

"I knew you weren't her and that you had some kind of relationship with the real person before you assumed her name. Other than that, I figure you'll share when you're ready." He paused, his mouth hardening to the point a muscle near his jaw twitched. "You don't like the way we operate, then now's your chance to bail."

And there it was. The honor she'd sensed in him from the beginning. Laying out who he was in the simplest terms. Take it or leave it. Maybe for someone else it would have been frightening, but after her years with Yefim—living and working with insanely powerful men capable of staring down a gun without so much as a wince—it was strangely comforting. A way of life she not only understood, but navigated easily. "Knowledge is power."

"Knowledge is everything. Especially when it comes to keeping the people I love safe."

She took a cautious step forward, anchoring herself in the moment with a loose grip on the doorjamb beside her. "Then you'll understand my question."

A wariness moved across his face, but he squared his shoulders just the same. "What question?"

She licked her lower lip. Need blossomed through her and blood rushed wild and frantic through her veins. To cover it, she stepped fully into the room and leaned her shoulders against the wall, crossing her arms beneath her breasts. "Why won't you let yourself go with me?"

His gaze dropped to her mouth. "Don't go there."

"Why not? You're attracted to me. I felt it. You intercepted another man's advances, not just with words but with touch."

"I wasn't stopping him."

"Really? In Russia, a man only intercedes and lays his hands on a woman as both a challenge and a claim."

"I was giving you a choice."

"And I made it. I want you." She pushed off the wall and strolled toward him, channeling all the longing and desire she'd fought from the first day she'd seen him into the gentle sway of her hips. Excitement and certainty sparked hot beneath her skin.

"No, you don't. As choices go, I'm a worse bet than Seth."

"Why?"

"Because I don't do monogamy and I damned sure don't do relationships."

"What do you do?"

He held his ground, the gray of his eyes deepening with every step. "I fuck and make sure the women I'm with get off as much or more than I do."

She stopped just an arm's reach away, the impact of his carnal claim slicing straight to her core. Her answer came out ragged and breathless. "Okay."

Tension radiated off him, bonfire quality heat pouring into her and stoking her courage. "You don't mean that."

"Yes, I do." She pressed her shoulders back, drawing his attention to her breasts. Beneath his ravenous gaze they grew heavier, craving his touch. "Relationships aren't a good idea for me either."

"Because you're running."

"*Was* running. For now, I'm living. Every moment to the fullest."

His gaze shot to hers, the keen awareness behind his eyes piercing through her. "What's that supposed to mean?"

"It means I made someone a promise. Promised them I'd live enough for both of us."

"You mean JJ."

Darya nodded, a slow confirmation and reaffirmation of her vow all at once. She took his hand and guided it to her heart. Beneath his palm her heart thrummed a demanding beat. "Any day—in a second—that rhythm could stop. I want to live. To feel. I don't want a single regret chasing me into the grave. Especially not this one."

She flattened her hand over his and inched closer, pressing her free hand against his chest and savoring the matching beat she found. His warm breath fluttered against her skin and his wine and woodsmoke scent coiled around her in a daring embrace. This was right. Worth every risk. "I've made my choice. Now you need to make yours."

Chapter Eleven

This was a bad idea. The worst. He'd already hurt more women than he could count, every damned cut he'd given them slicing un-healable scars into his own soul. Hurting Darya, dealing the inevitable blow that always came when lines were crossed, would kill what little good was left in him.

But he still couldn't pull his hand away. Her heart pounded beneath his palm. Fast, yes, but strong and steady. Unable to help himself, he spread his fingers wider and skimmed the soft inner swell of her breast with his thumb.

She sucked in a shaky breath and arched into the touch, her eyelids slipping closed. "You want this as much as I do. You feel it."

Hell yes, he felt it. Had done absolutely nothing but rerun a host of fantasies since the day she'd walked into his office, a fact that made dialing up anyone else for relief and a shot at quality sleep unpalatable.

The smart thing to do was walk away. Get his ass on his bike and find someone, anyone else but her, to take the edge off. He braced himself for the disconnect, an act he was pretty damned sure was going to sting as much as a severed hand.

Her eyes opened, the pure cloudless blue nearly consumed by her dilated pupils. "Please." A whisper, thick with need, spoken with perfect soft pink lips. Exactly what he wanted to hear when he sunk into her wet heat.

The image popped all too vividly in his head. Darya splayed out on her bed, those creamy thighs of hers spread wide while she took his cock.

Fuck.

He fisted his hand in her shirt, yanked her to him and claimed her mouth, forcing her lips apart with his own and slicking his tongue inside. He moaned into her mouth, palming the back of her head to hold her immobile and deepening the kiss. Sweet baby Jesus, she tasted good. Honey sweet and dangerously addictive. A teaser course guaranteed to wind him up and amp his thirst until he finagled his mouth between her thighs.

She jerked his T-shirt up and out of the way so her hands had unhindered room to work.

And work they did. Smoothing along his skin in confident, tempting strokes. This was a woman who knew what she wanted and went for it, giving as good as she got along the way. A total fucking turn-on for a man like him, but also a bullet train to getting him off.

He captured her hands, pinned them behind her and backed her toward the wall.

She wiggled and tried to yank free of his grip, groaning against his mouth, "Let me touch you."

Her shoulders met wall and he ground his pelvis against hers. "Later." He nipped her chin and licked and sucked his way down the column of her neck.

"Not later." Breathy and edgy as though she wanted to fight but couldn't quite muster the strength. She tilted her neck to give him better room to work. "Now."

"You'll get your turn." He gave into one of many impulses that had ridden him all night, cupped one breast and squeezed. "But I'm a greedy bastard so I'm taking mine first."

Her head dropped back against the wall and her back bowed. "Knox." A plea. And damned if his name slipping past her lips like that didn't turn his dick from humdrum concrete to the fucking Rock of Gibraltar. Man, he was so screwed. She wasn't even naked yet and he was primed to blow.

He rolled her nipple between his finger and thumb, and a delicate tremor moved through her. Like the carnal contact had jump-started a dormant passion. If she was this responsive with this many layers of clothes between them, he couldn't wait to get his tongue on her clit. "Look at me."

Slowly, she opened her eyes. Her hips rocked against his, each undulation matching the back-and-forth tug he gave the hard bud between his fingers.

The words that sat on his tongue stung, but not saying them wasn't an option. Taking this step was already fifty kinds of stupid. No way was he not giving her one last out. "You get what this is?"

"Sex." Her voice was the living embodiment of the word she'd spoken, the tail end of it humming with a pleasure soaked hiss. "Good, hard, sweaty sex."

Right. Fucking. Answer.

He jerked her away from the wall, yanked her T-shirt up and over her head and crushed her against him, devouring her mouth as he backed her toward the bed. One quick pinch of his fingers and her bra *snicked* open. He'd barely curled his fingers around the silky black straps to pull them free, when her legs hit the edge of the bed and she tumbled onto the bloodred comforter.

Christ, what a sight. All damned night, she'd drawn men's attention. Hell, he'd had a hard time keeping his own dick from saluting every time she'd so much as looked at him. But seeing her now, her creamy skin and white-blonde hair against those decadent sheets and the way her tits jiggled on impact, it'd take five lifetimes before he got that image out of his head.

She pushed herself up on her elbows and cocked one knee as though she wasn't entirely comfortable with the feature presentation she'd found herself in. "You're staring."

"Fuck yeah, I'm staring." He toed off his boots, not daring to take his eyes off her for fear she'd bolt. "Been thinking about seeing you exactly where you are now for the last week. You think I'm not gonna pause and pay homage, you're out of your mind."

The comment earned him a naughty smile and damned if she didn't push her shoulders back with a lot more confidence.

Done shucking his socks, he tugged his T off and popped the buttons on his fly, giving his straining cock some much needed breathing room. "You like that? Watching me look at you?"

Her gaze dropped to his torso then farther to where his dick stretched tall and proud behind his black briefs. "Yes, but I think I like looking at you more."

He chuckled and put a knee to the bed. "The feeling's mutual, sweetheart." He worked the button/zipper combo on her jeans and tugged them down her hips. "Now, ass up, because I'm gonna get a full frontal before I dive in and see if your pussy tastes as good as your mouth."

She lifted for him, but she did it on a low moan, squeezing her legs together like he'd already got his face between her thighs.

The second the denim cleared her bubblegum-pink painted toes, he was up on the bed, knees anchored on either side of her and hands skimming up her slender hips then in to cup her breasts. Fitting for her ballerina-lithe body, they barely filled his palms, but were one hundred percent Grade-A perfect with watermelon pink tips to match her lips.

Her fingertips danced across his pecs, then lower to his abs.

"Oh no, you don't." He caught her at both wrists and guided them to her chest. "You want to play with something, you play with these."

She pouted and opened her mouth.

"You don't like me bossy in the office," he said before she could argue, "you're gonna hate me in the bedroom. Now, get your hands engaged and show me how you play with your tits when you've got that box of toys out from under your bed."

Her eyelids grew heavy and her voice rasped through him in all the right places, "I don't want my hands, I want yours. And your mouth."

"Oh, you're gonna get my mouth." He maneuvered himself between her thighs, slipped his hands behind her knees and splayed them up and wide. "My mouth, my fingers and every inch of my cock."

He should have braced. Or at least had the common sense not to let his gaze trail down to her exposed sex. Beautiful. A thin strip of closely cropped blonde as white as the hair on her head and her pretty pink center just waiting for his undivided attention. Her clit was already so hard it peeked out from its hood and her labia glistened in the lamplight. He dove in, bypassing all preamble in favor of a direct assault and licking straight through her slit.

Darya bucked against his mouth and cried out, not one of the Russian words she uttered anything he understood, but sounded fantastic spilling from her lips. She widened her knees and her fingers tangled in his hair holding him in place. As if there was a snowball's chance in hell of him moving from this spot before she came on his tongue.

With another long swipe, he slowly lifted his gaze and nearly came at the sight.

She watched him. Openly. Her lips parted as her breath sawed in and out on heavy pants. A shining angel caught in a debauched moment.

He flicked her clit with his tongue and plunged one finger inside her. "This what you want?"

Her eyes widened and she rolled her hips. "More."

Now, *that* was a word he understood. He added a second and pumped deeper.

She moaned and fisted her hands in his hair. "Yes. Just like that." Her hips rocked, over and over, eyes riveted to his work. She licked her lower lip and her voice dropped to a husky pitch that drew his nuts up tight. "I imagined this. Wanted it."

God, so had he. Though, not once had he imagined she'd be this candid. This comfortable and direct in her sexuality. Combined with her responsiveness, she was a fresh new addiction just waiting to happen. "Yeah?" he muttered over her sex, his warm breath ricocheting off her flesh and eliciting a tiny whimper. "You come from my mouth in your fantasies, or my cock?"

"Both." An instant answer and insistent demand all rolled up into one.

He lifted his head just enough to grin up at her, crooked his wrist for just the right angle and growled against her clit. "Then sweetheart, that's exactly what you're gonna get."

The pads of his fingertips brushed the dimpled sweet spot along her front wall just as his mouth closed around her and suckled deep.

Her back bowed in a beautiful arch and her pert nipples jutted straight for the ceiling. With every brush of his fingers, her hips jerked and the muscles around his fingers quavered. So close. So damned close. He slipped in a third finger, her slickness easily letting him play and stretch her for his cock. He hummed and gently grazed her clit with his teeth.

"Knox!"

Hard and fast, her pussy contracted around his fingers, the sheer strength of the reaction making his shaft throb in anticipation. Her scent and taste engulfed him. A lethal mix of sin and sweetness. Not giving her a chance to level out, he replaced his fingers with his tongue, spearing deep to gather every drop while he rubbed out her release. Fuck, but he needed inside her. Needed that fierce catch and release rippling up and down his cock.

He nipped the inside of one thigh and landed a sharp smack on the outside of the other. "Hands and knees. Now."

Rather than follow his instruction, she slid her fingers between her legs, milking out the dregs of her release with a slow pump and glide. Her lips held a languid smile and her eyelids hung heavy like a milk-drunk kitten. Her husky voice mixed with her accent made her sound like a film noir starlet. "You're being bossy."

He pushed off the bed, shoved his jeans and briefs free and snagged a condom from his pocket in record time. His cock bobbed tall and eager, so engorged with blood it was a wonder he could stand at all. "You feel good?"

Her gaze dropped to his cock. "Oh, yes."

He grinned and ripped open the condom. "Then I'd say bossy's working just fine." Gloved up, he crawled onto the bed, grabbed her at the waist and flipped her over. "Now, ass up, face to the mattress. I've got work to do."

On his knees behind her, he couldn't see her face, but her low and wicked chuckle said *game on*. Sure enough, she slowly widened her knees and lifted her perfect heart-shaped ass. If that wasn't a drop dead sexy enough move on its own, she tossed her head, peeked at him over one shoulder and glided her fingers through her slit, picking right back up where she'd left off. "You work. I'll play."

Hell, yeah.

He palmed her hips and nudged his glans against her entrance. His whole damned body lit up on contact, a powerhouse current jolting through him that could have powered all of Dallas for a solid twenty-four hours.

She arched her back higher, offering herself in the most carnal way.

The sight was hands down the most erotic thing he'd ever seen. His thick cock, dark and insanely hard, poised and ready to tunnel into her soft pink pussy. But more than that, the moment felt huge. Life altering in a way he couldn't have stepped back from even at gunpoint. He pressed forward, the whole damned world narrowing down to that single moment. To the feel of her sex taking him in and making him whole.

"Knox." His name on her lips sounded like a prayer, which was good because he needed one. A huge one if he had any hopes of keeping his balance with this woman. Her scent. Her breathy moans. The forthright way she owned her sensuality and grabbed for what she wanted. It was intoxicating. A fix no man in his right mind would ever want to kick.

He worked himself inside, slow and steady at first then building to faster and longer strokes. Smoothing his hand up her spine, he wrapped one hand in her glorious hair and tugged her upright. It was primal, completely out of line with a woman who barely knew him, but Darya came willingly, dropping her head back against his shoulder with a sigh that pulsed straight down the center of his shaft.

"You like it hard?"

"Yes."

He cupped one breast, plucking the tip while the other shook with each smack of his hips. "Dirty?"

"God, yes." The way she said it, an edge of relief and utter gratitude mixed with wrenching need, cut straight through him. Untethered what was left of his control.

"Good," he said between heavy breaths, "because that's where we're going and we're going there fast."

She rolled her head toward him and opened her lust-drunk eyes, a triumphant smile tilting her lips. "I can't wait."

Fuck.

He tumbled them both forward, one hand holding his weight while the other pinned her at the back of her neck to the bed. Thrust after thrust, he powered deep and damned if she didn't lift her hips for more. Every detail crowded around him in the sharpest focus. His dog tags resting against her spine. The slap of flesh on flesh. Their ragged breaths. His dark hands gripping her pale hips and the way her hair spilled down her back. So many layers. An intricate, erotic labyrinth that lured him deeper and deeper.

Her sex fluttered around him, the promise of her release so close he nearly shot his own. He fingered the ample wetness between them and slicked the moisture up to her swollen nub. "Need you to get there." His sharp pants buffeted off her neck and against his face. "Need your cunt milking my cock the way you came on my fingers."

Her hips jerked and she cried out, the sweet pulse of her pussy fisting unmercifully around him. He tried to hold it. Drove his pelvis flush against her ass and stilled every movement save the gentle back-and-forth of his finger over her clit, but the clench of her muscles was too strong. Too potent.

His nuts drew up tight and his hips bucked on reflex, his release shooting down his shaft and jetting free so hard the rest of the world ceased to exist. All that that mattered was the silky glide of his cock inside her. Her winter-rose scent on his skin and the lingering musk of sex.

Slowly, he pumped in and out, leisurely exploring her slick folds with his fingers while his heart scrambled to find a steady rhythm.

Her body trembled beneath him and her breath shuddered out on a long sigh.

He eased some of his weight off her and nudged her to her belly with his hips. "Lay flat for me."

Instantly, she obeyed, for once not giving him lip or questioning why. He kept their connection, though, blanketing her back with his body. He kissed her sweat-dampened shoulder. "You okay?"

"Mmmm." She opened her eyes. No remorse shone back at him. Only sated pleasure. She stirred her hips beneath him and generated a fresh wave of aftershocks. "Quite happy, actually. Sweaty, but happy."

He grinned, swept her hair to one side and blew a cold stream of air along her spine. "Better?"

She shivered and giggled. "Stop that. I'm Russian. We appreciate heat."

Man, did he understand that, especially with his softening cock still nestled deep in the heart of her. He should move. Deal with the condom and give them both space before she read more into the moment than she should. Hell, before *he* read any more into it.

He kissed the top of her spine, taking one last second to savor the taste of her skin before he moved away. An act that, in and of itself, said just how dangerous this woman could be for him. Not one of his lovers had ever called him callous, but he'd always made a point to watch the affection afterward. Blurring the lines with sex was too easy, and yet with her, he couldn't help but trail more down her back as he pulled away, his dog tags dragging along her skin. "Gonna hit the bathroom. You want anything while I'm up?"

She hissed as he left her and slowly rolled to her back, a wanton sex goddess replete on a bed of sin. "No.

I'm perfect." She waved him away with a soft smile. "Go. Deal with business. Let me rest."

Dismissed without so much as a flinch. Definitely a good sign, but for some reason it stung. He ambled to the bathroom and tossed the condom. His reflection stared back at him. Same man. Same safe routine, but the image looked empty. Flat.

The lamplight from Darya's room clicked off.

So now what did he do? Normally, he covered the ground rules well before he got near a bed and made sure whoever he was with was good with him crashing long and hard while his brain disengaged, but he'd been so amped up and in denial when he snapped he'd leap-frogged right over logistics.

One thing was for sure, he needed the shut-eye. Badly. But on the other hand, if he woke up and found her wrapped around him he'd have a whole different mess on his hands.

He flipped off the light and padded to her bedroom. Only a trace of light slipped from the parking lot through her blinds, but enough to show her curled on one side of the bed, her blonde hair spilling across her pillow. She yawned and the seductive sound of her skin moving against the soft sheets slipped through the room. "Sorry," she said on the tail end of her yawn. "This is my side. You'll have to take the other."

So easy. Almost too easy.

But for a good night's sleep he'd take it at face value and worry about the rest in the morning. He peeled back the sheets and stretched out beside her. Her scent was everywhere, mingled with his own and the rich aftermath of sex. He closed his eyes and the blessed languidness that eluded him most nights crept in fog-thick around him. His heart slowed and his breath evened out, matching Darya's beside him. So close to sleep. "Darya?"

"Mmm?"

The darkness rolled closer. Heavier. "You were right. No regrets."

"No regrets," she whispered back.

And then, blessed sleep.

Chapter Twelve

Off and on, Darya's computer cursor blinked back at her, a blank screen all she had to show for the last hour she'd sat behind her desk. Not surprising considering how long it had taken her just to read through the first lesson in the second module, and she still wasn't sure any of the information she'd studied made sense.

8:14 a.m. beamed from the corner of her monitor, as steady and accusing as the cold nuns who'd handled her education growing up. She huffed out a frustrated breath, flipped back to the lesson in her browser session and snagged her lukewarm coffee for another sip. Focusing on a task had never been this hard before. Even when she'd first landed in the US, she'd been able to zero in on whatever she needed to without distraction so long as her environment felt safe. Then again, she'd never had Knox asleep in her bed, or his delicious scent blanketing every inch of her. As diversions went, he was apparently her Kryptonite.

God, the things he'd done to her. Said to her. She closed her eyes and squeezed her thighs together, the needy pulse she'd fought all morning building strength at the memory of last night. She'd tangled with powerful men before, but never one who took control in the bedroom as Knox had. Complete confidence, total focus and a wicked mouth.

Perfect.

Hand shaking, she set her mug aside and loosened her robe enough to let some much needed air-conditioned air sneak beneath the neckline. No doubt about it, risking Knox as a mentor had been worth it. She could teach herself if she had to, but experiences like that were once in a lifetime. Though, something told her if she kept her distance and maintained a professional demeanor she just might get a repeat. Or two. And God, did she want a repeat.

Through her open bedroom door, a sinfully sexy inhalation sounded followed by the swoosh of skin against sheets.

Goose bumps fanned out across her flesh and her nipples pebbled in anticipation. Not exactly the best start at presenting a disaffected front. She nabbed her mouse and scrolled deeper into the lesson, the words little more than a black-and-white blur.

The mattress let out a soft groan and footsteps whispered across the carpet. Movement registered in her periphery, but she kept her gaze trained on the screen and paired it with what she hoped came across as rapt concentration.

As soon as the bathroom door *snicked* shut, she let out a shaky breath. This wasn't a big deal. At least it shouldn't be. They'd had sex. Albeit, great sex, but she couldn't make any more of it than that. He'd been as blunt as possible from the start and she'd readily agreed to his terms, but never in her life had she felt like so much rode on how things progressed in the next few moments. As if one right or wrong step could tip life's scales from showing her everything she'd ever dreamed of, or plunging her into a fathomless abyss.

She bit her lip and scrolled back to the top of her lesson. Probably not a good idea to get caught toward the end with nothing to show for her work but a blank page and zero comprehension. He couldn't possibly know she'd been up since five. Or that she'd spent the first thirty minutes before she quietly slipped out of bed soaking in his unguarded features while he slept.

No, better to let him think she was barely ahead of him and just diving in for the day.

The toilet flushed and the water faucet kicked in shortly after.

A fine sweat broke out along the back of her neck and her heart took off at a leisurely jog. Maybe a half a pot of coffee hadn't been such a great idea. Or thinking about all the other things she hoped she'd get a chance to challenge him into trying the next time around.

With a tiny squeak from the hinges, the bathroom door swept open.

Don't look.

Focus on the screen.

Be calm.

Knox padded into view, hesitating on his path to the kitchen only long enough to check her computer screen. "You been at it long?"

Way too long. Though considering none of it took the first three times, she wasn't going to beat herself up too much for a tiny fib. "Just starting." Keeping a casual demeanor, she lifted her mug, twisted in her chair enough to give him her undivided attention and barely stifled a moan.

He wasn't completely naked, but with just his black

briefs on and standing in profile for her hungry gaze, it was the next best thing. With the same comfort he had the last time he'd been here, he popped open the cupboard and reached for a mug.

Between the lamplight and her lust the night before, she'd not had a chance to fully appreciate his tattoos, but in the bright light of morning they were something to behold. The shoulder closest to her was completely covered in an intricate mosaic of Nordic-styled dragons, intricate knots and richly detailed armor. The picture stretched to just below his bicep and swept down most of his abs at an angle until it faded out near his belly button.

She sipped her coffee to cover her open appreciation then managed a husky, "I thought you weren't a good sleeper."

He shut the cabinet and clunked his cup to the Formica countertop. "I'm not."

"Really? You slept pretty hard last night." She paired the snarky retort with a raised eyebrow and smirk. After all, the attitude had prodded the tiger out of his cage once. Now she knew what JJ meant by *If it ain't broke, don't fix it.*

Not looking up, he grinned and slid the coffeepot off the warmer. "After sex is the only time I can pull that feat off."

Now, that was an interesting detail and a terrible predicament for a man who shunned relationships.

He finished pouring his coffee and spun enough to hold up the pot. "You want a touch up?"

Don't say anything stupid. Just keep your mouth shut and act blasé. She held her cup up. "Please."

In three steps, he was right in front of her, the dog

tags that had slipped and jingled against her back as he'd pounded into her dangling between his pecs. They weren't military, though. The cut and detail was too thick and etched in the center was the same masculine H and tribal tree tattooed on his forearm. He was gone too fast, taking his sculpted abs with him before she could find an excuse to touch.

So, now what did they do? Pretending nothing ever happened seemed the coward's way out, and if she'd proven nothing else last night, she was most assuredly not a coward. She blew across the top of her coffee, eyes to him as she crossed her legs. "You said you're not monogamous and don't do relationships. Is that why? So you can have sex and sleep?"

He paused midway with the cup to his mouth as if she'd caught him off guard. "That's part of it," he said, then followed through with a leisurely drink. He leaned his ass against the counter and curled one hand around the lip, the other hand casually holding his mug in front of his stomach. It was a straightforward pose, one that practically dared her to look her fill.

She forced her gaze to stay locked with his. "What's the other part?"

"I've just learned relationships are best avoided."

A hard shutdown. The same kind she used when people started prying into her past. She spun back to the computer. "Sounds like an interesting story."

"Not unless you consider a middle-aged teacher fucking a senior in high school, making him think it was something more than it was, then claiming coercion when the principal found out interesting."

Her fingers clenched around her mouse and her stomach lurched, threatening to expel the coffee she'd just swallowed. The pain behind his words was tightly leashed behind a careless delivery, but it was there nonetheless, sharp enough it lashed against bare skin.

"Don't try to analyze or fix me," he said. "Been a slew of women before you who've tried and it doesn't work. I like sex. I sleep with women who think like me and it all works out. Less trauma and no drama."

She blanked her expression as her years with Yefim had taught her to, glanced at him over her shoulder and shrugged. "Your past. Your call." With that, she forced herself to re-read the first paragraph in her lesson for the fifth time.

She heard more than saw him sip his coffee behind her. "Speaking of pasts, how about you share a little about the real JJ."

"I'd rather not."

"I figured as much, but it ever occur to you if I knew some of the details I might be able to help?"

Her fingers hitched just the tiniest bit in scrolling down the screen and her breath caught in her throat. She'd definitely thought about it. Countless times. The fact that the Federal government had reached out to him on several occasions said loads about his capabilities.

"I'm aware of your skills and your connections." Hopefully, he didn't catch the subtle tremor in her voice, the quaver tightly woven with the hummingbird thrum of her heart.

"Then you know they could work to your advantage."

"I do. But I've already asked enough of your time and I've yet to learn if you're willing to take that much on. Creating a future where I can support myself is more important than adding more weight on top of everything else." Everything else being the awkward situation she'd created between them by tossing a match into the flammable chemistry between them.

Silence settled between them. Even without her eyes on him, his stare pulsed like a living, breathing entity around her.

"Look at me." A command. As powerful and un-yielding as the ones he'd given her last night and every bit as seductive.

She twisted her neck only enough to meet his gaze, her body still squared to the computer.

"All the way around," he said. "The attitude is hot as fuck and likely necessary to hold your own with me, but we've got a lot of ground to cover without your sass distracting me."

So he was ready to give her his answer. Or maybe multiple ones. Whatever topics he had in mind, left stark severity etched on his face. She swallowed and swiv-eled in her seat, squeezing her knees together tight and folding one hand over the other to cover her nervous-ness. "All right. I'm listening."

His gaze dipped to her knees and his expression softened before he shuttled his focus back to her face. "Relax. I'm not dropping any bombs." He paused as though questioning the thoughts running through his head. "You want me to teach you, I'm in."

Her shoulders sagged with relief and the breath she hadn't realized she'd been holding rushed out before she could mask the reaction. "Thank you."

He chuckled at that. "Don't thank me yet. I'm still an asshole to work with."

She tried to fight the smile, but failed miserably so she ducked her chin instead. "You are quite bossy."

"I am. But I'm good at what I do. As fast as you catch on, you could be too if you can tough it out."

The bold comment jerked her head back up as sure as if he'd fisted his hand in her hair and yanked. "You mean that?"

"I do. So, when I tell you that teaching you puts little to no weight on me and possibly gains me an asset in the long run I mean it." He sipped his coffee, never taking his eyes off her. Once done, he set it aside and crossed his arms over his chest. "Now, tell me about JJ."

For months, she'd faced her past alone. Within the safety of her home and beyond prying eyes. But here, with one simple demand, Knox swept aside the veil and let all the glory and discovery of her time with JJ drift through. The room faded to little more than a haze, only Knox's rapt presence tying her to the here and now. "When I landed here, I had no one. No name to use beyond the ones I made up. Only the cash I'd been given to live on."

The crush of mold and stale cigarette smoke that permeated the extended-stay hotel she'd lived in those first few weeks engulfed her like no time had passed at all. She'd not dared to pay too much attention to the floors or the comforter that covered her bed, sheer exhaustion the only way she'd managed any sleep. "I purchased newspapers the first few days looking for work. Then found a local library and searched for online advertisements."

Knox's hushed voice slipped through her memories and pulled her back to the present. "Where were you?"

"San Diego." The same wistfulness she'd felt her first day there swept in fresh and cleansing. "It's beautiful there. Heaven on Earth compared to Russia."

He said nothing. Merely offered her an understanding smile and waited patiently for her to continue.

"I answered a job posting," she said. "One of those classified websites with everything from personal ads to job postings. Jeannie needed a housekeeper and an assistant."

"And she hired you?"

Darya nodded. "Despite my insistence that I could only be paid in cash." She chuckled at the memory, remembering the suspicious glint in JJ's eyes. "Looking back, I think it was *because* of my insistence." She refocused on Knox. "She knew what it meant to run and helped me because of it."

Knox frowned and cocked his head. "Jeannie Simpson shows as a native US citizen."

"Yes. She was. But not everyone who runs flees the country and not everyone flees forever." It felt strange to share someone else's story. Almost as if she were filching on sacred vow, but JJ would have wanted this for her. Would have told the story herself if she were here. She pulled in a deep breath and let it out on a slow sigh. "She had no living family. Only a husband who deemed it his right to force his will on her in the way of his fists." She smiled. "If you knew JJ, you'd know that arrangement didn't last long."

"What happened?"

She shrugged. "When authorities proved to be unhelpful, she took care of herself."

"She ran."

"Yes."

"Anything else?"

Darya rolled her lips inward, torn between sharing what she believed to be the truth and keeping her silence. "She never told me more than that, but I did look enough to know that her husband no longer lives."

Knox dipped his chin. A simple acceptance without uttering a word. "So where is she now? There's no death certificate, so she's got to be breathing somewhere."

And here was the hard part. The part that still left a lingering weight on her soul. "Jeannie died nine months ago. Brain cancer." She swallowed around the gargantuan knot in her throat, the ugly tan carpeting beneath her feet all she could bear to look at. "It came on quickly and ended mercifully fast. But in that time—in the early months before it stole her spirit—she made arrangements. Leveraged contacts built throughout her life and made it so that I could take on her name and, hopefully, stop running."

"Those must have been some powerful connections."

She grinned despite the sadness seeping through her. How could she not? For someone like Knox to appreciate what she'd done would have sent JJ squawking for days. "There is only one loose thread from her arrangements— the funeral director she bribed to handle her cremation. And even he doesn't know my real name."

"So, you're relatively safe."

"Relatively. For now."

Seemingly satisfied with her story, he slid his mug from the counter and ambled back to the coffeepot. "From who?"

Quick, but casual. Designed to slip beneath an average person's defenses. Except she wasn't average and hadn't been for a long time. "That part of my past is best left alone."

He slid the coffeepot back in place, braced both hands on the counter for a handful of seconds then pushed upright and took a drink. He studied her over the rim, some mysterious emotion moving behind his eyes. Something powerful still unspoken.

Instinctively, she braced.

He lowered his mug. "All right. Then let's talk about sex."

Pleasure speared straight between her legs and her sex fluttered, the mere word making her whole body jolt with awareness. More than anything, she wanted to lick her lip and suggest they do that rather than talk, but something told her she'd be better off keeping her cards tight to her chest. "What about it?"

"You get all it can be for me is sex? No strings? No expectations?"

"I think I got that, yes."

"And you think you can work within that arrangement?"

"It's sex. Physical release. So long as the arrangement works both ways, I'm fine with it."

Something primal flashed behind his eyes, there and gone so fast anyone not watching him closely would've missed it.

But she'd been watching. Closely. "Is that a problem?"

"No." Zero hesitation, but voiced with an edge that said otherwise. "You have any problem with me crashing after?"

This time she gave into her need to play. To tease and nudge her predator just a little. She cocked her head and gave him a sly smile. "I should hope not. If you can easily walk out the door, that means we weren't doing it right."

He chuckled at that and lifted his mug in salute. "Point taken."

Looking at him nearly naked and bantering about sex without indulging was too much, so she spun back to her desk, scrolled back to the top of her lesson for the *sixth* time and started over.

His coffee mug clunked against the Formica and his bare footsteps sounded on the kitchen's cheap linoleum. A second later, he braced his hands on either side of her, one on her desk and the other on the back of her chair. Black currant and woodsmoke wrapped around her, and his body heat licked against hers. He checked the screen for all of two seconds before he turned his face and murmured close to her ear. "Not making much progress."

"I was distracted."

"Mmm."

A simple hum. Nothing more. But she felt it everywhere. Deeply.

He straightened and her whole body cried out at the loss. Before she could formulate a witty response, or at least refocus on her lesson, he cupped her far knee and spun her in her chair.

"What are you doing?" Mindless to anything but the lingering aftershock of his unexpected touch, the question came out as a whisper.

Thoughtfully, he skimmed the back of his knuckles along the exposed skin above her neckline then farther down along the edge of her robe. When his fingers reached her belt, he crooked them beneath and tugged until the fabric slipped free. Slowly he pushed her robe apart with both hands and sucked in a low breath that bordered on a hiss.

"Knox?"

"Hmm?" Totally focused. A hunter undistracted from his prey.

Still, she tried again, scrambling to find some mental footing in the midst of the sensations his perusal stirred. "What are you doing?"

He palmed her knees, slowly pressed them apart and crouched between them. Rolling to his knees, he gripped her hips, jerked her to the edge of her chair and lifted his hungry gaze to hers. "Wanted to do this the last time I was here."

He wouldn't. Dear God, if he put his mouth to her here, she'd never get anything productive done at her desk ever again. "But I have to work."

He grinned. A wolf's smile that sent ripples fanning out in all directions. "So do I." He cupped the back of one knee, lifted it up and as wide as the desk beside her allowed and lowered his mouth toward her sex. "Now, brace, because I'm about to give you thanks for a solid night's sleep in a way you won't soon forget."

Chapter Thirteen

Knox had a ton to do. Between the time he'd taken off Saturday night and his inability to concentrate on Sunday, he was way the fuck behind, but he still couldn't stop staring at his screen.

It had taken half of last night and most of the morning, but finally he'd found the thread, and now the man Darya had apparently worked for was staring back at him. The picture was black and white and grainy as hell, but she was right behind the guy. Dressed to the nines, she had her head down as though trying to blend into the background.

Like that could ever happen. He'd left her place over twenty-four hours ago and he was still juiced. Not just by the things they'd done, but by the mother of all miracles that had happened when he'd gotten home. Hell, he still couldn't believe it. The taste of her had still been on his tongue and his dick so hard it hurt to walk. He'd refused to get off with her again—no more condoms and a need to walk out with *some* kind of upper hand had driven him to leave shortly after she'd come against his mouth. But he'd been naked and flat on his bed in all of five minutes of walking in his front door, stroking one off with the previous night's details as clear as if they were happening all over again in real life.

He'd come. Hard.

And then he'd fallen asleep.

For four fucking hours.

That shit never happened by his own hand. Ever. Especially after he'd just had eight solid hours the night before. He'd woken with dried spunk on his belly, her scent all over him and his dick ready and raring to go again.

Yeah, he had his work cut out for him keeping his distance. Hell, he wasn't even sure a repeat was a good idea, no matter how well he'd slept after.

The door handle clicked behind him and he flipped the display on his screen to his email. That was another problem he needed to fix and fast. No one ever snuck up on him. Especially not here with cameras mounted at every conceivable angle. And yet, Beckett strode in behind him with a box of donuts and a monster cup of joe.

Beckett slid the box onto the desk beside him and dragged one of the chairs from his working table up beside Knox. "What's new in the land of cyber goodness?"

Well, at least that much was a safe topic. God knew he was going to get his ass handed to him before Beckett ambled back to his own office. "Got the goods on Darya. At least at a high level. What she said about being born and educated in Yekaterinburg checks out. So does the move to St. Petersburg after."

He pulled up the picture of Darya's boss and angled his primary screen toward Beckett. "Went to work for this guy. Yefim Mishin."

"Doing what?"

"Personal assistant. A pretty coveted job from what I can tell."

"And what's Yefim do?"

"An accountant on paper, but some of the articles paint him as more of a financial guru. Right hand to an oligarch."

Beckett's easygoing demeanor went stone-cold in a snap. "You think she's running because she stole from the guy? The way I understand it, oligarchs are barely a step up from the mob."

Knox shook his head, his focus drawn back to the picture of Darya as sure as if she'd reached out and guided his face by her own hand. "If she's got money, she's not using it. Not even a dime. Her stuff is quality, but all secondhand or very old."

The image of her in her desk chair, her body drawn in on itself and her voice barely more than a whisper as she'd shared her first weeks in the US, boomeranged back to him. She'd felt every word. Relived every memory. No way the emotion that had been behind her story had anything to do with nefarious deeds. "Not thinking she's not the type to steal."

"Well, at least you've dropped the idea of her being some dastardly killer."

"Yeah, I found out about that, too." He pulled up the best of the old social media pics he'd found of the real Jeannie Simpson and put it side by side with the ones officially linked to Darya's passport and driver's license. "Darya shared the details on JJ. She hired Darya shortly after she landed here. They made a connection. When JJ was diagnosed with brain cancer she took it on herself to set Darya up to carry on with her identity before she kicked it. The woman was smart. Did just enough altering of Darya's facial features to match her own. Smart move to throw off facial recognition."

"Damn. That's one hell of a fairy godmother."

"Tell me about it."

Beckett leaned in, popped open the box he'd brought in and snagged a donut. "So, when did this treasure trove of information come out? When you dropped her off last night, or the morning after?"

And here comes the ass-handing.

In one last dodge to avoid the whole scene entirely, he flipped open his email and scanned the list of senders without really clocking a word. "She's coming in this morning at ten. I need you to handle getting her prints and retina scans. Show her around and introduce her to the rest of the crew while you're at it. I already talked to Katy. She's gonna get her hooked into handling some app support tickets."

"Why me? Darya's your employee."

Goddamn Beckett. He never could just come out and say what he wanted to know. Had to prod and dig until a person finally confessed just to be free of the bastard.

Knox dragged his billfold out of his back pocket, peeled out the stack of hundreds he'd grabbed on the way in and plunked them down on the counter. "One large. You win."

Even monitoring him out of the corner of Knox's eye, Beckett's sly grin was too big to miss. "Oh, yeah. That's what I'm talking about. In less than two weeks, too." He smacked his hands together, effectively dusting the crumbs from his annihilated donut off his fingers and celebrating in one fell swoop. He snatched the cash, folded the wad with a whole lot of I-told-you-so attitude and stuffed it in his back pocket. "So? How was it?"

Knox dropped all pretense of work and slumped back in his chair. "Really? We gonna comb each other's hair and giggle, too? Maybe we can take a little extra time and spring for a mani/pedi." Whatever the fuck that was. All he knew was that the moms, Viv, Gabe and Nat had a standing appointment for the damned things every two weeks.

"Ah, come on, man. She's hot. The way you practically threaded Seth on a spit, I figure you had some crazy aggression to work off."

Yeah he had. And Darya had not only taken every scrap of it, but had turned around and goaded him for more. He refocused on his screen and hit reply to an email he hadn't even read for the sole purpose of having something to do. "Just do me a favor. Show her around. Get her set up. Make sure she gets one of our computers and secured VPN access so I can keep closer ties on what she's up to."

Beckett chuckled, reclined against his seat back and hooked one steel-toed boot heel on the rung of his chair. "She rung your bell. Hard."

Goddamn it. Knox anchored his elbows on the desk and dug the heels of his hands into his eye sockets. "Brother, just do me a solid and handle this. I need distance with this one." He looked up and met Beckett's too shrewd stare. "Give her an office if you want, but encourage her to work remote."

"You don't like people to work remote. You're the kingpin of micromanagers and don't trust anything you can't see with your own security cams. Hell, you'd hover over every one of our employees if you could figure out how to pull it off and still get work done."

"Yeah, well, I'm not gonna hover over her. I already

muddied the lines. I don't need to make it worse and I need you to help me the fuck out."

Beckett studied him a minute, one elbow planted on top of Knox's desk and his finger doing that push/pull thoughtful tell along his lower lip. Knox was just about to stand and bail when Beckett dropped his arm, nudged the box of donuts closer to Knox and stood. "Have a donut, brother. You look like you could use the sugar rush."

With that he ambled toward the exit.

"Are you gonna cover this?" Knox called over one shoulder.

Beckett waved him off without so much as a glance. "Don't sweat it, brother. I've got your back."

Chapter Fourteen

A new day and a new start. Yesterday, Darya had let herself nurse the mother of all sex hangovers as long as she'd wanted, but today was fresh. All business.

Or at least that was the goal.

With one last slow exhale, she closed her eyes and pictured herself detached. Professional and calm. She'd used the same visualization to get her through all kinds of tense conversations at Yefim's side. Negotiations that covered ridiculous sums of money and thinly veiled references to murder. Surely the tactic would work on a man who made her sex weep with a single dirty look.

She popped the handle on her Challenger and stepped into the late-July heat. Even at ten 'til ten in the morning, the air was thick with the promise of a scorching afternoon.

The security latch clicked open on the tinted double doors before she'd even lifted her arm to open it, and a second later the super-chilled air from inside wafted against her skin.

"The new victim arrives!" Katy stood behind her desk and held out her hand. "I mean trainee, of course, but you'll appreciate the term *victim* by the time Knox deems you ready for prime time."

Darya shook her hand, grateful for the levity as well as the warm welcome. "I don't mind hard work. And he speaks very highly of you."

"Only because I'm as stubborn as he is and stuck at it until I proved he'd be better off with me than without me." She sat back down, held up one finger and snatched the phone from its cradle. After she'd pushed a few buttons, she anchored the earpiece in place with her shoulder and said to Darya, "Knox gave me the rundown this morning. Said you already had your assignments for the next few days, but asked me to teach you the ropes on app support."

Before Darya could respond, she snapped to attention as if someone had answered the other line. "Hey, Beck. Darya's here." She smiled at whatever he said then volleyed back with, "Yeah, got it." She slid the phone back in place. "Beckett's on his way up."

"Beckett?"

"Yeah, he's gonna handle your scans and get you set up in the office. Just head back this way when you're done and I'll walk you through our ticketing system and how we triage everything."

Beckett.

Not Knox.

Not even so much as a hello.

It shouldn't have hurt as much as it did, but the realization packed an immense punch. An unprotected blow square to the center of her belly. But could she blame him? He'd told her no strings and no expectations, and she'd agreed. Had even implied her feelings ran the same way. Now it was time to do her part, even if it was all a load of crap.

Katy motioned to Darya's outfit. "You know, the

dress code's casual here. Jeans, sweats—heck one time, Misty showed up in flannel pajamas. Though, in fairness, that time she was just popping in before she had to run an errand for Knox."

Darya scanned her linen sheath dress. The cut was simple and the buff color soft against her skin, but dressing for the office had helped her distance herself mentally. Still, cutting back on the dry-cleaning bill would be good. "Who's Misty?"

"Knox's assistant. She's not exactly technically savvy, but she's wicked good at keeping everyone's rabid squirrels in a row."

The heavy steel door to her right chunked open and Beckett ambled out. Of all the brothers, he'd always seemed the scariest in pictures—tall enough nearly everyone looked up to him with impressive muscle to balance his height. His dark chocolate hair was cropped close on the sides, only marginally longer on top, lending more severity to his strong, square jaw, but it was the quiet lethalness that emanated from behind his blue eyes that put people on edge. A deadly panther always poised and ready to pounce.

Yet today a huge smile split his chiseled face. "Hey, JJ."

Nine months she'd carried her friend's name and accepted it as her own, but hearing it now felt clunky. Wrong. As though she'd slipped her shoes on the wrong feet and gone for a stroll regardless.

He motioned to Katy. "Katy's already got most of your information entered in the system. We'll just need you to confirm your social and all the other details."

Oh. Right. Just because she'd shared her real name with Knox and his brothers didn't mean she could do the same with the rest of the world. Mistakes like that would crush what little normalcy Jeannie's gift had created for her. "Thank you. Of course."

He crowded close, the nearness more what she'd have expected from Knox after the night they'd shared than a man she barely knew. His voice dropped to a low rumble. "You ready to get set up so you can get to work?"

The words were right, but a suggested undercurrent wiggled beneath them. She inched backward. "Yes, absolutely."

Beckett grinned as though he'd not only registered her discomfort, but that she'd somehow done exactly as he wanted. He motioned her toward the door he'd appeared from. "Well, then, let's get busy."

Weird. Something was off. Not quite big-bad-wolfish, but definitely something that told her to tread carefully. She nodded to Katy and cautiously started out in front of Beckett. "I'll see you soon."

If Katy had caught on to whatever was going on with Beckett, she didn't show it, simply ducked her head back to the screen while her fingers flew across the keyboard. "Yep. I'll be here when you're done."

At the door, Darya tried to open it, but remembered the hand scanner to one side when it wouldn't budge.

Beckett moved in tight behind her and splayed his huge hand on the black pad. "Just relax," he muttered low near her ear. "Trust me."

Trust him? To do what?

The lock clicked open and he pulled the door wide.

She opened her mouth to ask her thoughts aloud, but he shook his head, a movement she'd have missed entirely if her gaze hadn't been rooted on his face.

Definitely weird. Still she proceeded forward, her heels clicking delicately on the industrial tile.

"We're headed to the last door on your right. Once we get your prints uploaded we'll get you a computer and access set up."

"Where's Knox?" She hadn't meant to ask it. Had promised herself she wouldn't, but between Beckett's odd behavior and her general first-day nervousness it leaped right out.

Beckett chuckled, a satisfied rumble that stopped just short of a caveman beating on his chest. "Don't worry about him. I'll take good care of you." He splayed his hand low on her back, reached around her and opened the door so she could proceed him inside. "I promise."

And so it went. Touch, tease and wink-wink all through the orientation process. Not once did he cross an inappropriate line, but by the time they'd scanned her prints and retrieved a computer from a tech lover's utopian supply room, a soft breeze could have sent her leaping from her skin.

They'd just fired up her new equipment, Beckett leaning close over her shoulder while he pointed to her screen, when a low buzz sounded from somewhere.

Beckett grinned and murmured so low she could barely hear it. "Took him long enough." He straightened and dug his phone out of his back pocket. "Yeah, what's up?" He focused on the floor, his expression completely blank. "Not sure what you're talkin' about, brother. Just gettin' our girl set up like you asked." His lips twitched and he turned his back. "Now, why the hell would I do that? And even if I did, what difference would it make?" His shoulders shook, but when he spoke there was no trace of the laughter she'd expected alongside it. "Yeah,

yeah. Got it. Message received." He twisted enough to catch Darya's stare and winked. "Later."

He ended the call.

"Who was that?"

Ignoring her for the first time all morning, he stuffed his phone back in his pocket, typed a string of commands on the DOS screen, then pushed her computer back enough he could lean one hip on the edge of her desk. Gone was the man who'd flirted, cajoled and outright teased her all morning, replaced with the casual man she'd gotten to know Saturday night. "Okay, so you good on how the VPN works?"

"Umm." She stared at her computer and gave her mind a few precious seconds to reboot. "Triple authentication. Use the fingerprint scanner, the key fob for the single-use password, then the pass phrase."

"Perfect." He stood and motioned to her desk. "You can work remote if you want, but my advice, you want to get on Knox's good side, hit the office."

Really? That surprised her. He seemed more of a work anywhere and all the time guy. Plus, if he wanted them to keep distance between them, coming into the office would make for more of a challenge.

Still, she agreed with the suit up and show up routine. The act of preparing and physically going to work, no matter how casual the environment, always sharpened her focus. At least it did when Beckett wasn't crowding her space. She nodded. "I'll be here. Every day."

"Good call." Beckett jerked his head toward the main lobby. "Katy worked late every night the first year she was here. Refused to leave until after Knox did. Totally paid off with her. He trusts her almost as much as he trusts me and that's saying something."

Interesting. Far more information than was appropriate for someone new and untried. Her instincts prickled.

Beckett stared back at her, steady and unwavering.

"Put in the hours," she whispered.

"Definitely," Beckett said back, though it sounded like he was asking more than telling. "You do, I gotta hunch it'll be worth it."

He stood and started typing a new DOS command. "A word to the wise, this unit's got cameras and mics on all the time." He hit the enter button, closed the command window he'd been typing in and straightened, the tone of his voice shifting to something more appropriate for discussing the weather. "You need me, you know where I am. Knox's office is right next door."

He ambled toward the door.

So that's what he'd done with the DOS prompts. Killed the mic and camera long enough to share his advice. And he'd put her office right next door to Knox. Close to his brother.

"Beckett?" she said before he disappeared into the hallway.

Pausing with one hand on the jamb, he looked back at her and lifted both eyebrows. So innocent looking on the surface, but his eyes practically danced with mirth.

He was trying to help her. And not just on a professional level either. How she knew it she wasn't sure, but the thought was there, drifting through her soft as windswept cotton. "Thank you."

The stare he returned was intense, a demand and a plea all rolled up into one. He stepped back into the hallway's shadows and dropped his voice low enough the camera mounted in the far corner would struggle to pick up his response. "Whatever you're doing, keep doing it. Don't give up."

And then he was gone.

Chapter Fifteen

Darya hustled into her blessedly cool apartment, juggling her duffel bag full of workout clothes, her laptop bag and purse as she quickly shut the door against the brutal afternoon heat. She leaned against the door and huffed out a tired breath. The persistent *beep beep beep* of her freshly installed security system matched the still pounding rhythm of her heart. Thirty minutes it had taken her to drive home from Knox and Beckett's office and she still hadn't recovered from Beckett's merciless workout routine. He'd said continuing her self-defense classes was a job perk, but her sore arms and ass said otherwise.

She pushed off the door with an ugly *oomph* and punched in her alarm code. Her conversations with Knox over the last week had been limited at best, only an hour here and there to go over her lessons and endure gruesome code reviews, though there had been one unguarded moment where he'd ranted for the better part of thirty minutes about how her landlords were "certified fucking idiots." Hence, the reason she had only the most basic of systems instead of something that could control a third-world country. A fact that Knox was clearly not pleased about.

Her bags sat like anvils around her feet and sweat trickled down her spine. Never in her life did she think she'd ever experience triple digit heat, but as if Mother Nature had decided to celebrate the arrival of August, her thermostat had firmly shown 101. Truly, summer in Texas was hell on Earth.

She scooped up her bags, trudged past her makeshift office to unload her laptop and purse, then tossed her duffel into her bedroom on her way to the bathroom. Her haggard reflection stared back at her, hair dampened around her face with chunks that had escaped her long braid plastered to the back of her neck.

"Just keep doing what you're doing."

At least once a day, Beckett had found a way to reiterate the message. Sometimes with words. Sometimes with a pointed look.

She wasn't so sure the detached and dedicated worker bee approach was working, though. Every day she strode into the office never knowing which Knox she'd bump into—the one who seemed frustrated just to be in the same room with her, or the one who looked like he was contemplating fucking her against the nearest wall.

Her vote was definitely for the latter. Time and distance hadn't helped her forget that night or the morning after in the least. If anything, the memory had stoked her need twice as high and left her irritable and edgy. The only consolation was that he seemed to be in as bad of shape as her. Or worse. He covered it well, but his eyes didn't seem nearly as sharp, and she'd busted him countless times either raking his hands through his hair or gouging his thumbs against his eyes.

Sighing, she peeled off her tank top, ditched her yoga pants and sports bra and cranked the tub faucet to full blast. If nothing else was meant to happen between them she'd live. And she'd do it knowing she'd not only maintained her professionalism, but survived learning from the best.

Because Knox Torren was absolutely the best at what he did. No doubt about it.

A ping sounded from the bedroom, the sound so faint it was nearly drowned out by the rush of water.

She poked her head out of the bathroom, checked to make sure the living room blinds were fully closed and scampered to her hastily discarded purse. Rummaging past her sunglasses and cosmetic case, her fingers closed around her phone near the bottom.

The green text bubble flashed Knox's name and one line of text a second before the automatic print reader unlocked the device and sent her to the main app screen. Hands shaking from workout fatigue and an onslaught of fresh adrenaline, she flipped to her texts and nearly dropped the phone when the message came into focus.

Knox: Have you eaten?

Finally.

Her arms trembled, her palms so slick she had to grip the device with both hands to keep it steady.

Darya: No.

Simple and straightforward. Nothing he could read into one way or another and lobbed things right back into his court.

The answer came faster than she expected.

Knox: Are you hungry?

She smiled to herself, her heart picking up steam as she wandered back to the bathroom.

Darya: I thought we'd established I'm always hungry.

She leaned one hip against the vanity and bit her lip, the rush of the water splashing ferociously against the old porcelain tub as tumultuous as the blood coursing through her veins.

Knox: Can you cook?

Darya: I'm not a gourmet but I can hold my own.

Knox: Good. Then unless you tell me otherwise, I'm coming over with groceries.

Why wouldn't she tell him to come over? Unless he was just coming to eat and nothing else. Or maybe he was coming over for work.

Darya: Why would I say no to food?

For the longest time, she stood there, staring at the screen and waiting for the answer that refused to come. She was just about to toss the phone to the counter and let her sore muscles soak in the nearly full bath when the little dots that promised an incoming message danced along the bottom of the window.

Knox: Because after you feed me I plan to fuck you until you don't know your name. So, what's your answer?

Her heart seized then tumbled back to a jagged rhythm. On the surface, the response was crude. Utterly disrespectful and harsh. But something told her there was more behind it. The same frustration and need she'd combated for seven very long days veiled beneath a bold dare.

And he'd left the ball squarely in her court.

Surely she could keep herself in check. She *had* to. Because saying no to him wasn't an option. Not even something temporary and decadently shallow. Her body needed it. Demanded it.

She straightened away from the vanity and let her thumbs fly across the keyboard.

Darya: Technically, I have two names. You'd have your work cut out for you.

The little dots popped up right away and she held her breath.

Knox: Challenge accepted. Be there in thirty.

"Yes!" Her triumphant exclamation bounced off the stark white tiles, bringing with it the reality of what she'd just read.

Her head snapped up to the mirror. The bold and energy efficient LED bulbs shone down on her, spotlighting her bedraggled appearance. Thirty minutes was nothing. Barely enough time to get her hair dry let alone make an impression.

As soon as the thought ricocheted around in her head, another more calculated one slid in behind it. Only a woman out to tempt a man would race to make an impression. An indifferent one would be herself. She smiled back at her reflection. She could do indifferent. In fact, she knew just the right way to pull that off.

Chapter Sixteen

Knox stomped up the last few steps to Darya's apartment, shifted the sack of ingredients he'd pilfered from his and Beckett's pantry to one hip and knocked on the front door.

Darya's muffled voice sounded through the thick wooden door. "It's open."

"You gotta be shittin' me," he said under his breath and curled his hand around the knob. Sure enough, the damned thing twisted smooth as butter and whisked open without a sound. Even the POS security system he'd had Danny put in was silent.

He shut the door behind him, threw the bolt and punched in the code. "You want to tell me why your front door's unlocked?"

The rush of running water sounded from her bathroom, but no answer came.

Knox stomped toward the open bathroom door. "Darya?"

The water stopped. "What?"

"Why the hell did you leave your front door unlocked?"

She stepped into view, not a stitch on except a fluffy white towel wrapped around her chest. "Because I just got out of the shower and I still needed to brush my teeth." Her hair was wet, but combed through and swept to one side so it spilled over one breast and her face was completely void of makeup.

Fuck, she was beautiful. Stunning just the way God made her. He clenched his hand tighter against the brown paper bag filled with food and fought the need to toss the lot of it to the ground. To rip the offensive towel away, plant her ass on the sink behind her and sink his dick inside her right now.

"You're running from someone," he said instead.

The easy smile on her face disappeared, replaced with caution. "*Was* running."

"What if whoever it is is still looking? I changed those locks and put that system in for a reason. You think it's a good idea to just leave yourself exposed?"

She cocked her head and lowered her voice. "I saw you pull up in the parking lot. It was only unlocked from the time you got out until the time you walked through the door." She gripped the top of the towel and shifted it as though making sure it was properly in place. "I wouldn't take unnecessary risks."

Of course, she wouldn't. She was too smart for that. But he'd sure shown his ass storming in and jumping her shit. He dipped his chin and stepped away. It was either that or pull her against him and hold her there until his heart stopped its angry tantrum. "I'll get the stuff set up."

Not waiting for a response, he strode to the kitchen. He had everything unpacked and a skillet and casserole dish ready to go by the time Darya strolled toward the counter. He dumped the ground beef into the skillet, watching her from the corner of his eye.

She tilted the jar of spaghetti sauce back enough to check the label then shifted her attention to the crumpled and food-stained piece of paper beside it. Gently tracing one side, she said, "Whose recipe is this?"

"Momma McKee's."

Her head snapped up. "Who's Momma McKee?"

He put the lid on the skillet and forced himself to face her. The full-on experience sucker punched him hard. Her feet were still bare, but she'd put on pale gray leggings that looked as soft as his down comforter at home and a worn oversize button-down that begged a man to unbutton it. Slowly. And it was thin. So much so, the light behind her just barely outlined the lower swell of one breast.

He cleared his throat and forced his brain back online. He'd just jumped all over her ass without even a hint of provocation, and here he was planning out how and when to get her undressed. "Axel's mom."

She smiled, the genuineness of it so open and sweet it moved through him like a cleansing rain, forgiving him and luring back out into the sunshine all in one sweep. "I'm not sure what is more surprising. That Axel has the type of mother to share recipes, or that you actually use them."

He laughed at that, all the tension that had gripped him the last five minutes melting away along with it. "Actually, Sylvie almost never shares her recipes. She'd rather cook for us than make us self-sufficient, but she knows I've got a thing for fat and cheese." He nodded to the piece of paper loosely pinched between her fingers. "She calls that one Bachelor Lasagna."

Her mouth twitched. "So, you've actually made it?"

"Several times." He backed away from the stove and

motioned her into his place. "You think you can finish up while I work?"

She scanned the counter and glanced at the recipe. "I don't see why not."

He nodded and started to amble back to the living room and his backpack, but hesitated before he got more than three steps in. "Darya?"

She looked up from the stove, a spatula in one hand and the skillet lid in the other.

"I'm sorry I jumped your shit. I just..." Didn't like the thought of some asshole getting his hands on her. Hell, he didn't like the thought of anyone's hands on her. Which was precisely what had driven him here tonight in the first place. "You need to be careful."

Her gaze slid back to the stove, but not before he caught the surprise in her eyes. "Believe me. I'm very, very careful."

Before things could dive any deeper into awkward, he snatched his backpack off the living room floor and unpacked his tools. As televisions went, hers wasn't very big, but at least it wasn't ancient. It was also light-weight, making sliding it and the ebony particleboard stand it sat on a breeze.

"What are you doing?" Darya said from behind him.

He froze for a second, considered tossing her some bullshit excuse then decided against it. "Fixing your lackluster cable selection."

"But I can't afford anything more than basic."

She might not, but he could. And while he'd tried like hell to fight it the last seven days, he'd be blowing sunshine up his own ass if he didn't admit he had every intention of spending at least a few more nights here. "You're not going to pay a dime. Consider it a job perk," he said to the now exposed connection. "Payback for putting up with my attitude this week."

Her presence behind him stayed locked in place, but she kept her silence. At least at first. Then she nearly knocked him from his crouch to his knees with her soft voice. "You're who you are and you're taking a chance on me. That is benefit enough." Her footsteps padded away a second later, leaving him alone with his swirling thoughts.

He really had been an ass. Cold. Insanely distant. But what the hell else was he supposed to do? He didn't dare give in and make himself available for the same affection she gave everyone else. Let alone reciprocate it. That path spelled a hard ending that would kill him because he actually liked this woman. Respected the hell out of her intellect and her wit. Not to mention wanting to lock her up in a room, curl around her and indulge himself on her body.

Shaking off the round-and-round in his head, he screwed the faceplate back in place, gathered up his tools and put her furniture and TV back to rights. By the time he'd stowed things away and ambled into the kitchen to wash his hands, she'd already stowed the six pack of beer he'd brought, started building the layers in the casserole dish and had the skillet soaking in the sink. "Oven pre-heated?"

Her gaze slid to his hands under the cold water and her lips twitched. "Yes."

What? She thought he had the manners of an oaf or something?

Well, okay. Maybe that had been the case the first few times he'd walked into Ninette and Sylvie's kitchen, but they'd fixed that shit in short order. He killed the

water and dried his hands. From this angle, her shirt
didn't give so much as a glimpse of what lay hidden beneath, but the hem danced around her mid-thigh with
every move. He cocked his head, a dangerous but oh-so
delicious idea blossoming in his head.

He snatched the foil she'd left on the opposite counter, slid it next to the casserole dish and moved in close
behind her. "Thought you might need that."

"Thank you." So breathless. Very aware of his presence.

That was the best part, especially with Darya. The
anticipation. The snap and burn that fired every time
he so much as looked at her. He smoothed his hands
down her hips then gathered the shirt up inch-by-inch.

Her back-and-forth as she spread the sauce on her last
layer slowed, the spoon quivering in her grip. "What
are you doing?"

Grazing his lips along the bared side of her neck, he
inhaled deep. Her scent was stronger today. Must be
the soap she used that gave her that winter rose smell.
Or maybe her shampoo. Whatever it was was addictive.
He hooked his fingers in the waistband of her leggings
and eased them down, taking her panties with them.
"Keep working."

"Knox—" Her spoon clattered to the Formica, pasta
sauce and cheese splattering the otherwise pristine surface. She gripped the counter's edge tight and let out
a shaky breath.

Dragging the plush fabric along her skin, he slowly
crouched behind her. "Focus."

"But you're—"

"You get the food ready. I'll get you ready. That simple." He tapped one ankle. "Lift."

She did as he asked then repeated the process for the other leg. God he loved her legs. Had ogled them in her insanely fuckable shoes every day at work, but seeing her barefoot like this—her delicate feet and bubblegum-painted toenails—he needed them wrapped around him, her heels digging into his ass. He smoothed his hands up the outside of her legs then teased the inside of her knees with his thumbs. "You're not cooking."

"I can't..." Her hips tilted just a fraction, an innocent invitation he had no intention of taking. Yet. "It's hard to think."

"You don't cook, we don't eat. We don't eat, we don't fuck." He pushed upright, taking his time as he did and making sure she felt every inch. Pressing tight to her back, he nuzzled her ear and murmured, "And I'm very much looking forward to the fucking part." Giving in to the hard edge buzzing beneath his skin, he smacked her hip just hard enough to rip a gasp from her then forced himself to the fridge.

Beer in hand, he didn't look back. Didn't dare for fear he'd give into the impulse and take her right then and there. She'd already had fast and furious from him. Tonight he'd take his time and build her up. Build them both up until it was either come or combust.

He powered up the TV, ditched his boots and socks, and tucked them neatly out of the way. Even with a host of stations to keep him occupied, his mind seemed more in tune with the sounds coming from the kitchen than any visual on the screen. The muted creak of the oven door. Running water as she washed the dishes and the soft patter of her feet on the cheap linoleum as she tidied up the countertops.

The cable box glowed 7:45 p.m. in soft neon blue.

Fifteen minutes since she'd put the food in to bake. A long time for a woman as efficient as Darya.

He took a slow pull off his beer. Distance between them was smart. He'd been the one to insist on it all week and she'd easily followed suit, but right now it sucked. Too much to ignore. "You gonna come out here and sit with me, or hide in there the rest of the thirty minutes left for it to cook?"

Silence answered back from the kitchen.

"Darya?"

She glided around the corner, the same indifferent smile she'd kept in place while working firmly in place.

Oh, fuck no. At work yes, but not here. Not now. He crooked his fingers. "C'mere."

Gauging his place dead center on the couch then the two empty spots on either side of him, she crept forward. "What are you watching?"

Hell if he knew. All he'd done was punch the up button about a thousand times. "Nothing worth stopping for."

She reached for the throw pillow beside him and moved it, making extra room for her to sit beside him.

He snatched her wrist before she could land, set his beer on the coffee table and guided her in between his legs.

She tried to tug her hand free, for all the good it did her. "What are you doing?"

"Got time to play. I'm going to enjoy it." He tugged harder.

"But there's not enough room."

Easy enough to fix. He snatched the huge pillow that served as the back couch cushion and tossed it and the smaller pillow still in her hand to the floor. "There is now." He scooted back, turned her with hands at her hips and pulled her ass down right between his thighs.

Her back was still ramrod straight, hands splayed on his knees as if she'd bolt at any moment.

Smoothing his hands up her arms, he worked his thumbs along the muscles between her neck and shoulders and urged her to recline against him. "Just relax."

Bit-by-bit she gave in, melting against him on a soft sigh but keeping her head lolled forward to give him better room to work.

He chuckled and deepened his strokes. "Beck's a task master with the workouts, huh?"

"Mmm." As if his touch had totally unplugged her mind and left her floating on some distant cloud.

Which was completely weird, considering he'd never once touched a woman this way in his life. Not unless there was an orgasm imminent and her ass, tits or clit were the objects getting his attention. "You look good."

The second it was out he nearly bit his tongue in half.

She tried to twist toward him, but he held her in place and kept rubbing. "What do you mean?"

Well, to hell with it. He'd already shown his hand anyway. "With the self-defense. You look good doing it."

Her fingers pushed and pulled against the denim on his thighs, a mix of nervousness and a kitten kneading its soft bed before she settled in. "When did you see me?"

Fess up, buddy boy. You are who you are. "Only four rooms that don't have cameras at work—the bathrooms and mine and Beckett's offices." He dragged his thumbs along either side of her spine down to her shoulder blades. Oh, yeah. Definitely no bra. And didn't that make his dick give a celebratory high-five.

"You watched me?"

All. The. Damned. Time. Probably a little too much information, though. Better to hedge. "I watch everything."

She nodded, but it was more of a tacit agreement not to push any more than confirmation she understood.

He didn't blame her. Sometimes his incessant need to watch over the people he loved didn't even make sense to him. Not that he loved Darya. She was just a good person he felt compelled to look out for. No different than any of his other employees—except for his obsessive need to be inside her.

"You and Beckett seem very close," she said.

Knox shrugged and refocused on soothing the tight muscles along her delts. "He's my brother."

"But you've known him longer than the others."

He froze, the unexpected observation jolting him out of the languid place they'd settled into. No one at the office knew about his history. No one period, save his family. "What makes you say that?"

She let her head fall back against his shoulder and lifted her beautiful blue gaze to his. "I don't know. Maybe because you act like you've always known him."

There it was. The astuteness that always amazed him. That grabbed him by the nuts as sure as her own hand. "Since I was ten."

Her lips curved in a small smile, sweet as if he'd just given her a thoughtful gift. Before he could fully enjoy it, she rolled her head forward again and closed her eyes. "Were your families close?"

The chuckle that slipped free sounded bitter even to his own ears. "We didn't have families. Not really."

"Then where did you live?" Completely conversational. As if they were doing a code review instead of dredging up the worst stretch of his life.

But this was good. Maybe if she understood where he came from, she'd understand his lines a little better. Would excuse some of the harsh boundaries he needed to survive. Surely he could give her that much.

He swallowed hard, eyes on the beer his throat desperately needed, but in absolutely no hurry to lose the weight of her torso against him. "Hung out at Beckett's house a lot. His mom bailed before I met him. His dad was a nasty drunk, but so long as we stayed out of his way he left us alone."

"So, you lived with him?"

"Not officially, no."

"Then where?"

He ran his palms along her shoulders, her uber-soft cotton top tickling his hands. It wasn't a big deal. Or at least it wouldn't be if he didn't make it one. He forced his voice to stay even. "Foster homes."

With the back of her head resting easy against his shoulder and her eyes closed, he watched her. Waited for some kind of response. A flinch or a scowl.

Her serenity never slipped. Not so much as a blip. "What happened to your family?"

"Don't know who my dad was. Mom died when I was three. Drug overdose."

Her eyes snapped open, locking on to his almost as fast. "Is that why you don't take anything to help you sleep?"

Oh, yeah. Very astute. Dangerously so. As in time to get her on a different topic altogether.

He pulled in a slow breath, dipped his hands along her sides and splayed one against her belly. "You want to talk, tell me about your family."

She drew in a shaky breath. "My life was very simple growing up. Poor, but simple. I was an only child, but I knew much love when my parents were alive."

"They're both gone?" Back and forth, he skated his thumb just inches below her breasts.

Her shoulders pressed gently against his chest. She wanted more. Badly. But she was fighting it just as hard as he was. "My father worked as a machinist. He died when I was thirteen. My mother secured me schooling in St. Petersburg shortly after."

"Secured how?"

She squeezed her eyes shut and a shudder worked through her, this one having nothing to do with pleasure.

He froze. "Darya?"

She rolled her lips together, swallowed and opened her eyes. She met his stare head on. "My mother was very beautiful. With my father gone and no money, she felt it was better to use her assets in a way that would benefit her daughter than keep her pride. She traded herself in exchange for my education and my keeping."

Jesus Christ.

He'd never had a family. No one but Beckett until Axel and Jace found them. But at least he'd never lost one. He pressed his palm against her belly, doing his best to let her know he was there and that he understood without crossing more lines than he already had. "Sounds like she loved you very much."

"It was a tremendous gift." A ferocity lit behind her eyes, the power of it billowing up like some determined goddess. "One I will never let go to waste."

His hand moved without conscious direction from his head, sliding up between her breasts until he clasped her throat. Beneath his fingers and thumb, her pulse pounded through her carotid. But all he could focus on were her lips. Could only remember what they felt like against his. Soft and yet firm.

He never kissed. Not without sex and this was most definitely *not* sex. This was intimacy. Landmine-ridden, terrifying intimacy.

And he still wanted to claim her mouth. Devour and get lost in her taste.

The kitchen timer buzzed, an angry *zing* that barely penetrated despite the dangerous terrain. His gaze slipped to his possessive grip at her neck. Amazing how dark his skin was compared to hers, how rough against her soft flesh.

"I should get that," she whispered.

She should. Because after that all bets were off. "Oh, yeah. It's time to eat."

Chapter Seventeen

The dishwasher was loaded. The leftovers were put away and the casserole dish washed and stored in the same brown grocery bag Knox had brought it in. None of it should have been the stuff of foreplay, but with Knox teasing and touching at every turn, Darya's sex was not only drenched but aching.

The television went silent and the lights in her living room went dark.

She wiped down the counters, skin prickling with awareness. Never in her life had she been so uncertain about how to act around a man. So ready and yet cautious at the same time.

Then again, she'd never been with a man like Knox.

A click sounded from her bedroom and a quick glance over her shoulder confirmed that he'd clicked on the lamp beside her bed.

He strolled into view a second later, a lazy jaguar navigating foreign terrain as easily as if it were his own. His hungry gaze locked on to hers and he flipped off the light switch to her pseudo office, leaving her only in the pool of light coming from the smaller fixture overhead.

Her heart kicked. She slid to the sink and rinsed out

her sponge, desperate to affect the same casualness he portrayed.

He moved in behind her as she turned off the faucet, his hands unerringly slipping beneath her shirt's hem along her thighs and skimming up to her hips. While he anchored one at her waist, the other splayed soft at her belly.

Beneath his touch, her muscles quavered, poised and ready for his fingers to delve lower.

Instead he nuzzled the back of her neck. "Place is locked up. You need anything?" The silent *before I fuck you* hung unspoken in the silence, twice as powerful than if he'd actually voiced the words.

She shook her head, too gripped by the moment to actually speak.

He inhaled deep, slipped his hands from beneath her shirt and turned her with hands at her hips. Still in touching distance, but not crowding her as before, he cupped the side of her face with a tenderness that stole her breath. "Moved too fast last time. Didn't take the time to talk things out."

Talk? She could barely think right now. Let alone string together a sentence that would make sense. "About what?"

His gaze dropped to her mouth and his hand drifted low enough he could skim his thumb along her lower lip. "I think you were clear you're good with rough and open to dirty, but is there anything you absolutely *don't* want?"

Oh, boy. Definitely a dangerous topic to traverse with her mind so distracted.

Trailing his hand lower, he traced tempting patterns

down her neck then across the exposed skin above her neckline.

Her eyes slipped closed, every scrap of attention focused on his touch.

The fabric shifted and the first button slipped free, cool air slipping against the inch of skin he'd revealed. She swallowed hard and willed him to keep going. To peel the soft cotton off her over-sensitized skin and press his body against hers.

"Darya?"

She opened her eyes and his fingers moved on to the next button.

Right. They were talking. About things she didn't like. Though it wasn't as if she'd built up a wealth of experience to draw from before she'd run, and the last three years she'd settled on her toys versus potential exposure. "No pain."

"That include my hand on your ass when you piss me off?"

"Bozhe moi." My God, she whispered before she could stop it, clutching the counter's edge behind her as a visible shudder rippled through her.

Knox chuckled at that and slipped the last button free. "I know zero Russian, but I think I can interpret that as naughty girl spankings getting a pass. Anything else?"

She shook her head. "I haven't explored that much. I just know what we did felt good."

He nudged her shirt, leaving her mound exposed and the sides barely covering her nipples. "You ever play with other toys? Nipple clamps? Ropes?"

She couldn't look at him. Could only watch him

drag the backs of his knuckles from her sternum down, down, down.

"Darya, look at me."

It took every scrap of courage she had, but she did it, her lungs hitching as her gaze locked on to his.

He was hungry. Ravenous, despite what his outward confidence and calm alluded. And all of that need was aimed squarely on her. "You want to explore?"

God, yes. With him she'd try almost anything. "Yes."

He held her gaze. "Saw the plug in your box. That something you get off on often?"

"Sometimes."

"Toys only or men?"

"Toys. I never—haven't been with anyone I trusted."

Something fired behind his eyes. Challenge, maybe. Or perhaps a promise. He nodded, though whether it was for her or an answer to whatever dialogue was taking place in his own head, she wasn't sure. "Fair enough." His gaze dropping to his fingers skimming closer to her mound. "You promise me you'll share if we do something you don't like?"

Faster than she would have thought possible, she stopped his hand with her own and squeezed tight. "I will never allow a man to hurt me or push me into something I don't want. Ever."

He smiled in a way that said he wasn't just relieved by her answer, but was proud as well. "That's my girl." He slid the hand she'd captured free and wrapped his arm around her waist. His free hand cupped the side of her neck and his lips whispered close enough her own tingled. "Anything in particular you want to go to the top of the list?"

She gave into temptation and let her hands steal

under the hem of his T-shirt, the worn soft cotton a stark contrast to the hot hard muscle beneath her palms. "The last time you never let me take you in my mouth. I want to start there."

His mouth curved in a wicked grin, a wolfish response that promised she'd get what she wanted, but likely not the way she'd imagined it. "Okay, sweetheart," he murmured against her lips. "Let's play."

She'd wanted his kiss. Craved it.

Instead he pulled away, captured her hand and led her into the bedroom. The toss pillows were already on the floor and the comforter pulled back. "I think you did more than lock up."

"I had incentive." He moved in behind her and peeled her shirt off her shoulders. "If I'd known we were gonna start with your mouth on my dick, we might have skipped dinner altogether." The fabric whispered against her calves before it pooled around her ankles, and he cupped her breasts. "Remember what I said. You get uncomfortable, say the word and I'll stop."

The statement made no sense. It was just oral sex. Intimate, yes, but not exactly the most deviant act.

Before she could voice her thoughts, he nudged her toward the bed. "Lay down for me."

Now that made no sense. She put a knee to the bed, then another, crawling until she lay on her side in the center. "Shouldn't you be the one laying down?"

He grinned and snatched a pillow. "Not the way we're going to do it." He moved his finger in a circle and headed toward the foot of the bed. "Turn around. Head toward me." He laid the pillow at the edge and waited.

The slow and agonizing pulse she'd fought with every teasing touch and dark look through dinner, deepened to an aching throb. She crawled forward, a heady mix of uncertainty and utter thrill sending champagne tingles through her veins. She paused on her hands and knees in front of him. "Like this?"

He cupped the side of her face, a tenderness she hadn't expected creeping in then disappearing just as quickly. "On your back. Head on the pillow."

She looked at the pillow, then to him and swallowed. "Okay." The comforter welcomed her in a cool, slick kiss and the pillow whooshed as she released her weight into its downy goodness. The second she looked up, his intent registered. In this position, she'd be utterly at his mercy. Open not just to his hands, but his undivided attention.

He crouched next to the bed and rolled the pillow beneath her neck. He wasn't just gentle, he was thoughtful. Careful and attentive.

"What are you doing?" she whispered, her quiet question stirring his always tousled hair where he hovered upside-down above her.

His eyes locked on to hers and his hands framed her face. "I'm getting you settled so I can feed you my cock like you asked."

Her sex clenched, the power of it bordering on an actual orgasm, but without the gratifying release that came after. She whimpered and squeezed her thighs together so tightly her body trembled.

"Easy." His lips caressed hers, the touch soft and heart-stoppingly reverent. He licked into her barely parted lips, coaxing not just her mouth to open, but her body to release. To give herself into his care and throw away her fears. This was the kiss she'd craved from him. Even at the odd angle, it was perfect. Maybe more so because of it. Ravenous and yet caring and solemn. As though he was thanking her simply for laying herself bare.

He lifted his head only enough to slide his mouth back and forth against hers. His warm breath fanned out against her face and neck, the accelerated huff behind each exhalation the only clue he was as affected as she. "How is it I never hear you cuss? At all."

The question caught her completely off guard, not simply for the topic, but for the timing as well. "Because my father said it wasn't appropriate for a woman. That he'd be disappointed if I started such a habit."

He smiled at that and smoothed her hair away from her face, gently combing the strands so they hung off the edge of the bed. "For the record, I'm not your father. And if you ever tell me you want to suck my cock or beg me to fuck your pussy, I promise you I will not be disappointed." He sealed the proclamation with another kiss, picking up right where he'd left off, but letting his hands roam to her breasts. Molding and shaping the mounds and interspersing each touch with demanding tweaks to her nipples.

She moaned and arched for more, fisting her hands in his hair.

He growled and pulled away. "You keep that up, I'll come before you ever get a taste." He guided her hands to her sides and stood. "Keep those there until I tell you."

"What? Why?"

If he hadn't pulled his shirt off and stalked into full view on one side of the bed, she'd have scrambled upright and started a rousing protest. The sight of his muscled torso and beautifully defined abs stilled her thoughts.

He dug into his front pocket and laid something aside on the nightstand. "Because I'm not ready to let go yet and your hands have a tendency to make me want to short-circuit my plans."

They did? That was good information. Definitely a strategy she'd have to employ more often, at least in the bedroom.

He bent beside the bed and something *whooshed* against carpet.

This time she did pop upright, her eyes widening at the sight of her black box of goodies. "What are you doing?"

He slid it next to her hip and popped the top button on his jeans. "I said I'd give you what you want. Doesn't mean I can't play while we were at it." He shoved his jeans and briefs over his hips. His cock stretched thick and tall nearly to his belly button, bobbing as he stepped free of the constricting denim. Unlike the other men she'd known intimately, he was completely free of pubic hair, leaving all of him on prime display. "You rethinking what's at the top of your list?"

"No." Not the most convincing answer, especially voiced as little more than a broken rasp, but she couldn't tear her gaze away from his shaft. From the prominent veins that ran up his length and the shiny wetness gathered at the tip. Slowly, she took him in. Truly savored every inch of his magnificent body. Only when she locked on to his stare did she lay back and cup her aching breasts. "I'm not rethinking anything."

He prowled closer, totally comfortable with her open perusal. As if he knew how much pleasure just looking at him gave her and was more than happy to indulge her. Not one physical touch traded and yet twice as potent as traditional foreplay. "Your hands aren't on the mattress."

"They're not touching you."

"Ah, but they're stealing my fun." He braced his feet on either side of her head and her thoughts disintegrated. His tight sack hung just inches from her mouth, the soft and dusky skin that surrounded the most vulnerable part of him unveiled. It was primal. A dangerous predator demanding submission in the most carnal way possible. Never in her life had she felt anything so raw. So powerful.

He guided her trembling hands to her sides and his shaft danced above her lips. Her haggard breaths ricocheted against her face. "But how will I... I mean..."

Straightening, he took himself in hand, his tender yet watchful gaze locked on to her face. "I'll give you what you need." He pumped his length once. Twice. Then slicked the tip against her lips. "Open."

The command speared through her, setting her core alight. She arched her neck and obeyed, craving that first taste. The velvet hardness of him against her tongue and lips. Yet, instead of sliding inside he slicked his precum against her lips. She moaned and lapped the tip, licking and sucking the taste from both him and her mouth in greedy, desperate pulls.

He hissed above her and undulated forward, dragging the underside of his cock against her lips as he leaned forward and filled his hands with her breasts. His voice grumbled low and thick. "Had too much time to think. Too much time spent thinking about feeling your mouth just like this."

So had she. Maybe not as creatively as he had, but oh, how she liked the way his mind worked.

He plucked and teased her nipples, his breath coming heavy and shorter. "Time to put your hands to work, sweetheart. Lift your knees."

She heard the words, knew they required action, but had a hard time nudging her body to behave, her attention too centered on the leisurely exploration she'd begun with her lips and tongue. She must have at least managed to get the job partway done right, because his big hands gripped her high on her shins and splayed her thighs wide.

"Hands behind your knees."

Oh God.

Part of her couldn't move, but the far more adventurous part of herself wanted to disconnect from her corporeal form and watch the decadence in all its beauty. She dug her fingertips into the soft flesh behind her thighs, licked along one prominent vein on his shaft and bared herself completely.

"Just like that." So awed. Proud. His strong fingers teased the soft flesh along the back of her thighs.

She relaxed the muscles along the back of her neck into the pillow, licked past the base of his cock to the tight sack beneath and whispered against his most tender place, "Knox."

His hips jerked forward and his fingers tightened on her thighs, but still he chuckled. "I see you've learned how to play dirty." The bed shifted and the snap of her toy box rang overloud in her ears. "Think that means we can step it up a notch."

He dragged his hips backward, gliding his hard rod against her mouth as he went, and holding up his hand in her line of sight. Her pink finger vibe was already snug against his middle finger. "This little guy get much attention this week?"

Oh, boy. This was about to get really intense, really fast. Heart hammering, she licked his glans and grinned up at him. "No. I used the dildo and imagined it was you."

His cocky attitude slipped, replaced with a feral growl that danced across every inch of her. He toggled the vibe to life and feathered it across one nipple. "It's getting no play tonight, 'cause the only thing going inside you is me." He palmed his cock with his free hand and nudged her lips. "And I'm starting right here."

Finally. Days, she'd imaged this. Re-ran the night they'd had together and wished with everything she'd demanded the chance to taste him. To reciprocate the pleasure he'd given with his own mouth, not once, but twice.

He shifted forward, carefully guiding his length in and out while he teased the buzzing toy atop her mound, but not quite reaching her clit.

She widened her knees and moaned around his shaft. "More?"

God, yes. Not that she could say as much with her mouth stuffed full of his thick cock. Somehow the helplessness made the moment that much more powerful. More heightened and pronounced. She whimpered instead.

A second later his finger dipped between her drenched folds, dragging her essence up to her swollen clit and circling in with an insistent pressure. "Don't come."

No way could she hold off her release. It was too close. Barreling toward her with such ferocity her heart labored to keep up. She released her hold on one thigh, gripped his hip and dug her nails into his flanks. Tightening her mouth against his soft flesh, she sucked with all she had.

He jerked his hips away, slipping his length free of her mouth. "Fuck!"

She rolled to her stomach and tossed her hair out of her face. Poised on her hands and knees, her arms and legs shook on the overdose of adrenaline he'd built, but no way was she backing down. Not now. Not this close. "Yes, let's do that. Now."

Chapter Eighteen

Wild. Utterly uninhibited and ravenous. Braced on all fours with her moon-colored hair spilling down her back, Darya was pure primal temptress. A snow-white tigress eager for her claiming, but just as hungry for the fight.

And her hungry gaze was rooted solely on him.

Mine.

Knox jolted forward, catapulted out of every rational thought and spurred like some untamed beast intent on a wild hunt. In the space of seconds, he'd snagged a condom from the nightstand, flipped her to her back and pinned her thighs up and wide with his hands behind her knees. He couldn't think. Didn't want to. Only wanted her under him. Her skin against his, her mouth and tongue dueling with his and his cock buried inside her.

His cock lay thick and throbbing against the top of her sex, the soft patch of neatly trimmed curls whispering against the base of his shaft. He dropped the unopened condom on her belly, his heavy panting stirring the hair around her face. "Put it on me."

Her eyes widened and her mouth rounded on a surprised O.

"You want to fuck, get me ready," he growled. The

command was hard. Likely too hard, but what little bit of his conscience was left was already strained to the breaking point. Too focused on keeping his strength in check and holding back his release.

She smiled, slow at first then deepening in its wickedness as she eagerly fumbled for the packet and got to work on her task.

His cock jerked in anticipation, the need to feel her nimble fingers working over him drawing his nuts up tight.

He couldn't come. Not yet. Not until he was balls deep and her cunt milked him dry.

Quickly, she rolled the condom in place then gripped his hips. "Please."

Those hands. Goddamn it, those hands of hers were going to kill him. More dangerous than her mouth, her touch had the power to bring him down. To draw him into that vulnerable place barbed with pain and disappointment.

He pinned her wrists with one hand above her head and slicked his cockhead through her folds. "That dildo make you feel good? Give you what you needed?"

She shook her head, her pelvis lifting in invitation. "No." Her eyes closed and the rest of her words came out on a low groan. "Never enough."

He notched himself inside her and gripped her thigh, angling her hips for maximum penetration. "No," he said, eyes rooted to her sex. "I'm what you need. My cock." He powered deep and her back bowed off the bed, the sweetest cry of relief bouncing off the walls around them.

Nothing else mattered. Not the loss of his carefully cultivated distance. Not his fears or the twisted past

that had created them. Only the heat of her. The flutters rippling around his dick and the scent of sex. Over
and over, he pounded into her, her breasts jiggling with
each merciless stab and her hips undulating against his.

She opened her eyes, the slow and weighted movement unveiling her bright blue eyes like a goddamn
gift from the heavens. A healing benediction that bur-
rowed straight to his soul. "Knox." So much said with
one word. Hope. A plea. A promise.

He crushed his mouth against hers, chasing the sound
of his name on her lips. Greedy for the taste of it. He
released her hands and speared his fingers in her sweat-
dampened hair, holding her steady for his feast. "Give
it to me," he snarled against her mouth, licking and nip-
ping her kiss-swollen lips as his hips pistoned ruthlessly
against hers. "Give me what's *mine*." He punctuated the
claim with a powerful stab.

Her nails bit into his shoulders and her heels dug
into his flanks, her neck arched as she cried out her
release. "Knox!"

His cock jerked in answer, the punch of his orgasm
so sharp his whole body shuddered. There was nothing
but the moment. The press of Darya's skin. The flex
and release of her slick sex around his cock. Her trembling arms and legs coiled around him. This was what
he needed. What he'd craved and fixated on for days.
Since the first time she'd glided in to his office on her
long as fuck legs and crooked her lips in a shy smile.
No restraint. No barriers. Just the most carnal, genuine
connection. Intimate and honest.

He rested his forehead against hers, both of their
eyes closed and breaths choppy as they slowed to an
easy, languid rhythm. The air around them pulsed and

bit by bit the room's chill settled against his skin. The warmth of her mouth teased his own, bringing with it the memories of the last week.

Seven days he'd watched her. Seen how open she was with everyone. How innocent and bright she was. Everyone flocked to her. Men and women alike. It would be so easy to give in. To take her mouth in a slow kiss and reach for the one elusive dream left unrealized.

Instead, he lifted his head.

Her eyes remained closed and her mouth barely parted. A gorgeous flush marked her cheeks, neck and chest, and her body lay completely replete beneath him.

His voice came out ragged and so low it sounded as if it came from the soles of his feet. "Please tell me you're okay."

Lazily, she rolled her head and opened her eyes. "English is my second language and even I know better than to use *okay* for what we just did."

"I didn't hurt you?"

She smiled and tenderly cupped the side of his face. "You did what you promised and gave me what I needed." So easy. No attempts to draw him deeper, only open acceptance of what he had to offer.

Bracing himself on one forearm, he covered her hand with his and turned enough to kiss her palm. Just once. One brush with the dream before he locked it away and buried his heart with it. Yet as he laced his fingers with hers and tugged her hand away, it didn't seem like nearly enough.

Chapter Nineteen

A car door slammed in the distance, nudging Knox awake.

Don't move.

Don't think.

Not yet.

He blanked his mind and visualized nothing but pure white light. Willed the blessed quiet of sleep to close over him. He felt too good. Too warm and relaxed to ruin it with the restlessness of reality. Especially with Darya's winter rose scent all around him, her sleeping body soft against his.

His eyes snapped open, every synapse firing with alacrity. Darya was next to him.

No—scratch that. *He* was next to *her*, his body spooned tight against her back and their legs intimately tangled.

What. The. Fuck.

Sheer reflex and panic whipped through him, so powerful he nearly bolted upright. Just as fast, something far more instinctive locked him in place. Hell, cuffs around both his wrists couldn't have bound him to Darya's still-sleeping body more effectively.

He let out a slow, measured breath. His heart stomped and kicked with the fury of a sugar-loaded two-year-old, and a cold sweat broke out on the back of his neck, but beneath it all was an unfamiliar calm. As if her presence beside him had somehow muted the pain and disappointment of his past enough to loosen his restraints and draw his first full breath in years.

Relaxing his head against the pillow, her silky hair tickled his nose. Funny. Normally, he hated that sensation. Wanted to bat the offensive strands away the same as he would if he walked into a man-sized spider web. This time he nuzzled closer, inhaling her scent and the peace that went with it.

Faint sunlight seeped from behind the closed blinds, a soft buttery glow reserved for early sunrise. It took a good minute, but his heart settled into a steady rhythm. Too bad his mind couldn't follow suit. While his body relaxed into hers, his thoughts did their best Indy 500 imitation, lapping round and round until the room spun. Intimacy with a woman outside of sex was a bad idea. A single hollow-point bullet loaded in an otherwise empty revolver just waiting to hit pay dirt. With Darya? Yeah, he might as well load up both barrels on a sawed off shotgun and open fire.

The smart move would be to pull away. To leave a note or do something nice for her so he felt like less of a selfish ass then high-tail it to neutral territory before she woke up.

He splayed his hand against her belly instead and let his eyes slip closed. Only one other time in his life he'd felt this.

Once.

Reflexively, his arms tightened around Darya, spurring a deep inhalation and a peaceful sigh.

No, he couldn't do this. Couldn't risk it. No matter

how good it felt. No matter how natural. He pressed a kiss to her bare shoulder, savoring the soft skin beneath his lips for dangerous seconds before he untangled himself from her warm and welcoming body and slid from between the sheets. He dressed quickly, the ease and well-practiced silence behind the routine grating mercilessly against his conscience. God, he was so screwed. Just being in the office with her was hard enough to keep his balance, let alone sleeping with her. And calling anyone else? Yeah, that idea wasn't tracking. His brain and his body wanted the sweet Russian she-wolf curled up in the bed.

Never in his life had he seen anything so beautiful as the sight in front of him. Darya asleep on her bloodred sheets with her blonde hair trailing out behind her beat any landscape or classic masterpiece, hands down. Hell, the seven wonders of the world had nothing on her.

Beckett would call him a coward for leaving without waking her. Without giving her respect.

And Beckett would be right, you dumbass.

He paused long enough to brace himself, prowled to her side of the bed and sat beside her hip. Soft so he didn't jar her out of her peaceful sleep, he smoothed a wayward chunk of hair away from her face. "Hey."

Her eyelids fluttered open, disoriented at first then quickly sharpening on him. She took in his clothes, twisted to scan the room behind her and then settled back on her side. "What time is it?"

Hell if he knew. Although, the fact that he'd gone about his early-morning freak-out without so much as a glance at his phone said how close his past's demons were to taking a chunk out of his ass. "Early."

He cupped the back of her neck. So many women

he'd shared this particular space with, but only one of them made it hard to leave. He traced her jawline with his thumb. "I need to go."

She nodded. Her lips didn't move but her eyes said plenty, not one scrap of accusation or hurt behind them. If anything, they shone with understanding. Maybe even sympathy.

Man, this woman deserved so much more than him. And he owed her huge. If not for the sleep, then for the gift just waking up next to her had been. "I don't want you to think you don't matter. That what we did—last night or anything else—is just some random hookup. I just... I can't—"

"I know." Soft. Simple. No explanation needed.

He leaned in, knowing the second his trajectory registered what a monumentally horrid idea it was, and chucked his rules out the window anyway. His lips melded with hers. Easy. Lingering. More than anything, he wanted to lick between hers and wake her up differently. To take his time and show her the side to himself he kept hidden.

He pulled away instead and stood, locking his focus on her palm pressed against the sheets rather than the hunger in her bright blue gaze. "You don't have to come in today if you don't want to."

"I want to."

He looked. He couldn't have stopped it if he tried. No more than he could have stopped the words that slipped past his lips. "I want you to, too."

Chapter Twenty

Four days he'd made it. Four long, grueling days Knox had kept his shit centered and his hands off Darya. His focus shifted off the suspicious log entry on his main screen to the server room security feed on his left and gritted his teeth so hard a sharp twinge pierced the spot where his jaw hinged. Vance was a good kid. One of the best server guys he'd ever hired.

But if he didn't stop touching Darya soon, he was gonna be minus both arms.

His office door clicked open and Beckett's heavy footsteps lumbered in. "Hey, man. Jace and Axel called. The rest of the guys are hangin' at Crossroads tonight. You wanna go?"

Shifting his gaze back to the task at hand, Knox punched in the IP address listed in the most recent hit against their mail server. "Not sure. Got someone who started pinging our servers last night."

"Brother, the last thing I'm worried about is anyone getting past your traps." He pulled out a chair and made himself right at home. "And what's with the shit mood anyway?"

"I'm not in a shit mood."

"Uh, yeah. You are."

"Nope. I'm good." Fuck. Now he wasn't just lying to himself, he was lying to Beckett, too. "Just wanna know who's knocking so I can shut 'em down."

"Thought you said those honeypots and triggers you set up blocked 'em automatically."

"They do. Usually." Except the number of attempts had been twice as high in the last twenty-four hours, which made him itchy.

"Good, then finish up your cyber God routine this afternoon, and we'll meet back at our place after close. Danny's gonna meet up with us, too. It's Friday. Time to work out the kinks."

Movement in the server room feed caught his attention, and he caught the backside of Vance following Darya out the door. She'd work late. He'd bet last year's earnings on it. But then Vance probably would, too. And what the fuck was she doing hanging around with Vance anyway? The last time he'd checked in with Katy, Darya had been knee-deep in some low-priority code defects.

Beckett's deep voice boomed a little louder. "Yo. Earth to space cadet."

Goddamn it. Hell of a time for him to get caught eye-balling Darya. Though, Beckett was a little out of his direct line of sight. Maybe he hadn't caught the slip. "I don't know. Let me see how this goes for the next few hours and I'll let you know."

"You'll let me know." Beckett's deadpan mimic had more than a little sarcasm to it. He rested one forearm on the edge of Knox's desk and drummed his thumb against the chrome surface. "The only time in the last six years you've ditched your brothers when you didn't already have something to do was when three servers went down and you felt bad about letting Vance fly solo."

"So?"

"So, I wanna know what's wrong."

Knox slid his hands away from the keyboard, let his eyes slip closed and rolled his shoulders to work out the tension in his neck. He loved Beckett. Loved all his brothers. But right now, he needed time alone to make sure his emotional game was packed up good and tight. Not to mention, the usual pickup routine they'd all expect of him at Crossroads gave him the scratch. He swiveled his chair to Beckett and met his heavy stare head on. "I told you. Someone hits us this many times in one day, I want to know who's behind it."

"Bullshit. Someone hands you a puzzle, you get a boner. Not stressed out or pissed. And, brother, I'm very aware you've been one or the other all week, so what's really eating your lunch? You not sleeping?"

"No less than normal. Got a solid eight a few nights ago."

Beckett grinned and snickered the same way he had when they'd scored their first *Playboy*. "That the same night you disappeared over at Darya's place?"

Motherfucker. "You tracked me?"

"Why the hell not? The beauty of GPS and all that, right? Besides, you do that shit to us all the damned time. Don't get your panties in a wad when we return the favor." He shrugged, reclined in his chair and kicked one foot up on the edge of Knox's desk. "Get pissed if you want, but you weren't answering your phone. Just wanted to make sure you were someplace safe."

Tucked up next to Darya and sleeping like a damned baby, yes, but safe? Yeah, that was debatable. He still hadn't been able to shake how good waking up next to her felt. "Yeah, Mom. I even made sure to double check the windows and doors." He was just about to tack on a smart remark about missing his blankey when voices sounded in the hallway.

Darya's voice. That animated tone she used that made everyone feel like they were the center of the universe, tinged with her sweet accent. The only thing he hated was Vance's goofy laugh wrapped around it.

They walked past a second later, both casting surprised glances at Beckett and Knox. A reasonable response considering Knox never left his door open unless he knew someone was coming.

"Hey, boss!" Vance waved and shoved his thick black glasses back up on his nose. Why the guy never got around to sizing the things right, Knox couldn't figure. "I'm taking JJ over to Wing Bucket. You guys want anything?"

Bigger than Dallas, the memory of Darya licking her fingertips when she'd helped herself to a plateful of ribs at the Bikes and Blues rally hit him out of nowhere. So not an image he needed to remember right now. Especially knowing Vance would be eyeballing the same thing if she got a serving of wings. "Nah, I'm good." He shifted his gaze to Darya. Hell, maybe he should go out with Beck and the guys. God knew he'd be up to no good hanging here with her. "Don't let him talk you into the 19th Sauce."

She smiled and, swear to Christ, he felt it everywhere. Like she'd somehow reached inside him and unhinged all his tension. "Okay." She shifted her attention to Beckett and waved, but he'd swear the lost connection hurt her as much as it did Knox. "See you later."

"Yeah, JJ," Beck answered back, easily using the identity they'd all agreed she'd be wise to keep in public. He chin-lifted to Vance. "Take care of our girl."

The metal door latched hard behind them, the brutal sound echoing up and down the hallway with way too much finality.

Knox spun back to this keyboard just in time to watch Vance usher Darya to his white Jeep Wrangler.

"So that's it." Beckett's statement was packed with a whole lot of *aha* and even more *gotcha*.

That was okay. Knox was used to Beckett sniffing and could play shit off with the best of them. "What's it?"

"Why you're in a shit mood."

He glanced over his shoulder at Beckett and feigned an incredulous expression. "At Vance?" He scoffed for good measure and put eyes back to this work. "No way."

"Not at Vance. At Darya *with* Vance."

Knox shook his head, all too aware that if Beck got a straight-line view of his face, he'd see the glare aimed at his computer screens. "It's not like that."

"Yeah?"

"Yeah."

In one smooth move that shouldn't be possible for a guy with Beckett's kind of bulk, he dropped his foot, sat up and crossed his forearms on Knox's desk. "You sure? 'Cause you were sporting the same nasty look yesterday when you walked in and found me and Darya sparring in the workout room."

Yep, that had pissed him off. Especially when Beckett had thought it'd be a good idea to spend extra time teaching her how to break out of a choke hold—an exercise that had put him up against her way too damned long.

"Come to think of it," Beckett said, "Danny got the same look Wednesday afternoon when you busted her hoppin' off the back of his bike."

That hadn't pissed him off. He'd just been jealous as hell. At least Danny didn't paw her nonstop. "No harm in her makin' friends with my family."

"Nope. Though I gotta wonder why she doesn't show the same affection for you that she does with everyone else. The way I figure it, you're either a horrible fuck and she doesn't want to encourage you, or you drew an ironclad boundary and told her to keep her hands off outside of sex."

"Stop diggin', brother."

"Who says I'm digging? Maybe I'm just thinkin' out loud."

"Well, think with your mouth shut."

Silence boomeranged back at him, but Beckett's stare pressed as steady as a gun muzzle at his temple.

He opened a new command screen and started typing. "Don't you have something to do?"

When Beckett spoke, his tone had taken on a whole new range. The one saved for when he was either scared shitless or focused on something that meant the world to him. Considering Beckett had been afraid maybe twice in his whole life, it had to be door number two. "Nothing more important than me figuring out how to get my brother to pull his head out of his ass and see what everyone else in his family saw inside of ten minutes."

All the frustration Knox had buried lunged to the surface and he spun fast enough Beckett actually flinched. "What? That she's great? Yeah, I get that, too. But *you know* where my head's at with relationships."

"Yeah. I do. Like I said, your head's stuck up your

ass. And worse, you're an idiot to boot, because you're so wound up in those bullshit rules you hold yourself to, you don't see the way she looks at you when you're not looking."

"I'm her boss, that's it."

Beckett snapped closer, his face heating with a rare display of anger and nearly going nose to nose. "She doesn't look at you like you're her boss. She looks at you like you're the goddamn holy grail."

Knox jerked his head back, the reality of Beckett's statement as potent as a bitch slap. Surely she didn't feel the same way he did. She couldn't. If she did, then that meant…hell, he didn't want to think about what that meant.

Beckett huffed out an ironic chuckle and shook his head, all the tension that had ridden his big body seeping out in one rush. "Jesus, you really are an idiot. Knox, you need to listen and listen good. Fate, the universe or God almighty is raining all kinds of goodness on you, and you're so fucking whacked out by your past, you're throwing it away with both hands."

He stood, pushed his chair back where he'd found it then leaned in close. When he spoke, his voice was serious as death. "Do yourself and her a favor. Wake. The fuck. Up."

Chapter Twenty-One

"Hey, JJ." Vance poked his head around the corner to Darya's office, his customary open smile firmly in place and a few chunks of his tidy short brown hair askew at the front. "Me and some friends are gonna hang out at my place and do a movie marathon. You wanna come?"

He was such a nice guy. Everyone in Knox and Beckett's office was the same way. Friendly and willing to do whatever they needed to give you a leg up. Though, Vance had gone above and beyond. Enough so Darya was starting to wonder if it wouldn't be smart to work a few days remote, even if that meant going without seeing Knox.

God, just thinking about not seeing him wrecked her. Doused the determination and drive she'd vowed to tackle life with since the day she'd watched her mother walk away that last time. This wasn't healthy. Not for her or for Knox. The sheer pain on his face every time she looked at him sent tiny fractures splintering through her heart. Not touching him—not pulling him into her arms and holding him close—was killing her.

She gave Vance what she hoped at least looked like a genuine smile. A hard thing to do when her insides felt as though they weighed twice her body weight. "Thank you for asking, but I think I need tonight to recuperate from this week." And get her mind together. To find her courage and face the truth about her and Knox.

No matter what she'd hoped for, the odds of him changing were slim. He'd told her as much from the start. Had been brutally honest. Now she owed it to herself and her future to be honest with herself. Three people had already given of themselves at great risk and pain to offer her a better life. No matter how good—how electric and precious each moment with Knox felt—she couldn't waste their gift on a man who wasn't open to giving her everything.

Vance cocked his head and his smile shifted to a flirtish quirk, giving her a peek to the man beneath the thick glasses and the nonstop work ethic. His brown eyes sparkled with playful orneriness. "You sure? You'd like my friends. No pressure. We'll just hang out. Relax." He paused a second and when he spoke again his voice was just a fraction lower. "Whatever you want."

Oh, yes. She definitely needed to recalibrate with Vance and quickly. It was hard enough keeping her emotions in check with Knox plaguing her every thought. Adding guilt on top of the thick longing she barely kept at bay would break her.

Before she could politely reiterate her refusal, Knox's voice rumbled low from behind Vance. "She said no." It wasn't a threat. Not exactly. But it brooked no argument.

And it felt like a claim. A physical possession without boundaries that marked every inch of her from the inside out.

Vance stepped back, bringing Knox's brooding face into view. "Hey, boss. I was just seeing if—"

"I know." Knox's focus stayed rooted on Darya. "But she couldn't even if she wanted. She's busy."

She was? She tore her gaze away from Knox's heavy stare and blinked her screen into focus. She didn't think she'd missed any assignments, but then she'd been worthlessly combing through what looked like perfect code for the last hour trying to find the root cause behind some elusive defect.

Everything in her email was sorted and the ticketing system they used to track assignments showed nothing new.

"Go home." Knox stalked into the room and positioned himself between her and Vance. "I'll make sure JJ gets what she needs. Enjoy your weekend."

Okay that one wasn't nearly as subtle. The words were nice enough, but the way he'd faced off with Vance and his squared shoulders looked an awful lot like her coworker had fried Knox's last nerve.

"Uhh." Vance's face blanked. "Okay." His gaze shot to hers over Knox's shoulder. "I guess I'll see you Monday?"

"Sure," she said.

Knox fired back with a, "Doubtful," at the same time.

Oh, boy. That wasn't good. The shock that zapped across Vance's face before he ducked his chin and backed away confirmed as much. "Right. Okay, well... g'night."

And then he was gone, leaving her alone in the silent room with an unimpeded view of Knox's tense back.

For long seconds Knox didn't move. Simply stood there, staring down the dark hallway as though tracking Vance's moves even though he'd long disappeared from sight.

The steel door to the main entrance *kachunked* open then slammed closed.

Knox fisted his hands and lowered his head.

Bracing.

No. Not that. Please God, not that. Not yet.

No matter how much she knew breaking the physical relationship between them needed to happen she wasn't ready for it. She sucked in a slow breath, her mind scrambling for some way to distract him. Or better yet, how to extricate herself from the moment altogether. She cleared her throat and started gathering her things. "I should probably go home, too."

"No."

She froze, her fingers locked around the notepad she'd hastily snatched from her desk with the intent of cramming it in her backpack. One word he'd spoken. One simple word, but it sounded as though it eked from the lips of a man long caged in a dungeon.

Slowly, he turned and lifted his head.

Pain and fear stared back at her, so stark and brutal in its intensity her heart stuttered under its weight. But there was something else there, too. Something that urged her to throw all caution aside and hold him close. "What do you mean, no?"

He prowled forward. Unlike the confident gait she'd grown accustomed to, each step was cautious. A dangerous animal comfortable in his own strength and skill, but not daring to underestimate his opponent. "I mean, I don't want you to go home."

"You have something you need me to handle here, then?"

He shook his head and stopped so close his leg

brushed her knee. Sitting as she was, he towered over her. "No."

She laid her tablet aside and folded her hands in her lap, forcing them to remain loose no matter how much she wanted to clench them tight. "I don't understand."

His gaze dropped to her hands in her lap and he swallowed so hard his Adam's apple bobbed. "I'm not sure I do either, but I'm tired of fighting it." He scanned her desk then locked his focus on her computer. Before she could gauge his intent, he punched the power button and held it down, forcing it to close.

She bolted upright and knocked his hand away as if the delayed movement might somehow save the work he'd just thrown away. "Knox, I didn't save that."

Lightning fast, his fingers coiled around her wrist. "Work doesn't matter." He inched closer. "There's nothing I can't help you fix anyway." He used his hold to turn her, the movement gentle despite the power of his grip. His gaze was locked on the point of contact, a mesmerized look on his face. Only when her body was squared to his did he lift his head and meet her eyes. "I don't want you to go to your home. I want you to come to mine."

Home.

Part of her wanted to hiss and rail at the request. To lift her chin and tell him she was done with all his rules and carefully cultivated distance. But another, far more instinctive part, stilled and honed in on the word still reverberating through her thoughts. This meant something to him. Something huge given the caution that gripped his every action.

Maybe it was time for the truth. Even if she hadn't taken the time to prepare herself. To mourn a connection incompletely formed. She covered his hand still coiled around her wrist with her own, needing the contact even if it crossed a line he didn't want her beyond. "I'm not sure I can do this anymore. Not without going somewhere you don't want me to go."

His grip loosened enough to skim up her arm and over her shoulder until he cupped the side of her neck. His gray gaze burned into hers, pure terror and vulnerability reflected back at her. "What if I said I want you to go there?"

The words were so soft, so carefully spoken and ragged she wasn't even sure she'd heard them right at first. She braced her trembling hands against his chest. Beneath her palm, his heart raced. She smoothed her hands against him, the need to soothe whatever caused the wildness as inherent as drawing her next breath. "Why would you say that? I thought you said—"

"I know what I said." He urged her closer, both hands framing her face. His lips hovered so close her own parted, and his heat blanketed her from breasts to thighs. "I don't know what I'm doing. I just know what worked before isn't working now, and I want you *with* me."

The emphasis he chose yanked her resolve out from underneath her and fanned the barely repressed desires she'd tried to ignore. "What are you saying?"

His mouth tightened and the rhythm of his inhalations accelerated. "I want strings. Ropes. Chains. Whatever it takes to bind you to me. And I want you in my bed. Mine. Not yours."

A delicious swoop and spin whispered through her belly, and her skin tingled on a flash of adrenaline. He wanted her. Not at a distance. Not on a purely physical basis, but *bound* to him. Just replaying his words in her head made her cheeks burn and her heart race.

It was still a risk. By his own admission, he didn't know what he was doing and had limited if any experience with relationships. To be the first he attempted such a feat with in God only knew how many years was dangerous. A step that could leave her bruised and battered when everything was said and done.

Live enough for both of us.

This was living. Nestled close to Knox, his strength and emotion prickling against her skin, was the biggest thrill she'd ever experienced. And if she came out on the other side broken, then so be it. She'd bandage herself up, face life's next challenge the same way she had all the others and make all the sacrifices she'd been honored with worth it.

She skimmed her fingers along his jawline, the light stubble tickling the pads and causing a flutter up her arms. She rolled up on her toes, softly meshed her lips against his and whispered, "Then take me home."

Chapter Twenty-Two

Knox pressed his fingertips tighter against Darya's scalp, needing some kind of physical confirmation she was really here. That her lips were really against his and his mind hadn't somehow conjured her response.

Her tongue slicked along his lower lip, a tentative touch over and gone in a second, but every bit as powerful as her words still ringing in his head.

Then take me home.

He answered back, taking her mouth the way he'd always craved. Leisurely feasting without thought to anything more than her taste and sharing all the emotion he'd kept buried.

This was what he'd missed. What he'd avoided with nearly every woman for over ten years and only allowed himself with Darya in the most vulnerable moments. A simple unguarded kiss. So much more innocent than the other things they'd done together, but the rawest intimacy.

He wrapped her up, banding one arm around her waist and palming the back of her head.

Her silky hair slicked across his knuckles and down his forearms and her ragged breaths puffed against his lips between each pass of his own. He'd meant what he'd told her. He didn't have a clue what he was doing. Had never faced anything in his life as terrifying as laying himself out like he had tonight.

But here—with her in his arms and the rest of the world completely out of focus—the risk was worth it.

He nipped her lower lip, lingering long enough to chase the hungry gasp the action earned him with one last graze of his mouth, then rested his forehead against hers. His arms shook. Hell, his whole body shook, so flooded on adrenaline and endorphins he'd be lucky if he slept for a month. "I was an ass."

It was easier to admit than he'd expected. A relief, actually, leaving the weight he'd lugged on his shoulders a few bricks lighter and sweeping fresh air into the musty places inside him he'd forgotten existed.

She pulled away enough to search his face. "I thought you were quite sweet."

Of course, she would. In the three weeks since she'd first walked into his office, she'd built solid relationships with everyone she worked with and had done it by focusing on the good in every one of them. He, on the other hand, immediately isolated every person's character defect and catalogued how it might come back to bite him, or where it might run afoul of his or his brothers' business plans. With Darya, he'd known inside of two seconds, just how low she could bring him. All he'd garnered by holding her at bay was lost time and the creation of trust hurdles he'd now have to dismantle. "Not sure my manning up in the eleventh hour makes up for the rest of my jackass antics." He smoothed her hair back and cupped her face, soaking in the closeness. "I'll make it up to you."

Her lips quirked and a playful gleam danced behind

her beautiful eyes. "Does this mean I only have to do the work of one employee instead of two?"

There she was. The lighthearted and quick-to-frolic woman he'd watched with everyone else through the cameras. Except this time, he was the recipient. The one to earn her smile and revel in his sweet angel's voice.

Finally.

He was tempted to spill the beans and tell her yes, but he smirked instead and said, "No. If anything, you'll have to up your game and pull the weight of three people."

Her eyes popped wide and her mouth opened and closed at least twice before he chuckled and pulled her against him.

"Relax." He kissed the top of her head and filled his lungs with her perfect scent. "I know a guy that can help you with whatever your asshole boss dishes out."

She hugged her arms tighter around his waist and giggled, her laughter the brightest and most amazing sound he'd heard in ages. "Would that guy happen to be a little over six feet tall and have dirty blond hair?"

"He's dirty, all right. Especially when you factor into his thoughts, which is about every other second." On cue, his mind coughed up the fact that the woman he'd fantasized and fixated on for the better part of three weeks wasn't just plastered against him, but had willingly accepted taking a chance on him despite his fucked up behavior. His easy laughter died off and the significance of what he'd asked her filtered back to the top of his consciousness.

He cupped the back of her neck and pulled away enough to meet her gaze. "Come home with me." She couldn't realize what a huge deal this was for him. Not yet. But it was a start. A big one.

She nodded and uncurled her arms from around his waist, her movement hesitant as though she'd rather not let go. "Just let me get my things."

It was weird how easy things shifted. How they moved in sync without saying a word. Him slipping her laptop bag from her hand. Her moving in close to his side so his hand could settle at the small of her back. Even as he moved through the hallways, checking each room and shutting down the lights, she flowed beside him as though they'd done the routine together count-less nights.

All this time he'd missed this. Damn near lost his chance at it if he'd read the pain and hesitancy in her eyes right before he'd nutted up and reached for the brass ring.

The drive to his place was mostly quiet, sprinkled only with likes and dislikes on music once he encouraged her to take control of the radio. More than the genres represented on his preset selections—which she seemed to heartily agree with—she seemed fascinated by the number of stations available via the satellite ser-vice.

He'd just finished exiting I-35 when she finally made it through the last of the channels he'd programmed. "You seriously drive a recent model Challenger and you're not using satellite over local channels?" he said.

She flipped to the first set of six for a fresh lap through the stations and smiled as the chorus for Death Cab for Cutie's "Black Sun" filled the interior. "Not all of us are wildly successful app developers with a mysterious past in hacking. I have to watch my pennies and save."

Okay, he'd give her that one. Though, with his brothers and their diversified investments, his income wasn't limited to just what he made on Listalyzer or his other programs. "It'll come," he said, leaving her be with the rest of her exploration. It wasn't an empty promise either. As hard as she'd worked the last three weeks, she definitely had the drive to be successful. Plus, she'd just cemented a hard-core backer whether she realized it or not.

He pulled into the underground garage for his and Beckett's complex. Ten to fifteen years ago, the stretch of dilapidated warehouse buildings southwest of downtown Dallas was an iffy place to buy anything, but now it was on an upward trend. The fact that he'd been smart enough to talk Beckett into buying one of the old warehouses meant they'd more than tripled their investment value in the five years since they'd renovated the space.

Darya straightened in her seat and scanned the parking garage. "This is where you live?"

He nodded and steered them toward the row of ten reserved spots they'd kept for themselves. "Beck and I own the building. The top floor is ours, but we renovated the other four floors into two-bedroom lofts." Thankfully, renting it out to a host of yuppies and successful artists added to their already growing income stream.

Come to think of it, they had a unit open on the floor right below theirs. He could move her there, chalk it up as a job perk and give her a hell of a lot more security in the process. Or he could just keep her in his bed. She'd be even safer there.

The thought rattled him almost as badly as the sight of not just Beckett's Vette, but Danny's deep purple '69 Chevelle beside it.

Fuck.

He pulled into his spot and yanked the emergency brake. So much for stepping into new and scary without eyewitnesses.

Always perceptive, Darya's soft voice cut into his thoughts. "Everything okay?"

"Yeah." Or it would be. He'd already wasted too damned much time dodging what his instincts had told him was right from the get-go. All he had to do from here out was put one foot in front of the other and see where it led him. Or rather them.

Besides, it wouldn't be the first time Beckett razzed him about something, and it wouldn't be the last. He killed the engine and popped his door. "Hold up and I'll get your door."

If she noticed his tension on the way up the elevator she didn't show it, though the security was tight enough to keep her more than amused. Every floor was secured with keycards, but his and Beckett's required the same scanners they used at the office. Keeping one hand braced at the small of her back, he guided her through the small private landing to the main door.

He opened the front door and the lock's stout *clack* ricocheted off the loft's exposed brick walls. For the first time since he and Beckett had started renovations, he tried to view their bachelor space the way a woman like Darya might see it. The original concrete floors would've been fine for just him and Beck, but Sylvie and Ninette had taken one look at the place and ordered all kinds of area rugs to cover the wide-open space.

Steel gray, muted blues and dark chocolate, they all co-ordinated, but each had different textures and patterns. The final effect looked pretty damned cool.

The industrial metal door slammed shut behind them, drawing Beckett and Danny's attention from the open kitchen at the far side of the room. A huge concrete covered island was the only thing that demarcated the culinary wonder from the rest of the space and doubled as a decent poker table when the rest of the guys came over. Why they never used the monster dining room table situated off to one side he couldn't figure. When they'd bought the dark wood piece it'd reminded him of something out of *Game of Thrones*, but despite its cool factor hardly anyone sat behind it.

With both his and Darya's bags looped over one shoulder, he gripped her arm and ambled forward with as much casualness as he could muster. Yeah, the hold on her was more Neanderthal than thoughtful man, but it was either keep himself grounded with her presence, or get them both the fuck out of there before the questions started. "Thought you were going with the guys to Crossroads," he said to Beckett and Danny.

At a distance, he'd not been able to clearly make out Beckett's smug expression, or Danny's shock for that matter. The closer he got, the more things came into focus. Whatever they'd been discussing before he and Darya had walked in, it was long forgotten now.

"Had to wait for Danny to finish a job," Beckett said. "Thought we'd have a beer and then head over together." His gaze shifted to Darya and he cocked one eyebrow. "You comin' with us?"

"We're staying in," Knox said before Darya could answer. She might be sharp, but Beckett was a ruthless son of a bitch with ferreting out details when he wanted them, and judging by the curiosity on his face, he very much wanted them.

Beckett smiled as though Knox had just informed them he'd single-handedly breeched Pentagon security. He knocked back the rest of his beer, chunked it in the thigh-high stainless steel trash can that always seemed to be full and smacked Danny on the shoulder. "Come on, brother. We gotta go."

Danny sputtered and volleyed his attention between Beck and Knox. "Man, I just started this beer."

"Toss it," Beckett said as he rounded the island. He'd changed into a nice button-down, but had kept his faded jeans and a pair of black boots that would make Trevor proud. "Pigs just flew out my front door. I'll buy you another one to celebrate when we get to the club."

Still utterly clueless, Danny poured out what was left of his Bud and tossed the bottle. "What the fuck's that supposed to mean?"

Beckett glanced at Knox then zeroed in on Knox's hand still coiled around Darya's arm. "I'll explain on the way to the club."

Of course, he would. And not just to Danny, but to all the other guys, too. But then the rest of the guys already knew his history. The only surprise they'd get was learning Knox had shown up at his home with a woman in tow.

It wasn't until Beckett prowled closer and eyeballed Darya that Knox realized how he'd positioned himself in front of her.

Beckett stopped right in front of them and planted both hands on his hips. "You gonna let her out from behind you so I can say hello, or act like a fucking caveman all night?"

Caveman sounded good. Especially if it stopped his brother from making any bigger of a deal of things than he already had. Okay, granted it was a *huge* deal, but still.

Knox shrugged and stepped to the side.

The second Beck had a clear path to Darya, he stepped in, wrapped her up in one of his big bear hugs and kissed the top of her head. "Welcome to the family, sweetheart."

Darya's gaze shot to Knox, her eyes wide and loaded with questions he didn't have a clue how to answer.

"Think you're rushin' it a bit," Knox grumbled.

"Really? I'd say I've been bettin' a thousand on this run. Just wished I'd thought to go double or nothing while I had the chance." He chin-lifted in lieu of a good-bye and ambled to the front door, Danny trailing in his wake. "This mean I need to call rally?" he said without looking back.

"Leave it alone, Beck."

That earned him a quick grin over Beckett's shoulder. "Now, where's the fucking fun in that?" He dipped his head at Darya and opened the door. "Have fun."

The door clunked shut behind them.

Darya adjusted her purse strap on her shoulder, one of those uncertain I-need-something-to-do-with-my-hands moves women always did when they didn't have a clue how to move forward. "Well, that was interesting."

"What it was, was Beckett being a pain in my ass." The weight of their backpacks slung across one shoulder finally got some processing time in his frontal lobe and he motioned to his half of the loft with a jerk of his head. "How about I offload our stuff and show you around? Not sure what I've got to eat, but we can order delivery if you want."

She nodded and fell in beside him. Hearing her heels softly click against the concrete was strangely gratifying. As if a little of the unrefined bachelor fog had been lifted simply by her presence. She craned her neck this way and that, taking in every detail. "What did Beckett mean?"

Fucking Beckett. One of these days he was going to have to find a way to mute the guy's voice box. He opened the door to his suite and dodged the best he could. "Which part?"

"He said pigs flew out of your front door. Did I misinterpret something?"

He laughed louder than he had in days and veered to the right of the double-sided bookcase that served as the primary divider between his office and his bedroom. Through the wall of windows opposite them, the sun had just dipped beneath the horizon, leaving only a fiery orange in its wake. He set both their packs beside his desk. "Jesus, your English is so good I forget sometimes it's your second language."

Circling in one place, she perused the open space. Compared to the contemporary edge of their office, the traditional style was probably a shock, but he'd always told himself if he got a place of his own, he'd trick it out like some fancy English lord. Low and behold, he'd made it happen. She finished her open examination of the space and lifted her eyebrows in silent encouragement to continue.

"It's hyperbole," he said, then realized that probably

wasn't going to be much help either. "An exaggeration for a miracle happening. Like when hell freezes over."

"A miracle?" She meandered over to his bookcase. The bobbleheads he'd collected for as long as he could remember lined the whole center section, except for two shelves packed with pictures he'd saved of him and his brothers. His family.

She nudged his Milton bobblehead from *Office Space* then seemed to realize he hadn't answered. "Knox?"

Well, what the hell. Beckett would share the news inside of another thirty minutes anyway, which meant he'd get all of a two- or three-day grace period before the moms swept in. "I brought someone home."

Her smile slipped, a mix of confusion and sorrow moving across her face. "You've never done that?"

He shook his head. Or at least he tried to. Given how tense the muscles in his neck and shoulders were, he wasn't sure how good the movement turned out. His voice wasn't much better. "I never had a place to bring anyone before high school. My foster homes were either too crowded or not welcome to me having company."

"But surely after…once you got your own place."

A slow, uncomfortable panic crept in, casting an unwelcome shadow he had no intention of letting overcast tonight. "Never." He snagged his backpack off the floor, unzipped the main compartment and pulled out his laptop.

She moved in beside him and laid a hand over his forearm just as he sat in his big wingback and centered the computer in the middle of his desk. "Why?"

He shrugged and captured her hand in his. Smoothing his thumb along her knuckles, he let the memories surface. "Another way to keep women at a distance, I guess. Once you've had enough disappointment, you find ways to limit the damage going forward."

Edging close enough her knees brushed his, she gently combed her fingers through his hair. It was such a giving touch, full of heart despite its simplicity and so potent it quaked through every part of him. "It was the teacher who disappointed you? The one you mentioned that first morning after we…"

She dropped her gaze and bit her lip, all the comfort and ease she'd shown since Beckett and Danny's departure disappearing under uncertainty.

Oh, no. That wasn't happening. His pain was one thing, but she wasn't suffering through it. Not by his hand and damned sure not tonight. He tugged her hand enough to draw her off balance and guided her tumble forward so she landed in his lap. "You mean the morning after we started something I cannot find an ounce of regret for?"

Her smile was brilliant. Totally the stuff of spring mornings without a single cloud to blemish its beauty. Talk about a way to pump his ego up into Empire State Building range. "Not an ounce?"

He traced her jawline and marveled in the moment. Never in a million years did he think he'd find the courage to take this chance, but now that he was here, he wasn't going back. Not for anything. "Nada."

She studied him, her fingers cautiously moving above his sternum. "Do you think…would you tell me about her?"

It was a reasonable request. One he had every intention of mirroring back at her when the time was right. No matter what her past entailed, he'd make sure it never came back to bite her. But if he expected her to share her secrets, he'd have to grab his own by the nuts and show her he was worthy of knowing.

He swallowed huge, the action hindered by the fist-sized knot in his throat. "I was big for my age. Cocky as hell and looking for trouble anywhere I could find it." He chuckled as some of the lightness from those days filtered through. "I told you, Beckett and I really didn't have a ton of supervision, so we didn't really have to look hard."

"I found a picture of you." She giggled as she said it, but it had a husky edge of confession to it, too.

"You found a mugshot. Hardly my best look."

"But you were handsome." She snuggled a little closer to his chest. "My guess is trouble jumped in your lap."

Actually, she wasn't far from the truth. Beck had been just as eager as he had to explore the physical wonders the girls at school afforded them, but Knox had tackled getting them off with the same tenacity he spent penetrating firewalls. "I got a bit of a reputation, yeah."

Darya waited, patiently watching him while he tried to find some way to ease into the uncomfortable topic. As if sensing his lack of direction, she offered, "What was her name?"

"Tami Henderson." It was weird saying her name out loud after all these years. Weird, but not nearly as traumatic as he'd expected. "She was my history teacher. Had her for sixth hour. All the kids loved her because she wasn't the uptight stick-up-their-ass type and really loved what she did for a living."

"You were attracted to her?"

He grinned at that. "Uh, yeah. So was every other guy at the school. She was in her mid-thirties, but had a smokin' bod and wasn't the least bit shy about show-ing it."

"So, you approached her?"

Cold crept through his veins, starting at his toes and fingertips and winding its way toward his torso. He hugged Darya tighter to fight it off. "No. I was ballsy as hell, but not *that* ballsy." He anchored his gaze on her and ripped the Band-Aid off. "Just after Christmas break, she asked me to stay after class one day. From there, things just happened."

Her face softened and she cradled his cheek with one hand. "She meant something to you."

He hesitated for a second, trying to find the right way to explain it. "I didn't have anyone growing up. Not until I met Beckett. And yeah, I love him the way I would a brother by blood, but a man can only give you so much." He tugged her shirt free of her prim skirt and slipped his hand against her warm flesh, needing the contact to ground him. "I never had a mom. Never had affection. Tami gave me that. I thought it meant some-thing to her, too. Had shit all planned out. Happily ever afters and everything. Totally pussy whipped."

"But she didn't feel the same?"

He scoffed. "If she did, she dusted me off quick enough. We'd kept it quiet all of second semester, but one of the other kids caught wind of what was going on and spilled to the principal. We had one week left before graduation. One week before I thought we could be on the up and up and wouldn't have to hide this great thing between us anymore."

"What happened?"

Pulling in a long bracing breath, Knox met her stare head on. "When the principal called us on it, she said

I'd coerced her into the affair. That I'd threatened her with physical force if she didn't comply. Not quite a rape allegation, but close enough things got dicey for a day or two. The cops were even called in to investigate." He pursed his lips, the memory just as bitter now as it was all those years ago. "In the end, she graciously opted not to press charges. Mighty kind of her, right?"

"She betrayed you."

That she had. And he'd vowed the day he walked out of that school he'd never let anyone else close—a vow Axel, Jace and the rest of the guys had practically taken a battering ram to get through.

Funny, having said everything out loud, his reasons for acting the way he had seemed silly. Like the act of sharing with Darya had shone a huge spotlight on his shadowed closet and found nothing but empty space and cobwebs where he'd though a host of skeletons rattled. "I guess if I'm fair, it wasn't just her that did me in. I was ripe for disappointment. I told you the only homes I knew were foster placements, but everyone I went to I hoped I'd find a place. A family. When Tami gave me all the affection I'd ever wanted and talked about long-term, I gobbled it up." He scratched his chin and huffed out an ironic chuckle. "Pretty sure there's some psychobabble analysis a shrink could have a heyday with in all of that. Confusing the need for a mom with intimacy and all that."

"Our past makes us who we are. Yours made you appreciate the family you earned later and strong enough to accomplish more than most people ever dream of." Softly spoken, her words were still thick with emotion and loaded with the protectiveness of an alpha she-wolf.

She lightly trailed her fingers through his hair along one side. "Thank you for sharing your story with me."

He caught her hand in his and laced their fingers together. "You know I'm going to ask the same thing."

Fear flashed in her eyes and her body tensed.

"Easy." He tucked her head against his chest and smoothed one hand down her spine. "It doesn't have to be tonight. Not tomorrow or next week, but someday." He paused enough to let her focus and really hear what he had to say next. "I want to earn your trust. For you to figure out I won't judge you no matter what your story is and let me keep you safe."

She nodded, but didn't look up.

Maybe he shouldn't have brought it up. God knew, he hadn't skipped into sharing his details whistling Dixie. What he could do was get shit back in lighter territory and take a stab and being a regular guy without a fuck-load of hang-ups. "So, I'm new to this whole normal relationship routine. Any idea what we do next?"

Her giggle was the prettiest sound he'd heard in ages, second only to the sound of his name on her lips when she'd come around his cock. She lifted her head and bit her lip. "You could feed me."

The temptation to follow it up with a saucy quip about fucking her afterward danced on the edge of his tongue, but that was his usual MO. After all the hurdles he'd put them both through, she deserved better. "You okay with pizza? Momma McKee usually keeps us stocked with decent leftovers, but the way Beckett works through food, my guess is there's not much left."

"Chicken supreme with jalapeños?"

"Sweetheart, you could ask for anchovies and I'd say yes. Which, if you knew how I felt about ancho-

vies, you'd know that meant I'd also walk through hell
for you." He tugged his phone out of his back pocket
and thumbed up the nearby pizza place he kept in his
favorites. "What else should we do?"

She cocked her head. "I still haven't seen *Airplane*."

"I think I could swing that." He punched the call
button and tucked the phone between his shoulder and
ear. "On one condition."

"What's that?"

"We eat it and knock out the movie just like this."

She cocked one eyebrow. "At your desk?"

"No. Spread out on the couch out front, but with
you close."

A lady answered his call and rattled off the name of
their establishment, the racket in the background promising they had at least an hour's wait ahead of them.

"No distance," she whispered.

He smiled at that. Leave it to his woman to sum
things up the most precise way possible. He held the
mouthpiece away from his lips and murmured against
her lips, "No distance. Those days are over."

A deep, rumbling voice and a soft but firm nudge to
Knox's shoulder jogged him out of sleep. He cracked
heavily weighted eyelids. The monster TV mounted on
the wall beamed the main menu of his movie library
back at him, pooling soft white light on him and Darya
and the brown suede sectional where they'd spent their
night. The rest of the room was dark.

Darya lay curled sleeping against him, her head
heavy against his chest and her bare legs tangled with
his. He grinned at the sight of his T-shirt almost reaching her mid-thigh. Never in his life had he let a woman

wear his clothes, but seeing her pad from his bedroom after their massive pizza annihilation in nothing but the soft navy blue cotton was hands down one of the most gratifying sights of his life.

He closed his eyes, ready to let the blackness pull him back under.

Another chuckle sounded on his right, followed by another nudge. This time his brain managed to categorize the voice. "Hey, get your woman in bed," Beckett said. "You two will sleep for shit out here."

Knox's addled mind finally got in the game enough to realize Beckett was probably right, then followed up by pointing out just how much of his woman's legs were on prime display for Beckett's appreciation. Cranking out the mother of all ab curls, he carefully cradled Darya against his chest and stood with her in his arms. "Thanks, man." He paused as he rounded the edge of the oversize sofa. "Can you get the TV?" he said quiet enough not to wake his sleeping cargo.

"Already on it," Beckett fired back.

A second later, the screen went dark, leaving only a single stream of light filtering from Beckett's suite at the opposite end of the loft to guide Knox to his own rooms.

Darya inhaled deep and shifted her head against his shoulder, her warm exhalation whispering against his bare chest and neck.

This is what you were waiting for.

It was a random thought. Completely out of left field and the absolute last thing he'd expected his drowsy brain to conjure up, but deadly accurate. Holding Darya—feeling her weight in his arms and seeing to her comfort—felt *right*. Like after years of hacking and kicking a firmly locked door, he'd finally unlocked an elusive place inside himself and gained a whole new level of balance.

Beckett's deep voice crept through the darkness a second before he shut the door to his suite. "Hey, Knox."

Knox backed up enough to bring his brother into view and raised both eyebrows in silent question.

The shadows were deep, but there was still enough light to show a deadly seriousness on Beckett's face. "Not sure it's registered yet, but you were *asleep*."

One heartbeat.

Then another.

Only on the third did Beckett's emphasis finally connect.

He'd slept.

Not because of sex. Not because of booze or one of those soul-freezing pills. But just nodded off like a normal Joe, loaded on pizza, laughter and all that was Darya.

Slow and featherlight, a comfortable peace settled over him, so profound in its impact all he could do was stand rooted in place, dumbfounded.

"I wished someone like her for you almost my whole life." Beckett's mouth crooked on one side, a shaky smile riddled with a solemnness equally reflected in his raw and grated voice. "Happy for you, brother." With that he ambled toward his suite, closed the door behind him and left Knox standing speechless in the dark.

Happy.

The word resonated hard. Right up there with *content*, *settled* and every other pansy-ass word he'd lobbed at Jace, Zeke and Trevor the last year and a half. But now he got it.

His arms tightened reflexively around Darya's bone-less weight and he hefted her higher against his chest, a surge of protectiveness burning through his otherwise relaxed muscles.

Carefully, he made his way to his bed and laid Darya in the center.

She stirred as he pulled his arms from underneath her and her eyelids fluttered open, bright blue eyes reflected in the soft moonlight. Pressing one hand into the mattress, she levered herself up and scanned the room. "I missed the end?"

He shucked his jeans and crawled in beside her. "We'll watch it again in the morning over donuts and coffee." He drew the covers over them and pulled her close so her head rested on his chest. Her hair spilled like silk against his arm and her soft breath whispered against his sternum. Hell, he could have gone without any covers at all and been content with just her weight to warm him.

"Knox?"

He closed his eyes and savored her soft voice. "Mmm?"

"You're okay? To sleep?"

Outside his windows, the drone of cars speeding up and down the interstate hummed one step up from generated white noise. For once, it didn't bother him. Didn't grate his nerves and prod him to get up and pace. He traced his fingers up her arm and let them tangle in her hair. "I'm good."

"You're sure?"

He smiled into the darkness, the fog of sleep creeping in just enough to make his cheek protest the response. "I'm absolutely sure." His heart slowed and his muscles uncoiled. Whether or not he spoke the words that filtered through his head after that he wasn't sure, but they were the last he had before the darkness took over. "I have you."

Chapter Twenty-Three

"So, now all you do is click commit and your code will merge into the main branch," Katy said, her attitude as blasé as if she'd asked Darya to pass the salt instead of potentially hosing the core code from Knox's top-ten selling app.

Darya slid the cursor to the bold green save button and hesitated.

Beside her, Katy chuckled. "Really, it's not that big of a deal. If you don't think His Royal Highness doesn't have at least ten backups stored in at least that many different places, you're nuts." She waved her hand toward the screen. "Go on. Click it."

Well, she had a point. She'd heard the expression *a belt and suspenders guy* before, but never had she met a man who fit the description better than Knox. Before she could overthink it, she clicked the button and waited. When the confirmation message popped up on the screen she barely bit back a self-satisfied whoop and ridiculous fist pump.

"See?" Katy said. "I told you it'd be no big deal. The code was solid and we both tested the heck out of it. Now it'll go out with the rest of this week's updates over the weekend." She sat back in her chair and snagged her ever-present Starbucks to-go cup. "So? How's it feel to be a bona fide developer?"

Darya rolled her eyes, closed out of the application and opened her email. "It was a bug fix. Hardly worthy of calling me a developer."

"Hey, everyone's got to start somewhere, and the best way to dive in is fixing what's broken." She sipped her drink and studied Darya over the rim. "So, I suck at dancing around topics. Though, I'd like to point out I made it two and a half work days before I brought it up."

Darya kept her eyes trained on her screen and tried to keep her face passive. Not an easy task since she had a pretty good idea where Katy was headed. "Brought what up?"

"That you're seeing Knox."

Like it always did when she was reminded of her new blossoming relationship, her body resonated with a subtle tuning fork buzz and any semblance of coherent thought fluttered right out the window. She rolled her lips inward and forced herself to face Katy.

"Oh my God!" Katy laughed and planted her drink back on the desk with enough force Darya was a little surprised nothing sloshed out the top. "You can't seriously think we didn't know. I mean, it's not like he's made it a secret."

"He told you?"

"With words? No. But everyone here has worked with Knox for two or more years, and he's never so much as touched a woman in front of us except to shake hands."

Okay, the touching *had* been excessive the last few days. Crazy possessive excessive. Especially around Vance, who barely managed to make eye contact with her anymore. It was such an about-face from the way they had been, that the claiming yet gentle touches still caught her a little off guard.

Katy propped one elbow on Darya's desk, leaned in and waggled her eyebrows. "So?"

"So?"

"How'd it happen? What's he like? Is he as bossy one-on-one as he is at work?"

Knox spoke from the doorway. "When you weren't looking and none of your damned business on the other two counts."

Darya jolted taller in her chair and Katy's eyes bugged out.

Before Darya could summon up an explanation or at least derail Knox's focus to something other than Katy's questions, he prowled up beside her, leaned in and pressed a lingering soft kiss to her lips. "You get your fix in?"

Her fix?

Oh. Right. Her job. As in the thing that she and Katy were supposed to be working on instead of gabbing about their boss and her...well...whatever he was. She nodded, fingers curling reflexively in his soft T-shirt. Today's was soft gray with the Stay Puft Marshmallow Man smooshed between two graham crackers and a slab of chocolate. She nodded and fought the urge to answer with another kiss instead of words. No small feat with his handsome face still inches from her own. "Yes, just now."

"Good." He straightened, grabbed her hand and pulled her up as well. "'Cause you've got about two minutes to brace yourself and that's only if Katy does a bang-up job of running interference." He shifted his attention to Katy. "Front desk. Now. The horde is on the way in."

Katy shot to her feet and tagged her coffee. "All of them?"

"The whole lot. And since they're in one of our Escalades, my guess is Beckett helped 'em plan the attack."

Katy saluted and scurried out the door. "I'm on it."

"On what?" Darya urged Knox to face her with a firm grip on his shoulder. "What kind of attack?"

Despite the conversation alluding otherwise, Knox grinned in a way that said he was more tickled than worried. "You're about to meet my moms."

For a second, Darya's brain wouldn't compute. Just sat there, more unresponsive than the first time she'd tried to compile code with the wrong executable. "Your mothers are here?"

"Well, technically they're Jace's and Axel's moms—Ninette and Sylvie—but I claim 'em as mine and they seem all right with it, so yeah…my moms."

Panic set in, her arms trembling even more than the frigid office temperature called for and her palms growing clammy. She glanced down at her jeans and T-shirt. Of all the rotten times for her to finally cave and dress like everyone else at the office, she had to pick the day she'd make a first impression on the two women he cared about enough to call mother. Heck, the only thing decent she had on were the cute Jimmy Choo sandals she'd picked up secondhand on eBay. "Knox, I can't meet them like this. I look terrible."

He guided her face to his with soft fingers beneath her chin. "They'll love you. Promise." He smirked and wrapped her up with both arms around her waist. "And trust me when I tell you they're not your stereotypical mothers."

The thick metal door at the far end of the hallway chunked open and a cloud of feminine voices billowed right behind it.

Her face must've blanched or reflected the sheer terror coursing through her, because he swooped in fast and sealed his lips against hers in a chaste, but lingering kiss. "Relax," he murmured softly as he lifted his head. "You met Viv, Gabe and Nat already. They'll be with you, too."

"With me for what?"

The voices drifted closer, Katy clearly leading the way while she chattered about something Darya's mind was too numb to track.

Knox kissed her nose and whispered. "It's Wednesday afternoon. That can only mean one thing."

Before he could actually share what that was, Katy strode through the door with two gorgeous older women on her heels and the other three ladies Darya had met weeks ago behind them. "Hey, Knox. You've got company."

"Och, we dinna come for him, lass." The sassier looking of the two women she'd yet to meet intervened and sashayed toward Knox. While her shoulder-length auburn hair wasn't a color anyone would ever classify as natural, the spunk behind it matched her thick Scottish accent and the playfulness in her vivid green eyes. "We came ta meet our boy's new lovely."

Katy snickered, shook her head and quietly made her way out of the room.

As if he'd long grown accustomed to the routine,

Knox faced Sylvie and opened his arms in welcome. "Hey, Momma."

She patted one side of Knox's face and kissed the other. "Ye've been keeping secrets."

"No, he's been hoarding," said the other woman as she moved in for her own welcome. Where the red-headed woman was all fire and boldness, this one moved with refined elegance. Her hair was a platinum gray every woman prayed they'd develop with age, but rarely obtained without help from a rock star hair dresser. But even more impressive was the shrewd awareness that burned in her blue gaze as it moved across Darya and landed on Knox.

The elegant woman lovingly batted her friend out of the way and kissed Knox's cheek. "You know how the boys get when a woman fires up their possessive streak." She glanced back at Vivienne and winked. "The only reason we knew Viv existed those first few weeks is because Jace kept her under lock and key at Haven."

"Well, in fairness," Vivienne said, "I had a bullet hole in me, or that wouldn't have been the case."

Darya snapped her attention to Knox, her spine hopping from mere first-impression discomfort to full-alert and ready to bolt. "A bullet hole?"

"Long story," Knox muttered close to her ear then wrapped his arm around her waist. To the beautiful gray-haired woman he said, "You think maybe it might be smart to let her get comfortable with the lot of you before you air our dirty laundry?"

The woman grinned and her eyes sparked with pure mirth. "Don't you worry about us. We'll get her very comfortable and make sure we spill all *your* dirty laundry before we dive into anyone else's." She cocked one eyebrow. "Assuming you ever get around to introducing us."

Knox ducked his head and ran his fingers through his already tousled hair, but from Darya's angle beside him there was no missing the chagrined expression on his face. "Yeah. Right." He lifted his head and pulled her partially in front of him. He motioned to the one closest to him. "Darya, this is Jace's mom, Ninette. Behind her is Axel's mom, Sylvie."

Darya extended her hand to Ninette, hoping her palms weren't as shaky or clammy as they felt. "I'm Darya Volkova. It's very nice to meet you."

"Darya to family," Knox interjected with a quick glance at the hallway. "For everyone else it's JJ Simpson, so watch yourself."

"Oh!" Sylvie brightened and tapped Ninette's arm, shooing her out of her way. "Will ya listen to the lass's voice?" She opened her arms, pulled Darya in for a huge hug and whispered conspiratorially. "Take my advice. Wield that accent every chance you get. When they're in a snit, it'll unwind their tantrums every time." She pulled away and winked.

"You get I'm right here and heard every word," Knox said, a smile in his voice.

Sylvie shrugged like she couldn't care less. "And as sure as I'm standin' here, it'll work every time."

Still standing by the doorway with Vivienne and Gabe, Trevor's wife, Natalie, cleared her throat. "Um, not to cut short the one-upmanship brewing between the two of you, but if we're going to make our appointments we need to load Darya up and get a move on."

"What appointments?" Darya said.

Gabe smiled with a mix of shared orneriness and

sympathy. "Wednesdays are mani/pedi days. Otherwise known as mandatory Haven-gal gossip days."

"We do more than gossip," Sylvie fired back.

Ninette chuckled. "Right, but I'm not sure there's a way to categorize picking through the latest plot details from *Game of Thrones* and *Vikings*." Her gaze shifted to Darya. "We try to pay attention. Really, we do. But between all the accents, hot men and blatant sex it's hard not to get sidetracked."

"She's right," Sylvie added. "*Sons of Anarchy* was much easier ta keep up with."

Darya was lost. Unequivocally and helplessly lost. She twisted and peered up to Knox, rooted firmly behind her.

His hands rested easy on her hips and his low, soft laugher surrounded her on a comforting embrace. His voice rumbled at her ear. "Just go with it. You'll catch up. Eventually."

"But what about work?" She turned enough to meet his eyes head on. "You gave me all those new defects to research."

"Bugger that," Sylvie said. "What's the point o' havin' a man like our Knox if he can't handle the fort while we take some time ta play?" She motioned toward Darya's desk. "Grab yer purse, lass. Time ta get pampered and let us get ta know ye."

She hesitated and cast a questioning look at Knox.

He widened his eyes and held out his hands in a classic pose of male surrender. "If you think I'm gonna argue with 'em you're crazy. Sylvie makes a mean care package, and I'm not risking my leftovers."

"Men," Ninette said from behind her. "Everyone claims they think with their little head, but nine times out of ten, their stomach rules the roost." She splayed a hand on Darya's shoulder. "Get your things, sweetheart. Any girl who can snag this stubborn knucklehead deserves some pampering. Besides, I wanna see if I can drag out of you why you've got a secret alias."

Pampering sounded divine. When she'd lived in Russia, trips to the spa were an expected part of her routine. A perk Yefim insisted on as part of her food and clothing allowance. The only time someone other than herself had tended to her hands and feet since landing in the US had been a trip to a local spa with JJ two months before she'd died. "You really don't mind?" she asked Knox.

He stepped in close and cupped both sides of her face. His voice was quiet, but rich with the same sincerity he'd melted her with the night he'd invited her home. "I don't know where this is headed, but I know it's important. That means me opening up not just where I live, but sharing you with the people I love, too. So, yeah. If you're game for giggles and whatever conversation causes the laughter, then I'm absolutely on board."

The shock of what he'd shared—not just with her, but in front of witnesses—must have registered on her face, because he chuckled, kissed her forehead and pulled her into a hug, bracing her cheek against his chest. "Put everything on the joint account," he said to the women behind her. "If you're good enough to take my girl into the fold, the least I can do is spring for the trip."

"Now we're talking," Ninette said. She urged Darya out of Knox's arms, held up the purse Darya had stashed beside her desk and winked. "Suddenly I feel the need for deluxe everything."

Chapter Twenty-Four

Laughter, loads of food and everyone that meant a damn in Knox's life all in one place. Not exactly how he'd thought tonight would go. Or where for that matter. But by some quirk of fate they'd ended up re-routed to Dave & Buster's of all places, the details behind how that had happened a mystery still uncovered.

The bonus? No Haven meant the family only rule didn't apply. Which also meant his woman was beside him, her face animated and hands gesturing as though to paint the picture created by her beautiful voice.

"Have you seen the pictures of the canals in Venice?" she asked Trevor's son, Levi, across the table.

Levi stuffed another French fry in his mouth with the finesse of a hyped up eight-year-old boy and bobbed his head, a chunk of his longish blond hair falling over one eye. "Yeah, they use those skinny boats and guys in funny clothes steer 'em around."

"Yes, well, in St. Petersburg they have canals as well. The Neva River runs all the way through it and connects to the Baltic Sea. It is quite beautiful in the summer, but in the winter it freezes."

"Wow! We never have things freeze here."

"Oh, it can get very cold there and we have snow for much of the winter."

"Is it cold where you grew up, too? That Yekat..." He frowned and changed course. "That other funny sounding place?"

"Yekaterinburg," she said, beaming her sweet angel smile at him. She crossed her arms on the table, just as comfortable chattering back and forth with the unstoppable and candid eight-year-old as she'd been with Ninette and Sylvie when they'd first walked in the building together. "It's similar. A little warmer, but I found St. Petersburg more interesting. More things to see and do. More art to enjoy."

Levi opened his mouth, undoubtedly to launch yet another question.

Before he could voice it, Natalie cut in. "How about we let Darya get a solid breath in before you ask her anything else."

"Yeah," Trevor said. "Besides it's time to get our Skee-Ball championship underway. The man with the most coupons is the winner."

"Hey," Ninette said from her place to Darya's right. "What makes you think it'll be a man? I'll have you know I was quite the Skee-Ball expert in my day."

Levi straightened in his chair and re-engaged with Darya. "I'm the best at Skee-Ball. We always play games at family night and everyone gets a turn picking food and games. Tonight was my turn for games, so when Dad told me Uncle Beckett picked Dave & Buster's for food, I challenged everyone to a Skee-Ball championship."

Knox swiveled his head to Beckett beside him and muttered, "So *you're* the reason we're here. I don't sup-pose you made that decision the same time you helped Sylvie and Ninette plan their mani/pedi invasion?"

Beckett shrugged and bit into a wing. "Waitin' on you is like watchin' grass grow. More fun to nudge."

Darya drew him out of his sidebar with Beckett with her innocent question to Levi. "What is Skee-Ball?"

The look on the kid's face was priceless. Like he couldn't possibly comprehend anyone had gone through life without such dire information. "They don't have that in Russia?"

"Well, I don't know. We might call it something else."

Levi twisted in his chair and shot puppy dog eyes at Natalie. "Can I show her, Mom?" Not waiting for an answer, he spun back to Darya. "It's way cool. They've got these balls made out of wood. Or maybe not real wood, but they look like wood and feel like it, too. Then you roll it up this ramp and try to get the ball in different holes. The harder the hole, the more points you get."

He paused for all of one beat, seemed to realize he'd yet to get an answer and turned back to his mom. "Can I? I mean, Darya gets a chance to play, too, right? So, someone needs to teach her how to do it."

Natalie tried to fight back her laughter, but with Levi's enthusiasm she'd have had to be the devil to pull it off. "I'd say that's up to Darya." She shifted her attention across the table. "Do you *want* to learn how to play Skee-Ball?"

"Well, if I'm going to learn," she said, her pretty gaze locked on Levi, "I'd do best to learn from a champion."

"Awesome!" Levi jumped to his feet and held out his hand to Trevor. "Can I have my game card now?"

"Don't look at me. This is Uncle Beckett's thing."

Axel chuckled from the end of the table and raised

his scotch in salute toward Beckett. "The price of matchmaking, brother. Fork over the loot and let the lad win our girl over."

Darya leaned close to Knox and whispered, "What does he mean by that?"

Knox cupped the back of her neck, her silky hair playing over his knuckles. It should have scared him, how easy it was being with her. How natural it felt to have her beside him at a time reserved for only family. But seeing her smile—feeling her presence beside him—was more natural than anything he'd ever done in his life. Made more sense than any line of code or tricky riddle. "It means family night is usually just for family because we do it out at Jace and Axel's ranch, but Beck knew I'd want you with me, so he changed venues."

"Who said it had anything to do with you?" As soon as Levi got within arm's reach, Beckett forked over a stack of game cards big enough to tire out a whole brood of kids. Levi promptly started divvying out one to each person, but Beckett kept talking. "Maybe I'm biding my time until she figures out I'm a better bet so I can slide in and reap the rewards."

"And here I'd thought I was gonna make it a whole day off without having to stitch anyone up." Zeke wrapped an arm around Gabe and took a pull off his beer.

Jace chuckled, but it was Vivienne who spoke, her attention focused on Darya. "You see? This is why we can't have family dinners in public. Too much testosterone gathered in one place. I can never tell if they're going to beat their chests or each other's faces."

"At least they're old enough they're not beating something else all the time," Sylvie said under her breath.

No matter how quiet she'd said it, it still garnered a table full of laughs, even from Darya who didn't seem the least bit put off by the crude reference.

"Now, *that's* a picture I didn't need," Danny said.

Ninette stood as soon as Levi finished rounding the table, cupped his shoulder and motioned Darya toward the arcade area. "Come on, Darya. The Skee-Ball master's getting impatient, and these guys look like they're gonna marinate in their after-dinner drinks awhile longer."

"All the better for us," Sylvie said, standing as well. "The more the sots drink, the worse their coordination."

Despite the amused but slightly overwhelmed expression on her face, Darya stood and pushed in her chair, following Sylvie's lead.

Sylvie scanned the rest of the table, her gaze resting a little longer on Viv, Natalie and Gabe. "How about the rest of you ladies? Care ta team up and trounce the lads?"

"Oh, yeah." Viv tossed her napkin on the table and stood, spurring Gabe and Natalie to do the same.

"You realize you're still outnumbered by three," Jace said, his eyes lingering appreciatively on Viv's ass.

"Nope, only by two." Natalie leaned in and gave Trevor a kiss on the cheek. "We're gonna sweet talk Levi into pinch-hitting for us."

"Don't do it, son!" Trevor shouted over his shoulder as the group migrated from the table, Darya casting a quick wave over her shoulder as the women herded her into the sea of games.

Axel grinned and lifted his scotch for another swig. "Too late. The lad's got that gleam in his eye that says he's already smitten."

"Just like his dad," Jace added. "Can't help bein' a knight in shining armor for the women."

"Like you don't buckle the second Viv crooks a finger," Trevor said.

"True, but my armor's dirty."

Zeke chuckled and set his beer on the table. "Something tells me it's the dirty part she likes best."

The quip drew a full round of laughter, the overall tenor of it a little empty without the women's lightness to round it out.

"So…" Axel eased back in his chair and crossed one leg over the other. As usual, he stood out from the rest of them, his tailored brown slacks, shiny loafers and crisp white button-down rolled up at the sleeves making him look like a corporate CEO caught in a casual moment. Even with his wild russet hair knotted up tight at the back, he still made the look work. "Darya seems to be settling in."

And there it was. The nosey prodding he'd halfway expected the second he'd learned their family night had been relocated to a public place. Well, they could prod all they wanted. He wasn't ready yet and until he was, there was nothing to talk about. "Yep."

The table got quiet, all of his brothers looking from one to the other.

Not surprisingly, Jace was the one to break the silence. "That mean we need to talk about her future?"

"Hers or mine?" Knox said.

"Maybe both." Beckett peeled his attention off Darya where she stood beside Levi across the room at the end of a long line of Skee-Ball machines. "The two don't have to be exclusive."

Letting out a heavy breath, Knox snatched his beer and tipped it for a healthy draw.

"For a guy that looked as comfortable as you did about fifteen minutes ago, that sound doesn't jibe," Trevor said.

"Sure it does," Zeke said before Knox could answer. "Or did you forget how long it took for him to figure out we weren't gonna leave his ass swingin' in the wind? The only thing Knox does fast is type and hack into other people's business. Everything else he has to stew on and overthink twice as long as the rest of us."

"That true?" Danny asked. "We pushing where we shouldn't be?"

Knox set his beer bottle on the table and shrugged. "You're not asking anything not already in my head. I'm just not ready to go there. Not yet." He anchored both forearms on the table and grappled for some way to share what was in his head without coming off like a ginormous pussy. "She knows about me. My past. All of it."

"You ask me, that's the biggest hurdle you've got," Axel said.

"For me, yeah." Knox studied his brothers, letting his gaze rest on each of them for a split second before moving to the next. "But I don't know hers. I'm the only one standing out there full Monty, and until she's ready to do the same, I'm not willing to bring my family into it."

"We're already in it, brother." Jace sat forward, mirroring Knox's pose. "We always will be. Doesn't matter if you've got a toe in or the whole damned enchilada. We're *always* with you."

"Not like you to beat around the bush, though," Axel

said. "If not knowin' her past is the only thing holding you back, just ask her."

It wasn't like him. But then nothing he'd done since laying eyes on Darya had been status quo. He met Axel's steady stare. "Is it whacked I want her to give it to me?"

The hardness in his green gaze softened, understanding and a shit ton of compassion reflected back at him. "Not whacked at all. Surrender's the sweetest gift a woman can ever give a man. Worth the effort to earn and the wait that goes with it."

"So, we wait," Trevor said, the easy drawl in his voice belying the stout vow behind his words. He rocked forward, guiding the front two legs of his chair back on the floor, grabbed his beer and lifted it in salute. "But we do it together and give your girl a safe place to share."

The rest of the guys grabbed their drinks and lifted them as well, a mixed chorus of agreement echoing back at him.

God, they were a motley group. Every one of them incredibly different and fallible on their own, but unbreakable and steadfast as a whole. And they were his. His brothers. The family he'd always wanted patiently waiting and willing to support his future however he chose to build it. He lifted his own drink. "Yeah, we do it together."

Chapter Twenty-Five

As routines went, the one Darya had developed with Knox was not only surprising, but strangely comfortable. For a guy with the energy of a sugar-hyped two-year-old and the brain power of a rocket scientist, he'd proven to be a bit of a domesticated homebody.

Work. Dinner. More work peppered with ample music or movies. Sleep and repeat. For just over a week, the pattern had varied very little, only events with his brothers or the weekend offering diversion.

The sex though…that was a whole different story. *Predictable* wasn't a word that could ever coexist with Knox's sensual nature. Well, except maybe that they were guaranteed to bookend every single day with anything from languid, brutally teasing sex to nothing short of wickedly carnal fucking.

Forcing herself to focus on the search results detailed on the screen, Darya slowly scrolled down the list of known residences for the most recent skip she'd been hired to find. Despite Knox's attempts to get her to work with him on the couch, Darya always felt more focused behind her desk. More centered in her purpose.

Not that it was helping tonight. She was too distracted. Too aware of the shirtless man stretched out long across the couch cushions and the number of times she'd caught him watching her.

No, not watching.

Studying.

Calculating.

Which was doubly weird because after dinner, Knox was a machine when it came to work and focus. Nothing distracted him. Not music. Not her phone calls to clients or the endless movies that streamed across the television screen.

Well, there might be a *few* things that could distract him. The night she'd strolled out of the bathroom post-shower with nothing on but a towel, he'd ditched his computer and taken her from behind braced against a wall. Or, like tonight, Denzel in *The Equalizer* might get his attention. She still hadn't figured out why he loved that movie so much, but if it was on, he always stopped and watched it to the end.

Although, he wasn't really watching it tonight. Even without turning her head to confirm it, she felt his thoughtful gaze on her as sure as a tap on her shoulder.

She should tell him about her past. The way things were shifting between them he deserved to know. To truly understand what he was risking by being with her. Heck, if she was smart, she'd use the movie still playing on the screen as the perfect opening. To leverage some of the uncanny truths it portrayed to break her silence and share why she was running.

But she wasn't ready. Not yet. Not until they had more time.

She copied the skip's most recent address, pasted it in her report and hit save. In the background, Denzel's confrontation with the *vor* he'd tracked down at the end of movie filled the otherwise comfortable silence. Another few seconds and the bad guy would get it.

Knox loved that part, but a quick glance his direction confirmed he was completely detached from the action and centered solely on her.

Dropping her hands in her lap, she pushed away from the desk and frowned at him. "I can't focus when you're watching me like that."

"When I'm watching you like what?"

"Like you're crafting devious plans."

The dirty grin she'd come to not only love, but eagerly anticipate tilted his lips. "I thought you liked my devious plans."

Oh, she liked them, all right. Particularly the ones where the two of them ended up naked, sweaty and boneless from toe-curling sex. Commandeering the mouse again, she punched the back button on her browser session. "I can't afford devious plans right now. I'm behind on my contract jobs and if I don't get some information out to my skip clients tonight, they're going to start threatening to use someone else."

The grin shifted to a smirk. A seriously, self-satisfied smirk that said she'd all but danced right into the terrain where he wanted her. "Let 'em."

It was a dare, one thrown with a soft voice, but thick with challenge.

How she kept from looking at him—from meeting his gaze and letting the hope he'd fired with his simple words shine bright—was a miracle. Instead, she scrolled down the screen, not seeing a single thing that passed her focus. "I'm not ready yet."

"Yes, you are."

Three simple words, but hearing them from Knox

was the highest praise there was. At least in her book. She met his stare. "You mean that?"

"Have I ever blown smoke up your ass?"

No. Absolutely not. Knox could be extraordinarily thoughtful. Giving and detailed to a fault, but a bullshitter? Never.

Not waiting for her to answer, he motioned to the computer on his lap. "I just looked at the app rewrite you sent yesterday. The idea might not have been yours, but your execution was spot-on and you streamlined shit I didn't even think to catch. All you need is your own idea and you're off to the races."

Her own idea.

Her own opportunity.

Her own future.

But, she had to be practical. To set a solid foundation that would give her plenty of room to grow. And that meant staying the course until she had at least a handful of salable products. "Maybe. But giving up the solid income is reckless. Better to experiment and build on the side while my skip jobs pay the bills."

"It's not reckless if you come to work for me full time."

She froze, rewinding his words in her head even as she studied him for clues she hadn't misheard. "What?"

He closed his laptop, slid it onto the coffee table with the casual confidence of a man utterly certain of his actions and stood. "Come to work for me." He stalked toward her, the low waistband of his jeans accentuating the sharp V at his hips. "You're already pulling full-time hours. If you ditch the skip work you'll have extra time to brainstorm and work up prototypes." He braced one hand on the back of her chair and the other on the desk, leaning in close. "Plus, you'd have the added benefit of some very hands-on coaching."

Damn, but his voice was a weapon when he wielded it that way. Within kissing distance it was even headier, the smooth baritone of it scattering the few productive thoughts she'd managed to construct and stirring a whole host of tingles low in her stomach.

But she couldn't lose her focus. Not with a topic as important as this one. She focused on his lips and her heartbeat shifted to a hummingbird flutter. "It's the hands-on part I'm worried about."

"Really? Because I think we've got that part down pat." He teased his lips against hers, a barely there touch that made her own part, ready and impatient for more. "Give me one good reason why you shouldn't work with me."

Reason? There wasn't one. At least not one capable of overpowering the very tangible physical need he'd nudged to the surface. Fear, though, was another matter. One she'd be foolish not to broach. "What happens when this is over? When you're ready to move on? What if that makes our work life untenable?"

He smiled against her lips, palmed the back of her neck and kissed her with a firmness and depth that said he not only appreciated her honesty, but encouraged it. By the time he backed away enough to look her in the eye, she'd nearly forgotten her question. "Untenable will never happen. You just proved it. No matter what happens, you trust me enough to tell me the truth. To say what's on your mind. So long as we're talking, there isn't anything we can't figure out. Not with work or anything else."

"You really believe that?"

"Want me to prove it?" The glint in his eyes was irresistible. The irrepressible bad boy dangling the promise of something both decadent and divine.

A quiver speared low in her belly. Whatever he had on his mind, her body was more than ready and her mind adequately piqued. "Prove it how?"

Snagging her hand as he straightened, he pulled her from her chair and tugged her toward the bedroom. "Oh, this is a show, not a tell."

She half-heartedly dug in her heels and glanced back at her computer. "But I haven't finished."

"You're finished. You just haven't admitted it yet." With that, he swung her around, backed her against the edge of the bed and devoured her mouth.

As diversion tactics went, his kiss was the ultimate ploy. Especially, those when he took complete control.

And he was definitely in command now. From the hand at the back of her head holding her firm for his mouth, to the other one anchored on her ass, there was zero give in his embrace.

Not that she cared. In that second, the whole damned building could have crumbled around them and she'd have hesitated in finding shelter. His kiss was that good. A drugging caress that smoothed all the wrinkles of reality away and left only a silken pallet for her spirit.

With a casualness developed over their recent days and nights together, he had her T and sleep shorts off in short order and her body humming and primed. That was the thing about Knox—in life and in sex, he defined what he wanted and went all in. And oh, how she loved it when what he wanted was her, mindless and aching for whatever he wanted to dish out.

She reached for his waistband, keen to return the favor.

He snagged her hands, spun her and pinned both wrists behind her back. "Nope. Not yet," he growled near her ear. "I'm not done getting you ready."

She wriggled her ass against his more than ready cock, just hearing the promise in his voice enough to leave her drenched. "Ready for what?"

He snagged two of her thickest pillows, stacked them in front of her on the side of the bed. "Bend over, sweetheart. We're gonna put our communication skills to the test."

As tall as the pillows were stacked and the way they'd angle her ass for him, she seriously doubted there'd be any communication beyond her saying, *Yes,* and, *More.* Still, she leaned forward, rested one cheek against the soft comforter and peeked at him over her shoulder. "The last time you took me from behind the neighbors weren't happy with our enthusiasm."

"Which just proves your walls are too thin. Gonna deal with that inconvenience after I get you to see reason on work." He smacked her ass and nudged her feet apart. "Right now, I want you to spread for me. I need room to work."

Like he'd need to ask her twice for that one. Fingers, mouth or cock, Knox worked her with the same proficiency he did everything else. One hundred percent dedication and vehemence.

He crouched behind her and squeezed the firm grip he'd kept on her wrists. "Lace your fingers and keep your hands behind your back. You know how I hate distractions."

"That's so not true. You're a distraction junkie."

He chuckled and spanked her other cheek, this one packing enough sting her sex clenched. "Keep it up, sweetheart. Seeing your skin pink from my hand's a fucking huge turn-on."

She did as he asked but wiggled her butt while she did. "Then you should probably stop talking and give me more."

"Oh, I'm going to give you more." He skimmed his hands down the backs of her thighs, then the swish of plastic sliding against the carpet sounded from beneath the bed. The next thing she knew, he was standing behind her and the plastic tub she kept stowed beneath the bed was beside her on the comforter. "The question is how far you're going to let me go."

Dimly, her mind registered him moving behind her and the weighted rustle of his jeans tossed to the floor, but the bulk of her attention was centered on the box. Or more accurately, the toys inside it.

The front of his muscled thighs pressed against the backs of her legs and he skimmed his hands in an indolent caress up along her hips. "Anything in that box that's off-limits?"

Her heart kicked so hard she swore its pulse echoed through the mattress beneath her cheek. It wasn't *anything* in that box he was asking about, but one thing in particular…because they'd used all but one already.

But she'd sure thought about the one item remaining. Had imagined him working the slender plug inside her. How it might feel to have even more.

Only one man had ever inspired such thoughts. And now was her chance. "Nothing."

A low, approving rumble filled the room and he

guided his impossible hard cock along the seam of her ass. "What about what's not in the box?"

She groaned and rolled her head so her forehead pressed against the mattress, angling her hips up and back for more of his teasing strokes.

"Love the sound of that, sweetheart, but it's not an answer." His fingers delved between her folds and slicked the ready wetness up and around her clit. "Give me limits, or give me a green light."

Limits? With Knox? Maybe if he'd asked her before he'd touched her. Before he'd kissed her senseless, stripped her bare and bent her over like a conqueror ready to stake his claim. But right now, she couldn't come up with any boundaries. Not in her mind or her body. "No limits."

The rumble escalated to a growl and he pumped two fingers inside her sex. "You sure?"

Yes.

No.

Maybe.

All three were answers that pinged in her head, but her libido took the reins and gave the response it wanted. "Shut up and fuck me, Knox."

The sass earned her a sharp smack straight between her legs, the sting mingling with the cool air against her slick folds. "Just for that, I think I'll skip the plug and stretch you the old-fashioned way."

All too readily, her mind conjured a picture to match his words, and a shudder rocked her so hard her knees nearly buckled.

The crinkle of a condom wrapper sounded, followed by an appreciative hum.

And then the thick head of his cock nudged her sex.

"Christ, Darya. Need to find a way to fuck you like this so you can see what I do." His shaft sunk deep and she rose up on her toes, lifting for more. "Just like that. Your pretty pink pussy taking everything I give it."

"Knox!" Too frustrated with his slow and deliberate pace, she released her hands, braced them on either side of her head and pushed back into his thrusts.

As second later, his hand was at her nape, pinning her in place, and his heavy voice grated near her ear. "Be still."

Holy hell, that was hot. The complete mastery behind his simple command and the thick stretch of his cock in her sex nearly pushing her over the edge.

Slowly, he rebuilt his rhythm, still slow like before, but each stroke filling her completely. With her face angled away from the box, she couldn't see what he was doing, but something thumped against the hard plastic. "Love it when you get greedy, but tonight you take what I give you. Understand?"

"Then stop talking dirty. I can take your cock, or your filthy mouth, but not both at the same time."

He chuckled and a muted click of hard plastic sounded behind her. "You sure?" Cold moisture dribbled at the very base of her tailbone and slipped between her cheeks.

The lube.

God, this was really going to happen.

The click sounded again and the bottle landed beside her on the bed.

"If I can't talk while I fuck you then I can't give you a visual." As if he had all the time in the world and no clue how taut and ready to explode she was, he coated her in the moisture. Up and down, circling her anus and pressing ever so slightly, before dipping across her perineum and repeating the hypnotic path. "You always tip your hips for me like this, but tonight you're begging for it."

"Knox, stop it."

His thumb stilled, but not his hips, the thick head of his shaft scraping deliciously inside her. "Stop?"

"Just your mouth. Everything else, keep going."

"Hmmm." Spoken like a man who had no intention of listening. He circled his thumb again, but this time added more pressure and didn't retreat. "You sure you don't want to know? Because I'm committing the way my thumb looks slipping inside your ass to memory."

He pushed inside and she whimpered. Her pussy trembled around his thick girth in a way that promised the orgasm rushing toward her would be huge. "I'm going to come."

"Not yet." He shifted his hand and eased two fingers inside her, insistently stretching her. "Hold on to it for me."

"Knox." She fisted the comforter and moaned. "Please. It's so close."

"Oh, baby. So am I." The stretch in her ass increased and the ache between her legs escalated to a demanding pulse. "But I want to be right here when you go off. Want to be the one that makes you come this way the first time."

"Then do it." She'd meant it to sound more demanding, but it came out as a plea, her voiced as tight and ravaged as she felt. Sweat coated the back of her neck and the stretch of skin where his quads brushed the backs of her thighs. Every inch of her body quaked. Primed. Ready. *Wanting*.

Still pumping his shaft slow and methodically, he

eased his fingers free and he picked up the lube. "Do what, sweetheart?"

God, she didn't know whether to kill him or praise him. For all his devious machinations, he always knew exactly the right approach to push her to the very edge. To wring every last sensation from their play. But she wasn't without her own skills. Her own power. Which was exactly the point he'd set out to make. "Take that glorious cock and fuck my ass with it. Now."

The sound he made as his cock slipped free of her pussy and prodded her anus was pure primal predator. A barely leashed animal, hungry and intent on claiming its prey.

He drizzled more of the cold lube along her crevice and slicked it where he wanted it with his shaft. "Glorious, huh?" He tossed the bottle back to the bed and palmed both cheeks, fully exposing her for his perusal. Somehow just knowing his eyes were on her, watching as he prepared her, pushed her that much closer to the edge. Made her wish she could watch as well. "Can't deny you when you put it that way, can I?"

The fat head of him slipped past her tight ring and she whimpered, braced for the stretch and the burn.

"Easy." He smoothed one strong hand along the base of her spine, the gentle touch a stark contrast to the vise-like grip of his other on her hip. "Relax and let me give you what you want."

She let out a shaky breath and his shaft sunk deeper. Filling her. Claiming her in a way she didn't dare acknowledge.

"Perfect." A dark encouragement. Praise and temptation from her very own blond devil. "Slow and easy until you take it all."

His words moved through her, the subtle sub-context stirring possibilities she'd fought hard to ignore. To keep ideas of the future locked up tight until things were more stable between them.

But he was right. She trusted him. Physically. Emotionally. No matter what happened between them, he'd act with integrity. Honesty and openness.

And she wouldn't fight him.

Not in work. Not in sex. Not with her heart.

He slid to the hilt and her body sung with completeness. As if the physical connection served to confirm what her mind and emotions already accepted.

Holding himself in place, he squeezed her hips and ground out, "Talk to me."

"No talking." She moved what little she could within his unrelenting hold, reached back with one hand and dug her nails into his hips. "Please give me what I need."

He moved. Slow and shallow at first, but escalating quickly. Reading her response and building on it. Rolling his hips and driving inside her as though his only thought was to her pleasure. Her needs.

Pushing up on her forearms, she met each thrust, letting the foreign, but delicious contact sweep her deeper. Beyond thought. Beyond constraints or worry for the future. Beyond anything but right here and now and the impending explosion between them.

She slipped one hand between her legs, the light touch of her fingers against her throbbing clit almost painful. "I'm done waiting."

"Fuck. So goddamn greedy." With nothing short of a snarl, he fisted her hair, yanked her upright and collared her throat with one hand. With his other hand, he knocked her questing fingers out of his way, not once breaking the compelling rhythm of his cock inside her. "Oh, no you don't. This pussy's mine." He slicked his demanding fingers through her drenched folds and circled her clit. "When you come, it'll be because *I'm* the one that took you there."

He plunged two fingers deep and powered harder inside her ass, each stab commanding her to relent. To surrender.

And her body obeyed.

Her sex pulsing and clenching around his fingers. Muscles quivering with the onslaught of endorphins. Mind and soul drifting on a black velvet sky broken only by garnet, emerald and sapphire shards.

"Yes. Love it when you come. That's *mine*." He pumped once. Twice. Then plowed to the root and held himself deep, his cock jerking inside her. He buried his face at the crook of her neck and ground his hips against hers, his breath coming fast and hot against her skin. Despite the tension in his arms, he leisurely screwed his fingers in and out of her sex, drawing out her release with each precise stroke. "Mine because you trust me. Because what we've got works."

He was right. He'd proven it just as he said he would. But he was also a dominant man used to getting his way whenever he set his mind to it, and her past had already been impacted by too many men like him. If she took this step it would be because she chose it. On *her* time and no one else's.

Easing her so her torso was once more braced on the bed and him blanketing her, he gently swept her hair off her back and nuzzled the sweet spot at the base of her neck. Only when she'd fully relaxed and let out a soft sigh did he speak again. "You okay?"

Fabulous. Empowered and confident, and yet sheltered and protected, too. The combination was heady. Disconcerting and pleasant all at once. "I'll be sore, but it'll be the good kind," she murmured.

"There's a good kind?"

She shifted and peeked back at him. "I'll feel it, and I'll smile because I'll remember."

He grinned and nipped her shoulder, clearly pleased with her explanation. "How about if I run you a bath and you can soak for a bit before we call it a night?"

"I still have work to do."

"No, you don't."

"Knox—"

Still buried inside her, he rolled his hips and claimed her mouth to silence her. "You know this is right," he said after a long kiss. "Say yes, and I'll run you bath."

"Run me a bath and give me a week."

The calculating glint in his eyes reignited, and he skimmed his lips along her jawline. "Three days."

Stubborn, genius, beautiful man. "One week."

"Five."

Five days was reasonable. Especially considering she already knew her answer.

"And I want to ditch the condoms," he added before she could agree. "Whatever you need to be comfortable going there, I'm in. Zeke can test us, or we'll find someone else to do it."

Flutters rippled through her belly and the space behind her sternum swelled as though her heart had doubled in size. Just the thought of feeling him inside her like that—of feeling his slick release mingled with her own—nearly made her cave. "A bath now and five days for my answer, but we lose the condoms faster if we can."

He smiled huge, palmed the back of her head and pressed a triumphant kiss to her lips. "Then I guess I'd better get my butt in gear and get you a bath, because we've got a deal."

Chapter Twenty-Six

Knox scrolled through what felt like an endless list of log entries, the black text against his dimmed white background not even penetrating his otherwise occupied thoughts. The clock in the upper right-hand of his screen showed 3:23 p.m. A whopping five minutes later than the last time he'd checked the time and going nowhere fast. Kind of the same feeling as when he couldn't sleep and the night went on forever. Except instead of staring at the ceiling and thinking about everything from app ideas to possible data vulnerabilities, this time all he could think about was the answer Darya had promised him by the end of the day. Two more hours—three at most—before she'd let him know if she'd dump her skip tracing gigs and join his crew full time.

Shoving his mouse out of the way, he pushed back from his desk and stared out the thick tinted windows with a straight-line view of the busy street out front. Over two months, she'd poured herself into the training and opportunities he'd given her and made more ground in that short time than even the most gifted coders he'd worked with. To say that watching her devour information was a turn-on was the grossest of understatements. More like serving up napalm to a guy determined to dance in a bonfire. Add to that how things had gone between them on a personal level in the last month, and he was more determined than ever to tie her to him any and every way possible. *Now* he got why Jace had taken the tack he had with Vivienne. Hell, if he'd known then what he knew today, he'd have just packed her shit and moved her in with him on day one.

He sighed and dropped his head back on the top of his desk chair. She still hadn't shared about her past, though. She'd come close a few times, the far-off look on her face and the way she'd chewed her lower lip before she'd abruptly steered them into lighter territory the stuff of secrets dancing on the tip of her tongue. At least he assumed the past was what was on her mind. It damned well better not be their future.

A soft knock sounded on his door.

Knox jerked his head up, gaze shooting straight to the camera feed with a straight-on shot of his office door.

Well, speak of one very gorgeous devil.

He spun in his chair. "Yeah."

The knob turned slow and silent, like a burglar was on the other side of the door instead of the woman he was half out of his mind for. She poked her head through the opening. "Knox?"

"Sweetheart, you know you don't have to knock."

"But your door was closed. I thought maybe you were in the middle of something and didn't want to be interrupted."

He motioned to the door with a lift of his chin. "You shut and lock that door then we'll both be in the middle of something I don't want interrupted."

Her coy smile matched the pretty flush that swept

across her cheeks, but her hips swayed with natural sensuality as she drifted closer. "I thought we had a no-hands policy at work."

The second she was within grabbing distance, he snapped forward, grabbed her around the waist and tugged her into his lap. "Oh, we've got a no-hands policy all right. You promise no-hands on any man but me and I promise no-hands on any woman but you. Between the two of us, it's a free-for-all."

Her husky laughter was the stuff of wet dreams, a sensual rasp against his ears that fired all kinds of dirty thoughts. She cocked her head to one side and peeked playfully up at him through her soft lashes. "You sure you don't want to talk business?"

Instant. Focus.

"Are we talking something you're trying to work out code-wise, or long-term career plans?"

Her gaze slid to his chest where her fingers were pressed above his heart. "Long-term."

Thank Jesus. He probably could have made it to the end of the day, but if she was willing to bring things to a head early he might actually be able to get some much needed oxygen to his brain. "Well, then that depends. If you're going to give me the answer I want, then we can talk. If you're not, then we'll take a sidebar so I can spend extra time extolling the virtues of being my employee."

Her mouth quirked in an adorable smile. "Perhaps you should tell me about those virtues regardless."

"Sweetheart, I won't be *telling* you anything. I'll be showing you. Likely with your ass perched on the edge of my desk and your thighs around my hips."

One second. One infinitesimal second and her eyes

grew weighted. Her lips parted just a fraction, a welcome invitation he was halfway tempted to take regardless of how serious the root of their conversation was—or where he wanted it to lead. He palmed her hip and cradled her closer instead. "Say yes. The skip jobs don't pay you anywhere near what I can, let alone what you're worth. And you said from the get-go you didn't like the work."

She pressed her hand more firmly to his chest, as though seeking something to steady her.

He tightened his arms and lowered his voice. "Take the jump. Let me catch you."

"I already jumped," she whispered. "Months ago."

Pure pleasure fired through his veins, a high-octane rush that even some of his more dangerous exploits couldn't rival. "Is that a yes?"

She dipped her head, keeping her gaze on him.

"Good, then you won't mind if I push my luck while I'm at it."

Her lips pursed in a cute little mew. "You always push your luck."

Hell, yeah he did. Especially with the physical aspects to their relationship. He might be hesitant to voice the depth of everything he felt for her, but he had zero problem expressing it sexually. In the weeks since they'd settled into a routine bouncing back and forth between her place and his, he'd not only put her meager toy collection to good use, but had built a more sizable arsenal at his place. "Then you know you'd be wise to give in now. I'll get my way in the long run anyway."

"Give in to what?"

He swallowed hard, the magnitude of what he was about to propose the biggest step he'd taken to date. If she said yes, postponing a deeper conversation with his brothers wouldn't be an option anymore—whether she'd opted to share her past with him or not. "Move in with me."

For long, gut-wrenching seconds she sat motionless in his lap, so still it was hard to tell if her lungs were even working.

"We spend half our time at my place anyway," he said. "We can't do anything without your neighbors hearing and I don't have nearly the room I need to work you in the shower. Not to mention the place is a security nightmare."

"But what about Beckett?"

"What about him? He adores you. And outside of him inhaling the food before either of us can get to it and hogging the late-night television, we never see him." Except maybe that was the kicker. Maybe she wasn't big on the idea of co-habitating with another guy besides him. "Unless you want a place of our own," he tacked on. "We can leave him that floor and take on another one for us. I own half the building so we can do whatever we want. Or I can buy something—"

"Shhh." She pressed two fingers over his lips and smiled that soft smile that always made him wonder if she wasn't more angel than human. "I don't mind being with Beckett. I like your place. I just don't want to do something that would make him uncomfortable."

"You're kidding, right? Most of my better memories come from making Beckett uncomfortable. I'd just have a partner in crime this time." He cupped the side of her face and pulled her in for a kiss. "Seriously. Just think about it. No pressure."

She pulled away from his lips and cast an incredulous expression on him. "No pressure? From you?"

"Okay, maybe a little pressure. In fact, I vote we spend the night at your place tonight so I can spend adequate time pointing out everything that's wrong with it."

God, her smile was beautiful. Just as powerful and blazing as the August sunshine outside his window, but tinted with the cooler hues of a full moon. "Okay. My place tonight. And before I give you an answer, you have to promise me you'll talk with Beckett."

Oh, he'd talk to Beckett all right. Along with all the rest of his brothers. "I'll talk, but he'll be on board." He patted her hip and straightened in his chair. "Now, hop up and get your butt to work. I want us out of here before the sun goes down this time, and I haven't got half the shit done I need to."

She swiveled in his lap, but paused before she stood to lean in and study his screen. "You're working on something new?"

"No, combing through log files."

"That doesn't look like anything out of an application log file. Those look like websites and IP addresses."

He chuckled at the confused frown scrunching her face. "They're login hack attempts against one of our mail servers. I set up honeypots to draw nosier types away from the real stuff. When they try to access the data, it fires an auto-blocking trigger for their IP. Reviewing them is about as exciting as overnight infomercials, but I like to keep an eye out for persistent attempts."

She reached for the mouse, but paused just before wrapping her hand around it and glanced back. "Can I look?"

He shrugged. "Sure."

Eyes back to the screen, she scrolled from the top of the screen. "What's a honeypot?"

He couldn't help it. Not with her lobbing up such an easy one for him to swing at. He slipped his hands between her thighs and rubbed his finger along the center seam of her jeans. Looking back, talking her out of wearing those prim skirts and the easy access they provided was a serious misstep. "Well, this is one of my favorite ones."

She giggled, squirmed in his lap and batted his hand away. "That's not what I meant and you know it."

Sighing, he sat back and let her refocus on the long stream of text on the screen. "It's exactly what it sounds like. A diversion. A lure. I set out fake data and draw the people interested in nosing into our business there instead of to the good stuff. When they bite, I block 'em."

She nodded, but the motion seemed distracted. Her finger stilled on the mouse wheel and a subtle but very real tension held the rest of her locked in place.

Knox sat up and looked at the screen. "Something wrong?"

Releasing the mouse, she stood and took two shaky steps away from his desk. "No, I just…" She smoothed her hands against her hips and cleared her throat, stopping just short of meeting his gaze. Her smile was about as empty as they came. "I just don't know what any of it means."

Bullshit. Not once in the time he'd known her had he ever got the feeling she'd lied to him.

Until now.

Maybe it was more avoidance than an outright falsehood, but it still stung. He'd given her everything.

Knocked down barriers he'd never even considered dismantling for anyone else, and she couldn't even give him this? He stood, tempted to prowl closer, cage her against the wall and demand answers. Instead, he fought it. He'd already told her he wanted her past and more than anything he wanted to earn it. To know she trusted him enough to give it. Still, if what she'd seen had shaken her this bad, he needed to know. "What did you see?"

She swallowed huge and her gaze slid to the screen behind him. "There was a word—*Koschei*." Just uttering the term made her face blanch.

He turned, leaned into his desk and scrolled through the list. "Yeah, what about it?"

"It's probably nothing."

Having isolated the line she'd called out, he highlighted the text, pasted it off on a separate document and scowled back over his shoulder. "You look like the boogeyman just flashed a heinous set of nuts on my computer. Don't tell me it's nothing. What's it mean?"

"It's a figure from Slavic folklore. Koschei is…" She circled one hand and her gaze grew distant, as though scrambling for the right mix of words to convey her thoughts. "Deathless." Her gaze sharpened and she locked stares with Knox. "He cannot be killed because his soul is kept separate from his body."

Knox straightened. "So, it's the folklore that shook you?"

Pain flashed behind her eyes, and for a second he thought she'd deflect with some bullshit excuse as she had minutes before. "No."

Fuck distance. Fuck waiting and worrying and everything else that came in between it. He stalked to her and wrapped her up close. "Whatever it is, just tell me. I can't fix what I don't know."

"You can't fix this," she whispered. Her attention slid to the screen then back to him. "Maybe it's nothing. I hope it's nothing. But you deserve the truth."

Finally.

"Okay. Good." He hugged her tighter and kissed the top of her head. "Let's shut down. We'll get out of here early and just chill at your house."

She pressed her hands against his chest and pulled back to meet his gaze. "No, you finish your work. We'll do our normal routine and talk tonight. Okay?"

An uncomfortable prickle danced down the back of his neck. Whatever thoughts were moving through her nimble head, he had a pretty good idea he wouldn't like them. Still, if she needed him to wait two more fucking hours, he'd give them to her. Then he'd make sure the demons from her past never darkened her thoughts again.

Chapter Twenty-Seven

A tear splattered on the back of Darya's hand, the helpless tremor that shook her arms sending it careening to the mound of clothes in her open suitcase. Since the day she'd watched her mother walk away, she'd known the day would come when she'd have to make her own sacrifice. Had known she'd only upped her debt against the universe when Yefim and JJ had been delivered to aid her once more.

Today was the day to pay that price.

She dashed the back of her hand across each cheek and forced her legs to keep from crumbling. At most she had ten minutes to gather her wits and be ready for Knox. Probably less given the clipped delivery when he'd called demanding to know why she'd left before him.

Fear far more potent than the prospect of the days that lay ahead lanced straight through her, the mere thought of what her actions would do to further destroy his trust nearly crippling in their power. He'd never forgive her. Never. And how could she blame him? She'd not only broken her promise to him, but would give him a fresh new layer of emotional brick to hide his heart behind.

She crammed in the last of her most essential clothes and jerked the straps to cinch them down tight.

The door chunked open and her heart punched so hard it hurt.

"Darya?" An urgent call. One filled with worry as well as anger. His quick footsteps sounded through the living room.

A cold sweat broke out against her skin, and no matter how hard she tried, she couldn't steady the ragged breaths chuffing out of her chest.

When he spoke again, his voice was as ragged as her own, the tone more of an accusation than a question. "What are you doing?" he said from behind her.

She forced herself to turn and nearly buckled at the stark vulnerability on his face. His attention wasn't on her, but on the three suitcases waiting on the bed. "I have to go." In that second, she'd have done anything to draw the words back. To rewind the last four weeks and take them slower. To savor every single second and not waste a moment on sleep. She'd thought she understood what JJ had meant about living, but now she understood. Really understood the meaning of loss.

"This has to do with what you saw in the log files." It was a confirmation, not a question.

She nodded. "Yes." She braced her hand on the open suitcase, needing something—*anything* to keep her upright and steady. "I checked the IP address. It's from Russia."

He inched cautiously into the room. "Sixty percent of our hack attacks come from Russia. That doesn't mean anything."

"It does when the name Koschei is tied to them."

His eyes narrowed, a predator who'd just watched his

prey take a full step into its trap. "That why you ducked out early and logged into our security apps remotely?"

Of course, he'd know. What Knox didn't glean from physically watching through the cameras mounted in every nook and cranny of his office, he monitored electronically through logins and God only knew how many code traps. She swallowed hard, hating the sludge of betrayal tossing in her stomach. "I wanted to believe it was a coincidence. I left early to think about what I wanted to say. How to share my past. On the way home I remembered the recordings. I thought looking would help calm my nerves. Help me realize I was probably overthinking things."

"And?"

"I wasn't overthinking things."

In a flash, his expression shifted. Raw fury eradicating any trace of fear or loss. "Show me."

The force of his directive jolted her into action, sending her on unsteady feet to the company laptop still poised on her dresser. It took three tries to enter her password, his scalding presence licking fire against her back. The second her password took, the screen displayed the frame she'd left the footage on. She pointed to a parking lot across the street and a cable company worker walking toward his truck. His dark hair was short and a well-trimmed beard covered his jawline. His eyes were covered with mirrored sunglasses. "This is wrong."

Knox leaned in closer. "You're packing your shit and running because a cable guy was caught on tape across the street from where I work?" He straightened and looked her in the eye, an incredulous fire burning behind his gray gaze. "Are you out of your mind?"

"He's not a cable worker, Knox. Look at him." She tapped the screen again. "Have you ever seen a cable worker wear coveralls? In August? And where are his tools? He has none. Never took any out of the van with him. In fact, all he ever did was disappear out of the camera's range for a short time."

A trace of comprehension seemed to register and she'd swear he stopped breathing.

Darya zoomed in the image. "I almost missed it, but once I looked closer, this made it certain." She pointed to the man's hand. A half monster, half man was tattooed on the back of it. "This is Koschei and the men who serve him all wear it."

"You said it was folklore."

"It is, but the man who is after me took the moniker for his own. He believes he cannot die. Believes he's invincible. And he wants me."

"Like a hit? Retribution? What?"

She met his stare and tried to swallow, the harshness of her reality stealing any moisture from her tongue. Never in a million years would she forget the way Ruslan had looked at her. She couldn't let him get her, but more than that, she couldn't let him hurt Knox. "No, he wants *me*."

She wasn't sure what she expected. More arguments, maybe. Or an elevation of simmering rage he'd already displayed. Instead a fierce determination slipped into place. Indomitable, resolute conviction. "He can want all goddamn day, but he can't have you."

Ice-cold terror cracked and splintered through her veins. "Knox, you don't know what this man is like. I promised you that first day my past would only come for me. Only I didn't know how things would end up between us. If Ruslan has so much as an inkling you and I are together, he'll kill you. Possibly hurt the other people you love just to make a point. I have to go and I need to do it quickly so I draw him away from you. From all of you."

"You really fucking think I'm letting you walk out that door? You think I'd let you throw away what we're building?" He inched closer, his voice deadly steady. "Sweetheart, I wouldn't leave an employee hanging out in a situation like this, let alone the woman who's sleeping full time in my bed."

Every scrap of frustration, anger and fear she'd buried since the day she'd escaped Russia surged in one unforgiving burst. "He'll kill you. Don't you get it?"

He opened his mouth.

Before he could speak, she cut him off. "Three people have given for me. Sacrificed so I could have a life. They did that because they loved me and now it's my turn. Do I want to leave? No. The last thing I want to do is be away from you, but I will not let Ruslan hurt the man I love or his family. *Ever.*"

One second.

That was all it took and the tension in Knox shifted. Where the air around him had practically sparked with aggression and untamed ferocity, now it hummed with a supercharged focus centered squarely on her. His voice was tightly leashed, a powder keg of emotion compacting his quiet words. "You love me?"

So vulnerable. A rawness she knew without a shadow of doubt he gave only to her. She cupped the side of his face and drew in his woodsmoke and black currant scent deep into her lungs, willing it to imprint deep for the lonely days and nights to come. "Another boundary I crossed, I know. But how could I not? You're you."

Faster than she'd ever seen him move, he jerked her against him. His arms banded around her, coiled unmovable steel pinning her flush against his chest. Fingers tangled in her hair, he held her cheek above his heart while his heart beat a frantic rhythm beneath her ear.

God, she'd miss him. Their physical connection for sure, but more than that, his mind and staggering capacity for goodness. No one within Knox's sphere wanted for anything. Not if he could help it. Especially her. Because whether he realized it or not, he'd given her the world just by being him.

She pressed her hands against his chest, but his hold wouldn't budge. "Knox, I have to go. If he finds you with me..." A shudder racked her from head to toe, the horrid stories gleaned from her days working with Yefim stirring unwelcome images in her mind. "Please," she muttered. "If something happened to you or your family, I could never forgive myself."

His arms loosened only enough to let him soothingly stroke her spine and lay a sweet kiss to the top of her head. He chuckled low, the beautiful sound completely incongruent with the moment, but beautiful all the same. "The guys were right. I should have just claimed you right out of the chute."

This time when she pushed against him, he gave her enough play to meet his gaze. "Claim me? What's that supposed to mean?"

His smile was pure confidence laced with wickedness. "Exactly what it sounds like. That you're mine. You, your past *and* your future."

She fisted her hands in his T-shirt, the faded red fabric so soft it was a wonder it didn't tear behind her brutal grip. "Didn't you hear me? I have to go."

"I heard you. Though, if I'd listened to my brothers four weeks ago, you'd know by now our women don't *sacrifice* anything for us. They live how they want. Free. Without fear. And that happens because we have the means and the fortitude to obliterate any threat to their happiness, no matter where that threat comes from."

"Knox—"

"No." Knox dipped close. His deep voice reverberated through her, a thundering vow delivered with an assassin's stealth. "I don't know who Ruslan is or what he wants with you, but your days of running are over. We're going to close those suitcases, get them *and* you in my car, and then you're going to give me the whole damned backstory while I take you home."

More than anything she wanted to do just that. To give way and let yet another person protect and shield her from the ugliness of her past. "I can't do that. Think of your mothers. Vivienne, Natalie and Gabe. Or worse, Levi. If Ruslan can't get to me, he'll use them."

Knox dropped his hands, slow as though he'd had to force the action, then stepped back. "I don't think you understand." He turned for the bed and coiled his hand around the handle of one packed suitcase. "The only place you're going is with me."

Chapter Twenty-Eight

Fifteen minutes and a string of continued arguments later, Darya was in the passenger seat of Knox's car. The top was up and the music down, both completely outside the norm compared to other times she'd ridden beside him. He'd also been frustratingly tight-lipped. Where long stretches of silence between the two of them were normally filled with comfort—two busy minds working silently yet seamlessly in parallel—this time the quiet made her fidget.

As if he sensed her discomfort, he shifted to the next gear then coiled his hand around one of hers fisted in her lap. "Whatever you're worrying about, let it go. I've got this."

She opened her mouth to argue, but closed it just as fast at the warning look he shot her.

With one last encouraging squeeze, he released her hand and plucked his phone from the center console. In the last four weeks, she'd rarely seen him use the device while he drove, but when he did, he used every hands-free feature available. This time, he turned off the Bluetooth and anchored the phone between his ear and shoulder.

"Hey," he said to whoever answered, checking his

rearview mirror. "Need you to reroute family night from Haven to our place and call rally. Darya's in trouble and I'm not leaving her."

So it was Beckett. Not surprising, really. For men who weren't actually born from the same womb it was shocking how close they were. Shocking, but beautiful.

"Yeah, it's *that* rally, but I need all hands on deck. If what Darya says is true, we need the women and Levi, too. Too risky to have them exposed until we have a plan." He paused long enough to let Beckett get a word in edgewise then glanced at her. "No details yet, but by the time we get there I'll have them. We need a sweep of the loft, though. The office, too. Darya found footage of a guy she says works for the goon who's after her outside our building. If they got that close we have to assume the worst and check for bugs."

Her lungs hitched and the choking bile she'd swallowed down since finding the damning footage pitched violently in her stomach. She hadn't thought about bugs. What if Ruslan had managed to plant them in her apartment? If he'd heard what she's shared with Knox, he'd kill Knox for sure.

Knox's gaze slid to each side mirror, the focus he put into the action more attentive than what was necessary for seven-thirty traffic on a Wednesday night. "Nope, no tail visible yet, but I'm taking the scenic route home just in case. Make sure the guys know to arm up. I might not know all the finer points, but the men we're dealing with aren't amateurs." He listened for a second, nodded at whatever Beckett had said and answered back. "Right. Got it."

He thumbed off the connection and tossed the device back to its place below the dash. "Beckett's changing up the protocols in the building. Security guards will be in place within the hour and camera ranges extended."

"Knox—"

"Sweetheart, if you start in with how I don't have to do this again, I'll tie you down the second we get home and fuck you until you forget how to speak altogether."

She sucked in a sharp gasp. Her body might be weighted and fatigued from the prolonged adrenaline rush, but her sex clenched and fluttered at the promise.

He chuckled and glanced over his shoulder, checking the lane to his left. "If I'd have known that was the way to distract you, I'd have leveraged sex thirty minutes ago." Settled in the HOV lane, he poured on the gas and wrapped his hand back around hers. "Now, spill. Who's Ruslan? What's he want?"

Countless times in the last month she'd thought about how to share what had brought her here. Had dress-rehearsed all kinds of scenarios and dialogue in preparation for this moment. Now that she needed to put voice behind them, they dried up.

He scowled at the road and squeezed the steering wheel so tight his knuckles turned white. Despite his open frustration, he kept the hand around her own gentle. "I've got a full tank of gas and can keep us moving for a good four hours before I have to stop, so you might as well get it out."

"It's not that I don't want to tell you. I just don't know where to start."

His thumb smoothed back and forth against her knuckles. "You went to school. What happened after that?"

Right. The beginning was easy enough. She opened her hand and laced her fingers with his. "I studied business in school and did well in my studies. Well enough one of my instructors shared my name with a man named Yefim Mishin. He hired me as a personal assistant."

He nodded like the news wasn't exactly a surprise to him. "If you studied business, why take a PA job? Why not something with more meat to it?"

"Oh, there was plenty of meat when it came to working with Yefim. As his assistant, I was with him constantly. Was included in every meeting and traveled with him extensively. And while I was rarely a voice in those meetings, I learned much by watching him work. It was a very coveted position. One I was not only blessed to be offered, but eagerly accepted."

"He treated you good?"

She smiled down at her lap, memories of the days before all hell had broken loose drifting in like a soft morning breeze. "He was like a second father to me. Indulgent in the extreme. Not only was I compensated more than others might be in a similar role, he mentored me. Took the time to review the nuances of each meeting and strategic move he made."

"And?"

Outside the car's windshield, the sun crept toward the horizon, not a single cloud to mar the orange and indigo ahead of them. A far different view than the dark ominous fog rolling through her memories. "And one day he took me someplace he shouldn't have."

Knox kept his silence for a moment, the same narrowed focus he always aimed at his screen when attacking troublesome code marking his face. "What kind of business was he in?"

"Not one business. Many businesses. Have you ever heard the term *oligarch*?"

He frowned at that, but kept his eyes on the road. "Top businessmen in Russia, right?"

She nodded. "A small number of entrepreneurs accumulated much wealth under Gorbachev. Yefim served as the closest advisor to one of these men. But he also was an associate of Anton Fedorov." She paused long enough to suck in a tight breath. "Anton is *mafiya*."

Surprisingly, the word didn't ruffle him as much as she'd expected. Beyond a slight lift of his eyebrows, he seemed utterly unperturbed. More like she'd told him an unexpected cold front was predicted to blow. "And this Ruslan guy who's after you works for Anton?"

Darya shook her head. "Anton is very traditional *bratva*. A *pakhan*, or boss, who lives the old life of *vory v zakone*. But as an advisor to Anton, Yefim was called to negotiate with another family. Their *pakhan*, Ruslan Sokolov, is reckless. Power-hungry. So much so, he killed his own mentor and assumed his place. His business deals often drew attention Anton and the other *pakhans* detested. Yefim was sent to negotiate boundaries."

"So, Ruslan and Anton are rivals."

"Yes."

Knox glanced over his right shoulder, shifted quickly at the HOV interchange all the way to the far right lane and took an upcoming exit at top speed. His gaze locked on to his rearview mirror, watching for anyone to repeat the unexpected exit. "So, you went with Yefim to negotiate. Did you do something to piss this Ruslan guy off?"

"No." She focused on his hand curled around the

gearshift. The lazy yet powerful confidence as he shifted from one gear to the next. Right now, she'd give a lot for that hand to be back in hers, holding her steady. "I didn't anger him. I caught his attention."

Knox whipped his head toward her, his attention lingering uncomfortably long considering how fast he steered them down the access road. "You're telling me you had to run from a guy because he wants you?"

"I don't think you understand how things work with men like Ruslan. Traditional Russian men are possessive. More primitive in the way they approach women than Americans are."

He cocked one eyebrow high. "Are you the same woman who's been in bed with me for the last month? Because I'm thinking most of what we've done belongs in the primitive category."

Leave it to Knox to draw a smile from her at the most frightening of times. "Yes. What we have is quite primal. Carnal." Her smile slipped. "But you've always given me a choice. There would be no choice with Ruslan."

He might have been calm before, even blasé at the mention of organized crime, but with her explanation Knox's face hardened with unforgiving fury. "You're telling me he'd just…what? Own you?"

She slowly dipped her head and her voice dropped, her mind instinctively treating the rest as though it were the gravest secret. "Men like Ruslan do not ask for what they want. They take by whatever means they need to get it."

Knox held his silence. Despite his eyes on the road and the uninterrupted navigation through the light traffic, there was no question she held all of his attention.

"Ruslan made his desire for me well known," she said. "I knew what that meant and the life it would result in for me. So did Yefim. That's why he helped me escape. He used his ties to Anton to procure me false identification to get me in the United States and staged an assault. The plan was that Yefim would be found unconscious, and I would be missing. Anton's people were to provide an unidentifiable body that would be presumed to be me."

"Did it work?"

"I don't know. I couldn't contact Yefim without potentially revealing my existence and putting him at risk, but after I assumed JJ's identity, I believed I was safe."

Knox zipped into an alley, drove to the far end of the warehouses on either side and whipped a hard right. Directly in front of them was the underground entrance to their loft's garage. Stationed next to the gate normally only controlled by card readers was a big man in a plain black T-shirt and black cargo pants holding an electronic tablet. With one look at Knox's car, the man activated the gate and nodded.

In another thirty seconds, they slid into Knox's reserved spot. As soon as he killed the engine, silence engulfed them. He shifted in his chair. "I get that you're scared, but I want you to listen and really hear me. You're safe. No more running."

"Knox, Ruslan is dangerous. He has no conscience. No honor."

"So?"

Needing the contact, she placed her hand on his forearm and squeezed. "You do."

Either he was certifiably insane or truly comfortable with the nastiness she'd brought into his life, because he smiled. Genuinely smiled. "Yeah, I've got honor. So do my brothers. But only when it's deserved. We can and will play dirty if it means keeping our own safe. And I don't give a shit how much muscle this Ruslan dick throws around—I'm a wily fucker when I want to be and right now I've got a shitload of incentive."

"Why?"

"Why what?"

"Why the incentive? I told you the best thing for everyone is for me to leave and draw them away from you and your family."

In a blink, his hand was curled around her nape and his face close enough to hers his breath whispered warm against her skin. "You love me?"

She nodded, barely capable of even that much behind the intensity in his gaze.

His fingers tightened against her skin. "No woman outside my family has ever said that to me. If you think I'm gonna let anyone even think about hurting the first woman who does, you are very much mistaken." Closing what remained of the distance between them, he pressed a firm kiss to her lips then eased away only enough to murmur, "Now, unbuckle and get ready to hop out. In case you missed it, four of my brothers and their broods are already here and waiting on us."

The comment jolted her from the pleasant cocoon his powerful words had created. Sure enough, the spaces that were usually empty around his and Beckett's slots were full—one massive silver truck, a classic '69 Camaro, an eggplant-colored Chevelle and a candy apple red convertible Corvette. Translation: Trevor, Danny, Zeke and Beckett. "They're here already?"

Phone stashed in his back pocket, Knox popped

opened the glove box. If there'd been a snake coiled up and ready to strike inside, she couldn't have been more surprised than she was seeing the holstered gun inside. He grabbed it, slipped the gun free and checked the safety. "Family doesn't lollygag when you need them. My guess is Axel and Jace aren't far behind." He popped his car door. "You wait there."

Like she could have done anything but sit in stunned silence.

Knox has a firearm?

On one hand, the idea wouldn't jibe, but another more instinctive part of her settled into the concept easily. After all, Knox was Knox. Yes, he'd pushed her relentlessly from the very first, but he'd also demonstrated a protective streak. And not just with her, but with everyone in his life. The fact that he'd be willing to extend that level of protection to a more dangerous level shouldn't surprise her at all.

Her door chunked open and Knox stepped in close, his hand extended to help her out. "Come on, sweetheart. I'll come back for your bag after we get you situated." He didn't say as much, but there was an undercurrent of *when you're not in anyone's line of fire* woven into his words.

Tension and overdrive-awareness riddled their trip to the top floor, even the air supercharged with an invisible current. Nothing at all like the playful banter and teasing touches they'd shared on previous nights coming home from work together. Instead, he corralled her to one corner, braced himself in front of her and activated the fifth floor via the biometric scanner. Only when the doors opened to their loft, did his shoulders relax a fraction. He stepped out of her way, splayed his hand low on her back and motioned her toward the private landing.

From behind the thick steel door, Levi's laughter rang out, followed by the abrupt zing of a power drill.

Knox dug out his keys, but before he could find the one he wanted, the door swung open.

Keeping one hand on the doorknob, Danny stepped back enough to bring a good chunk of the loft's main room into view. He motioned over his shoulder to Beckett and the gorgeous black man with dreads she'd met at the concert. Both were perched on ladders and hanging what had to be at least a fifty-inch flat screen on the wall where a beautiful landscape had been. Five other flat screens just like it were already in place. "You got here just in time. We've almost got the surveillance feeds hooked up. If you don't want bank vault locks and retina scanners on the front door, you better jump in now, 'cause Beckett's got a security threat boner."

As if he'd just realized she was there, Danny shot her his huge and totally disarming smile, leaned in and kissed her cheek. "Welcome home, sweet cheeks."

Four other men she didn't recognize strode into view, all of them dressed in the same black cargo and T-shirt combo the men outside the gate had worn and hefting everything from tools to computer wire. "Who are they?"

"They're on Beckett's crew," Danny said before Knox could. "Mine's working the perimeter."

Knox urged her into the bustling room. "How much longer 'til we're ready to go online?"

"Already are," Beckett said, proving that he was one hundred percent aware of everything going on around him despite having his hands full. He glanced over his shoulder and jerked his head toward the computers set up on the previously ignored dining room table. "Got all the feeds piped in first. Saw you pull in." His gaze shifted to Darya and he winked. "Hey, sassy."

Levi's bright voice shot from the open kitchen. "You're here!"

At his words, Trevor, Natalie, Zeke and Gabe all turned their attention on Darya. Unlike the rest of the people in the room, they'd made themselves at home around the giant island, Trevor and Zeke casually enjoying a beer while Nat and Gabe futzed over what looked like a snack tray.

She braced, expecting a frigid blast of frowns or glares.

One by one, her presence registered in their gazes, but it wasn't anger that burned behind them. It was the same, friendly greeting they always offered.

Well, expect for Trevor. He actually did frown, but aimed it at Knox beside her. "Jesus, brother. What route did you take to get here? We drove all the way from Haven and still beat you."

Not the least bit daunted by the wires strung all directions or the chaos around him, Levi hustled their direction, his boots loud on the concrete floors. "Isn't this cool? Uncle Beckett said he'd teach me how to use all his cool gadgets after he gets everything set up."

"Uncle Beckett's smokin' crack." Knox ruffled Levi's head and steered Darya toward the kitchen with a hand between her shoulder blades. "Anything with an electrical current is mine. He's just in charge of muscle. You wanna know how stuff works, you come to me."

Knox peeled Darya's purse off her shoulder and tossed it on the kitchen counter like it was any other normal night instead of one where they were bracing for lockdown.

Natalie waved toward the snacks they'd laid out on the island and headed for the fridge. "Grab something to eat. You want anything to drink?"

"Beer for me." Knox kissed her cheek and squeezed her shoulder. "I'm gonna check the feeds real quick. Have a seat and settle in. Grab something to eat."

Have a seat.

Settle in.

Grab something to eat.

Completely relaxed. No different than the other occasions they'd gotten together as a family except that this time the security was escalating to Fort Knox. No matter how much she wanted her mind to do something useful and offer up an explanation, it wouldn't budge. Nor would her feet, incredulous wonder keeping her locked in place.

"You okay?" Levi said.

She surfaced from her dumbfounded stupor to find Levi clutching her hand and Zeke beside her. Except the man on her right wasn't the patient and kind brother she'd come to know over the last several weeks. This was the doctor, his narrowed and assessing gaze roving her face.

"You're not mad?" She hadn't meant to ask it. Hadn't even really realized the fear she'd walked into the room with until her subconscious had set forth the question, but now that she had, she *really* wanted to know the answer.

Zeke's mouth crooked in a goofy grin. "Are you kidding? If someone in our family hadn't done something to perk things up soon, I'd have had to start doling out antidepressants." He looped an arm around her neck and motioned Levi toward the food. "Load her up, Levi. Doctor's orders."

"Right," Levi said with the single-minded focus she'd come to appreciate in the little boy. "Food fixes everything."

Trevor snickered and lifted his beer off the counter. "Well, it will for another year or two, then you'll find another delightful mood fixer."

Natalie popped the top off Knox's beer and scowled at Trevor. "Cut it out."

"It's okay, Mom. It's just sex."

Gabe and Zeke did their best not to let it out, but their chests both shook on a rich chuckle.

"What's so funny?" Knox said as he came up behind her.

Natalie handed Knox a beer and pursed her mouth in a rueful mew. "Trev's been bonding with Levi over the birds and the bees, and Gabe and Zeke are earning some serious karmic debt giggling about it."

Knox eyeballed Levi, total seriousness. "Remember what I said about coming to me for electronics?"

"Yeah."

"Same goes for sex."

"Don't listen to him, kid," Zeke said. "I'm the one with a medical degree. I know how it all really works. Especially the important parts."

Just when Natalie looked like she was about to grab Zeke and Knox by the ears and kick them out of the loft, the front door opened to a chorus of boisterous voices.

"Sorry we're late!" Sylvie bellowed, her arms full of grocery bags.

Ninette and Vivienne were equally loaded down

right behind her, while Jace and Axel brought up the rear. "Only woman I know who thinks a store run is mission-critical in a crisis situation," Axel grumbled, though his eyes danced with mirth.

Already halfway to the kitchen, Sylvie handed off her bags to Danny while Jace locked up the front door. "I've seen what these boys keep in their refrigerator. If we're holing up until we get a decent plan for whatever's going on, I'm not doing it without something to satisfy my stomach."

And that was that. In seconds, Sylvie had commandeered the kitchen and set all the women to different tasks. The men gathered round the makeshift control center on the dining room table, their voices low and attention zeroed in on the screens now lit up with every view of the building. The only person dazed and motionless in the room was her.

Ninette moved in beside her and motioned to the untouched plate Levi had left on the counter in front her. "Are you saving yourself for Sylvie's cooking, or is the general idea of food not something you're up for right now?"

One glance at the white ceramic plate and anyone would guess a child had prepared it. Only one cursory carrot, a celery stick and three red grapes sat isolated in one spot. The rest of the space was loaded with three different kinds of cheese cubes, crackers and Nacho Cheese Doritos.

Such an amazing gift. Levi's open kindness as genuine and unshaken as the reception she'd received from everyone else. Three times she'd had amazing people go above and beyond to help her. This time she had a whole team of guardian angels.

She lifted her gaze to the other women working in the kitchen, then slid her attention to the men. "I can't ever repay this," she said so quietly only Ninette could hear. "Ever. Not what they're doing. Not how everyone has treated me. None of it. It's too much."

Just as softly, Ninette answered back. "What makes you think we'd want repayment?"

It was a good question. One she'd never really contemplated before. Only knew how many times she'd been blessed and wanted desperately to share what she'd been given with someone else.

Ninette moved in tight beside her and slid her arm around Darya's waist. Together they watched the men as they worked, their low voices rumbling in a comforting cadence that somehow anchored all the activity in the room. "I'm not sure where you got the idea there's some karmic tally being kept, but to my mind, family doesn't work that way. Especially not ours." She paused long enough to dip her head toward Knox front and center with his fingers flying over the keyboard. "But if you're worried about payback, then take a good look at my boy and think about this. I've seen him happier the last many weeks than the whole six years I've known him. He's always been funny, but I've never seen him free. Not the way he is with you. So, if you ask me, any repayment's been made a hundred times over."

She met Darya's stunned stare head-on, jerked her head toward the island and winked. "Now, get your plate and plant your ass on a bar stool. If you need a stiff drink, I'll pour you one, but I'll be damned if I'm the last one who gets to hear all the sordid details of why we're on lockdown."

Chapter Twenty-Nine

The last straggler from Beckett's install crew closed the door behind him, leaving only Knox's family safe within the loft. For the last thirty minutes, Knox, Danny and Beckett had tweaked camera angles throughout the building via remote access controls on their computers, each man seated next to each other at the massive dining room table they'd finally found a use for.

Lined up on the opposite side with their backs to the row of six flat screen monitors, Jace, Axel, Trevor and Zeke looked surprisingly calm for the curveball Knox had thrown on family night. Despite all the chaos buzzing around them and the lack of information as to why Beckett was pulling out all the stops, not a one of them had pushed for answers.

Now that the coast was clear, they were about to get an earful. It also meant he was one step closer to having logistics over and done with and Darya next to him again.

On his left, Danny waited until the elevator doors closed on the install crew then nodded. "They're clear."

"Good." Knox twisted to see Beckett ambling back from a trip to the fridge with a fresh Bud in hand. Levi and the women were gathered round the island well behind him. "You checked for bugs, right?"

Beck chuckled and slid into his chair next to Knox. "Ninette's been draggin' details out of Darya for the last thirty minutes. Even with her sly references to cover what they were talking about from Levi and keepin' their voices low when outsiders were close, you think I'd let them talk if I hadn't swept the place first thing?"

So, he'd caught the same bits and pieces Knox had. Which meant the rest of his brothers probably had as well.

Sure enough, Jace leaned into the table and braced both his forearms on the dark-stained wood. "All right, brother. Break it down. What the hell's going on?"

"In a nutshell? Some jackass in the Russian mob named Ruslan Sokolov is after Darya."

Jace stared at Knox another beat, scanned the row of computers on the table, then glanced at the screens on the wall. "I take it the fact that you've got this place locked up tighter than the White House means things between you and Darya have shifted?"

"Oh, they've shifted all right. She's mine."

Axel chuckled and Beckett scoffed a classic *I told you so*. The rest of the guys shared a mix of knowing grins and eye rolls.

Jace just twirled his ever-present toothpick, the look on his face a mix between humor and pride. "Gotta say, when you go down, you go big. Care to share when you ramped from taking things slow to a quarter mile sprint?"

"About a nanosecond after I found her with her bags packed and ready to bolt."

Beckett's head whipped from the screen he'd been

looking at to Knox, the surprise on his face no different than if Knox had pulled a gun on him. "What?"

Despite the volume behind Beckett's question, the women kept on with their chatter, only Darya's gaze sliding to the men with a touch of curiosity.

Knox cast what he hoped was a reassuring smile her direction then refocused on his brothers. "Apparently, me sleeping with her makes me not only an automatic target, but a fluorescent one with landing lights pointed to it." He couldn't give a shit less about being a target, but remembering the punch that had come with seeing her bags packed on her bed kicked his heart up to an uncomfortable rhythm. "I love my family. With what she says this guy is capable of and the risk it could bring down on everyone else, it might have been safer if I'd let her go, but I can't." He scanned his brothers. "She's mine and I'm keeping her."

"Now, there's a lad who knows his mind," Axel said. He looked to Jace. "I'll back his play."

Beckett reclined against his seat back. "Took him long enough, but I'm in."

"Hell, yeah," Trevor said.

Zeke lifted his Bohemia Weiss. "Then the taken men officially outweigh the free agents, 'cause I'm in, too."

Danny twisted in his chair enough to lean one elbow on the table and met Knox's gaze head on. "If I vote yes, does this mean your little black book's up for grabs? If it does, you get my vote."

"Not thinkin' Darya'd let me within a city block of any woman I'd even thought about sleeping with, so yeah." He crossed his arms on his chest. "Although, I'm a little incensed you'd think I'd actually store the names and numbers of phenomenal hookups on paper."

Jace huffed out a low laugh. "Well, I'm not gonna say no to Knox nabbing himself a good woman, so aside from passing down Knox's top ten list, that only leaves one more thing to deal with." He locked gazes with Knox. "Tell us more about the Russian jackass we've gotta take out to get our girl safe."

For the next twenty minutes Knox did just that, rehashing the same details Darya had haltingly shared with him on the ride to the loft. How she'd caught Ruslan's attention. About her job with Yefim and how he'd used his ties with another *mafiya* family to help her escape to the US. How she'd tied the name Koschei and the security footage outside their building together and realized Ruslan was closing in.

"And she thinks this Ruslan guy would stoop to leveraging one of us to draw her out if necessary?" Trevor asked Knox.

"She was certain of it. Said he was cutthroat enough to whack his own boss to take over the family."

"Greedy," Danny said under his breath. "If he's ballsy enough to take that route, a woman or kid wouldn't even be a blip on his conscience."

"Nope," Beckett agreed.

Zeke nodded as well. "Makes sense to keep an eye on the women, but if you knew you were gonna claim her, I don't get why you came here. Yeah, you've got more gizmos and gadgets and a whole slew of new screens to keep an eye on things, but we've got a hell of a lot more room at Haven."

He'd thought about that. Had even started to point his car toward 75 North the second he'd pulled out of Darya's parking lot, but his instincts had taken over and steered him home. She belonged with him. Someplace where he not only knew every nook and cranny, but had eyes on them, too. Not to mention a host of escape routes and easy cover.

Axel chuckled and answered before Knox could wrap words around his thoughts. "Yeah, he's not budging on that one. Gonna be a while before the caveman lets his new prize out of his bed. Doesn't mean the rest of us can't spread out at Haven. Sends the wrong message for us to all be cooped up under one roof anyway."

"Right," Jace said. "Best way to tip our hand is to let on we know we're being watched by huddling under one roof. Better we split up tonight and make it look like it was just a family get together on the off chance you didn't catch their tail. The women and Levi can bunk with me, Axel, Trevor and Zeke at Haven. Danny, Beckett, Knox and Darya can stay here."

"That's not gonna fly with the moms and you know it," Axel said. "You saw the haul they brought in from the store. Darya's their new little chick. If she doesn't go to Haven with the rest of the women, those groceries aren't comin' out of the cabinets and their butts will be right here making sure she's got their kind of support until this shite is over."

Damn, but he liked that. Not just the fact that the women who'd all but adopted him approved of the woman he'd chosen for his own, but that Darya would finally have the maternal support she'd lost way too early in life.

"We can make that work," Beckett said. "Got a corner loft open right beneath Knox's suite that Danny and I can use to crash in when we need to. Ninette and Sylvie can have my rooms since this floor's secured."

"Think it's smart all of us stay visible, too," Trevor

said. "The idea of the women and Levi being exposed rubs me wrong, though."

"So, we limit the exposure," Zeke said. "If they go out without us, they do it only with backup."

"Well, we've got plenty of that," Beckett said. "I'll rearrange schedules and make sure our top guys are freed up for family detail when we need it."

Fighting the need to get up and pace, Knox snatched one of three pens he'd tossed to the table while unpacking his laptop and twirled it between his fingers. "So, what's our next step on Ruslan?" he said to Beckett.

"For starters, I want a visual on the guys following her. I want to know their pattern, how big a crew we're dealing with and where they're based out of."

"You trust your security team enough to farm that job out, or is that something we keep inside the brotherhood?" Jace said.

Beckett shook his head. "Better to keep what we're researching close to the vest. At least until we've got a solid way to spin it. Anyone on our staff guarding the loft will just assume me or Knox have pissed off someone new. If I start putting them on a tail without much in the way of explanations, curiosity might get the better of them. The last thing we need is someone talking."

"What about Ivan?" Trevor said. "He deep enough in we can leverage him if we need another body?"

Everyone turned their sights on Knox.

Well, that answer at least was a no-brainer. "The way he stepped up looking out for Natalie and banded with us against Wyatt? Yeah, he's solid. No way he'd lose his shit and tuck tail if Darya needed him."

Zeke scanned each man at the table. "We take this step, everyone going to be good taking a serious look at him long-term? 'Cause something tells me what we're dealing with this time around could end with some hellacious dirty secrets to contain."

"You already know my thoughts," Trevor said. "I'm the one recommending him, and nothing's changed on my end."

"I like him." Danny edged his laptop back enough to cross his arms on the table. "Never grumbles. Only time he ever balked when I asked for something was when he had a conflict with his kid, and he still tried to juggle."

"Hope you stopped him before that happened," Axel said.

"Hell, yeah, I did. Family first."

"Always," Axel volleyed back.

Zeke looked to Axel, Jace, Knox and Beckett. "You guys good with this?"

A round of nods and yeses echoed back before Zeke zeroed in on Jace. "Then I say we use him, 'cause I'm in, too."

Jace grinned at Danny. "Looks like you might not be low man on the totem pole much longer. How's that feel?"

"Truth?" Danny cocked his head, a little solemnity filtering through his easygoing expression. "Never once felt like a low man with you guys so I doubt things will change." He shot Jace his own ornery grin. "That said, I'll take another brother at my back any day."

A chorus of agreement billowed up, each man lifting their drink in salute and drawing a host of expressions from the crowd gathered round the kitchen island. Most of the women cast their usual eye rolls and smirks. Levi's frown said he was a little put out he wasn't with the rest of the guys, but Darya's face was harder to read.

Like she was okay where she was, but couldn't grasp the need for distance between them.

Understandable. Outside of introducing her to his clan and encouraging the weekly outings with the women, he'd done shit to clue her in to the deeper aspects of the brotherhood. Like how they kept their meetings separate from the women so they could honestly claim innocence if anything ever blew back on the brothers, or the depth of what actions they were capable of. Though, after the wide-eyed surprise he'd caught on Darya's face when he'd pulled a pistol from his glove box, she'd likely clued in on that last part. He'd give her the rest of the details, though. Tonight. Just as soon as they got their initial plans in place.

Beckett's voice cut through his thoughts. "Knox?"

Knox dragged his attention back to the men gathered round the table. "Yeah. Sorry. What?"

To their credit, no one gave him shit for the fact that his mind had wandered off, but neither did they waste time diving right back on topic.

Jace tugged his toothpick from between his lips and tossed it on the table. "Beck was askin' about you not seeing anyone on your tail coming here. You think that means they're just marking when Darya comes and goes?"

Knox looked to Beckett. "What difference does that make?"

"'Cause if I'm gonna track these guys, I gotta find 'em first. Helps to know where to start."

Right. Now was the time for logistics. Knox speared his fingers through his hair and fisted it at the top of his head, forcing his mind to rehash the confrontation he'd had at Darya's house. "With the footage she found, we know they're at least marking her usual stops. The guy she showed me looked like he was getting the lay of the land more than on surveillance."

"Yep," Danny said. "I found it after Beckett mentioned it. Yesterday afternoon. Nothing else that matches the same MO before or after. At least not in camera range."

"That ties with when the Koschei logins started. Early in the morning but same day." Knox frowned at Beckett. "If we're lucky, they're just starting to dig in."

"And if we're not?" Trevor asked.

Knox met his gaze then shifted his attention to Beck. "If they got past the deadbolts and security we put in her apartment, they could've had bugs."

"So we gotta run a sweep to rule that out. What else?"

"Nothing. We walked out of her place with a suitcase. Told her I'd come back for the rest of the bags she'd packed if we needed to."

"You afraid them seeing her with a bag in tow is gonna send a wrong message?" Axel said.

"I don't know," Knox fired back. "Maybe."

Zeke shook his head. "I don't think so. You left her car behind." He focused on Beckett. "If we can rule out bugs, they'd likely just take it as her going somewhere for a few days with a guy."

"And likely upped the target size on Knox's back if what Darya says about this guy is true," Axel said.

Beckett zeroed in on Knox. "If I saw a mark coming out of an apartment with a suitcase, I'd follow her. You sure you didn't see a tail?"

"Nope. Pulled every trick in the book to make sure of it."

For a solid three heartbeats, Beckett just studied him, his mind obviously running at top speed. Finally, he nodded. "Okay. Tonight Danny and I will do a little snooping around. See if we can't use the dark to our advantage and find who's watching her."

"I'll start digging deeper into Ruslan's background and the Koschei hack attempts," Knox said. "See if I can set up a trap for whoever's running Ruslan's technical end. If they're ballsy enough to slap their name front and center when trying to slip onto someone's servers, you gotta hope they're stupid enough to make a few mistakes along the way."

Jace nodded. "Right. We'll get the women we can pry away from Darya out to Haven and meet back here in the morning for an update and plan next steps."

Axel chuckled low and swirled his tumbler of scotch. "Poor Russian fucker. Doesn't have a clue what trouble he just bit into." Axel lifted his glass to Jace. "The Haven men branching out into international intrigue. I fucking love it."

Chapter Thirty

Almost eight hours since Darya had spied the word *Kos-chei* on Knox's screen. Five since Knox had stormed into her apartment, seen the suitcases and demanded the truth. Now they were only an hour away from midnight with the bulk of his family on their way to Haven—a ranch she'd learned Jace and Axel owned on the outskirts of Dallas where only those considered family were allowed.

She'd also learned that family now included her, the resounding message delivered through a string of bear hugs and brotherly kisses that left her more than a little dumbfounded. What exactly family meant to them and when the change had happened, she wasn't exactly sure, but none of them messed around with conveying their happiness about it. Through it all, Knox stayed stead-fast at her side, only relinquishing his arm around her when well-wishes required it. Now he stood behind her, a rock-solid comfort as she said goodbye to the last of those headed to the ranch.

Standing by Knox's front door, Darya hugged Gabe and muttered the same sentiment she'd shared with Nat-alie and Vivienne before they'd headed out with their men. "I'm sorry. For everything."

Gabe tightened her arms around Darya's shoulders

and chuckled. "You clearly haven't been to Haven yet.
If you had, you'd know spending extended time relaxing there is anything but a hardship. You'll know that
for yourself soon enough, though." She relaxed her arms
and pulled away just enough to grasp both of Darya's
shoulders and hold her steady. Her expression sobered,
a sincerity behind her pale blue eyes that penetrated
deep. "I know it's hard—coming into this group after
so much time spent alone and acclimating to the idea
you've got so many good people behind you. But believe me when I tell you, you will never be more loved,
or more accepted and protected than you are with us."

Knox stepped in close, his hands a calming weight on
Darya's hips and his heat a comfortable blanket against
her back. "She'll get it. We'll talk tonight and she'll understand we can handle whatever we need to."

Zeke chuckled and steered Gabe out of his way
enough to give his own goodbye. "Something tells me
talking won't be the highest point on the agenda. You've
barely let her go since rally ended." He kissed Darya's
cheek, stepped back and shifted his gaze to Knox behind her. "See you back here mid-morning."

"Yep. We'll be ready." Knox squeezed Darya's shoulders and had just reached around her to open the door
for the couple when Ninette's voice shot from the doorway of Beckett's suite.

"You two be sure to let us know when you get to
Haven." Padding toward the kitchen on bare feet,
Ninette had traded in the jeans and casual blouse she'd
arrived in for yoga pants and an oversize T-shirt. Like
Sylvie, who'd already set up camp on the huge sectional
in front of the TV, her face was completely void of
makeup, but glowing with a vitality most twenty-year-

olds would envy. "And make sure Ruger and Max get free run of the house tonight. Max might only be able to bark the house down, but Ruger will tear the nuts off any stranger stupid enough to step foot in my house."

Gabe snickered at that. "Yes, ma'am."

Of all the surprises that had been thrown at Darya throughout the day, learning that both of Knox's mothers had refused to return to their home in favor of keeping Darya company had been one of the most unexpected.

If you think we're leaving her here with a trio of men overdosed on testosterone, you're out of your damned mind.

As if she'd overheard Darya replaying the proclamation in her own head, Gabe winked and waggled her fingers in farewell over one shoulder. "Like I said, lots of love. Y'all have fun."

Knox closed the door behind them and flipped the lock.

She'd barely turned, mouth open to ask Ninette who Ruger and Max were, when she found herself backed against the front door and a solid slab of delicious man pressed against her front.

His nose skimmed the side of hers and his breath whispered warm against her face, the air around them blazing fire pit hot in a second. "Zeke's right. I know you've probably got a lot of questions, but I'm leaning toward loving you first and fielding anything verbal later."

"Knox," she whispered, her conscience all too aware of the microwave door latching into place and buttons beeping through the open loft behind them.

"Okay, scratch that." He slipped his strong hands beneath the hem of her T-shirt, the low and grated rasp of his voice amplifying the sensual brush of his fingertips against her skin. "Verbal's fine as long as it's you saying my name just like that. Or begging." He licked her lower lip and the carnal stroke echoed straight between her legs. "Fucking love the word *please* on your lips."

Her sex fluttered and every nerve ending along her skin fired bright, all the worry and adrenaline she'd fought throughout the day tossed carelessly aside in favor of the need he'd created with just his presence and a string of sensual words.

"Knox, your mothers... I should—"

He sealed his mouth over hers, swallowing the rest of her words.

Her conscience demanded she push away. Even got so far as to brace the heels of her palms against his hard chest, but her body vetoed the idea and sunk into the kiss.

Sylvie's semi-harassed voice cut from the living room. "Jesus, Mary and Joseph, son. Standin' up against a wall might be a fine display of yer strength and all, but it's been a bear of a day fer the lass. Lay her down and let her take a load off, why don't ye?"

Forehead pressed against hers, Knox huffed out a chuckle, but kept his body flush against hers. "You sure you don't want to go to Haven, Ma? I doubt Zeke's made it out of the parking lot yet."

"And miss the antics around here?" The tone of her voice shifted, suggesting she'd turned her focus back to the television. "Not a chance. Besides, someone needs to teach the lass how ta keep the lot of ye in line. Might as well learn from the masters."

Knox lifted his head. If he was the least bit put off

by being coached and sassed by the mother figures in his life, his face didn't show it. In fact, behind the still sparking intensity in his eyes was a wealth of barely contained laughter. He cupped the side of her face and skimmed his thumb along her lower lip. His eyes were locked on hers, but his words were for the other two women going about their business behind them. "You two need anything from us?"

Ninette scoffed, the indelicate sound punctuated by the microwave door slamming shut. About a second later, the buttery scent of popcorn filled the air. "Been fightin' off assholes since before you were born, Knox. Get your girl where she needs to be. We'll be fine."

All the levity on his face disappeared, replaced with the pleasure of a hungry predator who'd just leaped the last barrier to its prey. He backed away and coiled his fingers around Darya's wrist. "Yes, ma'am."

Before she knew it, she was trailing behind him toward his loft, his strides unhurried but loaded with purpose.

"Ivan's scans are in the system," he said with eyes on Ninette and Sylvie. "He'll be here in under thirty to watch the feeds while Beckett and Danny are out. Until then you see anything that tweaks you, you let me know."

Bowlful of popcorn in hand, Ninette ambled to the couch and waved them both off. "Yeah, yeah. Go. I'd say have fun, but we already got the preview, so that's kind of a moot point."

Darya dug in her heels, determined to at least get in a proper goodnight. "Knox—"

He spun, dipped until his shoulder met her belly and hefted her up like a sack of potatoes.

Her surprised squeal rang out through the loft and mingled with Ninette's and Sylvie's laughter. Knox was just closing the door to his suite when Sylvie muttered, "Well, I guess that's one way to get her off her feet."

Still reeling from the sudden shift, Darya braced her hands on Knox's back and tried to lever herself up. "Knox, put me down."

He palmed her ass and strode through the darkness. "No way. Been waitin' all night to feel you next to me. This way's faster."

She tried to get vertical again, but Knox counterbalanced the move by ducking forward and flipping her onto her back. He caught her head just before it hit the bed, the rest of his king-size mattress taking her weight with a soft *whoosh*.

As natural as water moving over a pebble-lined stream, he slipped between her thighs, his hips resting comfortably in the cradle of her hips.

She blinked her eyes into focus.

Moonlight and the soft glow of lights from the other warehouses streamed through the huge windows and highlighted his handsome face just inches from hers. "Waited my whole life for you."

Whatever she'd expected him to say, it hadn't been that, but the beauty of it pierced straight through the fatigue and worry that had needled her through the long night. Aside from their accelerated breaths, the only sound was the muted drone from the cars on the freeway and the steady thump of her racing heart.

He kept going, raining his uncensored words over her like morning sunshine after a month-long stretch of darkness. "After Tami and a string of bad decisions after her, I convinced myself it wouldn't happen. Shut myself down so I couldn't get hurt again, but deep down, I always wanted someone of my own. Someone smart. Passionate with a soft heart. Watching my brothers fall nearly killed me. Made the want deeper. Sharper." Elbows braced on either side of her, he framed her face, the ferocity of his gaze echoed in the reverent touch. "Hearing the words you gave me, every day I waited—every second—was worth it."

Her lungs seized. So many times she'd been blessed. Been given countless opportunities and seen amazing things at a high price to those who'd sacrificed and risked on her behalf. But in that second, every other moment of her life paled in comparison. She splayed her hand against his chest. "I'm not sure I deserve that. Not after what I'm putting your family through."

The softness in his gaze shifted, replaced with enough heat her skin grew flush in seconds. He covered her hand on his chest with his own. "You feel that?"

Beneath her palm, his heart beat a steady rhythm, as strong and powerful as the man he'd proven himself to be.

"It might as well have been empty before you," he said. "Yeah, Beckett and the rest of my brothers gave me the family I never had, but there's one void they couldn't fill." He tightened his grip on her hand and lowered his voice. "Swear to God, sometimes I think the reason I couldn't sleep all those years is because a part of me was afraid I'd miss my chance if it ever came."

But with her, he slept. Had done so every night from the day he'd brought her home and done it deeply, curled up tight behind her.

He smiled as though he'd actually seen the realization materialize inside her head. "I didn't miss my chance. I came close by bein' a stubborn idiot, but now that my head's out of my ass, I can tell you unequivocally you deserve *it all*. My skills, my contacts, my money…anything up to and including my life if that's what it takes to keep you safe."

She fisted her hand in his shirt, all the lightness of the moment surging to a fine point of fear. "Please, don't say that. I've already lost too many people I love in my life. I don't want to lose you, too."

With a tender smile, he tugged her hand free and kissed her knuckles. "Sweetheart, I just claimed you for my own. You couldn't shake me if you tried."

Claimed her? The part of her who'd seen one too many women lose their independence, if not their life, under the dictatorial hand of men balked at the statement. Made her want to scramble for distance and give her mind a chance to think and process.

The other, far more instinctive part of herself, blossomed beneath the idea. As though he'd wrapped her very spirit in the finest silk and laid the world at her feet.

He guided her hand to the bed and pinned it beside her head. "Now, I've waited all night to show you how much your words meant to me. Any questions that can't wait until I've shown proper gratitude?"

Oh, she had questions. Tons of them. Though, with the hungry way his gaze devoured her, few seemed important enough to warrant air—save one. "What do you mean, you claimed me?"

For a few, heightened moments he studied her, his shrewd gray eyes undoubtedly taking in far more than she wished. "I'm not him. Ruslan wants to put you in a cage. I want you to be free. With me. Beside me. Part of me." He released her wrists, slid his palms flush with hers and laced their fingers together. "I won't lie to you, though. If you ever run, I'll be right behind you. Not to lock you down against your will, but to win you back. Everything that happens between us is because you choose it. Because you deem me worthy." He paused a beat, eyes roving her face. "You understand?"

"I think so," she whispered, her throat too clogged with emotion to manage more.

"Good. Then I'll cover the other worry I figure is dancing around in your head while we're at it." He dipped closer, his voice nearly as hushed as her own. "You shared the kind of life Yefim lived. His involvement with dangerous men. So, I think you understand how men like that operate. Their mindset, what they're capable of and how they operate."

A weight settled on her chest and the pulse at her throat fluttered so fast she felt light-headed. She nodded. Or at least she tried to, uncertainty and fear making the simple motion a Herculean feat.

"Wherever you're goin' in that head of yours, come back." His lips quirked in a cocky smile. "We're ballsy bastards and not all that interested in rules outside our own making, but we're not *mafiya*. I only bring it up to give you an idea of what we're capable of. Their mindset— their tenacity and focus—is what we share. We've built a good life that provides for the people we love. Sometimes that means we play nice and color inside the lines drawn by other people, sometimes we don't. But whatever decisions we make, we make them based on our own code. On honor. No plays are ever made that might hurt an innocent."

"So, it's just business? Investments and connections?"

He held her gaze, silent and watchful. "Unless one of our own needs something more. Then all bets are off."

"Knox, please don't—"

His mouth slanted across hers, silencing not just her words but her swirling thoughts with his all-consuming kiss. Lips, teeth and tongue, he worked her mouth until every vestige of worry disintegrated, leaving her pliant and primed for more of his touch.

Still, he kept his fingers twined with hers, his weight pressing into her palms. Only when she moaned, bucked her hips against his and tried to slip her hands free, did he surrender the kiss. He rested his forehead against hers. His breath huffed heavy to match hers, a beast who'd not only chased, but snared his prey. "You trust me?"

"Yes." No doubt. No matter the atrocities she knew Ruslan was capable of or what fears she harbored deep, there was no one alive she trusted more than Knox.

He lifted his head and met her stare head on. "Then trust me in this. Trust me to know what we're capable of and to keep you safe. To make you free."

There were no words, not in English or her own tongue, worthy of the emotion swelling inside her. But she could show him. Could put everything she felt— every hope, dream and fear—into this moment and offer her surrender. "Knox?" she asked softly, a careful whisper against the room's silence.

In lieu of an answer, he tipped his head to one side and cocked an eyebrow.

She tugged her hands and surprisingly, he released them, letting her frame his face within her trembling fingers. "I think I'm done talking."

One second. One blisteringly perfect second, and

his whole demeanor changed. A caged tiger faced with freedom and poised to pounce. Yet instead of the consuming attack she'd expected, he pressed a soft, reverent kiss to her lips.

Weeks, they'd spent every night together. Tussled and explored each other's sexual desires with an endless, ravenous appetite. Always after, he was gentle. Attentive and present in a way he hadn't allowed himself to be at first, but during sex, he was always aggressive. Demanding and bold to the point their play sometimes ran deliciously rough.

But this was different.

Special in a way that went beyond words and tapped into the deepest part of her.

Back and forth, he skimmed his lips against hers, his breath mingling with hers for a delightful new level of intimacy. While his kiss was infinitely gentle, the air around them zinged with a supercharged energy that left her skin prickling in the most delectable way.

Coiling her hands around the back of his neck and lifting her head from the mattress, she tried to deepen the kiss.

Knox pulled away, not enough to ease his weight, but enough to rob her of his heavenly taste. Of all the expressions she'd seen on his face, this one was new. A trace of the vulnerability he'd shown the night he shared his past, but overshadowing it was a resolute solemnness. A vow given even before he spoke. "I'm not rushing this. Not tonight. What I want to give you, what I want to show you, deserves more than that."

Even after all the ups and downs of the day, her stomach still managed a swoop and twirl to rival an amusement park thrill ride and her breath caught in her throat.

She smoothed one hand along his jaw. "Whatever you want. You lead and I'll trust you."

His eyes flared at that, the same greedy expression of a covetous man who'd just stumbled on a cave full of lost treasure. He covered her hand with his, squeezed, then pushed back and sat on his heels, using his hold on her hand to pull her upright with him. In one smooth move, he gripped the hem of her T-shirt and pulled it up and over her head.

The room's chilled air settled against her exposed skin, raising goose flesh in its wake, but it was the awe behind the way he looked at her that stilled her thoughts. Like he was seeing her for the very first time. Experiencing the beauty of the two of them together from a whole new perspective. He skimmed his fingertips along the upper swell of one breast. "I should have known that first day."

"Known what?"

He lifted his gaze to hers. "That you were different." Taking his time, he peeled her bra straps off her shoulders, traced a teasing path from her rib cage to her spine and unsnapped the clasp. Not once did his eyes leave hers. "Just looking at you made me stupid. Made me want to forget I ever had a past. Forget all the hurt and throw my rules out the window." He peeled the silk free, tossed it to the floor and guided her to her back. "I should have known you were mine."

Mine.

Such a simple word, but it detonated inside her, unleashing a maelstrom of sensations in its wake. Beneath his gaze, her breasts drew taut and heavy, and tingles danced beneath her skin.

With achingly slow movements, he freed her of her

jeans and panties and tossed them to the floor. He stood beside the bed and studied her in the moonlight. "Beautiful."

So many times he'd seen her bare, but never had it felt this intimate. This exposed and raw. "You're not even touching me, but I swear I can still feel you."

He grinned at that, a little of the playfulness she loved about him slipping free. "Interesting. Care to share where?"

Oh, yes. Knox's mischievous side had definitely engaged and she was more than ready to play along. She cocked her knees to one side and teased her fingertips above her belly button. "It starts here. Sometimes a flutter. Sometimes something deeper. A tug or a pull."

He inched closer to the bed, his body angled as though drawn and desperate for contact, but holding himself in check. "Only there?"

"No." Engaging both hands, she gently cupped her breasts, the sensation greatly welcomed against her sensitized mounds, but still not the caress she craved. After the nights they'd spent together only his hands would do. The power behind them. The tightly leashed strength he wielded with each touch. "I ache here."

His gaze rained down on her, utterly devoted, lids heavy and lips parted. His hands opened and closed in loose fists.

She kneaded her breasts and rasped her thumbs across her distended nipples. "You like looking at me?"

He licked his lower lip and his voice came out low and hungry. "*Like*'s the wrong word."

"What's the right one?"

He lifted his gaze to hers. *"Necessary."*

Pleasure speared straight between her legs and she

whimpered, her hips flexing into the pulse building in her sex. Pinching and rolling her nipples, she amplified the sensation, each tug darting straight to her clit. "It's necessary for me, too, but you have on too many clothes."

With a frustrated grumble, he wrenched his T-shirt over his head. The second it cleared his face, his gaze latched back on her hands at her breasts and tossed the shirt to the floor. "Where else?"

She liked this game. Very much. A heady mix of visuals, temptation and strategy. And oh, how she loved looking at him. Appreciating the tightly compacted and defined muscles at his shoulders, arms and chest. Of all the ways he took her, her favorite was to see him above her, watching each ripple and flex of his abdomen as he worked his cock inside her.

Eager to push him more, she lifted one hand over her head and arched her back, offering herself to him even as her other hand smoothed toward her stomach. "I'll show you if you'll give me the rest of you. All of you."

The muscle at the back of his jaw twitched, the shadows from the bold moonlight streaming through the window making the move even more pronounced. "Want to give you slow."

"Then give me slow. But let me love you with my eyes the way I love you with my heart."

Something flashed across his face. Perhaps surprise at the reminder of her feelings, or just the unfamiliarity of the confession. Whatever it was spurred him into motion. He shoved the denim past his hips, pushing his black briefs down with them and unveiling his perfect cock. Hard and thick it jutted proudly toward his belly, the lingering movements as he stepped out of his jeans and kicked them aside, making it bob in a way that made her hands itch to cradle and stroke his length.

As if sensing the direction of her thoughts, he curled one hand around the base and squeezed. "Show me." The words rumbled up his throat as a command, but need was there, too. Her man starved for what only she could give.

She traced a leisurely circle around her navel then dipped lower, slowly moving toward her sex. In one blinding moment, everything shifted. What had started as a game—a sensual tease to heighten and build the moment—shifted to something bigger. An all-encompassing connection that coiled and pulsed around them even without physical contact. Her mind scrambled to process it all, but failed under the sensory input. The way he slowly pumped his shaft, the possessive heat in his gaze as he watched her, his shoulders pushed back and chest rising and falling on each deep breath. It all coalesced and consumed her. Pushed aside everything, but the need to feel him. His weight pinning her down. His skin hot against hers. His cock slicking inside her.

Teasing her fingertips through the tight curls atop her mound, she drew in a shaky breath. "I need you here."

Gaze locked on her fingers, he crawled on the bed, gently grasped her ankles and kneeled between them. He smoothed his hands up her shins and palmed her knees, opening her further for his unflinching study. "Keep going."

As if she could do anything else. The way he watched her, devoured every inch she covered, practically demanded her obedience. She slicked her fingers through her folds, the wetness she found matching the slow, pushing ache. "Knox."

"Just like that." He sat back on his heels and skimmed the flat of his hands down her inner thighs. "So slick for me. Ready." His thumbs skated only inches from her core, up and down, flaming her need until she could barely draw a decent breath. "Draw it up. Coat your clit with it."

Her thighs shook and the muscles in her sex clenched at his command, but she did as he said, circling the tight swollen bundle and flexing her hips into each stroke. Her muscles fluttered, release whispering just out of reach.

"Don't come," he growled. "Wait for me."

She moaned and added more pressure, gaze shuttling between the beauty of his muscled body kneeling tall above her in the moonlight and the rapt craving on his face. "I'm close."

"You'll be closer before I give you my cock." He gripped his shaft with one hand and squeezed her thigh with the other. "Slide your fingers inside. Show me where you want me."

Eagerly, she dipped her fingers and pushed two inside, desperate for the fullness she longed for, but finding her own touch sadly lacking. She whimpered and circled her hips. "It's not enough."

"I know, baby. But I want a taste and you're going to give it to me." He gripped her hips, dragged her close enough the fine hairs along his thighs tickled her ass and guided her hand to his mouth. "Best of both worlds." He licked one finger and teased the side of his cock against her clit still damp from her juices. "The

taste of you in my mouth and your hot pussy teasing
my dick."

Her hips surged on reflex, a low grated moan dragging up her throat as she banded her legs around his
hips. She lifted her hips, angling to catch the tip of him
at her entrance, but the one hand he kept on her hip held
her just out of reach. God, but she loved the feel of him
bare. Of all the changes in their relationship the last
few weeks, deciding they were ready for a commitment
befitting the trust of skin-to-skin contact had been the
most intimate. Until now. "Knox. Please."

Pulling both her fingers into the wet heat of his
mouth, he sucked her clean, eyes closed and savoring every drop. Through it all he undulated his length
against her swollen clit, driving her higher and higher
with every stroke. Only when he'd lapped and sucked
every inch, did he kiss the center of her palm and guide
her hand to his chest. He leaned over her, relinquishing his hold on her hip to anchor his hands beside her.
His dog tags fell on her sternum with a soft jingle, the
metal a welcome chill against the fire burning her from
the inside out.

Frozen in place, he stared at them a moment, thoughts
she couldn't identify moving across his face. "You're
mine now." He lifted his gaze to hers, the resoluteness
in his eyes searing straight to the heart of her. "Mine
to keep. To protect. Always." He shifted his hips and
she nearly wept at the tip of him prodding her entrance.

She flexed to take him, rolling her hips in welcome.
When he held himself back, she sunk her nails into his
shoulders and dug her heels into his ass. "Please."

He nudged forward just a fraction. Enough to make

her muscles flutter in anticipation, but not enough to ease the ache. "Take them off me."

She moaned and writhed beneath him, the odd command not penetrating beyond the need to feel his length inside her. "Take what?"

"My tags." He slid one hand behind her head and gently fisted her hair, forcing her eyes to open and her gaze on him. "Take them off."

Stunned by the intensity in his eyes, she forced her fingers to release the death grip she'd placed on his shoulders and smoothed her shaking fingers to the thick chain around his neck. "You never take them off." Not ever. Not in the shower. Not at night. Not when they were together. And from what the other women had said, the rest of the brothers were the same.

Never.

His hips pressed forward, notching himself inside her. "Do it."

She lifted the chain up and he ducked his chin. The second it cleared his head, he pinned his gazed on hers and commanded, "Put them on."

Oh. My. God.

She'd understood his claim. Understood the importance of tonight and what her words had meant to him, but until that moment, she hadn't understood what he was trying to say. What he was trying to show. Knox wasn't just claiming her, he was giving her himself. Showing his love the best way he knew how.

Fingers trembling, she lifted the chain over her head. The tags' heavy weight rested on her chest, a brand searing deep beneath the skin. She moved her hands away from their smooth surface and splayed her hands against his chest.

Pride and possessiveness filled his expression and when his focus shifted to her eyes it was as if something between them locked into place. He held her gaze and inched his hips forward. Filling her with agonizing slowness. "Mine."

She wrapped her hands around his shoulders, needing his inherent strength to anchor her through the moment. "Yours."

Deeper he pressed, slowly taking what she freely offered and burning it into her memory in a way not even death could steal. He filled her to the root and lowered his mouth to hers. "Swear to me, Darya. Swear you won't ever run and you'll let me keep you safe."

There it was. The vulnerability laid bare in the most intimate of moments. No matter what it cost her. No matter what the future brought the two of them, this was the moment she chose him for her own and took a stand beside him. "Never." She banded her arms and legs around him, tangling her fingers in his hair and holding his head to hers. "I'm yours. Completely."

In one consuming move, he took her mouth and ground his hips against hers, sealing her vow in the most physical and delicious of ways. Every sensation catapulted her to the very edge, hovering toward a monumental free fall. His kiss. His hard body moving against hers. His iron and velvet length tunneling in and out of her wet sex. No more was this about anticipation or sex. This was about two people becoming one. A joining of heart as well as flesh and vows spoken without a single word.

Groaning into her mouth, he shifted his weight back and slipped his arms beneath her, one banded low on her back and the other behind her shoulders. He straight-

ened, taking her with him as he went so she straddled
his hips as he thrust deeper inside her. From this angle
and the power behind each buck of his hips, his glans
brushed the sweet spot inside her and his pelvis ground
unrelentingly against her clit. Lips close to hers and
hearts pounding chest to chest, he fisted her hair at the
back of her head and growled, "Now. Take it. Come for
me. Make me whole."

She couldn't have stopped her release if she wanted,
not with the feel of him and his sweet words pooling
in her heart. Her sex clenched, the intensity behind it
drawing pulses from the very soles of her feet and billowing out in all directions. She cried out against his
mouth and squeezed her arms around his shoulders,
the metal of his tags digging into her flesh even as her
core milked his shaft.

His mouth crashed against hers and his hips surged
to the hilt, burying himself inside her and pressing his
hand at the base of her spine so there was no way to
move. No escape from his cock jerking and jetting his
release inside her.

No escape.

The idea would have terrified her with Ruslan, but
with Knox she welcomed it. Savored the precious shield
his claim created. The protection and love that came
with it. Because after this, there was no doubt in her
mind. Knox loved her. With everything in him—every
action since she'd uttered her feelings and shared her
past until this beautiful moment—he'd shown it. Given
her all of him, heart and soul.

His kiss eased along with his thrusts, what had been
wild and desperate before calming to languid, savoring strokes. Keeping one arm cradled around her back,

he cupped the side of her face. He rested his forehead against hers, his breaths wafting soft and warm against her face.

She opened her eyes and nearly wept at the vulnerability reflected back at her. Even with his eyes closed, he was completely bared to her, a gift she had no doubt he'd never given anyone in his mostly solitary life. She framed his face with her hands, utterly safe in the knowledge he'd hold her close. "You love me," she whispered.

His eyes opened. With just the moonlight streaming through the window, they seemed even more lustrous than in the brightest light. A foggy and mystical gray that reflected the magical moment. "If *love* is the strongest word there is to describe what I'm feeling, then yes. I love you. With everything in me."

Tears welled from out of nowhere and emotion clogged her throat so thick she could hardly speak. "Thank you for honoring me with that. For giving me you."

He smiled, the brightness of it outshining the moon and filling her heart to the point it ached. He leaned forward, keeping her supported with one hand even as he caught them both with the other, and eased her to the bed. "Told you I'd give you everything. Not much of a man if I can't own up to what's real."

And just like that, he leveled them out. Eased them into a comfortable space where they could simply enjoy the moment and linger in the delicious afterglow. One forearm anchored in the mattress beside her and his cock still nestled inside her, he smoothed her hair away from her face and traced the line of her jaw. "You want me to clean you up, or are we staying close?"

It was a question they'd experimented in finding the answers to in the week since they'd stopped using condoms, the change in circumstance being one neither of them had any experience in handling before they'd agreed on the deeper intimacy. Sometimes they showered. Sometimes he saw to her. Sometimes they merely let things be what they were.

Tonight she was going for the latter. "I'd rather not be away from you."

His quick grin warmed her. "No complaints from me." He rolled them to their sides and his shaft slipped free, drawing a sad whimper past her lips. He drew her leg over his hip and slid his thigh between hers. Every night they fell asleep this way. No matter how they woke, they started nose to nose and chest to chest, their breath mingled as sleep took them. "You going to be able to sleep?"

She took her time studying his face, letting the moment imprint deep on her memory. "With you, I think I can do anything."

Chapter Thirty-One

Knox stared up at his bedroom ceiling. Since sunrise an hour ago, he'd watched the buttery glow of another summer morning slowly stretch across the white surface, Darya's comfortable weight and the sweet press of her naked body against his the only thing stilling his need to take action. Not that his mind was inactive. For the first time since he'd brought her home, sleep had eluded him and he hadn't minded one bit. Some of his best ideas had come to him in the quiet hours before dawn, and right now he needed every slick inspiration his mind could dole out.

Snagging his phone off the nightstand, he checked the time.

7:53 a.m.

Which meant Ninette and Sylvie were probably up and around already, and with a little luck, Danny and Beckett were either back already or at least on their way with news on if anyone was watching Darya's house.

He slid the phone back against the nightstand's rich mahogany surface and rolled to his side, wrapping his woman up tight. Another benefit to a sleepless night was watching her sleep. Letting himself drink his fill of her classical face and burn every detail deep. He'd also figured out she liked having someone play with her hair. Whether she'd registered the contact in her sleep or not, he wasn't sure, but every time he'd taken to slicking his fingers through the silky strands, she'd almost purred and snuggled closer.

He kissed her cheek and muttered low beside her ear, "Morning, angel."

She stirred and her eyes fluttered open, the striking blue even more impactful with the sun's soft glow. At first her expression was a little dazed, her features still soft and unmarked by reality, but like everything else about her, her mind caught up quick and her eyes came into focus. "Is everything okay?"

"Perfect." He rolled her to her back and pressed a soft kiss to her lips. "I need to run some traps I laid out last night, but I didn't want you to wake up and worry where I'd run off to."

She traced an arc below one of his eyes. "You didn't sleep."

"I didn't want to. Was too busy enjoying the woman next to me." He snagged her hand and kissed her palm. "I'll get my work done a whole lot easier if I know you're happy and asleep in my bed, though."

"If I stay, will you promise me you'll sleep tonight?"

He couldn't help it. The lure of all the ways they could sexually work his over-thinking brain into off mode made his dick twitch and start to swell. "Oh, I'll make sure we're both so exhausted tonight we'll drop into a coma."

She smiled at that, one full of teeth and mischief to match his own. "I can work with that plan."

"Good. Now close your eyes and think about what's on your wish list for tonight."

She chuckled low and sultry. "That list keeps getting longer with you."

Fuck, but he loved this woman. Loved her heart. How sweet she was even to strangers. How easily she not only kept pace with him intellectually, but eagerly met him pound-for-pound with sex. "Make it as long as you want. Not gonna quit until you're sated, and then I'll still be ready to start over again from the top." He slid his nose alongside hers and breathed in her winter rose scent. "Sleep for me, angel."

Before he could change his mind and indulge himself and his ready cock in her sweetness, he rolled out of bed and grabbed his phone as he stood. He snatched his discarded jeans off the floor, tugged them on in short order and padded to the door as quietly as he could. The second he opened it, the rich, nutty scent of coffee and the even better promise of Sylvie's old-fashioned fried potatoes and bacon assailed him. His stomach growled in appreciation before he'd even shut the door to his suite.

Sure enough, Ninette was perched on a bar stool at the massive island while Sylvie manned the stove. For two women outside their normal environment, they looked right at home, both still fitted out in their TV-watching yoga pant and T-shirt combos. It was Ninette who spied him first, casting an easy good morning grin over her shoulder as she set her oversize coffee mug on the concrete-topped counter. "Look who's up and smiling like he ate a whole flock of canaries last night."

Well, hell. Who'd have known he could be twenty-nine years old and still blush like he'd just been caught whacking off to a *Penthouse* centerfold? He strolled past Ivan manning the screens and laptops lined up on the dining room table. "Hey, man. Anything?"

"Nope. Not a peep," Ivan said. "Got a call from Danny and Beck about half an hour ago. They're hittin' Krispy Kreme on the way back and called the rest of the crew in early. Jace and Axel just pulled into the garage."

Good news. An earlier meet meant less time to kill keeping Darya distracted. "Thanks, man." He headed on toward the kitchen and Ninette, who'd yet to take her eyes off him, her focus a little too narrowed for comfort.

She stood just as he reached her and wrapped him up in a familiar hug. "I'd ask if you got any sleep, but my guess is no. So how about I ask if your girl did?"

Knox chuckled and kissed Ninette's gray head. "She slept hard. Though, I'm hopin' she gets at least another hour in before she gives in to curiosity and obligation and drags her butt out of bed."

"She's a woman, Knox. A smart one who's just had it made plain she is well and truly taken. Only normal she'd instinctively feel the need to step into her place as woman of the house instead of resting where she should be." She stepped away, but kept her hands on his shoulders and scanned his bare torso. "I see you're missing something this morning."

Knox scoffed and headed for the coffeepot. "Like you haven't seen the lot of us hangin' out sans shirts a million times before."

The odd commentary must have caught Sylvie off guard, too, because she paused in stirring the potatoes long enough to twist and scan him head to toe.

Knox took advantage, leaned in and kissed her cheek. "Mornin', Ma."

When he pulled away, she was smirking back at him. "Ninnie wasn't talkin' about the shirt, love." She dipped her head toward his chest and waggled her eyebrows. "She was talkin' about yer tags."

Yep. Twenty-nine and both of them could make him feel like he was ten again. He covered the uncomfortable response by tackling the single-brew coffee machine.

Sylvie didn't seem the least bit troubled by the topic, because she kept going. "Ye know Ninnie and I would be more than happy ta help ye pick out a pretty ring fer the lass."

"Yeah, I thought we'd start by making it so she could walk out of the house without a psycho catching her before we started planning weddings and babies."

"Oh, babies!" This from Ninette who'd settled back on her bar stool. "The fact that word even came out of our boy's mouth says that shopping trip's not too far away."

Shit. She was right. Where the fuck had *babies* come from? Although, picturing Darya's belly big with his child made him stand up a helluva lot taller and pushed his shoulders back about as far as they'd go. Still, he kept his gaze trained on the coffee machine while it gurgled and churned out the last of his brew.

The loft's door chunked open, and Jace and Axel ambled in. It took the two of them all of two seconds to scan the open space, clock everyone's positions and settle in on razzing Knox. "Told ya he'd be up and chompin' to go," Axel said over his shoulder to Jace.

Jace aimed an ornery grin at Knox. "Yeah, but if he's half-dressed it hasn't been for long, which meant he had a damned good night."

"I'm in my own place and my woman's still in my bed," Knox said over his cup of coffee. "Be glad I put on jeans."

"Well, there is that." Axel ambled toward the kitchen while Jace peeled off to check in with Ivan. "Do I smell fried potatoes?"

"And bacon," Sylvie said. "Biscuits are in the oven, and I'll whip up the eggs once Danny and Beckett roll in."

Axel moved into Ninette's side, wrapped his arm around her shoulders and kissed her cheek. "Just like bein' at home."

"If my boys are there, it is home," Ninette said with an easy smile. "But speakin' of Haven, how's the rest of the crew?"

"Levi's on top of the world," Axel said. "Trevor stopped off at his place and picked up Lady, so adding Ruger and Max in the mix, he's in dog heaven. Plus, his aunt Vivienne and aunt Gabe have deemed it their duty to spoil him more than normal."

"As they should," Sylvie said. "Though, I've never met a lad easier to spoil than Levi."

The grate of wood against the concrete floor drew everyone's attention to the big dining room table. Ivan stood, shook Jace's hand and tossed a casual wave to everyone gathered in the kitchen. "I'm gonna head out and bunk down for a few hours. You guys need me before tonight, give me a call and I'll head over."

Knox met him halfway to the front door and offered his hand. "Appreciate you pulling a shift on short notice."

Ivan took it and met his stare head on. "Haven't gotten to know Darya much yet, but I know you. If she's yours, she's worth it." With that, he tipped his head to the women, opened the door and headed out.

"He's gonna be a no-brainer." Jace settled in behind the computers, but rearranged his chair so he could have a straight-on view of the kitchen as well as the laptop screens. He cocked one foot up on the rung of the chair beside him and cranked his head to Knox. "Any idea how far out Danny and Beck are?"

Knox threw the bolt on the front door and padded back to the kitchen. "Ought to be here anytime. Where are Zeke and Trevor?"

"Stayin' at Haven to keep an eye on things," Axel said. "We've got their proxy, but can call 'em if somethin' big comes up that needs their input." Lifting his own coffee mug, he dipped his head in the direction of Knox's suite. "Darya still out?"

"I hope so." Knox pulled out a bar stool next to Ninette. "Yesterday was a hell of a day."

"I take it you shared a few extra details on her new family?" Axel said.

"Enough she gets we can handle what needs to be handled."

"How'd that go?" Ninette asked.

Knox kept his gaze rooted to the countertop, but he was pretty sure everyone still caught the stupid smile on his face. "She took me like I am."

"Knew I liked that lass," Axel said with a chuckle.

Jace's voice cut from the dining room table. "Danny and Beck just pulled in."

"Right," Sylvie said with a nod. "Eggs are goin' on now."

Maybe it was the smell of all the food, or the chorus of male voices overpowering the room once Beck-

ett and Danny showed, but about fifteen minutes later
Darya wandered out of his suite. Her face was void
of makeup—a practice that had taken him about five
mornings to convince her he absolutely loved—and
she'd thrown on a loose pair of ice-blue cotton pajama
bottoms and a white tank. Dangling dead center between her breasts were his tags, right out where God
and everyone could see.

Fuck yeah, he was gonna catch all kinds of shit the
second his brothers got him alone. Probably three times
what Sylvie and Ninette had dished out, but damned if
he cared. They looked perfect right where they were.
Not to mention, they'd serve as a hell of a reminder if
she caught some wild idea about running.

The second she got within grabbing distance he
pulled her between his thighs and hugged her close.
"I take it we were too loud?" he murmured in her ear.

"My thoughts were louder." She anchored the heels
of her palms on his shoulder and leveraged herself
enough away she could see his face. "Plus, the food
smelled really good, so I gave in."

"Knox, let go of the lass and let her eat." Sylvie slid
a fully loaded plate next to the one she'd built for Knox
along with a napkin rolled around a full set of silverware. "Hop up and let her have your place. You men can
eat your food and do your business at the same time."

Axel grunted, nabbed his plate and coffee mug off
the counter. Despite the beleaguered sound, his voice
was full of mirth. "Sounds to me like the women want
us out of their hair so they can get the play-by-play
from last night." He winked at Darya as he rounded
the island then shot Knox a smirk as he headed toward
the dining room table where Jace, Danny and Beckett

were already situated. "Better hope you gave it your A game, brother."

Knox palmed her hips and squeezed, tempted to tell the lot of them to go to hell and cart Darya back to his suite. Instead, he lowered his voice just for her. "You good while I talk with the guys?"

Her smile was a sweet one. Soft like her morning kisses and a little bit shy, but void of the worry she'd wrestled the day before. "I'm good. I'll help your moms with cleanup then spend some time digging into work."

Work was good. Like him, she was all focus the second she dove into her code. Where they differed was once she walked away from the screen, she could easily detach. He cupped the back of her neck and kissed her, not giving two fucks about the fact that conversation had all but ceased around them. Only when she smiled against his mouth and pushed against his chest did he release her and move away.

"Tags, huh?" Danny grinned and shoved the empty seat next to him far enough away from the table Knox could slide right in. "You sure you don't want to go with something that would warn the male population off a little more clearly? Like, I don't know…a big honkin' ring?"

Eyes on the screen in front of him and fingers moving at about half the time what Knox was capable of, Beckett cut in with a chuckle. "Be glad he didn't haul her off to a tattoo shop in the middle of the night."

"Property of," Axel added.

Jace held Knox's gaze, but his low voice was for everyone else at the table. "Careful, brothers. What comes around goes around." He scanned the rest of the men and picked up his coffee. "The way I see it, you're all prime pickings to be in his shoes. Just a matter of which one's gonna fall next."

Yeah, Jace got it. Had been the first of the brothers to face all the unfamiliar sensations that came from claiming a woman for their own. The fact that he'd never thought to be in these shoes only made the moment sweeter. "They can give me all the hell they want. Only thing I care about right now is fixing shit so Darya and the rest of our women aren't cooped up inside four walls." He stretched his legs out long, reclined against the seat back and rested his forearm on the table, fingers coiled loosely around his mug's handle. Eyes on Beckett, he got down to business. "So? Anyone watching Darya's house?"

"Two," Beckett said. "Took a while, but found 'em backed into a driveway across from the complex. House was for rent and completely dark. Only thing that tipped 'em off was their shiny black Mercedes."

"Not exactly the best way to blend in in that neighborhood," Danny said.

Axel leaned into the table and sipped his coffee. "A good slip for us, though, if it means Beckett can get a bead on where they're operating from or how big their crew is."

"What about Darya?" Jace asked Knox.

"What about her?"

"If they're tracking movements then they'd have marked the two of you leaving with a suitcase in tow. They might buy you two headin' out for a little trip, but if she doesn't pop back up on their radar, they're guaranteed to start digging into you."

"Let 'em dig."

Jace hesitated, keeping his gaze steady even as he

gave his toothpick a quick swirl with his tongue. "Think you're missing my point. If she shows, it keeps them off track. They think we're still clueless and buy us more time to build a plan."

"No." As if his harsh shutdown wasn't enough, Knox focused on the screen in front of him completely cutting eye contact. "I'm not using her."

Situated on the same side of the table as Knox, Beckett shifted enough to see around Danny. "He's got a good point, Knox. No one's saying it has to be much. Just show back up at her place, drop off an empty suitcase and head out again."

Knox whipped his head around and glared with all he had in him. "Not gonna happen." He held Beckett's stare and tried bringing his breath in line with something less heavy than a marathon runner. Not exactly the easiest task considering his heart had taken off at a sprint with the mere idea of letting Darya outside the safety of his loft. He forced his attention back to his laptop. "I put out a new honeypot."

His brothers kept their silence, either too stunned by his outright refusal to say anything, or just giving him space to see where the new topic was headed. He was just about to share more when Axel grumbled, "What the fuck's a honeypot?"

Danny snickered. "It's a lure. Knox uses 'em to trick people nosing into our business. Fake databases with the promise of financial or personal info. They bite and he blocks."

Axel grinned. "Think I like my definition of honeypot better, but to each his own."

One quip and the tension was broken. But then, that was the thing Knox loved about his brothers. They might not always see eye to eye completely, but they always had each others' backs.

"I take it you're hoping this lure is gonna get us another inroad to Ruslan?" Jace said.

Knox nodded. "The goal's to find some way I can get them suckered into uploading a RAT."

Axel's head snapped back and he frowned. "A what?"

"Remote Access Trojan," Beckett answered. "Basically malware. It gets him administrative access to their systems."

"And from there I get whatever information on this prick we need to gain leverage." Knox hesitated. Of all the shit they'd done together in the years since he'd met them, what he was about to suggest was probably the most dangerous. "The little bit of research I did on Ruslan last night showed this guy's loaded."

"You wanna hit the fucker's accounts." Jace grinned huge. "You're a mean bastard when someone messes with your toys."

"Like you'd do anything different if it was Viv."

The grin died and the lethal side Jace barely kept banked on a good day roared to life. "I'd take his money, but only as a means to lure him close enough to cut his dick off and choke the son of a bitch on it."

"Then you see my point."

"Clear as day." He reclined against his seat back. "Still, you take that step, it'll escalate fast. We ready for that?"

"Not yet," Beckett said. "We will be. Just need to find where they're holed up and if Ruslan's even with them."

Danny perked up in his chair, eyes narrowed on his

laptop. "You got any tenants registered with a navy blue 750 BMW?"

Knox leaned over only long enough to confirm the model that pulled up in front of the building then checked all the makes and models listed by their renters. "Don't remember anyone with a BMW, let alone a 750."

"Brother, that's not just a 750," Beckett said. "That's an Alpina with blacked out glass I'd bet is bulletproof."

Danny zoomed in on the car and punched a few keystrokes on the keyboard. A second later the image flashed on one of the six flat screens on the wall just as the front two doors of the sedan opened. Two men dressed in dark pants and black oxfords rolled up at the forearms unfolded themselves from each side. Both scanned the immediate perimeter before the driver shifted to the rear door curbside and opened it.

Another man stepped out, this one dressed to rival Axel on one of his most tricked-out days. His gray suit reeked of money, and despite the muggy morning his white shirt looked hanger fresh. Come to think of it, with his dark shoulder-length hair and trimmed beard, he and Axel would have been double-trouble in the clubs. He glanced up toward the top of the building as though he felt the stares on him, fastened his double-breasted jacket and pushed his shoulders back as only a man comfortable with power could.

Jace swiveled his head to Knox. "Somethin' tells me our search for Ruslan just got a whole lot shorter."

Chapter Thirty-Two

That ballsy motherfucker.

Knox's chair legs grated harsh against the concrete floor as he stood, nearly pushing the damned thing to its back along the way. He opened his mouth to order the women to his suite, but promptly swallowed the command at Darya's startled voice.

"Oh my God." With a whole lot of shock and a twist of delight on her face, she slid off her bar stool and hurried to the dining room table, leaving Ninette and Sylvie wide-eyed and silent. Not once on her way toward Knox did her eyes move off the screen in the center. "What's Sergei doing here?"

Even after a night of recon, Danny and Beckett got their heads out of neutral faster than Knox, practically talking over each other.

"Who's Sergei?"

"That's not Ruslan?"

"Considerin' the lass is smilin', I'm gonna hazard not." Typical Axel, he chuckled and reclined against his seat back, stroking his fingers through his beard like he'd just stumbled on one hell of an entertaining show. "Whoever he is, the man's got style."

"Never a dull moment in this family," Jace added with a shake of his head.

On the screens, the two men who'd vacated the front seat stood with feet braced, shoulders back, and hands loosely clasped in front of them. The suit—or Sergei, as it seemed to be—trekked into the lobby toward the imminent two-on-one with Beckett's guards.

Knox stepped in close to Darya and turned her to face him. "You know this guy?"

Axel was right. Whoever this guy was, she was happy to see him. Maybe not doing cartwheels happy, but there was a definite tilt to her lips. Fuck if that didn't make him want to punch the bastard on principle. As if she needed one last confirmation, she glanced back at the screen then nodded. "Sergei helped me escape."

"I thought some dude named Yefim did that," Danny said from behind her.

Beckett's phone rang just as two more guards moved into the camera's view, each coming from the main stairwell's secured door. Sure enough, one of the main guards had his own phone to his ear. "Yeah, we see him," Beckett said in way of a greeting. He glanced up at Darya. "Just keep him there for now. Looks like we know him."

Understanding settled into her features and her mouth parted. "You thought he was Ruslan?"

Jace shrugged. "A dude in a suit pullin' up in a hundred and thirty thousand dollar car with two men for backup—not exactly a huge leap."

"No." She splayed her hand above Knox's sternum, an urgent touch he couldn't decide how to interpret. Either she was upset at the concern this guy's arrival had caused, or she was scared shitless he and his brothers were going to string him up by his nuts and was desperate to stop them. "I told you Yefim called on his own *mafiya* connections to help me escape. It was Anton's most trusted *avtoritet* who actually made it happen."

"Sergei," Knox said, hating the way the guy's name sat on his tongue. Which was thirty kinds of stupid considering if it hadn't been for the guy, Darya wouldn't be here right now. "This guy got a last name?"

She cocked her head and studied his face. "Petrovyh." With her accent, the bastard's name sounded way too sexy.

Great. One more thing to tweak his ego.

Her lips tipped as though she'd stumbled onto a secret and she moved in close enough to band her arms around his waist. When she spoke, her voice was low and only for him. "I have known Sergei for many years and I owe him much for his actions. But you should also know that he is fourteen years older than me and was raised by Yefim from the age of twelve."

"Meaning?"

"Meaning that in the time I knew him, he treated me as a little sister. Nothing more. And even if he'd had an interest in me, his position with Anton would have made any relationship nearly impossible."

Right. He'd seen the way men looked at Darya—old men and his own brothers included. No way this Sergei guy was any exception. Still, if all she saw in him was a big brother that was something. He hugged Darya flush against him and focused on Beckett. "I take it he's here for a chat?"

Phone still pressed against his ear, Beckett covered the bottom half of the phone with his big palm. "Lance says he asked for you and Darya specifically. Said you have a mutual acquaintance that needs attention."

"How the fuck did he know to come here?" Danny said.

"My guess is the best way to find that out is to ask." Jace twisted enough to study Sergei in the screen. "Sure as shit doesn't look like the guy's in a hurry to leave."

No. Not at all. In fact, if Beckett's four guards braced in front of him even remotely gave him the heebees, Sergei didn't show it. Just stood there with his feet planted hip width apart and his arms easy at his sides. Definitely ballsy.

Knox peered down at Darya. "You really trust this guy?"

She held his stare, her breath coming soft and even. "I will not lie to you. Working for Yefim, I met many dangerous men. None were more so than Sergei. He grew up in the life. Started working for Anton when he was only sixteen. He's smart. Very well educated. Loyal to those inside his realm. But also deadly." She paused a beat and twisted in his arms enough to speak to Axel and Jace. "I trust him not just with my own life, but with the lives of your family."

Jace twirled his toothpick.

Axel rocked back on the rear legs of his chair.

It was Ninette who broke the silence. "Oh, for fuck's sake." All the men turned toward the kitchen in time to see her power off the tablet she'd been surfing on and push it aside like she'd had enough of waiting for the men to pull their heads out of their asses. "If Darya says he's good, let the man up. We'll get a hell of a lot more answers that way than with the four of you beating your chest and sending smoke signals."

"Don't hold back, Mom. Tell us what's really on your mind," Jace said.

"I'll tell ye what's on my mind." Sylvie wiped her hands on her dish towel, laid it on the counter and dipped her head toward the flat screens. "The man wears a fine suit and is easy on the eyes. If the four of ye can't give the all clear, Ninnie and I will for the view alone."

"Amen to that," Ninette added.

"Jesus," Axel said under his breath as he sat up. He looked to Beckett and shrugged. "Do it. We'll get answers and make the women happy."

Still wrapped up in Knox's arms, Darya snickered.

Beckett scowled at each of the women, but peeled his palm away from the phone and growled into the handset, "Send him up."

The next few minutes passed in silence, Danny and Beckett heading out to the elevator landing with holstered weapons in plain sight while Jace and Axel kept their seats and their unflappable calm. Ninette and Sylvie kept on with their usual synchronized kitchen routine like they hadn't just welcomed up a known killer to the loft.

The top right screen showed the elevator swishing open and Sergei stepping into the plain gray space.

"You know they're gonna frisk him, right?" Knox said.

She squeezed the hand she'd laced tight with his the second the guards had stepped aside and let Sergei pass. "It's no different than what he would do. He'll respect the action more than be offended by it."

Knox shifted his attention to hers. "I could give a fuck what he thinks. It's what you think I'm worried about."

She smiled at that, her eyes alight with understanding and a little wonder. "I worry about what you think, too. Just remember what I said. He gave me much. Treated me like a little sister for many years. I could no more give him a cold welcome than I could your family." She skimmed her fingertips along his jawline and lowered her voice. "Will you trust me?"

Before he could answer, the loft door opened.

Danny ambled in first and jerked his chin up at Knox.

Behind him was Sergei with Beckett practically a lead blanket on his back. To his credit, Sergei didn't seem the least bit put off by the intimidation tactic. Just scanned the room in one cool sweep before his eyes locked on to Darya. *"Moya zvyozdochka."*

Two words Knox didn't understand for shit, but spoken directly to his woman with a low familiarity and warmth that made Knox grit his teeth.

Darya, on the other hand, beamed back at the guy. "Sergei." She started forward and solely by Herculean will did Knox let her fingers slip from his.

He followed her, though. Yeah, the guy might have saved her and deserved a decent hello, but that didn't mean Knox couldn't make it clear as day whose arms she was headed back to once all the hi-how-are-yas were done.

Rolling up on her toes, she threw her arms around Sergei's neck and hugged him tight, the gesture no different than the ones he'd spied her sharing with Beckett after a hard session of sparring. "It's good to see you."

Gaze sliding to Knox, Sergei carefully returned the hug, his big hands splayed firm, but high on her back and well away from her hips. Silver and black rings adorned three of his fingers and one thumb and black tattoos in a variety of symbols took up a good chunk of real estate on the backs of his hands and near his knuckles. A string of Russian none of them had a hope in hell of understanding slipped from his lips.

Darya understood it, though, and given the way she jerked out of Sergei's arms and scowled, it wasn't good.

Knox moved in, pulling Darya back into the circle of his arm. "Let's try that again. In English."

One side of Sergei's mouth quirked in an almost smile. His accent was much heavier than Darya's, but the words he strung together made it clear he had no problem with the language. "You have found worthy protectors, it seems," he said to Darya. "I shared as much with Yefim. He is pleased."

A mix of sadness and worry crept across Darya's face. "He's okay?"

"Quite well. Cantankerous as usual, but still fit and pulling too many strings." Sergei smoothed his hand down the front of his jacket, taking note of each person's placement in the room and the security footage marking every angle on the building. He zeroed in on Knox. "I'm sure Darya has already shared my name, but I will offer it myself." He held out his hand. "I am Sergei Petrovyh. I consider her former employer and patron, Yefim Mishin, my father."

"Knox Torren." Knox shook his hand. "Darya told us you're the person who helped her escape."

Sergei looked to Darya, a silent question behind his eyes.

"I have no secrets from Knox," Darya said quietly. "Not from him or his family."

"*Her* family," Knox corrected.

It took only a handful of seconds, but Sergei nodded and spoke to the room at large. "Just as well. It will make the news I have to share less tedious in the details."

Darya glanced at Ninette and Sylvie as though double checking to ensure they were still there. Both had forgone any pretense of busy work in favor of watching the scene unfold, but in that second, some womanly communication shuttled silently between the three of them. Darya turned her attention back to Sergei and rubbed her hands together in an uncustomary nervous gesture. "We have some coffee left. Maybe you could have a seat with Jace and Axel, and you can tell us what brought you here."

A pleasant buzz moved through Knox, a little warm fuzzy and a whole lot of male pride pushing his shoulders back a notch. As much as he'd grown accustomed to Ninette and Sylvie commandeering the bulk of their family gatherings, having Darya be the one at the helm slathered up his ego like nobody's business.

Sergei dipped his head in a regal nod and moved in beside Darya as she led the way.

It was only when Sergei approached the table, that Jace and Axel found their feet, each offering respectful handshakes and stern faces in greeting. Danny and Beckett fell in right behind them, introducing themselves in clipped, businesslike tones. In between it all, Darya snagged her coffee off the countertop and a fresh mug for Sergei, then aimed her ass for the empty chair beside Knox.

Yeah, it was a total caveman move, but Knox rerouted her before gravity could gain much headway and redirected her into his lap. The second her body settled into his, a good chunk of his tension unwound, leaving him as focused as if he'd settled into a code. He locked stares with Sergei. "The guards said we had a mutual acquaintance to discuss."

Sergei nodded. "My men noted you leading Darya from her apartment with a suitcase. They also noted heightened security at your building and that neither you or Darya left the building for work as is your normal routine. I can only assume from those actions that you've surmised she's being watched."

"By Ruslan," Knox said.

"Not by him. Not yet. But his men, yes. They arrived in Dallas Tuesday morning and immediately started tracking her movements."

"Okay, that explains why we're interested in him," Knox said. "Now share what makes him a mutual concern."

"Because he has become a detriment to many important families." Sergei's gaze darted to Darya long enough to consider his words, then refocused on Knox. "I take it Darya explained the term *pakhan*?"

"In the most fundamental way, I call him your boss."

Sergei pulled in a slow, assessing breath then let it out. "Too simple of a term and lacking appropriate respect, but close in essence." He circled the ring on his thumb. "Ruslan has drawn attention for years and disregards our code. Many *pakhans* have grown tired of his behavior and no longer wish to tolerate it."

Clearly tired of the slow and steady approach, Beckett cut in. "Still doesn't explain what you're doing here."

Before Sergei could even open his mouth, Axel answered, his voice deep and sinister. "Because he's been using Darya for bait and the bait disappeared."

The room buzzed with an eerie silence.

Sergei held himself freakishly still and, for a second, Knox worried Danny or Beck might have missed a concealed carry. Finally, eyes still locked on Axel, Sergei dipped his chin in acknowledgment.

Once loose and comfortable against him, Darya pushed tall in his lap. "What? Why? You know what my life will be like if he finds me."

Sergei redirected his attention to Darya. "I did. But his actions have escalated. As has his paranoia. He is never unprotected. Never vulnerable."

"You're his weakness," Jace said to Darya.

"Indeed." Sergei's lips quirked in an ironic smile and he scanned the men at the table. "Darya's disappearance was quite suspect. Nothing more demeaning to a man like Ruslan than a woman escaping his reach." He shrugged and smoothed a nonexistent wrinkle from his pants. "A body was found. Unrecognizable, but staged so that he could save face and accept it as hers, or besmirch his reputation by digging deeper."

From his place at the far end of the table, Danny filled in the blanks. "And since then he's gone off the rails."

"He is impacting business," Sergei answered. "He has no honor. No reason behind his actions save his ego. The families cannot afford to ignore the situation anymore." He zeroed in on Knox. "It is my job to address the situation."

"Only you can't do that if your bait's under lock and key," Beckett said.

Sergei nodded. "Precisely."

"Are you out of your fucking mind?" In that second, the only thing that kept him from surging to his feet and strangling the asshole was Darya's sweet body against him and the death grip she had on his thigh. "Darya's told me what this guy's like. How the women in his life end up. You actually think you're going to waltz in here and suggest we put her in a situation where this sick bastard can get his hands on her?"

"She has never been at risk," Sergei said. "Ruslan only left St. Petersburg yesterday afternoon after his scouters confirmed her existence and location. My men have looked over her since the day we leaked her presence in Dallas to one of Ruslan's acquaintances. They are the ones who diverted Ruslan's men long enough for you to leave her apartment without being followed." He cocked an eye at Knox. "They were even watching when you dared to break into her home."

White-hot anger seared through him, so fierce and overpowering his whole body jolted beneath its force.

But before his mind could rally with a physical or verbal retort, Darya fired off a string of words in Russian so clipped and biting it was a wonder Sergei didn't flinch under their attack. By the time her voice died off, her chest heaved and her cheeks were a mottled red.

Sergei stared back at her, a small smile playing on his lips. He must have realized his amusement didn't sit well with her, because he finally ducked his chin and schooled his features before he turned his attention to Knox. "My apologies. Darya has reiterated that there will be no secrets from her family, nor will she tolerate any disrespect."

Okay, the whole lady of the manor thing might have nudged his pride up a notch, but seeing her throw down for not just him but his whole family cranked his ego up bigger than the Jolly fucking Green Giant. Knox fought the need to pull her back against him or blow their unexpected guest off and show his appreciation in a far more thorough fashion.

Unfortunately, Sergei kept them all on track. "I must confess, I am curious. What tipped you off to their presence?"

"He tried to hit one of our servers," Knox said. "It looked like a random hack to me, but Darya recognized a word in the URL."

"Koschei," Darya said.

Already primed to collaborate, Beckett pulled up the footage Darya had found and directed it onto one of the screens on the wall. "She found this a few hours later. Footage just on the outskirts of our camera range." He zoomed in on the tattoo she'd shown him and freeze framed. "This look familiar?"

Sergei scoffed, obviously disgusted. "Unfortunately, yes. Though we didn't realize they were so foolish to be caught on camera. His men are as arrogant as he is."

"Or they think we're stupid."

Sergei cocked his head and gave his thumb ring another twirl. "We both know your intellect is the last thing in question. Your security is one of the few my men have been unable to access."

Son of a bitch.

Talk about your passive aggressive statements. Knox didn't know whether to smirk at the open nod to his security skills, or gut the bastard for having tried to get past his firewalls in the first place.

Thankfully, Jace redirected things before Knox could indulge either option. "So, your boss and his peers reap the rewards when Ruslan's gone. What's in it for you?"

Deadpan and without so much as a blip to his casual demeanor, Sergei turned his gaze on Jace. "I accomplish my task."

"That's shite," Axel said. "A hit this big, one you've put a nice lass like Darya at risk for, there's gotta be something sweet for you in the end."

Silence filled the loft.

Sergei held utterly still for long seconds until he turned his gaze on Darya, something Knox could only describe as approval shining behind his eyes. "You've chosen well in your new life." He folded his hands in his lap, a refined movement a father from some upper-crust family might take before he lectured a disobedient daughter. "Perhaps you could give me a minute with your protectors, *moya zvyozdochka*?"

Darya studied him a moment, then slid her attention to Knox.

Knox squeezed her hip, hoping she'd take the gesture as the encouragement he intended it to be. Yeah, it was her life and future that was predominately on the line, but if what Sergei had to say was bad enough to keep it a secret from a woman he considered a little sister, then Knox damned sure didn't want her exposed unnecessarily. He glanced back at Sylvie and Ninette and motioned toward his suite. "How about if you two help Darya get the rest of her stuff unpacked and figure out what else she needs from her apartment."

For once, neither Sylvie or Ninette added any snarky quips to Knox's not-so-subtle direction. But then, Sergei wasn't one of them, and one thing his mothers would never do was undermine family in front of a stranger.

With a soft kiss that went way too fast for Knox and a brotherly hug for Sergei, Darya made her way to Knox's suite, Ninette and Sylvie trailing right behind.

The door had barely shut when Sergei spoke. "You are correct. My reward is significant." He paused and stared out the row of windows overlooking the industrial district and I-45. "I was educated in the United States. You have much here to appreciate."

Always impatient with unnecessary theatrics, Beckett chimed in. "Not seeing how that ties to any kind of payback."

Sergei dragged his attention away from the windows and locked on to Beck. "It ties because I want to make your country my home. Dispatching Ruslan will earn me the right to start my own family. Here, in the place of my choosing."

Well, fuck.

Not exactly the gory info bomb he'd expected after politely asking Darya to leave the room, but still a bomb all the same. Especially since family in Sergei's context didn't mean a wife and two-point-five kids.

Jace cocked his head. "So, you'd be branching out."

Sergei nodded. "Indeed. And I would be indebted to the men who aided me in doing so."

"You can't seriously think I'd trade Darya's safety to earn future payback." Knox said.

"The payback, as you call it, would be a benefit, yes. But you forget who would benefit the most."

Darya.

Sergei didn't have to say it. Everyone in the room knew Ruslan had to be eliminated to make her safe. Still he kept going. "No more running. No hiding. Her name could be her own." He grinned and tilted his head as if throwing down the ultimate dare. "Or yours."

Chapter Thirty-Three

One thing Darya had learned about Dallas weather in the last many months was that it had a way of keeping you on your toes. True it wasn't as cold as Russia, but it wasn't predictable like San Diego either. More like a passionate child with a penchant for moodiness.

Curled up on the buttery soft leather sofa in Knox's home office, Darya stared out at the slate gray clouds coating the horizon. Where most of the day had shone with sunlight and heat so fierce it made the air waver off the tar-covered rooftop across the street, a powerful cold front had forged its way through near six o'clock, spawning a round of thunderstorms so fierce the thunder made the whole building shake. Now rain pelted the windows and every few minutes shards of lightning pierced the landscape.

The patter of Knox's fingers against his keypad served as a constant white noise. Almost nonstop, he'd been glued to his computer, pausing only long enough to check on her and stretch his legs. Even during his brief intermissions, his mind was obviously still at work. Never in the time since she'd worked with him had she seen him this focused. This fixated on one thing.

And she hated it.

Hated knowing that whatever he was buried in was because of her, but more so because she missed his lightness. His quirky sense of humor and razor-sharp wit.

Damn Ruslan.

Stretched out lengthwise on the sofa with her elbow braced on the back, she fisted her hand and pressed it against her mouth. Her whole damned life had been one defensive maneuver after another. First rebounding from her mother's loss. Then running from Ruslan and losing Yefim and JJ. True, she'd been shocked and a little terrified when Sergei had shared his reasons for leaking her existence to Ruslan, but the more she thought about it, the more she saw the wisdom in his plan. For once in her life, she had the chance to take the offense instead of mere reaction. There was power in that. Freedom.

She shut her laptop and slid it onto the chocolate leather ottoman beside her. From her place across the room, she couldn't make out any of the code displayed on Knox's computer screens, but she'd bet their future he was looking for a way into Ruslan's networks. Some foothold that would give him the advantage he needed to make her safe.

Another person taking a stand on her behalf. Several, actually, if you considered how his family had rallied around her.

I'm not sure where you got the idea there's some karmic tally being kept, but to my mind, family doesn't work that way. Especially not ours.

Ninette was right. There was nothing wrong with her wanting to give back after so many people had helped her, but there was also something to be said for holding your own. For standing up and making your own mark.

She palmed the dog tags hanging heavy between her breasts and squeezed them tight, the metal cool against her over-warm skin. "We need to talk."

Knox's fingers stalled the second she spoke and he canted his head just enough to bring his handsome face in profile. "Something wrong?"

Any other day, she'd have taken a different tactic. Would have started slow and moved in with logic. Today, if she had any chance of breaking through his need to shield and protect her, she'd have to go in guns blazing. "Yes."

He spun in his chair, worry instantly wiping the tenacious focus from his face. His gaze dropped to the closed laptop in front of her then scanned the room as if it might conjure up some clue as to what was wrong. He locked on to her hand fisted around his tags and his expression shuttered. "If you're thinking of leaving again, you can toss that idea out the window."

"I gave you my word and my love. Whatever we do, I want us to do together." Like a beacon, her gaze drifted to the screens behind her, gifting her with the words she needed. She refocused on him. "But we're not together in this. It's only you. You and your brothers. It's my future. *You* are my future. I should play a part in it."

He stood and frowned, more than a little wariness pinching his brow as he prowled toward her. "Babe, the things I'm doing take years to learn. And no way in hell would I recommend you hone your chops with some of the safeguards Ruslan's got in place." Reaching the couch, he sat and pulled her across his lap so she straddled his hips. "If you want to learn this side of my business, I'll teach it to you, but one misstep with this guy and he'll know we're digging."

"I'm not talking about hacking."

Silence stretched between them for two heavy heartbeats and his mouth pressed into a hard line, too stubborn to broach the subject.

"I think Sergei's plan is a good one," she said. "I could—"

"No." His chest rose and fell a little quicker, and his eyes sparked with barely contained anger. The loose grip he'd held on her hips tightened in such a way she wasn't sure if he'd jerk her against him, or push her away. "That's not happening. We'll find a better way. One that doesn't put you at risk."

"And what if I *want* that risk?"

His head snapped back and his eyes widened. "You can't be serious."

"I'm very serious." She framed his face and let her fingers tangle in his hair. It was always unruly after he'd spent time on his computer, but it was more so today, the quirk of running his hands through it as he untangled whatever riddle kept his focus leaving him with the look of a man who'd just had a healthy tussle in bed. "My whole life I've reacted to events. Been the recipient of others standing up for me or giving of themselves." She paused long enough to hold his sparking gray gaze. "I don't want to be passive this time. I want to make a stand. To take action and claim the future I want."

"I get that. I want it for you and I'll help you, but not at a time when taking that stand can mean you end up dead."

"You won't let that happen to me. Neither will your brothers. Or Sergei. I trust you. All of you."

His jaw slackened just enough to show she'd made a dent, so she forged ahead. "It's the right move. The cleanest, fastest and safest one for everyone involved. Me included. Sergei knows Ruslan. Would have already planned to accommodate every scenario, but with you and your brothers aiding him, we can get this over with and move on with our lives. You know this and you'd admit it if the woman in question was anyone but me."

He swallowed hard and his hands moved up her back as though he needed the tactile connection to ground him. "You don't realize what you're asking me to do."

"I do," she whispered, hating the wound she was asking him to inflict on himself. "I'm asking you to risk the future you've always wanted. But for me to walk into that future with you, I need to be whole. To know that I had a part in building it beside you." She paused only enough to ensure the weight of what she had left to say reached him with added emphasis. "You told me the women in this family are free to live the way they want. To make their own choices. This is me making mine."

He palmed her shoulders and squeezed, no doubt a host of arguments cued up and ready for flight on his tongue.

"Can you outwit him?" she asked before he could speak. "If it were anyone else—one of Danny or Beckett's clients—could you pull it off?"

There it was—the unflappable confidence and certainty that had governed his every movement from the day she'd first walked into his business flashing bold and beautiful to the surface. "That's a dirty play."

"Dirty, but accurate. You wouldn't hesitate. Not for a second."

He drew in a deep breath, dropped his head against

the back of the couch and let out a long sigh. He glared at the ceiling, the muscles at the back of his jaw ticking in a way that said he didn't much care for the logistics already setting up shop in his head. "You're right."

"Then you agree?"

It took forever before he answered, but when he did a cautious resolution filled his stormy gaze. "I'll talk to my brothers."

Chapter Thirty-Four

A day and a half later and Knox still hadn't found any peace with Darya's decision. Nearly forty hours' worth of planning and surveillance with Beckett's best men on the job plus Sergei's on top of it. Their approach was dead on. Solid and well thought out. Fucking brilliant, really.

And he still hated the whole idea.

He turned into the parking lot fronting Darya's apartment building, halfway tempted to pull a U-ey and head back to the loft. Darya sat in silence beside him. Usually, she'd man the radio and pepper him with random small talk about whichever bands came on, but today her posture had about as much give as a concrete post and her hands were fisted in her lap.

"We don't have to do this," he said for what had to be the twentieth time since they'd rolled out of bed. "They took the bait I set out online and I've got all the access I need to their servers to choke him financially. No one will think less of you if you opted for a technical attack. Hell, I'd be grateful."

Whatever she'd been thinking about, she shrugged it off, turned to face him and covered his hand on the gear shift. "Ruslan's here. We know where he's staying and we have a plan. To back out would be foolish."

Oh, they knew where he was staying. And about five minutes after Sergei had phoned in the details, Knox had access to the hotel's servers and knew not only what room he was in, but what the cocksucker ordered for breakfast. "I still don't see why Sergei didn't take the shot at the airport."

"He's got one shot at this, Knox. You know that. Taking a risk like that out in the open would have been nearly impossible to cover. And if they tried and his shooter missed, Ruslan would have gotten right back on his plane and taken off. This is better. Easier to contain."

Easier on cleanup maybe. Not so much on keeping Darya safe. Although, he'd felt a whole lot better after they'd learned Ruslan had landed at the same private airstrip Trevor used. Thanks to his brother's connections, Ruslan didn't stand a snowball's chance in hell of getting his bird back in the air. At least not until it got a little TLC from a qualified mechanic.

He whipped into the parking spot next to Darya's red Challenger and popped the gear shift into Neutral. Thank God, Beck's buddy Gia had agreed to jump into the operation they'd put together. No way he'd have kept from crawling out of his own skin without a top bodyguard like her watching Darya's back. "Remember what I said about your car. We couldn't check it without drawing attention from the guys watching your place, so stick to Gia's ride."

Darya nodded and grabbed her purse from between her feet on the floorboard. Cranked up to high to combat the stifling heat, the Audi's AC pumped hard enough to stir her hair around her shoulders.

"We can't talk about our plans again until I've swept your place for bugs," he added. "You want to run through the drill one more time before we head in?"

Her lips curved in a tired, but sweet smile. "We've gone over it so many times I could recite it in my sleep."

God, she was beautiful. Beautiful, smart and brave with the kindest heart he'd ever met. He curled his hand around the side of her neck. Her skin was damp against his palm, but whether it was from the oppressing heat or fear he couldn't know. "I love you."

She placed her hand over his, guided it to her mouth and kissed his palm. "It's going to be okay. This time tomorrow we'll be back at your loft and neither of us will have to think of this again."

He'd think of it. Hell, things hadn't even kicked into motion yet, but he already knew he'd have nightmares for months, if not years.

But right now she needed him strong and fully on board with the decision she'd made. She'd been right to call him on his promise. Haven women deserved to live the life they wanted and make the choices they deemed right every bit as much as the men did. If he couldn't honor and support what she wanted, he didn't deserve the future she offered. "This time tomorrow, I'll have you tied to my bed and so boneless from me working your body, you won't think at all."

She grinned at that, a little of the lightness they'd lost since the day she'd seen *Koschei* on his screen shining through her grim focus. "I'm looking forward to that." She leaned across the center console and kissed him, her winter rose scent flaming his fear of loss higher even as it calmed him. "Let's hurry and get this over with so we can get started."

Before she could pull away, he fisted his hand in her hair and took more of what she offered, slanting his mouth against hers and claiming her hard enough she'd feel it long after he was gone. Nothing came easier to him than kissing Darya. Not code. Not puzzles. Not even breathing. Just the thought of her lips against his—her taste on his tongue—disconnected him from reality and left him free to float on utter bliss.

His phone vibrated and chirped.

Darya dug the heel of one palm against his shoulder and pushed away. She licked her lower lip, and her eyelids hung weighted over her beautiful blue eyes. Beautiful. Even with the rest of the world ready and waiting for them to get their asses in gear.

Knox snagged his phone and thumbed the answer button. "Yeah."

Beckett's voice came sharp through the earpiece. "Know you don't want to do this, brother, but you've got an audience. I suggest you pry your ass out of that car and get on with the show."

Fuck.

He raked his hands through his hair. "Right. We're getting out." He killed the connection without waiting for a response and looked to Darya. "You ready?"

She nodded.

"All right. Let's do this." He popped his door and unwound himself from the low-slung seats. Summer was giving Texas all it had for the last few days of August. At just after ten in the morning, the temps were already nearing ninety, which wouldn't have been so bad if the humidity wasn't pushing ninety, too.

He snagged Darya's nearly empty suitcase from the trunk, rounded to her door and helped her out. Unlike Beckett, he didn't relish packing a firearm all the damned time, but guiding her up to her apartment door and knowing Ruslan's men were somewhere out there, he'd have felt a hell of a lot better with its weight holstered close to his side.

Once inside, he got to work with a physical inspection of every room, then hauled his scanners out of her suitcase and started in with an electronic sweep. Through it all they bantered back and forth about movies and music while Darya tricked herself out for her trumped-up afternoon out on the town with Gia.

He was wrapping up his scan of the bathroom and double-checking the mirror for any signs of hidden cameras when his phone buzzed in his back pocket.

Beckett: Gia's moving in. Men in position. Find anything?

He could do this. For Darya he could knuckle down and ignore the need to haul her back to his place. Every one of his brothers were in position and ready to protect his woman with their life if needed. He just needed to focus and do what he was good at until this was over.

Knox: All clear.

Less than five minutes later, Gia was in place and Knox was out of excuses to linger. He snagged Darya's hand in his and led her to the door. When he not only opened it, but steered her onto the landing with him, she dug in her heels and glanced back at Gia.

"Relax," he said as he pulled her into his arms. From where they stood, the men watching would have a flawless view of them both. "Just give your man a goodbye kiss to tide him over while we run this drill."

"But they'll see you," she whispered as though anyone but Gia could hear and tried to push out of his hold. "I told you what would happen if they find out we're intimate."

He banded his arm tighter around her waist and palmed the back of her head, holding her right where he wanted her. Running his nose alongside hers, he breathed her in and teased her lips with his. "You did. That's why I'm rubbing their nose in it. The odds of them taking the bait and going for me today instead of you are slim and none, but if it means I'm the one in the hot seat and not you, then I'm gonna take it." He licked her lower lip and growled, "Now give me your mouth."

She hesitated only a second, bathing him in so much goodness with one simple look it rocked him to his core. Then she kissed him.

Everything was in that kiss. Love. Need. Fear and hope. All of it woven together so thick the whole damned world could have imploded in a second and not a single thing would have touched them.

Behind them, Gia cleared her throat.

Knox forced himself to break the kiss and scowled at Gia over Darya's shoulder.

She waggled her phone. "Sorry. Beck says the plan was to establish a relationship. Not insight a bloodbath in the parking lot because the two of you had sex."

Fucking Beckett. For a guy who'd gone all fairy godmother getting him and Darya together, he'd turned into one hell of a cock blocker the last twenty-four hours with all of his planning sessions. "Fine." Knox pressed his lips to Darya's forehead and let her go. "Headset on.

Mics and trackers checked before you take a step out of this apartment."

"We've got this," Gia said before Darya could answer.

Hands down, walking away from Darya and not looking back was the hardest thing he'd ever done in his life. Hell, the only thing helping him get in his car and pull out of the parking lot was the frail hope Ruslan's goons would take the bait and follow him instead of Darya.

He'd barely made the on-ramp to I-75, his foot uncomfortable with the slow and easy routine on the accelerator, when his phone rang through the Audi's Bluetooth. Beckett's name flashed across the dash's center display. "Tell me they fell for it."

The line crackled with way too much emptiness. "Sorry, brother. You knew it was a long shot."

Yeah, he had. Rule number one when tailing anyone was never to leave your primary target. Not unless you had enough backup. The good news? If they only had two men watching Darya, that could mean the crew covering Ruslan was also limited. According to Sergei, only four men had followed him off his private jet. That meant six known triggers to contend with when push came to shove versus five from the brotherhood and Sergei's six. Eleven to six were damned good odds. He'd have preferred to have all his brothers for the job, but Trevor had to make sure Ruslan's plane stayed out of commission and Jace was the only one with a prayer of keeping Ninette, Sylvie and the rest of the women safe at Haven. Zeke would hang with Knox in the surveillance room they'd set up at the hotel for medical emergencies.

"Then on to Plan B," Knox said, taking the next exit and rerouting to the hotel. "But once we're in, Sergei better holster his weapon, because that motherfucker is mine."

Chapter Thirty-Five

After two solid hours shopping in one of Dallas's more elite malls, Darya could say with absolute certainty that Gia Sinclair kicked butt at her job. From the time they'd stepped outside Darya's front door until now, Gia had somehow kept an easygoing conversation moving with Darya while simultaneously listening and responding to Beckett, Knox and Danny's intermittent updates via headset. The constant chatter was enough to fry Darya's mind. Not unlike trying to cram for an important test while someone blared Metallica in the background.

Gia wasn't the least bit fazed. Not by the fact that two of Ruslan's goons had loosely trailed them for the last hour or that Knox had reported more men had left Ruslan's suite and headed their way. On the surface, she was just a carefree woman out with her friend and hell-bent on some serious retail therapy. Only the most subtle cues showed how carefully she gauged their surroundings.

They ordered fountain drinks from one of the fast-food places and found a table nestled against a square pillar. Gia took the seat with her back to it, set her open purse on the table and motioned Darya into the seat across from her.

Murmurs sounded in the headset, the distinct rumble of Sergei's accented voice carrying even though she couldn't make out the words. A second later, Beckett was back. "Knox, any luck getting a look inside Ruslan's suite, or is Sergei finding out how many we're up against the old-fashioned bloody way?"

"Not yet." From the grumble beneath Knox's answer, her man was none-too-pleased their plan to get a camera inside via a room service or housekeeping cart was stuck on idle. "After callin' up room service myself for lunch, I can't blame him for having his meals brought in from somewhere else, but you'd think the son of a bitch would at least need some clean towels by now."

Beckett chuckled. "Old-fashioned and bloody it is."

A cold chill that had nothing to do with the mall's supercharged air-conditioners snaked down her back. Ruslan might be unpredictable, but he was ruthless and the men who served him were no different. Getting any information out of them would take extreme measures.

"Think about something good," Gia murmured from her place across the table. Her mic was still on, so it reverberated with a surround sound effect, but also held a sharp command. "Our guys are coming down the walkway behind us. They haven't clocked us yet, but it'll be better if you don't look white as a sheet."

Her phone rang in her purse, dragging her out of her bone rattling worry. She dug it out and found her first genuine smile of the afternoon at the sight of Knox's name on the screen. "Hey," she said, wishing she had the ability to toggle her mic on and off the way Gia could. Unfortunately, she'd be under far more scrutiny with Ruslan's men than Gia would, which meant she'd been given a nearly undetectable headset with a wireless receiver only big enough to be cleverly hidden by her belt.

"You want out?" Knox said. "All you have to do is say the word and we'll shut it down." No preamble. No soft hi-how-are-ya-holding-up? Just straight to business. But then this was his future as much as it was hers. And if she'd learned anything about Knox in the two months since she'd known him, it was that he protected the people he loved with everything he had in him.

And Knox Torren definitely loved her.

"No, I want to finish it. Once and for all." She glanced at Gia who put on a good show of impatiently waiting for her girlfriend to get off the damned phone.

At first, silence filled the line. She braced, fully expecting to hear his voice shift to the earpiece and to have him shut the whole operation down with one word.

Instead, he spoke only to her and gave her the exact anchor she needed. "We're gonna kick this thing, sweetheart. You, me and our family. We'll deal with the lot of them and all this shit will be behind us."

You, me and our family.

So beautiful. No matter how many times he'd reiterated that very statement in the last few days, it still resonated deep.

"I love you." It was quiet, but she offered the simple words with all the emotion inside her and prayed it didn't hit him as a fearful goodbye—even if a part of her was terrified it was.

"Love you, too, sweetheart. You stay close to Gia, listen to what she says and hold the fuck on to her when shit gets real. Got it?"

"Got it."

He paused and in that second, she could practically feel the hesitation thrumming through him.

"I'm fine, Knox. Hang up the phone and work your magic. I'll see you at the hotel."

"I'm right here. Every step."

And he was. Flooding her spirit with his strength and confidence even from a distance. "I know you are." She braced and straightened taller in her seat. "I'll see you soon." Before she could change her mind, she ended the call and forced a big gulp of Coke down her desert-dry throat.

Gia planted her elbow on the table and rested her chin on her upturned palm. "I'd have ordered food, too, but I figure you'd just pick at it and give your anxiety away."

"No food," Darya confirmed. "Even if I ate it, I'm not sure I'd keep it down."

"Not me," Gia said. "I'm a stress eater. The higher the anxiety, the bigger the caloric content."

Knox's voice cut through the headset. "Ruslan's men just exited Park Lane and are circling back around to the mall."

"Gia?" Beckett said.

"Right." Gia stood, draped her purse over her shoulder and pointed down the mall's long corridor behind them. "Time to wrap this up."

Darya stood, though how she managed it with her legs shaking as much as they did was a miracle. Not even when she'd fled to the States with no idea if her false identification would work had she been this terrified.

Gia smoothed a comforting hand down Darya's back and stayed close to her side, but her words were for the men watching their backs. "Headed to the parking garage."

The trek was a short one that felt like a lifetime. They crossed out of the store into the mall's main corridor and a rush of chilled air slicked beneath her loose hair to kiss her sweat-slicked nape. A few stores ahead of them, Axel meandered across one of the wide bridges that connected the two walkways, his focus seemingly centered on his phone instead of where he was going.

From the murmured updates in her headset, she knew better. Knew that everyone else was in place ready to do their part as well. Every scrap of information registered clearly in her ear, but not a bit of it made a difference. Her brain couldn't process it. Couldn't do anything better than stay on damage control with her over-stimulated senses and ensure she kept pace with Gia.

The parking garage doors whooshed open and the oppressive August heat slammed against her with twice as much weight as before. This was it. No more running. No more hiding. Not from Ruslan or anyone else. Ever.

Five cars into their row, the sound of low masculine voices drew closer, their Russian accents unmistakable but the words not quite carrying enough clarity to give her direction.

Up ahead a black SUV with blacked out windows neared their row.

"Black SUV dead ahead," Gia whispered.

Beckett's voice was crisp and loaded with purpose. "We have visual. Plans are a go."

Gia wrapped her arm around Darya's waist and gave a friendly squeeze. To anyone else, they'd look like two women drunk on overcharged credit cards with an evening of shopping afterglow to indulge in, but the sharpness in Gia's tone as she leaned in was total focus. "Remember the plan. Grab on to me like you're terrified. They won't have a choice but to take us both without causing a scene."

Darya managed a jerky nod and kept walking.

The SUV made its turn headed directly toward them.

Behind them the men grew closer, their quick footsteps ricocheting off the low ceiling and cement pillars around them.

Gia glanced back and a mask of fear that in no way matched the confident grip she kept around Darya's waist slipped across her face just as the SUV screeched to a halt in front of them. Three men jumped from the car's interior, leaving them sandwiched.

"Five," Gia muttered so low Darya barely caught it even through her headpiece, but it was enough to let the team know what they were dealing with.

From there the scrambling came natural, fear and a very real need to escape pummeling Darya at all sides. With one arm she fought, slinging her bags with all she had in her and keeping her other banded tight to Gia. One man barked out a command in Russian, directing the others to take them both. The next thing she knew she was part dragged, part carried to the SUV's hatchback and tossed alongside Gia onto the cargo area.

Gia rolled, taking Darya with her so Darya's back was plastered against the rear seat and covered her with her body, but one of the men crawled in the cargo area, slammed the hatchback shut behind him and whipped a zip tie from his pocket.

The car doors upfront slammed shut and a voice yelled back, *"Blondinka yego. Ushibla, i on budet imet' golovu."* The blonde is his. Hurt her and he'll have your head.

Meaning, for now, she was safe, but Gia wasn't. Not until their own men made a move and she could engage with her gun.

Zip tie clenched between his teeth, the man with them in the back jerked Gia away and tried to roll her to her belly.

The car moved into motion, the smooth glide completely belying the struggle going on between Gia and their captor. She elbowed him in the jaw hard enough to earn a backhand across her cheek. It stunned her long enough the man flipped her to her stomach and wrenched both hands to her back.

Oh, hell no. No way was Darya letting that happen. Not when they were this close. She launched forward with everything she had, knocking the man off balance and filling the car's interior with an infuriated roar.

Unlike his brutal attack on Gia, he merely banded his arms around Darya's, holding her in an unforgiving grip as he tried to wrestle her to the floorboard. No easy task, considering Gia had teamed up and wrapped her arm around the guy's throat.

"In place." Sergei's voice sounded in her headset, thick with his accent and loaded with grim determination. A quick glance out the back window confirmed not only the black Mercedes that had followed them to the mall behind their SUV, but an industrial air-conditioning service van pulling out of a reserved spot.

Done with playing nice, their captor released Darya and threw Gia across the cargo space so hard her head snapped against the glass. She slumped, and for a second, Darya thought he'd knocked her new friend unconscious.

Just as Darya was about to crawl across the space to protect her, the car turned hard into the narrowed stall where the self-pay gate was lowered and jerked to a stop. The sudden stop threw her and the man beside her off balance.

The driver's window hummed as they lowered it and Darya scrambled to her knees, but her guard whipped out a knife and moved in between them. *"Peremeshcheniye i ona umirayet."* Move and she dies.

Darya froze, gaze sliding to Gia's slumped body. *"Ty yey bol'no. Vse, chto ya khochu sdelat', eto ubedit'sya, chto ona v poryadke."* You hurt her. All I want to do is make sure she's okay.

Through the front windshield, she spied the tip of the white gate raising up. Just a few more seconds. Enough to get both the SUV and the trail car wedged in the narrow aisle and they'd have help.

The SUV inched forward just as a white Cadillac Escalade sped forward and screeched to a halt in front of them.

Beckett's voice shot through the earpiece. "Gia go."

One second.

One freeze-frame moment, then Gia launched for the man beside her and all hell broke loose.

Chapter Thirty-Six

Too much noise and not information. Knox fisted both hands on the desk in front of him, his forearms pressed so hard on the high-priced furniture the wood groaned in protest. He didn't dare touch his laptop for fear he'd squeeze the ever-loving hell out of it or chuck the damned thing out the window.

Beckett, Danny, Axel and Ivan barked out feedback, but the details were too clipped to form a decent picture. It was still better than the Russian bullshit flying from the mouths of Sergei's crew, though. Those words he didn't stand a hope of understanding.

And not one peep from Darya. Only a few grunts and shouts from Gia beside her.

"Last one," Beckett said, followed by a loud thump that sounded like a car door slamming. "Danny with me. Ivan get the tail car. Axel back the Caddie up."

"On it," Axel said.

Another thump sounded. Then another.

Engines revved and tires squealed, but Knox didn't dare speak. The last thing any of them needed were distractions.

"You breathin', Knox?"

Zeke cut in first. "Only one thing you're gonna say that makes that happen."

"Well, time to start," Beckett fired back, more than a little satisfaction coating his voice even through his accelerated breaths. "Your girl's clear, men are contained, and we're on the move."

Fuck.

He tried to relax. Tried to force his hands to uncoil and his mind to unhinge from the terrified freeze-frame it had held for the last thirty seconds. "Where's Darya?" he finally managed, though how enough air made it up the back of his throat to ask he couldn't figure. God knew his diaphragm was still knotted up like a pretzel.

Fumbling sounded and a second later Darya's shaky voice sounded through the line. "I'm here." Heavy huffs filled what would have been silence, but the smile in her words lingered. "I lost my earpiece in the shuffle, but I'm fine." An adrenaline-coated laugh followed tight behind her claim. "We're all fine."

"Fuckin' A," Danny chimed in.

Already back in tactical mode, Beckett's voice sliced through the feed. "Knox, need you to check for any reports from police. Caught a few onlookers in the middle of it all. Sergei's got Ruslan's men in the cargo van behind us. Not gonna go good if he gets busted before we can get intel out of 'em."

As a way of getting his head straight fast, the need for intel worked like little else could have. Before his brain could even fully process the request, his fingers were flying over the keyboard, intercepting 911 dispatches the way he used to just for shits and grins as early as high school. "Two calls. Intercepted them both. No dispatches sent. How far out are you?"

"Just pullin' onto the service road, takin' it slow to blend in," Beckett said. "Axel, get on 75. We'll take the service road to give us more time. Sergei, you with us?"

"Keycards to Ruslan's suite and phones secured," Sergei said. "No outgoing calls after we engaged. Only two others before we moved in, none to Ruslan."

"So, Ruslan's got no ETA and no alert for what happened," Axel said.

"We hope," Beckett confirmed. "Better not to get too cocky. Not until they're out for the count and we're the only ones standing."

Knox magnified the camera feeds he'd kept pinned to the corner of his screen. "He's still got two guards outside the front door we'll need to deal with. You get a head count on what's waiting inside yet?"

"Give me thirty minutes." The low rumble in Sergei's voice ensured whatever went down inside that van in the next half hour wouldn't be pretty for the captured men, but Sergei was definitely looking forward to it.

"Darya, you got your phone?" Knox said.

"Um…" Movement sounded through the line along with a decent amount of rustling. "Yes, I have it."

"Good. Anyone needs me, ping Zeke. I'm offline." He tugged his headset free and punched her number on speed dial.

"We did it," was her answer. Part whisper, part overwhelming thrill. "You should have seen Gia. I thought the guy trying to tie her up had knocked her out, but when Beckett said, 'Go,' she sprung into an action hero. I want to learn how to do that."

"Sweetheart, after we get through the rest of this day, you can learn how to do anything you want to, so long as you don't do any of it without me next to you. Not until I can get over the last seven hours."

For a second, she was quiet. When she spoke again her voice was soft with need to match his own. "I miss you, too."

Knox sighed and fisted the hair on top of his head, elbows braced on the desk in front of him. "I couldn't see anything." The words came from the very pit of his soul. A confession and a plea for her to understand. "It took ninety-seven seconds. Over a minute and a half when the bits and pieces I heard wouldn't form a visual in my head, and you were in the thick of it. Without me."

"You're where you're supposed to be. Doing what you're good at."

Funny. Ever since he could remember, he'd had a driving curiosity to poke and prod at things. To break them apart and see how they worked. The habit had driven him into computers and he'd been devoted ever since. The code and the challenge of sneaking into places he shouldn't be had been his comfort. His way to escape and flip a mental bird to the people who'd been all too effective at keeping him out of their life. Now that he had Darya, he didn't need the solace. Didn't need to prove anything. "The only thing that matters anymore is taking care of you."

Zeke smacked him on the shoulder and pointed at Knox's headset on the desk in front of him.

Knox snatched it up, but directed his comment to Darya. "You got your earpiece on?"

"I'm putting it on now."

"Good. Remember the plan. And no more covert shit with you in the middle and me not beside you for as long as I'm breathing."

Her light laughter was the last thing he heard before Sergei's voice gut through their link. "Eleven inside including Ruslan. They sent more for surveillance than we thought."

Axel's low voice slid through the link. "Nice. You came in five minutes under."

"I'll bet that also means we've got a van to dispose of when this is all over," Beckett added.

Sergei's breath was slightly elevated, but his accent was twice as thick and there was grim satisfaction in his tone when he answered. "You would be correct."

"How much time do you need to head up?" Danny said.

"My men are gearing up now," Sergei answered. "Take your team up the stairwell and be ready."

"We'll need Gia's trigger to even out the eleven," Beckett said. "Gia, you good with that?"

Before Gia could answer, Knox cut in. "Gia covers Darya. I'm in."

"Knox, we need you on the controls," Axel said. "Besides, not a one of us are going in without vests. I know damned good and well you don't have one."

"Odds of anyone aiming at anything other than our heads are slim and a vest's not gonna help me there. And once we activate at the entrance, there's nothing Zeke can't handle here. He'll be prepped, but Darya's not stepping a foot in that door without full cover. If we need another gunner it's me."

Silence crackled through the line, though there wasn't a doubt in his mind that Axel, Danny and Beckett were all scrambling for one decent reason to keep his ass in his chair.

"Glad we got that straight," Knox said before any of

them could come up with anything. "Danny, I'll watch the feeds and meet the rest of you in the stairwell."

To his credit, Zeke waited all of ten seconds from the time Knox muted his mic before he spoke. "You sure you want to do this? If something backfires in there, they may need you behind this keyboard more than in the line of fire."

Under normal circumstances he'd agree, but Ruslan had bought and paid for the whole floor. No matter what went down in the next half hour, no innocent bystanders were going to be close enough to fire off any 911 calls. "I walked away from my woman seven hours ago and have sat in this chair ever since. I did it because this was the place I could do her the most good and it almost killed me. But right now, if it were Gabe walking into a room with guns firing off in all directions and we needed another trigger to even the score, where would you be?"

Zeke held his gaze and nodded. "Point taken."

In the garage camera feed, the service van's side door slid open and Sergei's men piled out, all but Sergei and his two best shooters heading to join Danny, Axel and Ivan already positioned in the stairwell. Beckett, Sergei and his men surrounded Darya and Gia, acting the part of Ruslan's guards.

Knox stood, switched his headset out for a mobile unit and checked his gun. "I'm up. All you have to do is keep a sharp eye on the guards outside the door and clue us in before they can signal any alarms inside."

"Yeah, that and make sure no one ends up dead." Zeke slid into Knox's vacated chair behind the desk and cracked his knuckles. "Do me a favor. Save me some overtime and avoid the bullets, all right?"

"Says the guy who went into a break-in for his own woman without a gun and came out with a trophy wound. At least I'm armed."

He reached the stairwell landing on Ruslan's floor, Danny, Axel, Ivan and Sergei's men already in place. Despite their slightly rumpled appearance and a few stray blood splotches on one of the men's shirts, the three Russians all sported bland expressions. The sort that said they were either so damned used to this line of work it didn't faze them anymore, or were doing their best to hide how much they hated the idea of working with a mixed crew.

With the door to Ruslan's suite just outside the landing, no one said a word.

Beckett's voice cut through the line. "Two floors away."

Axel stepped back and nodded.

Danny took his place in front of the door.

"Zeke, we good?" Knox said low enough not to let his voice carry.

"Guards are still in place, but look bored as shit."

"They won't be for long," Axel muttered.

The elevator ding sounded through the line. "Moving out," Beckett said.

As soon as Beckett spoke, Gia and Darya kicked into action. Even without a visual, the sound of their struggle reached through the steel stairway door. He might not understand a lick of whatever it was coming out of Darya's mouth, but the sound of it was vile. Perfect for their approach.

Sergei's voice cut in. A command in Russian.

"I've got the one farthest from the stairwell," Beckett muttered through the chaos. "Danny, you're on the one closest. Fifteen feet."

More Russian sounded, but this time it came through the guards on the other side of the door.

"They're gettin' itchy," Zeke said. "Think you'd better move."

Beckett's order came right behind it. "Danny, go."

Danny yanked open the door, snatched the startled guard outside Ruslan's suite and yanked him into the stairwell. Five seconds. It couldn't have been more than that, but every bit of it happened in a blur, Darya's and Gia's protests more than covering the guard's struggles and ending with the two of them in lifeless heaps on the concrete landing.

Darya's voice died off, her gaze aimed through the open stairwell door at the dead men and her face a sickly white.

Knox stepped in close.

"Guns up," Sergei said as he pulled the keycard they'd pilfered from Ruslan's men from his pocket.

Knox gripped Darya's chin tight. "Look at me. Focus."

Her eyes shot to his and she jerked a terse nod. "I'm good." She spun and said something loud in a string of Russian that made Sergei smirk.

He punched the keycard into the slot and Gia stumbled through the opening as though someone had shoved her. She pulled Darya along with her, fully clearing the door, dropping to the floor and rolling to cover Darya.

The unexpected entrance and the girls as a distraction gave them the jump they needed. The silencers on the guns might have muted the shots, but did nothing to muffle the instant mayhem. Terse commands in both Russian and English fired through the room mixed with the grunts, crashes and the thump of bodies hitting the floor.

Knox stepped in front of Darya and Gia, shielding the two of them while Gia hustled Darya deeper into the safety of the elevator landing. He was just about to head into the suite and engage when another door in the hallway behind him yanked open.

Connecting rooms.

The paranoid motherfucker had bought out the whole floor. Of course, he'd have an escape hatch if he needed one.

Two men surged out, braced shoulder to shoulder with Ruslan right behind them.

"Action in the hallway!" Zeke called out through the headpiece.

Gia drew her gun the same second Knox did and shouted, "Beckett!"

Shots fired all at once, Knox and Gia taking the two men in front. Knox aimed again, one heartbeat from taking the shot at Ruslan, but froze the second his brain registered Ruslan's gun trained on Darya.

Sergei moved in from the opposite side, gun drawn and aimed at Ruslan's head, but hesitated when he took in Ruslan's target.

"Pull the trigger and she dies as well." His accent was thick, barely intelligible, but Ruslan's steady hand and the maniacal gaze he kept locked on Darya was clear enough.

No one moved.

Ever since Darya had told Knox about Ruslan he'd wanted this shot. A chance to make her life safe by his own hands. But now all he wanted was a distraction.

Anything to get his woman out of the line of fire. She was one step away from him. One stroke of luck or a miracle was all he needed to cover her.

Zeke's voice slid through the earpiece. "Got a distraction coming. Be ready."

A low hum fired through the landing, the sound of an elevator approaching their floor filling the quiet.

"You've given me quite a chase, little dove. I look forward to all the ways I'll make you repay me for the time and trouble." Ruslan narrowed his eyes and motioned Darya toward the elevator with a jerk of his head. "Move."

For all of a second, Knox locked stares with Sergei still locked in place in the suite's entrance, but it was enough to make his intention clear. The elevator dinged and Knox growled, "She's not going anywhere."

The doors swooshed open and the housekeeping cart they'd stolen with the intent of getting a better look inside the suite shot forward.

Knox spun, shielded Darya with his body and took her to the floor.

Gunfire filled the landing, bullets splintering into wall, wood and metal all around them. Pain exploded in his right shoulder, a sharp stab that radiated down his arm and out along his upper torso, but he held himself in place, forcing both hands up and around Darya's head.

The gunfire ceased and footsteps stomped around them, Russian words coated with disgust coursing from Sergei across the room.

Darya pressed her hands against his chest and tried to get up, but Knox didn't move. Didn't dare before he got the all clear from one of the men.

"Oh my God!" Darya struggled harder beneath him. "Gia, help me. Knox is bleeding."

Quick footsteps sounded on the thick carpet and Gia crouched beside them. "Hold still, let me look."

"I'm fine," he managed. Whatever had hit him hurt like hell, but he could move his arm and his lungs were both working, so it couldn't be too bad. He pushed up on one forearm just as Beckett, Axel and Zeke stormed toward him, helped him off Darya and up to his feet.

In all of five seconds, Zeke ripped Knox's T at the neck and down the bloodied sleeve, peeling back the ruined sides for better inspection.

Darya all but linebacked Beckett out of the way for a better look. "Is he okay?"

"Shoulder wound. Probably ricocheted off the elevator, but nothing we can't handle at Sanctuary."

Sergei turned from issuing a command to his men and met Knox's gaze across the housekeeping cart still lodged between them.

"Tell me that fucker isn't breathing," Knox said.

With the coldness of a long-jaded man, Sergei shoved the cart aside.

On the floor, Ruslan lay sprawled on the floor, sightless eyes aimed at the ceiling and a puddle of blood building beside a gruesome hole where his temple had been.

Darya gasped and turned away, but Knox hugged her against his chest with his good arm and cradled the back of her head. Finally, she was safe. No more running or living with fear dogging her step. And while it hadn't been his bullet that had done the deed, she was breathing. In the end, it was the only thing that mattered. "He can't hurt you anymore. No one can."

Epilogue

Six months Knox had waited for this day. Twenty-one long weeks of dealing with the fallout from a dead Russian *pakhan* and another four spent in Russia letting the once missing Darya Volkova resurface while she resumed her volunteering at the nursing home, started on her new career and happily made her wedding plans. Needless to say, Ninette and Sylvie had been alongside her every step of the way for the latter, filling the motherly gap she'd grown up with twenty times over.

Across the huge reception hall, his wife stood resplendent in a soft white gown that made her look every inch a winter princess. As styles and fabrics went, he was clueless, but there wasn't a royal alive or dead who'd ever outshined her. Flanked by Gia, who'd not only become Darya's closest friend but had served as maid of honor, on one side, and Ninette on the other, Yefim urged her from one guest to the next and boasted of her great American adventures.

No one could take her from Knox now.

Darya Volkova Torren.

Actually, if he was honest, he hadn't waited six months. He'd waited his whole life. And every minute had been worth it.

Seated beside Knox at the heavily adorned head table, Axel stretched his legs out, draped his arm along the top of the gold gilt chair beside him and scanned the ornate reception hall. Unlike the rest of the groomsmen, he'd paired his tux coat with a kilt—a tactic Knox was still convinced Axel had taken to one-up Sergei in the style department. The look might have been completely unconventional among the rest of the crowd, but somehow Axel pulled it off and looked slick as shit doing it.

"You gotta say one thing about Russian weddings," Axel said. "They do not fuck around."

"No, they do not," Beckett said from beside Knox. "Hell, it wasn't even me getting shackled and *I* feel married."

He wasn't wrong. Planning aside, the affair had taken two full days. Day one had started with him retrieving his bride-to-be from Yefim's home and paying a ransom, or *vykup nevesty*. Considering Knox had already siphoned all but ten million of Ruslan's money to the elderly man for further distribution as the other families saw fit, he'd shown with a custom-made stuffed wolf, a diamond pendant he'd had fashioned in the brotherhood's symbol and chocolates for Darya instead of customary cash.

Well, she'd still gotten cash. Namely ten million setting in a bank account with only her name on it, even if she didn't know about that yet. But he'd tell her when the time was right. No way in hell was his woman ever not having something to fall back on again.

Strangely, after the ransom, they'd had to attend a civil service that officially registered them as husband and wife. Something about churches being more about symbolism than legally binding, and he'd be go to hell before he left Russia without being *very* bound to his woman.

Day two was the real kicker, starting with a traditional ceremony in a church Yefim had undoubtedly pulled strings to get them into. The thing had lasted well over an hour, incorporated crowns and a ton of pageantry that made no sense since they were spoken in Russian, but Darya had smiled so big through the whole thing, he'd have done four more in a row if it made her happy.

Their only time alone had been a quiet limousine tour through St. Petersburg after the ceremony, a solemn time where they'd paused at an older cemetery and left flowers on her parents' graves.

Now they were here. Surrounded by an indoor, manmade winter wonderland of soft blue and white lights and only hours away from boarding one of Trevor's Gulfstreams.

Alone.

With his wife.

Finally.

Danny shifted in his seat enough to check out the dance floor and the wealth of beautiful women enjoying the music. He might have balked at the idea of a tux when Darya had first brought it up, but once he'd figured out the attention it drew from the ladies, he'd dropped all his complaints. "Man, I am not looking forward to the flight back to Dallas, but I have to say I wouldn't pass up the experience."

"Fifteen hours is nothing." Trevor jerked his head in Knox's direction. "With the jump Knox and Darya are making to Maui, they'll spend damned near a full day flying."

With his arm wrapped around Vivienne's shoulders and his hand smoothing affectionately over her shoulder, Jace chuckled and eyed Knox across the table. "He's got the G6 with the bed in it. After all the hoopla the last few days, I'm not thinkin' he's gonna mind quality alone time with his woman no matter what altitude they spend it at."

The band shifted from one slow ballad to another and those crowding the dance floor traded places with a new crew. Zeke and Gabe were the first back to the table, followed tight behind by Levi and Sylvie.

Trevor held his arm out for Levi and pulled him tight to his side, pride an evident stamp on his brother's face. "You give Nanna Sylvie a good turn, bud?"

"I tried," Levi said, "but it's no fun when you can't reach over their head and spin 'em around like you do, Mom." He frowned and scanned the crowd, no doubt looking for the pretty eight-year-old blonde he'd been palling around with since yesterday. "Can I go see if I can find Anna again?"

Trevor scratched his nose and tried to hide his smile. In the year and a half since Levi had been introduced to all the brothers, Levi had done everything in his power to emulate his new dad and uncles, including the appreciation of beautiful women.

Before Trevor could give Levi a thumbs-up, Sergei strolled up with Natalie on his arm. "You're looking for Anna?"

Levi spun and beamed a huge smile up at Sergei. "Have you seen her?"

Sergei dipped his head in the direction of the overflowing dessert buffet. "Your mother and I passed her coming off the dance floor."

"Cool!" He knocked back a swig of his Coke and plunked it back on the table, ready and raring to go. "I'll be back."

"You stay on this side of the hall where me and your uncles can see you," Trevor said. "No leaving the building."

A smart move considering some of the men milling through the room were unquestionably dangerous.

Levi stopped dead in his tracks and looked back at Sergei. "That includes you now, too, right? Aunt Darya says you're like a brother, so that makes you my uncle."

The table grew quiet and every eye turned to Sergei.

If he was unnerved by Levi's open question, he didn't show it. Only held the boy's stare with the utmost solemnness. "You are my family. Never doubt it."

Like lightning, Levi's smile whipped right back into place. "Awesome! Another uncle." His gaze slid to Natalie, who'd moved in close to Trevor's side and rested her hand on his shoulder. "Next Christmas is gonna be huge!" With that, he was gone, his quick strides winding him in and out of the finely dressed couples swaying on the dance floor.

Zeke barked out a sharp laugh and rested his hands on Gabe's hips. "He's got a point. We keep this up, Haven's gonna need an expansion."

Eyes still tracking her son's progress, Natalie squeezed Trevor's shoulder. "I think I'll tag along just to make sure he stays out of trouble."

"I'll go with you," Sylvie said, moving around the table. She motioned for Gabe and Vivienne to join them. "Come on you two. They loaded up a new batch of *pastilas* while we were dancing and I saw a new cake I have to try."

Vivienne and Gabe traded good-natured eye rolls, slid their chairs back and stood, but it was Vivienne who spoke, her comment aimed toward Axel. "Your mother isn't safe for my waistline."

Jace caught her wrist before she could glide away, slid his hand low on her back and pulled her close. Even with the band behind them, there was no missing the growl in his voice. "You want to have a chance winning that argument, you're gonna have to stop wearing tight red dresses that say otherwise." Not the least bit fazed by the men gathered round the table, he kissed her belly through the shiny fabric and let her go, but not without a quick palm of her ass.

"You're very blessed men," Sergei said as he watched them go.

Never one to let an opportunity go, Zeke took advantage of the moment alone with the men to cover the topic that had been on all the brothers' minds. "Enough so I'd sleep a whole lot better knowing any blowback from the last six months never so much as whispers their direction."

Sergei's gaze slid to Zeke, then scanned the rest of the men at the table. He looked to the empty chair beside Knox and cocked an eyebrow.

He wasn't Haven. Not even close. But he was special to Darya and had brought a gruesomely gratifying end to Ruslan. For that alone, he had Knox's never-ending gratitude. "You said it yourself. You're family. Have a seat."

In all the time Knox had known Sergei, not once had he seen a full smile out of the guy, but the semi-smirk he'd seen on the rare times Darya got him to let go crooked one corner of his mouth. He sat, crossed one leg over the other and scanned the crowd. "Your family will not be touched. Only a few know of your involvement. Yefim. My crew. Anton and myself."

"Your crew had five men we don't know from Adam," Beckett said. "They know their shit in a crisis and how to go unnoticed, but how's that stop them from sharing with other interested parties?"

"Because they are loyal to me. Because they will travel with me to America." He met Beckett's stare head on. "But mostly because they respect the way you take care of your own."

Jace sipped his scotch and eyeballed Sergei over the rim. "Sounds like your relocation plans are a little less hazy these days. Got someplace in particular in mind?"

A satisfaction that surprised Knox slipped across Sergei's face. "New Orleans."

More than one set of eyebrows popped high and Danny whistled. "Man, that's a hot town."

Sergei shrugged. "It has character. Good food. Good music. Warm." He looked to Knox. "And close enough I can aid my family if they need me."

"Think we've proven we've got family covered," Axel said with a chuckle. "Though, you'll be screwed twenty ways to Sunday if you don't show for Christmas now that Levi's claimed you."

Sergei spied Levi back on the dance floor with Anna and his half-smirk popped back into place. "If he wants me there, I will not disappoint him." He met each man's eyes one at a time. "But my debt stands. If you need me, you need only call."

The newest song ended and a swell of applause rang up to fill its void.

Before it died away, the band's sultry female singer said something in Russian and the crowd parted.

Darya stood waiting in the center of the dance floor, Yefim standing beside her and holding her hand, waiting to hand her off to her husband.

Sergei tilted his head, his attention solely on Darya. "I believe the time for formalities and business is over."

Hell, yeah it was. No more pomp and circumstance. No more interruptions. Just him, the music and his wife. He stood and buttoned his tux, pride pushing his shoulders back and leaving him ten feet tall. "Brother, I believe you're right."

Darya had thought San Diego was heaven on Earth. She'd been wrong. Maui was the real paradise.

Especially with Knox.

On the horizon, the sun glowed a beautiful gold, no more than a half hour from touching the turquoise water. Late afternoon clouds billowed above it, blending with the warm rays to paint the skies with mango, purples and soft blue.

More content than she could ever remember being in her life, she watched another day slip into night, comfortably nestled close to her dozing husband in their cabana on a private beach. For a man who'd once struggled to find sleep, now he did it easily. Only waking in the middle of the night to indulge them both in the sweetest intimacy. As if he realized they both needed the reminder they were alive and very much together. Safe and making their future together.

The wind danced against her skin, gently streaming her loose hair across her shoulders. Overhead, the white linen cover that had shielded her fair skin from the sun's powerful afternoon rays gently wavered and the ocean lapped soft against the powder white sand.

Yes, this was heaven.

But then anyplace with Knox would be the same.

She lifted her head off his chest and smoothed her hand along his bare sternum. Beneath her palm and his Haven tags, the wolf he'd had tattooed above his heart stared back at her, solemn but beautiful. It had taken hours for the artist to complete it, but she'd sat with him throughout it, honored not only by the permanence of the mark, but the fact that he so proudly wore it. Her mark. Her heritage, now blended with his.

Never in her life had she considered taking such a step of her own, but watching him had changed her viewpoint. Now, the simple quote she'd once kept mounted above her kitchen sink lay coiled forever in graceful script around one wrist.

Dream as if you'll live forever. Live as if you'll die tomorrow.

From the day she'd heard Knox's name, she'd known he'd be a part of her dreams. The foundation for her future. She'd just had no idea how much.

"You're watching me again," Knox mumbled without opening his eyes.

She loved his sleepy, grumble voice. Deep, rich and thick with wickedness. "If your brothers saw you this still and so long away from your keyboards, they'd accuse me of brainwashing you."

His lips curled in a lazy smile and his eyelids lifted. In the setting sun, his eyes matched the gray tones of the softer clouds overhead. "They know better."

She cocked her head. "Know what?"

He cupped the side of her face, his thumb dragging

tenderly along the edge of her jaw and his gaze softening. "That I don't need it anymore. The code kept me entertained. The hacks gave me challenge. But at the end of the day, all I wanted was something of my own. *Someone* of my own. No need to build something new or break through a wall, when you've already got perfection."

Her stomach pitched and swirled to match the birds singing over the ocean, and her heart grew so light it was a wonder it stayed rooted in her chest. "You don't want to build anything new?"

He grinned and his eyes twinkled. "Do orgasms count? Because I'm pretty inspired to build plenty of those."

Boy, was he. From the time they'd boarded the plane in St. Petersburg, he'd made her pleasure and comfort paramount in all things. Totally indulgent in his sometimes overbearing alpha way.

But she loved it.

Dream as if you'll live forever. Live as if you'll die tomorrow.

It was right there. Winking up at her from her skin and offering encouragement. Daring her to bridge the one topic she'd been too nervous to bring up. But this was Knox. Her husband. Her foundation.

She focused on the beautiful script and pulled in a slow breath. "You know there are things we could build together."

At first, only silence echoed back at her, the soft wind and waves filling the space between them. She traced one ear of her wolf, her finger shaking as she waited.

He guided her face to his. "I'd build anything with you."

She swallowed hard and pressed her palm against his chest. "Even a family?"

An alertness she hadn't seen in him in days fired bright behind his eyes. Before she could gauge his intent, he pushed himself up on one elbow and rolled her to her back so he hovered above her. "Are you trying to tell me something?"

Oh, dear. She'd gone all the wrong way with this. Though, on the surface he didn't seem to be too upset with the direction things had gone, so perhaps the miscalculation wasn't a bad one. "I'm not pregnant if that's what you're thinking."

His gaze roamed her face and pure wonder lit his features.

Definitely not a bad reaction. One she could work with, if she dared.

She touched her finger to his lips and whispered, "But I'd like to be."

In a flash, the air around them went from cool and comfortable to supercharged and heated, the wind licking against her skin with the same intensity as his gaze. "How long does it take for those pills to leave your system?"

There he was. Her take charge, confident man awakened to a new challenge and ready to get things underway. She giggled despite the serious topic. "I have no idea."

"We'll call Zeke," he said, positioning himself between her thighs. With only his board shorts and her bikini between them, there was no missing his enthusiasm or willingness to get started.

She opened her thighs wider and cocked her knees, letting him settle into the cradle of her hips. "We don't have to do anything right away. I just wanted to know how you felt about it."

"Is your dream having babies?"

God, yes. To her mind there was no better gift—no better expression of love between two people than a child. "Someday, yes."

He rolled his hips against hers, the naughty gleam in his eyes gaining more depth. "How many?"

Her breath caught in her throat, the perfect press of his shaft against her sending her thoughts thoroughly off track. "I don't know. I'd be happy with one, but would like to have two."

The touch of his warm hand along her nape and the swoosh of her swim top coming untied wrenched her back to reality. "What are you doing?"

He peeled the fabric away, baring her breasts to the air's welcome coolness and palmed one mound. "Life's short. Dream big, right?"

Life *was* short. Perilously so. And with Knox every dream seemed bigger. Brighter. "We're outside," she whispered and arched into his touch.

"Don't care." He skimmed his lips against hers. "Besides, what's the point in a private beach if you can't enjoy a little decadence while it's yours."

She tangled her hands in his hair and wrapped her legs around his hips. He was right. If there was ever a time to chase her dreams with the man she loved, it was right now. Protected in his arms while paradise hummed around them. "You know I took a pill this morning."

He smiled against her lips and muttered, "You know how I feel about firewalls."

Laughing, she nipped his lower lip. "Think you can get one past the goalie, do you?"

"Maybe. Maybe not. But you can bet your sweet ass I'm gonna try."

* * * * *

To purchase and read more books by Rhenna Morgan please visit Rhenna's website at http://RhennaMorgan.com.

Acknowledgments

Diving into Knox's book was daunting simply because the mere thought of networks, firewalls and IP addresses made me whimper. Fortunately, I know this guy by the name of Jay Donovan who is all things techy-goodness. Not only does he keep my website safe and humming, but he's also happy to talk dastardly plots and cyber-shenanigans—a handy perk for an author faced with creating a wicked smooth character like Knox.

Once again, Angela James gets the giant-size high-five for having my back and making Knox and Darya's story totally rock. Swear to God, if anyone tries to take her away from me, I'm sending the brothers to intervene on my behalf.

And of course, I have to thank my rock-solid posse—Cori Deyoe, Juliette Cross, Kyra Jacobs, Audrey Carlan, Dena Garson and most importantly my *amazing* daughters. Without each of you to keep me grounded, laughing, and overflowing with love and support, I'd be utterly lost.

Go back to the beginning of the Men Of Haven in Rough & Tumble *by Rhenna Morgan.*

"*ROUGH & TUMBLE* by Rhenna Morgan will warm your heart and melt your panties."
—#1 *New York Times* bestselling author Audrey Carlan (Calendar Girl series)

Chapter One

Nothing like a New Year's Eve drunk-sister-search-and-rescue to top off a chaos-laden twelve-hour workday. Vivienne dialed Shinedown's newest release from full blast to almost nothing and whipped her Honda hybrid into a pay-by-the-hour lot in the heart of Dallas's Deep Ellum. Five freaking weekends in a row Callie had pulled this crap, with way too many random SOS calls before her current streak.

At least this place was in a decent part of town. Across the street, men and women milled outside a new bar styled like an old-fashioned pub called The Den, with patrons dressed in everything from T-shirts and faded jeans, to leather riding gear and motorcycle boots. Not one of them looked like they were calling the party quits anytime soon.

Viv tucked her purse beneath the seat, stashed her key fob in her pocket, and strode into the humid January night. Her knockoff Jimmy Choos clicked against the aged blacktop, and cool fog misted her cheeks.

Off to one side, an appreciative whistle sounded between low, masculine voices.

She kept her head down, hustled through the dark double doors and into a cramped, black-walled foyer. A crazy-big bouncer with mocha skin and dreads leaned against the doorjamb between her and the main bar, his attention centered on a stunning brunette in a soft pink wifebeater, jeans and stilettos.

The doors behind her clanged shut.

Pushing to full height, the bouncer warily scanned Viv head to toe. Hard to blame the guy. Outside of health inspectors and liquor licensing agents, they probably didn't get many suits in here, and she'd bet none of them showed in silk shirts.

"ID," he said.

"I'm not here to stay. I just need to find someone."

He smirked and crossed his arms. "Can't break the rules, momma. No ID, no party."

"I don't want a party, I want to pick up my sister and then I'm out. She said she'd be up front. About my height, light brown, curly hair and three sheets to the wind?"

"You must mean Callie," the brunette said. "She was up here about an hour ago mumbling something about *sissy*, so I'm guessing you're her." She leaned into Scary Bouncer Dude's formidable chest, grinned up at him, and stroked his biceps with an almost absentminded reverence. "May as well let her in. If you don't, Trev will spend closing time hearing his waitresses bitch about cleaning up puke."

Too bad Viv didn't have someone to bitch to about getting puke detail. Callie sure as heck never listened.

Bouncer dude stared Viv down and slid his mammoth hand far enough south he palmed the brunette's ass. He jerked his head toward the room beyond the opening. "Make it quick. You might be old enough, but the cops have been in three times tonight chomping to bust our balls on any write-up they can find."

Finally, something in her night that didn't require extra time and trouble. Though if she'd been smart, she'd have grabbed her ID before she came in.

"Smart move, chief." The woman tagged him with a fast but none-too-innocent kiss, winked and motioned for Viv to follow. "Come on. I'll show you where she is."

An even better break. The last search and rescue had taken over thirty minutes in a techno dance bar. She'd finally found Callie passed out under a set of stairs not far from the main speakers, but the ringing in Viv's ears had lasted for days. At least this time she'd have a tour guide and an extra pair of hands.

The place was as eclectic on the inside as it was out. Rock and movie collectibles hung on exposed brick walls and made the place look like it'd been around for years even though it reeked of new. Every table was packed. Waitresses navigated overflowing trays between the bustling crowd, and Five Finger Death Punch vibrated loud enough to make conversation a challenge.

The brunette smiled and semi-yelled over one shoulder, never breaking her hip-slinging stride. "Nice turnout for an opening week, yeah?"

Well, that explained the new smell. "I don't do crowds." At least not this kind. Signing her dad's Do Not Resuscitate after a barroom brawl had pretty much cured her of smoky, dark and wild. "It looks like a great place, though."

The woman paused where the bar opened to a whole different area and scanned Viv's outfit. "From the looks of things, you could use a crowd to loosen up." She shrugged and motioned toward the rear of the room.

"Corner booth. Last I saw your girl she was propped up between two airheads almost as hammered as she was. And don't mind Ivan. The cops are only hounding the owner, not the customers. My name's Lily if you need anything." And then she was gone, sauntering off to a pack of women whooping it up at the opposite end of the club.

So much for an extra set of hands. At least this part of the bar was less crowded, scattered sitting areas with every kind of mismatched chair and sofa you could think of making it a whole lot easier to case the place.

She wove her way across the stained black concrete floors toward the randomly decorated booths along the back. Overhead, high-end mini sparkle lights cast the room in a muted, sexy glow. Great for ambience, but horrid for picking drunk sisters out of a crowd. Still, Viv loved the look. She'd try the same thing in her own place if it wouldn't ruin the tasteful uptown vibe in her new town house. Funky might be fun, but it wouldn't help with resale.

Laughter and a choking cloud of smoke mushroomed out from the corner booth.

The instant Viv reached the table, the chatter died. Three guys, two girls and the stench of Acapulco Red— but no sister. "You guys see Callie?"

A lanky man with messy curly blond hair eyed her beneath thirty-pound eyelids and grinned, not even bothering to hide the still smoldering joint. "'Sup."

The redhead cozied next to him smacked him on the shoulder and glowered. "She's after Callie, Mac. Not stopping in for a late-night chat." She reached across the table and handed Viv an unpaid bar tab. "She headed to the bathroom about ten minutes ago, but be sure you take this with you. She stuck me with the bill last night."

Seventy-eight bucks. A light night for New Year's Eve, which was a damn good thing considering Viv's bank balance. She tucked the tab in her pocket. "Which way to the bathroom?"

The girl pointed toward a dark corridor. "Down that hall and on your left."

Viv strode that direction, not bothering with any follow-up niceties. Odds were good they wouldn't remember her in the morning, let alone five minutes from now.

Inside the hallway, the steady drone of music and laughter plunged to background noise. Two scowling women pranced past her headed back into the bar. One glanced over her shoulder and shook her head at Viv. "May as well head to the one up front. Someone's in that one and isn't coming out anytime soon from the sound of things."

Well, shit. This was going to be fun. She wiggled the knob. "Callie?"

God, she hoped it was her sister in there. Knowing her luck, she was interrupting a New Year's booty call. Although, if that were the case, they were doing it wrong because it was way too quiet. She tried the knob again and knocked on the door. "Callie, it's Viv. Open up."

Still no answer.

Oh, to hell with it. She banged on the door and gave it the good old pissed-off-sister yell. "Callie, for the love of God, open the damned door! I want to go home."

A not so promising groan sounded from inside a second before the door marked Office at her right swung wide. A tall Adonis in jeans and a club T-shirt emblazoned with The Den's edgy logo blocked the doorway, his sky blue eyes alert in a way that shouldn't be possible past 1:00 a.m.

Two men filled the space behind him, one shirtless with arms braced on the top of a desk, and another leaning close, studying the shirtless guy's shoulder. No wait, he wasn't studying it, he was stitching it, which explained the seriously bloody shirt on the floor.

"Got more bathrooms up front. No need to break down the damned door." Adonis Man ambled toward her, zigzagging his attention between her and the bathroom. "There a problem?"

Dear God in heaven, now that the Adonis had moved out of the way, the shirtless guy was on full, mouthwatering display, and he was every book boyfriend and indecent fantasy rolled up into one. A wrestler's body, not too big and not too lean, but one hundred percent solid. A huge tattoo covered his back, a gnarled and aged tree with a compass worked into the gothic design. And his ass. Oh hell, that ass was worth every torturous hour in front of her tonight. The only thing better than seeing it in seriously faded Levi's would be seeing it naked.

"Hey," Adonis said. "You gonna ogle my brother all night, or tell me why you're banging down one of my doors?"

They were brothers? No way. Adonis was all...well, Adonis. The other guy was tall, dark and dirty.

Fantasy Man peered over his injured shoulder. Shrewd, almost angry eyes lasered on her, just as dark as his near-black hair. A chunk of the inky locks had escaped his ponytail and fell over his forehead. His closely cropped beard gave him a sinister and deadly edge that probably kept most people at a distance, but his lips could lull half the women in Texas through hell if it meant they'd get a taste.

Viv shook her head and coughed while her mind clambered its way up from Smuttville. "Um…" Her heart thrummed to the point she thought her head would float off her shoulders, and her tongue was so dry it wouldn't work right. "I think my sister's passed out in there. I just want to get her home."

Adonis knocked on the door and gave the knob a much firmer twist than Viv had. "Zeke, toss me the keys off the desk."

Before either of the men could move, the lock on the door popped and the door creaked open a few inches. "Vivie?" Callie's mascara-streaked face flashed a second before the door slipped shut again.

Months of training kicked in and Viv lurched forward, easing open the door and slipping inside. "I've got it now. Give me a minute to get her cleaned up and gather her stuff."

Adonis blocked the door with his foot. The black, fancy cowboy boots probably cost more than a month's mortgage payment, which seemed a shame considering it didn't look like she'd be able to pay her next one. "You sure you don't need help?"

"Nope." She snatched a few towels out of the dispenser and wetted them, keeping one eye on Callie where she semi-dozed against the wall. "We've done this before. I just need a few minutes and a clear path."

"All right. My name's Trevor if you need me. You know where we are if you change your mind." He eased his foot away, grinned and shook his head.

"Oh!" Viv caught the door before it could close all the way and pulled the bar tab out of her pocket. "My sister ran up a tab. Could you hold this at the bar for me and let me pay it after I get her out to the car? I need to grab my purse first."

He backtracked, eyeballed Callie behind her, and crumpled the receipt. "I'd say you've already covered tonight." He turned for the office. "We'll call it even."

Fantasy Man was still locked in place and glaring over one shoulder, the power behind his gaze as potent as the crackle and hum after a nearby lightning strike.

She ducked back into the bathroom and locked the door, her heart jackrabbiting right back up where it had been the first time he'd looked at her. She seriously needed to get a grip on her taste in men. Suits and education were a much safer choice. Manners and meaningful conversation. Not bloody T-shirts, smoky bars and panty-melting grins.

Snatching Callie's purse off the counter, she let out a serrated breath, shook out the wadded wet towel, and started wiping the black streaks off her sister's cheek. A man like him wouldn't be interested in her anyway. At least, not the new and improved her. And the odds of them running into each other again in a city like Dallas were slim to none, so she may as well wrangle up her naughty thoughts and keep them in perspective.

On the bright side, she didn't have to worry about the tab. Plus, she had a fresh new imaginary star for her next late-night rendezvous with BOB.

Damn if this hadn't been the most problematic New Year's Eve in history. It wasn't Jace's first knife wound, but getting it while pulling apart two high-powered, hot-headed drug dealers promised future complications he didn't need. Add to that, two more customers arrested at his own club, Crossroads, in less than three days, and nonstop visits from the cops at The Den, and his New Year wasn't exactly top-notch.

Thank God his brother Zeke wasn't working trauma tonight or he'd have had to have Trev stitch him up. That motherfucker would've hacked the shit out of his tat.

"You 'bout done?" Jace said.

Zeke layered one last strip of tape in place and tossed the roll to the desk. "I am now."

"Took you long enough." Jace straightened up, tucked the toothpick he'd had pinched between his fingers into his mouth and rolled his shoulder. It was tight and throbbing like a son of a bitch, but not bad enough to keep him from day-to-day shit—assuming he didn't have any more drug dealer run-ins.

"I don't know. Our straitlaced partygoer didn't seem to mind me taking my time." Zeke packed his supplies into one of the locked cabinets, the same triage kit they kept at every residence or business they owned. It might have been overkill, but it sure as hell beat emergency rooms and sketchy conversations with police. "Thought for a minute there the sweet little thing was going to combust."

"Sweet little thing my ass." Trevor dropped into his desk chair, propped his booted feet on the corner of his desk, and fisted the remote control for the security vids mounted on the wall. "I'd bet my new G6 that woman's got a titanium backbone and a mind that would whip both your asses into knots."

Jace snatched a fresh white club T-shirt from Trev's grand opening inventory and yanked it over his head, the wound in his shoulder screaming the whole time.

"Based on what? Her courtroom getup or her uptight hairdo?"

"Like I judge by what people wear. You know me better than that." Trev punched a few buttons, paused long enough to eyeball the new bartender he'd just hired ringing in an order on the register, then dropped the remote on the desk. "You ask me, you're the one judging. Which is kind of the pot calling the kettle black."

The setback hit its mark, the Haven tags he wore weighting his neck a little heavier, a reminder of their brotherhood and the code they lived by.

It's not where a man comes from, or what he wears, that matters. It's what he does with his life that counts.

Twenty-seven years he and Axel had lived by that mantra, dragging themselves out of the trailer park and into a brotherhood nothing but death would breach.

"He's right," Zeke said. "You're letting Paul's campaign crawl up your ass and it's knockin' you off course."

Damn, but he hated it when his own mantras got tossed back at him. More so when he deserved it. He let out an exhausted huff and dropped down on the leather couch facing the string of monitors. "Play it again."

Trevor shook his head but navigated the menu on the center screen anyway.

"Not sure why you're doing this to yourself, man." Zeke pulled three Modelos out of the stainless mini-fridge under the wet bar and popped the tops faster than any bartender. God knew he'd gotten enough experience working as one through med school. "Paul's a politician with a grudge, nothing else. Watching this again is just self-inflicted pain. Focus on the real problem."

Jace took the beer Zeke offered as the ten o'clock

news story flashed on the screen. The third-string reporter's too-bright smile and pageant hairdo screamed of a woman with zero experience but eager for a shot at a seat behind the anchor desk.

"Dallas's popular club, Crossroads, is in the news again this New Year's Eve as two additional patrons were arrested on charges of drug possession with intent to distribute. Undercover police are withholding names at this time, but allege both are part of a ring lead by Hugo Moreno, a dealer notorious in many Northeast Texas counties for peddling some of the most dangerous products on the street."

"She's not wrong on that score." Zeke plopped on the other end of the couch and motioned to the screen with his bottle. "The number of ODs coming in at Baylor and Methodist the last six months have been through the roof. The guys from DPD swear most are tied to some designer shit coming out of Moreno's labs."

Trevor leaned in and planted his elbows on the desk, eyes to Jace. "You think Otter's going to hold out long enough to waylay Moreno?"

If Jace knew the answer to that one, he'd be a lot less jumpy and minus one slash to his shoulder. Pushing one pharmaceutical genius out of his club by strong-arming him with another was a risky move at best, but it sure as shit beat ousting Moreno on his own. "Otter's a good man with a calm head on his shoulders and a strong team. If he says he'll only let weed in the place and keep Hugo at bay, I'm gonna give him all the backing he needs. DPD's sure as hell not going to help. Not the ones in Paul's pockets anyway."

"Paul doesn't have any pockets," Trev said. "Only his daddy does."

Right on cue, the camera cut to an interview with Paul Renner as reporters intercepted him leaving another political fund-raiser.

"Councilman Renner, you've been very vocal in your run for US Representative in supporting the Dallas Police Department's efforts to crack down on drug crime, and have called out establishments such as Crossroads in midtown Dallas. Have you heard about the additional drug arrests there tonight, and do you have any comments?"

Renner frowned at the ground, a picture-perfect image of disappointment and concern. Like that dickhead hadn't been trying to screw people since his first foray from the cradle.

"I continue to grow more concerned with establishments like those run by Jace Kennedy and his counterparts," Renner said. *"It seems they continually skirt justice and keep their seedy establishments open for business. It's innocent citizens who end up paying the price, courted by heinous individuals peddling dangerous substances and amoral behavior. My primary goal, if elected to the House of Representatives, will be to promote legislation that makes it difficult for men like Mr. Kennedy and Mr. Moreno to escape justice."*

The toothpick between Jace's teeth snapped in half. He tossed it to the coffee table in front of him and pulled out another one of many stashed in the pocket of his jacket.

"It's official, now." Trevor raised his beer in salute and tipped his head. "You're an amoral son of a bitch leading innocent citizens to ruin."

Motion registered in one of the smaller security screens, the bathroom door outside Trevor's office swinging open enough to let Little Miss and her seriously drunken sister ping-pong down the hallway. The two were about the same height, but you couldn't have dressed two women more differently. Next to Little Miss, her sister was best suited for a biker bar, all tits, ass and wobbling heels. Not that she was bad to look at. She just lacked the natural, earthy grace of the sober one.

Damn it, he needed to pace. Or get laid. Just looking at the ass on Little Miss in tailored pants made him want to rut like a madman. Never mind the puzzle she presented. Trev wasn't wrong—she had a shitload of backbone blazing through those doe-shaped eyes. The combination didn't jive with her image. Nothing like a paradox to get his head spinning.

"Guess we found one way to get his head off Renner." Zeke knocked back another gulp of his beer.

"What?" He back-and-forthed a glare between his brothers.

Trevor chuckled low and shifted the videos so Little Miss's trek to the front of the bar sat center stage. "Zeke said the only thing you've done amoral was that freak show you put on with Kat and Darcy at last month's barbecue."

"Fuck you, Trev."

"Fuck her, you mean," Trev said. "No shame there, brother. You didn't even see her up close. If you did, you sure as shit wouldn't be sitting here rerunning sound bites of asshole Renner."

"Hell, no," Jace said. "A woman that uptight is the last thing I need. Or did you miss her casing not just Zeke patching up my shoulder, but the bloody shirt on the floor, too? You'll be lucky if the cops don't show from an anonymous tip called in."

Little Miss and her sister stumbled into the front section of the bar, the sister's arm curled around Little Miss's neck in a way he'd bet would still hurt tomorrow morning.

Nope. Sweet hips, fiery eyes and a good dose of mystery or not, she was the last thing he needed right now.

Two men blocked Little Miss's path.

The women stopped, and the drunk sister swayed enough it was a wonder she didn't topple onto the table beside her.

One of the men palmed the back of Little Miss's neck, and she jerked away.

Jace surged to his feet, grabbing his leather jacket off the table. "I'm headed to Haven. You hear more from Axel at Crossroads or get any more grief from the cops, let me know."

Both men let out hardy guffaws and waved him off.

"Twenty bucks says our buttoned-up guest gets some help on the way out the door," Trev said.

Zeke chimed in behind him. "Yeah, let us know if Sweet Cheeks tastes as good as she looks."

Bastards. The sad thing was, Trev was about to score a twenty from Zeke, because Jace might not be willing to curl up with Little Miss, but he wasn't watching men paw her either.

Chapter Two

Viv tightened her arm around Callie's waist and shook off the not-so-shy behemoth of a man gripping the back of her neck. His height alone was enough to make him intimidating, but paired with his shaved head and leathers, the scary vibe packed an extra punch. "I appreciate the offer, but we'll be fine."

"Ah, come on, darlin'." He stepped closer and shot a quick, conspiratorial grin at his cohort in crime, a much smaller guy who more than made up in the shaggy hair department what Cue Ball was missing. "Just trying to help out. Can't have a pretty thing like you out on the streets alone this time of night."

Stupid, stubborn men. One thing about guys who lived and breathed a hard life, they seemed to think the word *no* was a coy version of *maybe*. She feigned an innocent smile as best she could with Callie wrenching her neck. "Well, before I take you up on that, I should warn you, Callie's probably about five minutes from puking on anything or anyone within a twenty-foot radius. Seeing as how I'm right next to her, that would include me. You still up for helping?"

The mood killer worked even better than she expected, dousing the naughty gleam in both men's eyes faster than the people at the table behind them downed their shots. The big guy stepped back and waved her through without another word.

Viv half laughed and half scoffed, leaning into her first few steps to get some extra forward momentum.

Callie staggered closer and nuzzled next to Viv, her words coming out in a drunken, sleepy slur. "Thanks for coming to get me, Vivie." The scent of tequila and other things Viv didn't want to contemplate blasted across her nose and riled what little was left of the snack she'd pilfered at the New Year's Eve party. "You're a good sister. I can always count on you."

An uncomfortable pang rattled in her chest, memories of coming home to an empty apartment when Mom and Dad should've been there clanging together all at once. Family was supposed to be there for one another. To love each other and have their backs, not leave them to grapple with life all alone. "Yeah, Callie. I'm here. Always."

The bouncer who'd let her in took one look at her sister and stepped out of hurling range. "See you found your girl."

"I did, thanks." She shouldered the main door open and braced when Callie stumble-stepped down to the sidewalk. A little farther and she'd be home free, or at least in a place where she could battle the rest of the night barefoot in a comfy pair of sweats.

Behind her, the bar door chunked open, and a few of the people crowded in front of the bar called out goodnights and wishes for a happy new year to who-ever had come out.

Viv stepped out onto Elm Street, Callie pinned to her hip.

Midstride, Callie lurched and waved to someone across the street. "Stephanie!" The unexpected happy dance knocked them both off center. Callie fisted Viv's hair in a last-ditch grasp to stay upright, but wrenched Viv's neck before she went sideways.

Viv stumbled, heels teetering on the blacktop and arms flailing for purchase.

Callie smacked her head on the curb.

Viv braced for her own impact, but strong arms caught her, her back connecting with a warm solid chest instead of the painful concrete she'd expected.

A deep, rumbling voice rang out behind her. "Get Zeke and Trevor out here. See if Danny's still around, too."

She clenched the leather-clad arms around her waist and fought to catch a steady breath.

The bouncer hurried into the street and kneeled beside Callie, gently lifting her so her head rested on his lap.

This fucking night. This horrid, embarrassing, fucking night. Behind her, murmurs and giggles from bystanders grew by the second. Her mind pushed for her to get up, deal with Callie, and get home where it was safe, but her body wouldn't move, mortification and the flood of adrenaline rooting her in place.

The man behind her tightened his hold as though he sensed her self-consciousness. "We got this, sugar." The tiny movement made the leather of his jacket groan. His scent permeated her haze, a sea-meets-sun combination that made her think of Mediterranean islands and lazy days on the beach, not at all what she'd expect from a man coming out of the dive behind her. He sifted his fingers through her freed hair, moving it to one side of her neck, and a stray bobby pin clattered to the asphalt. "Your neck all right? Your sister gave it a hell of a snap."

That voice. Every word radiated through her, grated and deep like the rumbling bass of a stereo cranked up too loud.

He stroked her nape, the touch confident and not the least bit platonic.

Her senses leaped to attention, eager for more of the delicious contact. It was all she could do to hold back the moan lodged in the back of her throat. She swallowed and blew out a slow breath instead. "Yeah, I'm fine."

He lifted her upright, and the muscles in his arms and chest flexed around her, tangling what was left of her reasonable thoughts into a hopeless knot.

A man jogged up, hunkered down beside her sister, and opened up a leather duffel. Not just any man, the guy who'd stitched up the hottie in the office.

She surged forward to intervene, but firm hands gripped her shoulders and pulled her back. "Give Zeke a minute to check her out."

Viv twisted, ready to shout at whoever dared to hold her back—and froze. Her breath whooshed out of her like she'd hit the pavement after all.

Fantasy Man grinned down at her, a toothpick anchored at the corner of his mouth. His tan spoke of far more hours in the sun than the surgeon general recommended, and his almost black eyes burned with a wicked gleam that promised loads of trouble. And not necessarily the good kind, judging by the vicious scar marking the corner of one eye.

"Zeke's a trauma doc," he said. "Perks up like a bloodhound if anyone so much as stubs a toe."

Callie moaned, and Viv spun back around to find the doc prodding the back of her sister's neck.

"I know it hurts," Zeke said. "Can you tell me your name?"

"I don't feel so good," Callie said.

Zeke carefully moved Callie's head back and forth and side to side. "I imagine you don't. Still want to know your name, though."

"Callie."

"That's a pretty name." Zeke dug into his duffel and pulled out a penlight. "You know what day it is, Callie?"

Callie's eyes stayed shut, but she smiled like a kid at Christmas and threw her arms out to the side, damn near whacking Trevor as he sat on the curb beside her. "Happy New Year!"

Trevor chuckled and shifted Callie away from the bouncer so she rested against his own chest. "I got her, Ivan. See if you can't find the crowd something else to gawk at."

"You know where you're at, Callie?" Zeke checked her sister's pupils for responsiveness.

As soon as Zeke pulled the light away, Callie blinked and focused on Viv. "I'm with Vivie."

Fantasy Man's voice resonated beside Viv's ear, the tone low enough it zinged from her neck to the base of her spine. "Vivie, huh?"

A shudder racked her and she crossed her arms to combat the goose bumps popping up under her suit jacket.

His arm slipped around her waist from behind and pulled her against his chest, his heat blasting straight through to her skin. "You okay?"

Hell, no she wasn't okay. Her sister was hurt and

bystanders lined both sides of the street waiting to see what happened next, but all Viv could think about was how his voice would sound up close and in the dark. Preferably between heavy breaths with lots and lots of skin involved. She'd chalk it up to exhaustion, but her nonexistent sex life was probably the real culprit.

"I'm fine. Just tired." She forced herself to step away and faced him, holding out her hand. "And it's Vivienne. Vivienne Moore. Or Viv. Callie's the only one that calls me Vivie."

He studied her outstretched palm, scanning her with languid assessment, then clasped her hand in his and pierced her with a look that jolted straight between her legs. "Jace Kennedy."

Figured that Fantasy Man would have a fantasy name to match. It sounded familiar, too, though with all the pheromones jetting through her body she couldn't quite place where. Maybe wishful thinking or one too many romance novels. She tugged her hand free and stuffed her fists into her pockets. "Thanks for not letting me bust my ass in front of everyone."

He matched her posture and shuttled his toothpick from one side of his mouth to the other with his tongue. "Pretty sure I got the best end of the deal."

Zeke's voice cut in from behind her. "I think she's fine. Just a nasty goose egg and too much booze."

Viv turned in time to see the two men guide Callie to her feet. She weaved a little and looked like she'd fall asleep any second, but the pain seemed to have knocked off a little of her drunken haze. Her floral bohemian top was wrinkled and askew on her curvy frame, and her golden-brown hair was mussed like she'd just had monkey sex. Otherwise, she fit the rest of the crowd a whole lot better than Viv.

Pegging Zeke with a pointed look, Jace cupped the back of Viv's neck. "Check Little Miss out, too. Didn't like the angle her neck took when her girl went down." He focused on Viv and held out his hand, palm up. "Keys."

"What?"

"Keys," he said. "Give 'em to me and we'll bring your car around."

"You don't need to do that." She pointed at the lot across the street. "I'm just over there, and Callie looks—"

"It's almost two in the morning, your sister's hammered and you both took a fall. Fork over the keys, we'll get your car, pull it around and load your girl up."

Four unyielding stares locked on to her—Zeke, Trevor and Jace, plus a new guy with black hair and a ponytail nearly down to his ass. The way the new guy trimmed his goatee gave him a Ming the Merciless vibe. She shouldn't let any one of these guys near her, let alone surrender the keys to her car. "I think it's better if Callie and I handle it ourselves."

The muscle at the back of Jace's jaw twitched and his eyes darkened.

"I don't mean to sound ungrateful," Viv added. "I appreciate everyone jumping in to help. It's way more than you needed to do. I just don't know you guys. Have you watched the news lately?"

"That's fair." Trevor's focus was locked on Jace when he spoke, but then slid his gaze to Viv. "But this is my bar, your sister drank too much while she was in it and hurt herself on the way out. It's in my best interest to make sure you make it home safe. Anything bad goes

down between here and there, you could give me and
my new business a whole lot of heartache I don't need,
right?"

Trevor had a point.

"Give me the keys, sugar." Jace crooked the fingers
on his outstretched hand. "You've done enough solo
tonight."

She handed them over and Zeke stepped in, gently
prodding the muscles along the back of her neck. "Any
soreness?"

Viv shook her head as much as she could with Zeke's
big hands wrapped around her throat.

Behind Zeke, Jace handed off the keys to Ivan. A
second later, jogging boot heels rang against the asphalt followed by the chirp of a disengaging car alarm.

Zeke tested her movement side to side and front and
back as he'd done for Callie and checked her pupils. "I
doubt you'd feel it until tomorrow anyway. Probably
wouldn't hurt to take a few ibuprofens before you go
to bed." He jerked his head toward Callie, still swaying
next to Trevor. "Same goes for her. You'll have a hard
time keeping her awake and not puking with as much
as she's had to drink, but if she starts to act confused,
can't remember things or complains of ringing in her
ears, get her to an ER."

"You got anyone that can help you tonight?" Jace asked.

Trevor piped up. "I can ask one of the girls to stay
with you if you want."

"No, I can handle it."

Zeke gave her a knowing look, pulled a card out of
his billfold, and handed it over. "You need help, call.
We'll get her where she needs to be."

As in to an ER, or a place that had a minimum thirty-day stay? God knew, she'd begged her sister to at least try an AA meeting, but Callie and their dad had cornered all the stubborn genes for the family.

Her hybrid hummed up beside them and Zeke stepped away. "Lay her down in the back, Trev."

The bouncer hopped out of the driver's seat and opened up the back door for Trevor, who'd given up steering Callie and opted for carrying her to the car.

Jace moved in close and lowered his voice. "She get like this a lot?"

The men situated her sister in the back seat.

"Yeah." God, she was tired of this routine. She'd give just about anything to surrender, curl up into a little ball and let someone else handle Callie's tricks for a day or two.

Jace splayed his hand along the small of her back and urged her forward as a big, mean-looking bike with even nastier sounding pipes rolled up behind her car. "Danny's gonna follow you home and help you get Sleeping Beauty settled in for the night."

"I don't think—"

"If your sister passes out, can you get her in the house on your own?"

"No."

"Then stop thinking and let us handle this," Jace said. "Danny so much as breathes funny, you call the number on Zeke's card and we'll deal with it."

Another good point. After everything they'd done for her tonight, the odds of any of them having bad intentions were pretty slim. And her dog would leave even a big guy like Danny a heaping bloody mess if Viv so much as snapped a finger.

He opened the car door and she slid behind the

wheel, fastening her seat belt in a bit of a daze. "Thank you. For everything."

"Just doing what decent people do." He started to shut her door and stopped. Leaning slightly into her space, he seemed to listen for something, glanced at the stereo display, then eased back. He studied her car, Callie curled up in the back seat, then Viv. His gaze lingered on her hair and he ran a few fingers through the curly strands. "Like it better down. Kinda wild."

Her heart tripped, and the last bit of logic left in her brain poofed to nothing. She clenched the steering wheel and swallowed, grateful to find her mouth wasn't hanging open.

He winked and stepped back. "Take care, sugar."

The car door thumped shut, muting out everything but the quiet strains of Shinedown and Callie's muffled snore.

She put the car in Drive and forced her eyes to aim straight ahead. She wouldn't look back. He might've nudged her long-dead sex drive out of a coma, but he was bad news. Everything about him screamed danger and headstrong alpha, and she'd sworn she wouldn't have that kind of life for herself. One look in the back seat showed where that landed a person.

Still, making a right turn onto Highway 75 for her town house in Uptown instead of circling the block for another peek was tempting as hell.

Buy Rough & Tumble *by Rhenna Morgan now available wherever Carina Press ebooks are sold.*
www.CarinaPress.com